7.50

The Missile Lords

THE

JEFFERSON SUTTON

MISSILE LORDS

a novel

G. P. Putnam's Sons   New York

To my wife, Eugenia, who, as critic, editor-in-chief and girl Friday, certainly deserves top billing; and to Chris and Gale, who were ever so patient.

B721

Chapter 1

THE moment the seven A.M. news came on, Roland T. Bergstrom knew he was in for a bad day.

Congressman Stafford C. Slater blasts ICBM waste—that had been the gist of it, at least as far as Bergstrom was concerned. Not that the makers of the big weapon systems hadn't been blasted before. But this time the congressman referred to the Monarch Intercontinental Ballistic Missile, which the company was developing for the Air Force. With the president of Midwest Aeronautical Corporation's Western Aerospace Division and his director for space projects scheduled to testify before the House Appropriations subcommittee of which Slater was chairman, Bergstrom knew what lay behind the congressman's words.

Now, sitting across from John Vroman, Western Aerospace's vice-president for public relations and advertising found his premonition of a bad day confirmed, but not for the reason he had suspected.

"So that's it," Vroman was saying. "I'm calling it a day."

"I hope not, John." He spoke in an offhand manner to conceal

13

his dismay. Vroman, his department director . . . quitting? He echoed the thought silently, disbelievingly, conscious of the implications which lay behind the words. Vroman had steered the company's ICBM program through the welter of political and economic forces which had belabored it from the beginning—forces now becoming winds of intense proportions if he read the weather vanes correctly. It wasn't just Slater. Rumors, the occasional barbs of columnists, weighty editorials in the opposition press, by which he meant any newspaper or magazine opposed to all-out defense spending—a multitude of forces was at work to disparage the Monarch. With its initial launching scheduled in six weeks, a hundred-million-dollar production contract hung in the balance. And that was just the beginning. It was everything they'd worked for—he'd worked for. The future of the company depended on that one fact—landing the contract. A damned critical period. If ever he needed the gaunt man across from him, it was now. "I can't afford to lose you," he finished.

"It's nice to know you feel that way, Roland."

"How else could I feel, John?" Getting no answer, he continued, "Why the sudden decision? I don't mind telling you, it's caught me flat-footed."

"Health—peace of mind."

"Do we ever get peace of mind?"

"Not in this business."

"Especially not in this business." He noted the deepening lines, the thinning hair, the tense jaw muscles that told him the other was on the defensive. The gray eyes held a wary gleam. "You look in good shape," and as a second thought struck him, he added sharply, "Nothing serious?"

"No . . ."

Bergstrom caught the hesitancy. "If there's anything . . ." He left the thought unfinished.

"Only that I have to slow down . . . need a change."

"We all do, but we've still got the bird. Once we get it launched . . ."

"The bird." The director echoed the words dully.

"That's why we're here, John."

"I've never neglected that fact."

"No, you haven't. You've been pushing hard—too hard."

In truth, John Vroman had been shouldering a titanic burden. Bergstrom's own job was administration, policy-making —overseer of the division PR and advertising programs. But it had been the angular, aging man across from him who handled Air Force relations, created the slogans, manipulated words—sold the Monarch into an eminence almost the equal of its tested, established competitors. An untried bird at that. Aging? It came as a shock to recall that Vroman was only five or so years older than he—a few years over fifty. "You've got to learn to coast, let your men carry the load," he finished brusquely.

"It's more than that, Roland."

"Nonsense, we all feel discouraged at times."

"Not discouraged."

"What then?"

"It's not easy to explain."

"Something personal?"

"Yes, that's a fair statement."

"Then it's not health?"

Vroman hesitated. "Yes, that too."

Puzzled, Bergstrom regarded him. Health and not health, what kind of double-talk was that? He didn't appear troubled. To the contrary, he seemed calm, positive, and except for the guarded look, reflected the sureness that had always been part of him. What then? He had really said nothing at all, except that he was quitting, and for reasons quite obscure. Bergstrom began talking of the job again, encouragingly this time, then extended a bit of bait.

"I hope to move up the ladder someday, to corporation level. When I do . . ."

"I'd be in a worse fix, Roland."

"You've done wonders with the Monarch, with the Guardian space vehicle too. Everyone's been highly pleased, John."

"I've tried."

"A magnificent job."

"A killing one." Bergstrom caught the snap in his voice, not querulous exactly, but sharp, and eyed him searchingly.

"Has it been that bad?"

"Yes," Vroman said simply.

"We never expected it to be easy. The magnitude . . . complexity of the Monarch precludes that. The opposition. We knew it would be an uphill battle when we started. We're building an empire, John. You should draw a great deal of satisfaction from your part in it."

Vroman's gray eyes dwelt on him, but he sensed the other wasn't really listening—he was speaking into a vacuum. He tried to grasp what had happened. An executive didn't quit as casually as a factory hand might punch out. It didn't make sense. Especially now. Vroman knew the stakes. The Monarch was ready to go, but it still had to be sold. That was the rub. A development contract was one thing, quite different from a healthy continuing production contract—several hundreds of millions of dollars different. The initial contract was just the first bite. A year ago full-scale production had been a foregone conclusion, but in the interim, technology had advanced, racing faster than blueprints could be converted into steel. New liquid fuels—hypergolics as they were called—had surpassed the tricky kerosene and liquid oxygen combination which drove the Monarch. And solid fuels were edging to the fore. They'd have to fight every inch of the way.

He eyed the other covertly. "You've got to reach people" —that was Vroman's simple formula. He was trying to reach him now, put an end to his nonsensical talk. Perhaps if he laid the issue on the line . . . Debating, he said:

"This comes at a damned bad time, John. Titan II could throw a wrench in the works."

"It has strong support," the director agreed.

"Too strong. Aside from that, we have some big hurdles— the hot firing, the production contract . . ." He ticked them off. "The Slater committee."

"He'll cause some trouble."

"Damned right he will. He could sink us."

"Believe me, I've considered all that, but no man's indispensable." Vroman spoke earnestly. "Any of my section chiefs could carry the ball. Elliott, Garfield, Koepple . . . You don't lack good men."

"That's not the point, John. You've handled the reins, leading us through the wilderness, so to speak. You've been with the program almost since its inception—know the people, the pipelines, the steps we have to take. We can't gamble now. You say you're not indispensable"—he allowed his voice to soften —"but you're close to it. I can't risk putting someone else in your spot, not at this time."

"A new hand might prove better, Roland."

"With what we have facing us? It'll be one hell of a battle."

"Not if the bird goes."

"It'll go," he rejoined sharply. "I'm not worried over that, but it still has to be justified."

"Yes, it does."

"A lot of people claim the Monarch's obsolete," he went on,

disregarding the comment. "Look at the solid fuel propaganda. Believe me, management's concerned."

"I realize that."

"We have to push. Hard."

"That's why I'm calling it a day."

"This is no time to quit, John."

"Next year would be just as bad, or five years."

"That's the business," he replied shortly.

"That's what I'm saying, Roland."

"I know." He allowed himself a sigh. The director's set face told him his appeal fell on deaf ears. Vroman had prepared his defenses beforehand, just as he so meticulously prepared his publicity campaigns. Yet, somehow, he was different today. Failing to understand or reach him, Bergstrom felt as if some vital point were eluding him. Try as he would, he couldn't put a finger on it.

"Why rush it?" he suggested. "Take off a week or so. Rest up and perhaps you'll feel better."

"That won't do it, Roland. I've thought this over for quite some time."

"You're still being hasty," he warned.

"Perhaps." Vroman looked him full in the face. "I've given notice."

"You should have spoken with me first," he reproved.

"You'd have tried to talk me out of it."

"For your own good, yes." Annoyed, he let his eyes wander to a drawing on the far wall. The Monarch ICBM—"The Bird of Freedom." The man sitting opposite him had coined the slogan, now it was synonymous with the 96-foot stainless-steel monster being spawned in the factory across the way. One of the first of the missiles was in Florida being tested, checked, prepared for initial flight into the blue skies above Cape Canaveral. Once a dream, the Monarch was a dream no longer. It existed in steel . . . in reality. Engineers had given it form, factory workers had given it substance, but Vroman had given it life. The first launching . . .

Bergstrom found his irritation tempered by his own needs. The struggle to sell the Monarch would be hard, bitter. Opposed were key congressional members, military powers, competing weapon complexes. The indisputable fact was that he needed John Vroman. Drumming his fingers against the desk, he said slowly:

"All right, John. But I'll hold your spot open until after the hot firing. If you change your mind . . ."

The parent body of half a dozen divisions, Midwest Aeronautical Corporation manufactured just about every kind of weapon. Except stone axes. Or so Martin L. Byerkoff, chairman of the board, was prone to boast.

"Whatever weapons are needed, we manufacture; whatever weapons are proposed, we develop." That was Byerkoff's claim. Not that it had always been thus. In the matter of ICBMs, the corporation had been a latecomer, lagging behind such giants as General Dynamics, Martin and Boeing, a situation ascribed to the reluctance of Byerkoff's predecessor to accept the passing of the big bomber as the nation's prime weapon system. When it became apparent that the big military bomber was indeed passé, the board changed both its chairman and its policy, bringing to Byerkoff the fruition of a long dream.

Fortunately, the need of a new ICBM arose soon afterward, and Midwest Aeronautical Corporation received the development contract. More properly, an Air Force general named Lyman Stark had seen the need of another ICBM, "in order," he said, "to broaden the base of our industrial output to assure continued production under atomic attack." Supported by obscure but powerful forces, his view prevailed; the Monarch was born. This was the same Lyman Stark who, upon his subsequent retirement, became executive vice-president of Western Aerospace, the division created by Midwest Aeronautical Corporation for the express purpose of producing this new addition to the nation's arsenal. Since, the stockholders had little reason to complain.

Bergstrom saw the contract as veritable security, at least for a long period of time and for hundreds of millions of dollars. It would hold them until the next morsel. In the magic world of Cost Plus Fixed Fee, the government supplied much of the equipment and machine tools; the manufacturer was reimbursed for all costs plus a nice percentage. At the same time he was all too aware of the many weapons canceled, edged out by more competent rivals, or those with more political stature. Billions had been poured into such lost dreams. Cancellation was, in fact, a recurring nightmare.

Sitting behind the walnut desk in his luxurious office, he contemplated what the director's abrupt action might portend. Nothing really mattered, he reflected, neither myself nor Vroman nor anyone else, as long as the bird gets into operational production. He saw the Monarch as a symbol, not of awesome power, but of the corporation. Which, in the final analysis, it was. The corporation and not the bird was the real entity. Because the corporation was his whole life, he couldn't conceive that his subordinate could feel differently. He'd seen men quit before on the way up, lots of them. Wife, health, pressure—there were innumerable reasons. But what manner of man quit once he arrived? That baffled him. *Health—peace of mind.* What did Vroman really mean? Not health, certainly. His later arguments belied that. And what was peace of mind but a state of mind? Could he be worried over the hot firing? The big contract? He decided not. Those were constant pressures, the day-to-day kind that came as part of the job. It was more than that. It bothered him not to know.

His eyes lingered on the sketch of the Monarch. Done in color—one of Carole Janek's best—he could all but feel the heat of its fire trail. Newest and most powerful addition to the ICBM arsenal, or would be once it got into operational production, it was also the heart and soul of Western Aerospace, the sole reason for the big plant's existence. The Guardian space vehicle and smaller jobs were the gravy; the Monarch made Western Aerospace—comprised its bone and muscle, the blood that surged through its veins.

"We need a good first flight," he murmured. The words in his mind had a familiar ring. "God, how we need it." He felt a tinge of unease. The bird was great because it had to be great, for it had come into an age when nothing less than greatness survived. But greatness was a thing of words; of the missile itself, he was not so certain.

A missile is a creature of engineering—applied mathematics; but it lives only through words that give it meaning.

That was Byerkoff too, the old Egyptian philosophy that nothing existed until named. But the old man was right; added it meant SELL, the single-word slogan that hung in his office. Sell the Monarch. He mused over the drawing. The chameleon bird, the bird of a hundred roles. To the public it must represent peace, to the Air Force reliability, to the scientist technical advancement—to all, power. The philosophy backing the ICBM stressed the utility of deterrency rather than devastation. The awesome face of power depended upon size, number, dispersal, the logistics of quantity, the enemy's knowledge that the big weapon systems were too many and too widely dispersed to be destroyed at a single blow, that reprisal remained a certainty. Those were the unspoken ingredients of peace. The nation needed ICBMs; it especially needed the Monarch, the mailed fist which Western Aerospace had undertaken to supply. Or so he believed. It simply wasn't true that it was all gravy. Changing administrations, shifts among power blocs, economic peaks and valleys, technological breakthroughs, threat of disarmament—the company's risks were incalculable.

He stirred and lit a cigarette. No doubt Vroman would feel differently after a few weeks out of harness. Still, he'd have to play it safe, prepare a successor, and in the meantime try and get him back. And if he failed . . . ? He contemplated the next step. Vroman was right. He had good men. Henderson from Space Electronics, Garfield, Koepple, Elliott . . . He let the names filter through his mind. They were good. They wouldn't be here otherwise. But he needed the best.

He went back to the names, closing his eyes reflectively. Eugene Henderson was good, of that he had no doubt. He had done wonders for Space Electronics, the division created in turn by Western Aerospace when it had become necessary to farm out some of the Monarch's electrical and electronic systems. The youngest of his executives, he already bore the title of "director." Henderson's youth, vigor and, yes, opportunism certainly favored him. Of Vroman's men, it looked like a toss-up. Harry Garfield, a crackerjack of an idea man, was perhaps a trifle loud, but he certainly possessed aggression. He handled the audio-visual aspects of PR, and handled them damn well. Also, he had seniority—over twenty-two years with the company. That was not to be sneezed at. Arthur Koepple was another matter. Like Garfield, he had over twenty years' service; unlike him, he was quiet, mild, a small graying man who headed division advertising, and whom he considered absolutely tops in the field. If Bergstrom had to characterize him, it would be as a thinker, a man able to see to the core of a problem while others were concerned with the skin. Koepple had formidable talents.

And James Elliott. Bergstrom sat straighter. He had a momentary vision of a tall man, husky, with short, dark hair, a noticeable scar down one temple and a deceptively easygoing manner. Vroman had brought him over from the *Bulletin-News* several years before to head the news bureau. His capabilities were beyond doubt; Vroman thought highly of him, in itself a strong recommendation. He certainly punched out the news and articles, hewing tight to the company line. Close to Henderson in age—a few years older perhaps—he gave the impression of greater maturity and dependability. Not that it was true; Henderson was right up there. But Bergstrom certainly had to place Jim Elliott high on the list. Which of them was best? He didn't know. That was the trouble, he'd been out of contact. The price of administration. Well, there it was.

His buzzer sounded.

"Mr. Welkes would like to have you stop by if you're not busy," his secretary said.

"Thanks, Joan." Wondering what the president wanted, he scribbled a note and dropped it on her desk on the way out, instructing, "Shoot this to Cronkhill by wire." Hamilton Cronkhill, Midwest Aeronautical Corporation's senior vice-president for public relations and advertising, and hence Bergstrom's boss, liked to be apprised of key personnel changes in the division departments. Bergstrom never overlooked the fact.

"Yes, Mr. Bergstrom."

"It's confidential." As she glanced at the memo, he turned to head down executive row.

Bergstrom's secretary read the message twice, as if not quite certain of its contents, then glanced toward the door, feeling suddenly quiet inside. Assured he was gone, she lifted the phone and dialed rapidly.

"Space Electronics," a feminine voice answered.

"Extension two-one-one." Another ring came through the receiver and she waited impatiently.

"Mr. Henderson's office."

"Mr. Henderson, please. Mr. Bergstrom calling."

"One moment." Another click, and he was on.

"This is Joan." She kept her voice low.

"Oh . . . it's good to hear from you." The formality told her he was not alone.

"May I talk?"

"Yes, of course."

She announced carefully: "Vroman quit."

"What?" he exclaimed, startled. She could picture the expression on his face, see it change from amazement to calculation. It was a job he'd like; one she'd like him to have. Then, maybe . . . She was afraid to think.

"How did you find out?"

"A message . . . to Cronkhill."

"What did it say?"

"Nothing. Just that Vroman had quit."

"Anything else?"

"Nothing . . . yet."

"Keep me posted."

"I will."

"When. . . ?"

"Tonight?"

"That would be fine."

"Thank you," she said, and meant it. Placing the receiver in the cradle, she began to hum.

The home of the Monarch missile, a collection of white, crate-shaped buildings set on a 270-acre site in the southwestern part of metropolitan Los Angeles, resembled giant blocks tumbled randomly onto a flat plain. The administration, engineering and cafeteria buildings were bordered by carefully kept lawns and shrubbery, while the factory, laboratories, warehouses and various test installations were set amid a desert of asphalt that provided roadways, parking and outdoor storage facilities. The plant's chief architect had described it as "a study in functional beauty."

Shoestrings of neat, geometrical, three-bedroom, two-bath houses, all remarkably alike, hemmed it on two sides. Hughes, North American, Douglas, the Garrett Corporation and other large manufacturing concerns sprawled nearby, as did the mammoth International Airport. Western Aerospace Division of Midwest Aeronautical Corporation, a giant come to roost among giants, had picked its kind with complete disregard for aesthetics. Seen from afar, its white walls, lined with phalanxes of windows, were harsh to the eye, an effect calculated to be removed as scattered eucalyptus, olive trees and colorful shrubs and flowers flourished at its feet.

Western Aerospace came into being when Midwest Aeronautical Corporation received an initial ninety-million-dollar development contract for the Monarch, a fourth generation ICBM. The board of directors had promptly appropriated twenty-five million dollars to acquire the land and build the plant, while the government provided an additional twenty-five million dollars to equip it.

The seven-story administration building carried out the general theme of concrete and glass, but since the first summer's occupancy, more and more of the windows had been covered with translucent and even opaque materials as it became apparent that the utility of glass left something to be desired in a land of sun and heat.

Herbert P. Welkes, a vice-president of Midwest Aeronautical Corporation and president of its Western Aerospace Division, occupied a suite of offices on the southeast corner of the top floor, which was referred to by the less reverent employees as "Kingdom Hall." Firmly believing that the décor of an office should mirror its occupant's personality, his own was paneled in walnut, furnished with deep, red leather chairs with matching three-sectional couches and deep, deep rugs, all of which he considered as the trademark of the successful executive. His elegantly finished executive desk with its French-curve top was canted to face an artificial hearth, above which a mantel displayed several plaques attesting his contributions to the cause of air power. Their dates antedated the era of the ballistic missile. A Japanese Arisaka rifle and a Civil War powder horn hung from one wall.

His offices overlooked the thirty-odd buildings which comprised the remainder of the plant. Car-jammed Pacific Highway was visible to the south, but Welkes seldom looked in that direction. He was far more interested in the view underfoot—the rectangular four-story engineering building to the north, the great complex of testing labs which lay to the east, the huge, windowless box in the distance where the Monarch ICBM and Guardian space vehicles were fabricated.

Although the conglomeration of sizes and shapes gave the plant a haphazard appearance, he knew this was not the case at all. Each building had a bearing on the missile—warehouses to store parts, laboratories to test them, a factory to fabricate and assemble them; service structures, a beehive of offices to administer, plan, purchase, record, or in other ways shuffle the countless tons of paper which made the missile possible. The missile itself was the golden egg; the plant its fifty-million-dollar nest.

Occasionally Welkes gazed farther east, some two thousand miles farther, and envisioned another plant—Midwest Aeronautical Corporation, parent of this rambunctious offspring. That and not Western Aerospace commanded his true interest, for if things went right (if the Monarch were a success), he might someday be president of the other company, or even board chairman. The dream was clouded by the certain knowledge that in each of five other divisions a president had the same dream. Still, one of them had to come true; he never ceased to hope.

As a vice-president of Western Aerospace, Roland T. Bergstrom enjoyed a suite on the seventh floor. Not as large or as elegantly furnished as the president's, it infinitely surpassed, say, the offices of Paul Gaither, the chief engineer. For one thing, lacking the magical word "vice-president" before his name, the latter was located on the sixth floor; secondly, he did not enjoy the luxury of wall-to-wall carpeting. The sixth-floor location had the advantage of keeping Gaither readily available to the executive offices; at the same time, it stood as a constant reminder that regardless of the power and prestige associated with the title "chief engineer," it still held status below that of a seventh-floor dweller.

Oddly enough, although not a vice-president, Otto Kroeber's offices adjoined Welkes'; thus, physically, he stood a step closer to the president than did Lyman Stark, the executive vice-president. Although Kroeber's title was "director of space projects"—he was generally referred to as "the spaceman"—he enjoyed all the privileges accorded a vice-presidential level. As Welkes once explained:

"A missile plant's got to have a spaceman. It's a mark of the trade, a symbol of the future, and a symbol isn't worth a damn unless it's clothed in status."

He didn't say so but he knew the symbol had to bear a German name, preferably one that could be linked with a Peenemünde and the German V-2 missile, which in itself was a guarantee of its owner's genius in dealing with tomorrow's space world. Fortunately, Midwest Aeronautical Corporation had been big enough and rich enough to afford one of Peenemünde's outstanding scientists for its offspring; Otto Kroeber had worked on the V-2 airframe.

The division director for public relations and advertising, the position abdicated by John Vroman, did not occupy a spectacular suite in Kingdom Hall—the job was at secondary management level—but his offices were nonetheless imposing. Located on the third floor of the administration building, the PR offices constituted a study in potted plants, ornate drawings depicting the interplanetary adventures of Monarch-boosted space vehicles (it being considered poor taste to show a thermonuclear bomb erasing a city), and impeccably polished desks, each bearing a copper nameplate set in a mahogany frame. Exceptions were the names of the secretaries and file clerks. As hourly employees, their names were printed in block letters on cardboard backed by metal, a small but important difference that distinguished salaried employees from those who punched the clock. The offices of Vroman's section chiefs, exactly the same from polished desk to swivel chair, differed only in the personal items, which in time came to clutter all three alike. Neat signs at the entrances of the first two announced they belonged to Harry Garfield, chief of publicity, and Arthur W. Koepple, chief of advertising. The third office down belonged to James Elliott, chief of the news bureau.

Launching of the first Monarch ICBM moved a step closer today as the giant missile was erected in its gantry at Cape Canaveral, Florida, for a final pre-flight checkout. Developed by Western Aerospace Division of Midwest Aeronautical Corporation for the Air Force, the fourth generation ICBM was hailed by company officials as the Nation's newest guardian of the peace.

James Elliott paused to scan the copy. Although the missile had several weeks to go before it would be flight-ready, he hoped to pick up a few paragraphs of news. As he started to type again, John Vroman came in and sat across from him.

"Morning, Jim. Hard at it?"

"A squib on the Monarch," he explained. "They're erecting it in the gantry."

"Any art?"

"Not to mention." He paused, waiting for whatever the director had in mind.

"Bergstrom's curious about the Slater material," Vroman pursued. "He mentioned it this morning."

"It's coming along."

"He's anxious to preview it with Welkes. Slater cut loose a blast on the air that has him worried."

"Welkes?"

"Bergstrom." Vroman leaned back, extending his legs. "He thinks Slater's out to scuttle us."

"Isn't he?"

"He can make it damned uncomfortable."

Elliott considered the point. "I don't know what we can do about it. You can't gag a congressman."

"Welkes wants to be prepared, that's all. What do we have so far?"

"The usual. We show the Monarch in a definitely favorable light. Some of it's a lift from the testimony Welkes gave the House Committee on Astronautics and Science."

"He'll probably hit hardest on the question of the Monarch's necessity," Vroman conjectured.

"We're documented. We show the bird as a more advanced system, a step forward. Show that our later start gave the advantage of new technology . . . improved materials and fabrication techniques."

"We might have to defend our propellants against the new hypergolics."

"I thought of that, John. There's not much we can say except that our fuel yields more thrust per pound. I can't imagine he'll hit it too hard."

"Why not?"

"He's a solids man. I can't see him touting another liquid fuel."

"He might use the Titan II to undercut the Monarch. You can't tell how these things go, Jim."

"A missile's more than a fuel system," he countered. "We have better guidance and controls." As Vroman nodded, he added: "Our pitch is that the Monarch's an up-to-the-minute bird—a step into the future. We show it as both a missile and a space booster."

"The same applies to the Atlas and Titan," the director murmured.

"Ours is a better missile, a better booster."

"We have to show that, not just state it."

"I believe we do. We have some strong engineering data to go on."

"Yes, we have that."

"I also included data on our sea-launch capability."

"Classified, Jim."

"Not to a congressional committee. At least, if it comes up, Welkes will have the dope."

Vroman leaned back, regarding him a moment before saying, "We have a slight problem."

"On the sea-launch?"

"On what we claim for the Monarch," he explained. "Alex Barmon will be testifying for the Air Force."

"General Barmon? He's good."

"Very good, Jim, but he'll have to justify all of the ICBMs.

We can't afford to make any claims for the Monarch that run counter to his testimony."

"Do we know his pitch?"

"We've been in touch with him—Welkes and Stark both—but what he says depends on what Slater asks." Vroman frowned. "You'll have to play it straight, use plenty of supporting facts and figures. Slater doesn't buy words."

"It's hard to nail down, John. Facts are surmises and figures are guesses."

"I know. How about costs?"

"We're not too firm." Elliott shook his head. "What does a developmental missile cost? No one knows."

"How do we show it?" Vroman persisted.

"On a curve. The first prototype model comes at a round fifteen million, dropping to under two million each when we get into operational production. They're cheaper by the dozen," he concluded dryly.

"Sounds low."

"For the prototype or operational model?"

"Both."

"I don't know," he admitted. "I got the figures from contracts."

"An educated guess." When Elliott didn't reply, the director continued, "What are you doing about Kroeber's testimony?"

"Not much," he admitted. "You know Otto. He'd rather gather his own data . . . speak off the cuff."

Vroman shrugged. "There's not much we can do about it."

"Not a thing."

"It's a tough situation, Jim. Otto's not exactly oriented politically."

"He's sharp."

"Also honest. That's why they summoned him."

"I'll talk with him again."

"Do that. In the meantime, better give Bergstrom the package as soon as possible, get him off the hot seat."

"Okay."

"I have a call in for Sumner," the director continued. "Perhaps we can get some guidelines."

"It would help," he acknowledged. Bert Sumner, the local congressman, also happened to be a member of the House Appropriations subcommittee of which Slater was chairman. A junior member, to be sure, but at least he represented a friend in court. Bert Sumner could always count on Western Aerospace at campaign time.

Vroman glanced around, drumming on the arms of his chair. Knowing he had something in mind, Elliott waited, thinking he looked tired. His face, always gaunt, had acquired a waxen pallor that accentuated the fine web of veins splotching his cheeks, and for the first time he caught himself thinking of him as old. Silly, for he couldn't be much past fifty. Vroman brought back his eyes, saying, "There's one other thing. I'd appreciate your keeping it in confidence."

"Certainly."

"I've put in my resignation."

"Oh!" He uttered the word quickly, startled.

"Effective in two weeks," Vroman added.

"Why, John?" He felt a quick dismay.

"It's overdue."

"Hell, you're right in stride."

"I wouldn't say that."

"You've been carrying this damned program," he expostulated.

"As far as I could," he admitted.

"It'll be a helluva blow."

"That I doubt."

"I don't, John." He studied the other curiously. "From what

I hear, the big contract won't be so easy to come by. They're talking about more Minutemen—"

"I know, more of everything," Vroman cut in, "but I doubt if the company has to worry. It's got strong support, Jim."

"So have the others."

"Yes . . ."

"I'm damned sorry to hear it," Elliott said, thinking the other the best friend he had in the plant. The gaunt man opposite him had played it square, every inch of the way. He wouldn't get a better boss. He eyed him hopefully. "Any chance you'll reconsider?"

"None," Vroman said firmly.

"You might be sorry, John."

"No, it's the best thing I've done."

"Not for the company."

"Perhaps not."

He had another thought. "How did Bergie take it?"

"He didn't like the idea," Vroman admitted.

"I don't imagine he did."

"No man's indispensable, Jim. That's a good point to remember."

"It isn't a matter of being indispensable."

"Oh?"

"We've been letting you carry the load."

"No." Vroman made the denial quickly. "I've done what I've had to do, Jim. Now I'm at the end, that's all. It's as simple as that."

They talked for a while longer, and when the director departed, Elliott stared at the typewriter, the copy forgotten. The tall, stoop-shouldered man had been a good friend—*was* a good friend. He had brought him over from the *Bulletin-News*, had given him his start. That had been only two years ago. It seemed much longer. Vroman had been gayer, happier in those days. Perhaps they both had. Now that he thought of it, he could see the changes in him. Not a lessening of vitality perhaps, but the verve had gone, his heartiness replaced by a stereotyped kind of enthusiasm—a professional brand. Still, he remained as much a part of the plant as the bird itself. Certainly he gave the bird voice, personality; in many ways had created it, or its image.

Why? He lingered over the question. Not health, definitely. Unknowingly he echoed Bergstrom's words. But what if not health? Vroman had been on a tough grind, but hadn't they all? Like Otto Kroeber, he had worked night and day, often on weekends, devoting his energies to the big metal form that now stood in the gantry at Cape Canaveral. The bird. He felt puzzled until he realized that Vroman hadn't expressed the same enthusiasm for the Monarch the last . . . how many months? He worked, he slaved, but without the same fervor. But that couldn't be it. A better job? He rejected the idea immediately, even though he knew several of the big aerospace companies had approached him in the past.

More to the point, who'd take his place? The next thought staggered him. Himself? He weighed the idea, considering the pros and cons. This could be his chance. The Big Step. Hell, it couldn't be. Quietly he sat back. Youngest of the PR section heads, he'd gotten his job through Vroman—stepped right in at a level that had taken Garfield and Koepple years to reach. Not that he couldn't handle it; his solid newspaper background and subsequent industrial experience fitted right in with the job. Still, he was older than Henderson, who *was* a director. He'd have competition, but he was willing to place his own abilities in the balance. The key was Bergstrom—how to reach him.

Oddly, he felt he knew the vice-president well, even though he seldom worked directly for him. Vroman had been his shield, but he was extremely aware of the big, balding man upstairs. If he were to tabulate his characteristics, he would use such words as dedicated, determined, purposeful, a man willing to tote a big cross for a cause in which he believed. He would also use such words as unyielding, dogged, uncompromising, a man to whom a goal was a thing to be attained at whatever cost. The vice-president was a company man with all that it implied. Whereas Vroman once had displayed considerable enthusiasm for the missile, Bergstrom held the same fervor for the company.

He became aware of his unlit cigarette and reached for a match. Damned few men thought in terms of the corporation. Bergstrom did. To him the Monarch was merely a giant tool, a mechanism with which to push the corporation ahead. Men, tools, systems, entire weapon complexes, were but artifacts in the game of corporate expansion; and while he couldn't go along with that, he could go along with Bergstrom's dedication.

Where did that leave him? If nothing else, it gave a valuable clue to the vice-president's thinking and, as such, furnished guidelines which might well lead to the director's chair. Bergstrom would demand loyalty and he would give it, easily and gladly, for he believed in the Monarch—its necessity. Bergstrom would also demand top-caliber performance; and that, too, he felt he could give. But he would have bitter competition. Garfield, the oldest in service, was sharp and aggressive although prone toward cynicism, a man whose hat would come sailing into the ring and who could back his candidacy with a proven record of accomplishment. Koepple, less aggressive by far, was nevertheless a clear thinker, precise, given to detail rather than the overall picture. But he couldn't discount him. Although he bore the marks of time, he had scant doubt but that the chief of advertising would place himself very much in the running when he learned that Vroman's job was up for grabs.

Finally there was Eugene Henderson. He frowned, puzzled. Henderson was a different breed of cat. Polished and suave and, if the gossip were true, ruthless in his ambitions. He had gone to the top fast. It came to him that he didn't know Henderson at all. Bergstrom, in many ways enigmatic, was actually an open book; Henderson, frank and extrovertive, was a closed one. Or was it the other way around?

But the key to Bergstrom was accomplishment. Well, he'd show accomplishment. Unofficially he'd take up the reins Vroman had dropped. He felt a tinge of guilt. Not that he was taking his place. The older man voluntarily had relinquished the post. He'd willingly submerge his ambitions if Vroman reconsidered. But with the job open . . .

After a while he finished the Monarch release, slipped it into the OUT basket and went to keep his luncheon date with Carole Janek.

She was waiting by the fountain.

His eyes found her immediately, despite the throng of workers streaming toward the cafeteria. She held one hand to shade her eyes and a light breeze pressed against her skirt, revealing the bold outlines of her legs and riffling her corn-yellow hair. He liked the sight. Nearer, he lifted a hand in recognition.

"Keep you waiting?"

"Only a moment. Isn't it windy?"

"Off the desert." Touching her elbow, he guided her through the crowd.

"More beautiful than ever," he said when they were seated. "New dress?"

"You ask that every time. No."

"There's something different. Ah, I've got it. Your smile."

"What about it?"

"It's happy," he explained. "You know why? Because I'm taking you out tonight."

"You are not. We were out last night."

"So we were. Why not tonight?"

"Work."

"Again?" She nodded. "What this time?"

"A rush illustration for Kroeber."

"He's monopolizing you. I could dislike that man."

"Him? Never."

"Guess you're right." He eyed her warmly. Although she'd been with the company less than a year, her talent, imagination and ability to translate abstract scientific and engineering jargon into technically accurate yet eye-appealing illustrations had brought her to head a small art group specializing in promotional literature. As one of Vroman's section heads, she kept shop on the floor below the PR offices. He looked at the slightly crooked front tooth, the straight nose and calm blue eyes, and thought: She's beautiful. The thought was nearly a year old.

During a lull in the conversation he told her about John Vroman. She didn't appear surprised.

"You're hoping to get the job?"

"If possible."

"Oh, it's possible." She glanced away disapprovingly. Not that he had expected otherwise. Despite her own success, she considered Western Aerospace as a place to pause, not as a career. She had been vociferous on that point before.

He set down his fork.

"You don't think much of the idea?"

"You know how I feel."

"It's a good job, Carole."

"It's not a future."

"Vroman's job at my age? That sounds pretty good to me."

"Does it?"

"You're a pillar of strength today, Carole."

"I'm trying to be," she answered quietly.

"Did I hurt your feelings? I didn't mean to, but I can't stand still. Do that and I might as well quit." When she failed to answer, he pressed: "What's wrong with this place?"

"It's a huge disorganized beehive, Jim Elliott, and you know it—people rushing pell-mell, getting nowhere, and for what?"

"To produce a missile," he answered promptly.

"Killing themselves, you mean."

"I wouldn't do it that way," he stated, holding her eyes. He knew exactly what she would say.

"You'd have to do it that way. You couldn't work five days with Bergstrom working six. He wouldn't appoint a five-day man, as you very well know. It's not a five-day job."

"What am I supposed to do, make a future of the news bureau?"

"Don't be facetious, Jim."

"I'm not, I'm serious."

"It's not just the ungodly hours, Jim. It's what it does to one . . . the waste, the senselessness of it. It might be all right for some people . . ."

"I'm different?"

"You're a writer. You have talent. I have faith in that, Jim, but you're wasting it here."

"You don't have to stay at the bottom."

"Is the top any better?"

"Bergie appears satisfied."

"This is his life," she explained. "You're not Bergstrom."

"Don't look so serious, honey."

"Why not, Jim? It's a serious matter."

"Hell, I probably won't get it anyway, so why all the argument?"

"I wouldn't say that."

"Now you're on the other side of the fence."

"No, not a bit. I wouldn't like to see you take the job, but I think you have an excellent chance of getting it. There's a difference, Jim."

He smiled. "You make me feel good even when you don't want to."

"Do I?" She didn't sound enthusiastic. He looked at the slope of her cheek, the full lips. At times when he was near her—in the office, at a conference—he felt her presence as sharp as a physical contact. He felt it now, reflecting on their relationship. It had been like none he had ever known, gripping him as he knew it gripped her. Occasionally she remained apart from him for several weeks at a time. He understood these periods as self-questioning, and when they occurred, he respected her privacy. This he knew: She was a woman he wanted, badly and permanently. She could be frustratingly casual, and she could be—

"You're disappointed?" she asked.

"That you're not cheering me?"

She nodded. "I want you to know my side of it, Jim."

"You work here too."

Her voice was level. "For now, yes. There's not a rushing market for female illustrators."

"There's not a rushing market for writers either. Not many get this kind of dough."

"Is that what matters?"

"You have to live, Carole. I'm not old enough for social security."

She disregarded the sarcasm. "How about your writing, Jim? What's happened to that?"

He didn't answer immediately. It was true, he'd reached a point where he'd been selling almost regularly, but the last story had lain untouched for months. Not that he had shifted interest, but there simply wasn't time. He caught the expectancy in her face and dodged the question, asking, "What would you do if you quit?"

"Take a steamer to Rio," she responded promptly.

"Rio?" He wondered if she were joking. "And you think *I'm* silly!"

"What's so silly about that? I've always wanted to see the Avenida Rio Branco, Botafogo Bay, the Sugar Loaf." She flicked her eyes at him. "They say it's even lovelier than the Monarch."

"I'm being serious, Carole."

"So am I."

"How would you live?"

"I didn't say I'd stay."

"Then why go?"

"James Elliott, haven't you any romance in your soul?"

"You should know." He grinned wickedly.

She returned the look imperturbably. "I'd go to slow down —return to a kind of life where an hour is sixty minutes long instead of fifteen, where a girl can make a date and know the man will show up. I'd walk the beaches and swim and lounge in the sun, go to concerts and museums. Then, when I'd learned to slow down, I'd come back and start over, a different kind of life. I'd do the things I want to do instead of just dreaming about them."

"This isn't so bad," he remonstrated.

"No?" She gazed steadily at him. "Vroman's about killed himself. You know that. Kroeber's doing the same, so is Bergstrom. Everything belongs to the bird. At times I think it's a monument to ulcers and cardiac attacks. And for what? I don't want that to happen to you, Jim." She paused. "You have talent, Jim, but you have to develop it, let it flower. Creativity demands freedom of expression—self-expression with no restraints. It can't develop in an atmosphere of organized demands. It's like a spark. If you don't nourish it, it dies."

"There's plenty of talent around here," he objected. "The place is jammed to the rafters with it."

"Perhaps, but not much creativity, and what there is doesn't last. You know that."

"Perhaps." He gave her a long reflective look. "There are aspects you don't consider, Carole. It's a job that has to be done. The Monarch's important."

"Is it? Is it really, Jim?"

"You know it is. It's the next step in defense, and we need it. The Air Force is screaming for it, Carole."

"I don't know." She studied him closely. "At times I think it's all words . . . that its power exists solely as a description; that when it's finally tested, it'll be just another missile —perhaps not even necessary. It's like my space illustrations. Kroeber gives me a description, a few rough sketches, and from them I create a satellite or spaceship. They're paper spaceships, Jim."

"I don't get the analogy."

"I make a sketch of a moonship, but it's just a sketch, not something that'll go to the moon. Sometimes I feel pretty deflated."

"That's silly."

"Do you feel your words make the Monarch more powerful, more real?"

"It has to be sold."

"Does it?" She tossed her head, glancing away, and he stifled his reply. Lord, she should be able to see the opportunity—should be egging him on, cheering him. But she wasn't.

They finished the meal in silence.

2

Chapter 2

No!" Arthur Koepple exclaimed incredulously.

"It's true," Jane Cooper insisted.

"I can't believe it." Yet he knew she was right. So, John Vroman was quitting. Why? They were practically on the eve of the launching, of the final push for the contract. Why would a man strive so furiously, then quit at the critical hour? It was as if Bergstrom had quit, or Welkes. It didn't make sense. He probed the question for meaning, and finding none, moved on to the next step. With Vroman out . . .

He felt a stillness, and for the moment forgot the presence of Garfield's secretary. A dim hope flared in his mind, a small beacon in the sea of his thoughts which he once had believed forever extinguished, and a tingle of anticipation ran through his thin body, a stirring he hadn't felt for a long time. Now, after all these years . . .

"Who told you?"

"A girl in personnel."

"Is she certain?"

"She handles terminations," she replied smugly.

"Who else knows?"

"I'm the only one."

"And me." He chuckled nervously.

"And you."

"Not Garfield?"

"Not yet," she replied, oblivious of the fact that she had just stated her intention of telling him. "He's up in Bergie's office."

"What's he doing there?" He asked too quickly, but she didn't seem to notice.

"Something about some slides." Slides, hell. Garfield knew all right, was already making points. He was a regular ferret. He voiced his suspicions.

"I'm pretty sure he doesn't." Her voice plainly said she hoped she was right; she wanted the pleasure of telling him. He weighed her carefully: a gossip who got around, her information generally was pretty good, although she was prone to color it with tidbits from her own imagination.

"Esther Lynn surely knows."

"I doubt it." She didn't explain the reason for her belief. He debated, thinking it strange if Vroman's own secretary wasn't aware that he had quit. It could be tough on her.

He said, "That could leave her without a job."

"Well, she'd be transferred." Jane sounded as if she liked the idea. As secretary to the director, Esther rated a notch above her. "Whoever gets the job would probably pick his own girl," she surmised.

"Hear anything?"

"It's too early."

"Might be a job for you."

"I wouldn't have it." She tossed her head defiantly as if to disparage the prospect. He knew differently.

"It might be good . . . with a new man."

"Well, I don't know."

"You could handle it."

"There's nothing to the job. Esther doesn't do half the work I do—just sits around and answers the phone and takes two-hour lunch breaks. I think I'd get bored."

"Rather work for Garfield, eh?"

"It's all right." She canted her head, smoothing back her hair, and watching her, it occurred to him she could make a valuable pipeline.

"Garfield might be the boy, then you'd automatically get it," he pursued. She glanced quickly at him as if it were a new idea and he wondered if he'd said the wrong thing. He was relieved when a dubious expression crept over her face.

"I hadn't really thought about that, but somehow I can't picture it."

"Going along with Garfield?"

"No, he'd be glad to have me."

"What can't you picture?"

"His getting the job."

"Why?"

"He just doesn't seem like the type. You know what I mean. He's, well, not like Vroman, or anybody like that . . ." He let her flounder. "Maybe it's just that he's always working. The director's job is more meeting people, taking them to eat at places like the Sycamore Tree and all that jazz. He just doesn't strike me as the type."

"Entertaining isn't everything." He eyed the wrinkles gathering at the corners of her eyes, the lines that powder couldn't quite conceal. All at once he wanted to be rid of her, to be alone, to think. "Let me know if you hear anything."

"Depend on me." She straightened, smoothing her skirt over her hips. "Don't say anything."

"I won't." Watching her go, the stillness came again. So, Vroman was leaving. He wasn't too surprised; he'd seen it coming.

Vroman wasn't the first. The long hours, no overtime at that level, Bergie's constant pressure—those had been the straws. He looked through the empty doorway. It was true, all right. There was no secret so tight it didn't flow like water among the girls. Now he was gone—the dour, tired-faced man who had been his boss, who had gotten the job he should have had in the first place.

He plucked at his memory, recalling his bitterness when Bergstrom had brought Vroman in from the outside. But he couldn't do that now; there wasn't time. He'd need someone who could step right in, take over, handle the storm cloud brewing over the growing budgets, the dollar that had to be split between space and defense—someone who could defend the Monarch's none-too-firm position in the ICBM hierarchy. Vroman had been a driving fireball, had ended the same way. Ashes. He had almost seen him disintegrate as he drove faster and faster; a crash had been inevitable. The old aspirin-vita-min-nupercainal routine. Vroman hadn't learned to take it slow, conserve his energy, delegate responsibility. Now he was out.

Vroman, and Bergstrom too, considered Koepple methodical, a careful man, a planner. He believed in schedules, detail, precision in the mechanics of moving work as well as what went into the work itself. He was methodical now, holding down his hopes while he examined the matter of Vroman's successor, mulling over the possible candidates—Garfield, Henderson, Elliott.

Finally, almost fearfully, he sat back to examine his own situation, aware of a slight tremor in his hands. He studied them, startled at their thin, veined appearance. Not enough sun, exercise. Should get out more—hike, fish, play golf. Yet he knew it was idle speculation, for in truth he did none of those things; there simply wasn't time. But the job? He found himself half afraid to explore the question. *Ah, damn my baffled soul.* He had read the line years before and for some reason it had remained with him; now, after all these years, he knew why. It expressed his present predicament perfectly, and when he meditated upon it, it also expressed his past. He had been picking his way through a maze, probing for a door that opened into the light, and had encountered blind alleys. Now, for the moment, he glimpsed the light. *Why not himself?*

Excited, he tried to evaluate his position objectively. He had lived with the missile a long time, since it had existed simply as a dream and a hope, fortified with a clutter of crude blueprints. He had watched it grow, knew its strengths and weaknesses—how to exploit the former and conceal the latter. He didn't contemplate anything miraculous when it came time for the big metal bird to fly. The history of first flights sufficed to tell him that. But the point was, he knew the bird, how to handle it, how to paint it in other people's minds.

More important, he understood Bergstrom, and how he believed the missile should be handled. The missile was everything, yet it wasn't; that was the knowledge they shared. The missile formed a gigantic façade, dwarfing the company which had created it; yet the creator was of far more importance than the creature spawned. The difference, subtle, was one he attempted to exploit in his work. The ultimate objective was to build, not a missile, but a missile-making empire; the Monarch formed the means toward that end.

By the same token, it became necessary to maintain and foster the turbulent environment necessary for the big bird's survival, for it could only exist on stormy waters. Not that a real threat didn't exist. He was too prescient to believe otherwise. But the threat had to be slanted, made to appear that only a certain brand of weapon sufficed to answer it. Speed, distance, accuracy, megatons—those were the parameters of survival, parameters which could only be met by ICBMs, and particularly by the Monarch. Armies, navies and even manned aircraft became brushfire weapons, inadequate when forests flamed.

At the moment, the big metal bird dominated the scene, caught the headlines, captured the imagination. The company formed a scarcely seen neutral background . . . sort of a sky across which the missile thundered, or at least thundered on paper. Yet long after the Monarch had been interred in its dozens of silos in the northern tier of states or had been floated to waiting places in the sea, the gray mass of the company would continue its growth. When the day came that the Monarch was no more—hopefully replaced by still another ICBM— the corporation would continue its way, growing, dividing, spreading. But the company must never take the feature spot. It must appear on the edge of the circle of light, just close enough to be recognizable; the product itself, in this case the Monarch, must hold the center of the beam. As in the case of a politician who connives his way into a photograph of the president, the company must seek its greatness through association. By the same token, the Monarch must prove an unqualified success, for it carried both the company's prestige and made possible its growth. He appreciated the tightrope Bergstrom had to walk.

But that was one thing. His own job was something else. It wasn't splashy enough, not the kind that made people sit up and take notice. He couldn't make a fast impression like Garfield. His was the day-to-day plugging, with long-range returns. That's why he'd pushed the tie-in ads and articles— they gave him a chance to branch out, use his talents. Only, the material he planted today might not appear for months; by then everyone forgot where it came from.

And there was his personality. Looking objectively at himself, he could very well see what had happened. Faced by blasted hopes, trading ambition for security, he had withdrawn from the race, satisfied, or so he had thought, with his present position. But there had been specters, shadows of unclear meaning, so that he had become fearful, withdrawing even more. Now he was "Koepple, chief of advertising," a title with a terminal ring. No longer was he counted among the battlers. His name could easily slip past, unnoticed by Bergstrom as he examined his empire for John Vroman's replacement. But was he through? He pulled his thin shoulders together, striving for strength. His last chance. Could he do it?

Harry Garfield learned of John Vroman's resignation from his secretary, Jane Cooper, and since, the rumors had been flying: Vroman had quit, had been fired, had been hired by Boeing at double the salary—NASA had grabbed him. Everyone had a different story. But one thing was certain: it had come out of the blue.

He wasn't nearly so interested in what had happened to Vroman as what might happen to his job. Eighteen or twenty G's, a tidy sum that carried with it a goodly amount of prestige: the privilege of the executive dining room, attendance at top management meetings, use of the executive barbershop, a future—all things he could use. It rightfully should have been his when Bergstrom hired Vroman, and the memory still galled.

A couple of stiff highballs at the Sycamore Tree hadn't prevented a restless night. Now forty-five, he had been with the company twenty-two years; this was his last chance for the top. Muff it and he'd hack out his life in the twelve-G bracket. But he wouldn't muff it. Last time he'd lost out because of Vroman's friendship with Bergstrom; he had convinced himself of that. Now the job was open. It required a firm hand, an old hand who knew the company and its ways; someone like himself. Harry Garfield, director of PR. He liked the sound of it.

Bergie couldn't wait long. With the hot firing coming up, the big contract, he'd have to move fast. Henderson and Elliott were too new, he reflected, and Koepple was washed up. He could see it in the ad chief's wasted body, his chronic fatigue. He looked like an old, old man, too old to hope. The thought struck him there was a difference of but few years in their ages, yet, he reflected, there was a world of difference. He had youth, vigor, was just getting into stride. Youth plus maturity.

Contemplating the happy twist of fate, he headed toward Bergstrom's office to present a new idea and, incidentally, plant the thought that Vroman's abrupt default really posed no problem: he was there, available. He considered Bergstrom a plodding man with definite ideas, one who seldom acted until every card was covered. Yet he was sharp, disconcertingly so at times. His eyes, polished and blank, could become excruciatingly penetrating. Long ago he had analyzed the vice-president's decision-making behavior, deciding it revolved around one point: what could it do for the company? Well, he could do plenty for the company. But he'd have to push fast, hard, catch Bergie on the rebound.

He walked slowly, stopping several times to sip from a cup of coffee he had obtained from one of the machines. He knew Bergie too well to make a blatant pitch. Instead he'd concentrate on the idea he had to offer, get him enthused, then gently plant the idea of himself as director and let it flower in Bergie's mind so that he would come to think of it as his own. He'd push other ideas, build them up, pyramid them, overwhelm the big stolid man upstairs until he had no recourse but to appoint him. And when he got the job, he'd initiate a PR program that would make the present one look like a pitch for a Sunday school picnic.

Leaving the elevator, he threw the paper cup into a trash container, squared his shoulders and walked into the vice-president's office.

"Greetings, beautiful. Is the boss man in?"

Joan Wesley gave him an artificial smile. "He's busy."

"Alone?" She nodded. "I'll just pop in."

The vice-president glanced up at his entrance.

"Morning, R. T. Got a minute?"

"I have a meeting with Kroeber shortly."

"This won't take long. Just an idea I want to get rolling."

"All right." Bergstrom sounded reluctant. Garfield slid into the chair opposite him.

"As you know, we—my section—have been working damned hard to sell the Monarch to the community, and I believe with some success. But I feel we've been missing a good bet—the future." He watched, alert for a reaction, and saw none.

"The future . . . as represented by our youth," he continued. "I've always felt the schools offer the most fertile ground for this sort of thing. Sell the missile to the kids and they'll sell it to their parents. That's the whole idea. But to get to the kids, we have to get to the educators—hit 'em hard with something that'll make 'em sit up." He gazed expectantly at the heavy, balding man across from him, forcing him to nod.

"Today's students are tomorrow's workers so, in a sense, we're feathering our own nest, preparing the soil for tomorrow's crop, so to speak. I've talked with Carson in employment and he's hot for the idea, thinks it's great. We can cut down recruiting costs by orienting these kids ahead of time—make the Monarch their goal."

"The Monarch?"

"The corporation," he amended. "I'm just using the Monarch as a symbol—of WAD and MAC both." He noticed the vice-president grimace, and remembered he detested the contracted forms for the division and corporate names, even though widely used. (Vroman liked to point out they fitted nicely into headlines.) "I have an idea how we can do it," he finished.

"I have no doubt."

"It's surefire, R. T."

"Perhaps."

"I have the package ready, laid out."

"You probably have a good idea, Harry, but right now, with the launching scarcely six weeks away, we have more pressing problems."

"Certainly," he responded quickly. "I've been concentrating on the hot firing, but this is the routine kind of material we have to build—the kind that keeps the machine going from day to day. It's not something that would interfere with our key efforts. I hadn't intended that."

"Granted your idea's good, we can't afford it, Harry. Right now our future depends on getting a damned healthy production contract. We should be bending every effort in that direction."

"We are," he stated firmly. "We're paving the way, a steady buildup—whetting the public appetite, so to speak. Don't worry about the publicity, R. T. We're playing it like a striptease—not too much at once." He caught the unrelenting look in Bergstrom's eyes, and quickly added, "I was going to suggest we get together, let me show you what we have laid out."

"Sounds fine."

"A positive approach."

"I'm happy to hear it, Harry."

"About this other program—"

"I don't want to hear about it," Bergstrom cut in. "I don't want to hear about anything but the Monarch."

"Yes, of course."

Bergstrom glanced at his watch and Garfield eyed him indecisively, wondering if the time were opportune to mention the director. Harsh, austere, the vice-president's demeanor offered no encouragement. Feeling the seconds slip away, he blurted: "By the way . . ."

"Yes?" Bergstrom lifted his eyes.

"What's this rumor I hear?"

"What have you heard?"

"About Vroman."

"Well?"

"They say he's quitting." Bergstrom's face remained unchanged and Garfield felt the weight of six or seven seconds before he replied.

"I know of no rumor."

The frosty smile didn't escape Garfield. His need to push the subject, make his pitch, ended in a cold knot inside him. Smacking his lips, he said in a too-loud voice, "Well, it doesn't make much difference. It's just that I have a dozen projects on the fire. I don't want to be held up for lack of authority."

Bergstrom answered softly, "There won't be a lack of authority, Harry."

Esther Lynn was doing her nails when she heard someone at the door and looked up, startled to see Bergstrom. She dropped her hands guiltily.

"Hello, Esther." Appearing not to notice, he came in and sat across from her. She felt a stab of unease. The visit, following so closely on the heels of Vroman's resignation, portended no good. Perhaps he had come to tell her he had a new director —that the new man had requested his own girl. The unease turned to dread but she managed a smile. Glancing toward the door to assure himself they were alone, he asked casually, "Doing anything this evening?"

"Not a thing." She felt sudden relief.

"Perhaps you could help me out."

"I'd be glad to, Mr. Bergstrom."

He nodded. "We have a visitor—Colonel Hammond from Washington. He's in the plant now with Elliott. Perhaps you've seen him."

"Just a glimpse."

"I had hoped to entertain him this evening, but unfortunately, a second appointment somehow got onto the calendar."

"Oh, if I can . . ." She felt the familiar tingle of anticipation.

"It would be appreciated."

"I'd be delighted."

"I thought I might take him over to the Sycamore Tree for an early highball. Perhaps . . ."

"I'd be quite happy," she murmured.

"Just a cocktail or two."

"Of course."

"It would be of immense help, Esther." The dark eyes held a mocking gleam but she didn't mind, had never minded. A vast knowledge lay between them, wordless, but shared. Why had she worried?

"He's looking over our operation—getting information for General Barmon."

"Oh?" She searched her mind.

"Ballistic Systems Division," he explained. "Hammond handles his liaison with the Pentagon. Barmon's scheduled to testify before the Slater committee." As their eyes met, he added, "Along the same lines we are, I hope."

"What time?" She watched him steadily.

"Around six."

"Fine, I'll have time to change."

"Make it casual."

"Yes."

"Everything else all right?" he asked.

"Yes, fine."

"Need anything?"

"No, everything's fine." She waited expectantly.

"You might as well take off now."

"Thank you, Mr. Bergstrom." As he rose to leave, she felt a pang of disappointment that he hadn't mentioned anything about Vroman, or her job. His stopping in, the few casual words, the abrupt departure—it was like the first time and all the times since. Aside from the first occasion, there had been no mention of overtime. Now she automatically put in for it, just as it was automatically approved. Vroman had never mentioned the subject, but she had always sensed his chill disapproval as he initialed the requests. She was glad he was gone.

Bergstrom turned back at the door, wearing that curious half-smile she knew so well and found so baffling.

"I'm certain you'll leave a much better impression than I could."

"I'll try, Mr. Bergstrom."

"Thank you, Esther."

"Over there's the factory, half a million square feet," Elliott told Colonel Otis Hammond, indicating a huge boxlike structure across from them. They had just come from the metallurgical laboratories, where they had spent an hour or so watching test engineers torture steel during its submersion in liquid hydrogen at minus 423 degrees Fahrenheit—bending, ripping, twisting, tearing it apart with powerful steel talons in the ceaseless quest to obtain better space-age materials.

Entering through the big rolling factory doors, they walked between rows of wire-meshed tool cribs, past punch presses and metal-processing booths toward the fabrication and assembly line. Elliott liked the factory. Here he could see the gigantic missile hulks in various stages of manufacture, or nestled in the end docks like a row of submarines berthed side by side as they awaited shipment. They appeared heavy, ponderous, completely incapable of boosting themselves from the face of the earth, let alone of riding the rim of space at fantastic speeds. Thick of girth, flared at the tails, still they possessed a peculiar grace. He supposed it lay in their symmetry.

Hammond cupped his mouth and yelled, "Noisy."

"Damned noisy," he shouted back.

"I feel half deaf."

"You'll get used to it," he encouraged. Odd, Elliott had scarcely noticed the noise until the other mentioned it, but it was true, the squat building vibrated with sound—the smash of huge drop hammers, the whine of high-speed drills, clanging overhead cranes and clanking noises—ten thousand sounds that drowned all but the loudest and nearest human voices. Yet the sound, too, had a pattern, a steady pulsating throb that underscored the harsher noises—like a giant heartbeat, he thought. From time to time Hammond stopped to peer at something or ask questions concerning one of the operations. Middle-aged, slender, bespectacled, he somehow reminded Elliott of a bird dog.

Elliott enjoyed this part of the tour. This was the domain of the green badge—the hourly worker who lived by the clock, ate from a battered lunch pail instead of in the spick-and-span cafeteria, and spent a great deal of time reading union handouts and waiting for coffee breaks to begin pitching rings. The badges formed a caste system—he had discovered that early. The whites were the Brahmins, the gods of the missile, and like gods they seldom mixed with lesser mortals. No more than necessary. When they did, they descended but a single step, gave their orders to the blues, who passed them down to the red-blues. (But there were grades of blue; his own badge was low blue.) The greens were the untouchables, the men who, around him now, bit by bit fabricated and assembled the tens of thousands of parts that gave being to the big metal bird. Shirtsleeved supervisors wearing bow ties and sweat-stained collars strolled here and there, as if their presence alone sufficed to guarantee proper work procedures. Soiled hands, grimy clothes, strange scents of chemicals and greases, forklifts threading along crowded aisles, the metallic voices of loudspeakers competing with bells, buzzers, gongs, the agonized shriek of metal passing under a saw blade—he liked it all. Occasionally someone nodded or waved and he answered without recognition.

Faces interested him. They all tended to merge into one, which he identified as "the face of America"—which, in fact, it was. The sheer multitude of faces robbed them of individuality. Faces from Los Angeles, Long Beach, Santa Monica, Burbank, from as far away as Santa Ana and Ventura; from places with names like Altadena, San Marino, Arcadia and Garden Grove. These were the faces of native sons and out-of-staters, of Greeks, Mexicans, Germans, Japanese, Italians—a medley of nationalities, statures, dress. Here and there girls wearing tight slacks assembled small components or worked in walled nooks that served as offices. DANGER, KEEP OUT, NO ADMISSION WITHOUT SAFETY GLASSES, HIGH VOLTAGE, TESTS IN OPERATION, DANGER, DANGER, DANGER—warning signs, direction signs, first-aid signs; bulletin boards filled with union and management news, recreational posters interspersed with lurid pictures depicting workers blinded, cut or otherwise maimed through failure to heed the safety rules.

Hammond stopped to inspect a stubby tank.

"Guardian space vehicle," Elliott explained.

"I know. It resembles the Agena."

"Somewhat," he agreed. "It has a different purpose." The colonel didn't answer, and they moved on.

The fabrication of the Monarch ICBM began in one corner of the factory. Starting as a roll of thin, tough, stainless steel, it grew by accretion as it passed through the various fabrication and assembly areas until it reached the opposite end of the building, by then ready for weighing, shrouding and lifting aboard one of the huge tubular steel transports for delivery to the airfield, from whence it would be flown to one of the static test sites, or to Cape Canaveral. But it was here in the factory that the missiles gestated. Huge, wingless, they resembled prone giants, their bright steel bodies glistening in the glare of the overhead fluorescent lights.

They paused to watch the weld heads move over the great circular bands of steel, binding them together to form the Monarch's tanks. There was something eerie about the scene, Elliott thought—the great curving planes of metal, the masked welders, goggled eyes peering into the blue flames, the constant movement of machines and people. He walked over to one of the foremen.

"How's it going, Herb?"

"The same." The foreman grinned. He was a beanpole giant with red hair, a bent nose, and eyes that were as blue as the heliarc flames. His shirt collar was drenched with sweat and he wore a sporty gold and brown bow tie. Elliott had done an article on him and Herb thought the PR man tops. Elliott introduced Colonel Hammond.

"How does the Air Force like this bastard?" Herb asked.

"Fine."

"Better than the Atlas and Titan, eh?" Elliott felt discomfited but Hammond smiled at the blunt question.

"We'll have to see," he said.

"Wait'll she flies. You'll see. This baby will plaster the moon with Guardians."

"That's NASA," Hammond replied dryly.

"Sure, NASA, but she'll sure carry a nice bomb, eh?" He winked. "She could sure plaster Moscow."

"We're not planning on that." Despite himself, Hammond's face became wreathed.

"She could, Colonel. I got a feeling about this baby. Look at her. Power. She stinks of it. Goddamn, she's a beauty. You going to see her fly?"

"I expect to." Hammond's eyes told Elliott he was enjoying the talk.

"Man, I wish I could. All I see is this goddamned part here . . . welding the tanks, some of the plumbing, hanging on the sheet steel, then pushing her over to final assembly. I wish to hell I could see her go."

"You sound enthused."

"Damned right I'm enthused," Herb exclaimed. "I feel like I built the damn thing. Those people over there"—he waved toward final assembly—"just hang on all the crap, but this is where the bird's really built. The tanks and plumbing, Christ, that's her guts. You know what? Sometimes I go out on the apron and I look at the finished babies and I think: Holy Jesus, I built that. It sure gives me a good feeling."

"It gives the Air Force a good feeling to know the people here feel that way," Hammond said.

"Hell, yes, we feel that way. This baby's like a woman," Herb said. "We go over her the same way."

Hammond said earnestly, "I'm sure you do."

"Amen." Herb winked. "It's the plumbing that counts."

They walked down the line, inspecting the seemingly endless machines that forged, extruded, spun or otherwise shaped the long sheets of raw metal, spewing out their products to workers who added them to the growing hulks. Finished, Elliott led the way to final assembly, a raised dock where the plumbing, pneumatic and hydraulic systems were attached to the tankage and the huge booster and second-stage engines installed. Brackets, pressure lines and cables were added, then came the electrical and electronic systems—guidance, autopilot, telemetry, propellant utilization.

"Like a jigsaw puzzle," Hammond commented as they reached the end of the dock.

"Over forty thousand parts." He showed him the rows of electronic consoles jamming the bays beneath the docks, explaining, "Test equipment. Every part is tested as the missile is built—subsystems, systems, the entire missile."

"And still we lose them."

"You can't say we don't try."

"Yes," Hammond agreed, "we try."

Elliott led the way past a guard into a walled-off area marked RESTRICTED, and paused before a huge bottle-shaped form that nearly filled the large rectangular room.

"The Monarch mock-up." When the other didn't comment, he continued, "A carbon copy of the missiles on the assembly line—all but the reality."

This time Hammond said, "Quite a replication." Elliott tapped one of the giant engines, producing a hollow sound.

"She's made of wood, metal and plastics," he explained.

They studied it silently. Over ten feet in diameter and ninety-six feet long, it lay cradled on a three-section trailer. Designed to compress time and distance beyond anything presently produced, it was hailed by its backers as the technological wonder of the missile age. Hammond studied the thick, ungainly mainstage with its huge twin engines, the slimmer, single-engine second stage, the tapering nose cone. He poked and peered at the various parts—the flared tail nozzles, the electronic pods, the adapter ring that fitted the nose cone to the second stage.

Herb was right, Elliott thought, she was a goddamned beauty. The shop man had expressed his own feelings exactly. Viewing the mock-up now, he imagined the way it would be someday with the bird. Great clouds of steam would swirl upward as she struggled to break free of the pad, her mainstage engines shooting a fiery exhaust into a flame bucket cooled by the injection of thousands of gallons of water per minute. Freed, she would compute her way through the loneliness high above the earth, sensing every force which affected her body. She would measure gravitation, acceleration, angular velocity, compute these as units of time, perform complex mathematical equations, translate these into guidance commands to enable her to find her way unerringly over the South Atlantic; and someday, perhaps, a third of the way around the earth—an assignation with total destruction.

But not all of the rocket would make the trip.

High up in the atmosphere small explosive bolts would fire, push free the second stage; the mainstage would follow for a short while before curving back into the denser regions of the air to turn to a molten torch. The second stage would continue to ride the upper rim of the air, attaining a speed of nearly seventeen thousand miles per hour before a small brain caused the big sustainer engine to shut down, instructed smaller trim rockets to adjust velocity and trajectory; finally freed, the reentry vehicle would speed on alone. For the first and second stages had but a single purpose—to drive the nose cone to its target. He wondered if the man now peering at the mock-up saw this drama. Or was the Monarch just a stark weapon to him —a tool for annihilation?

The ear-splitting screech of the factory whistle brought an end to the din beyond the wall. The reflection of blue heliarc flames blinked out, the snarling screech of saw blades biting through the metal ceased, leaving an almost eerie silence. Then came the shuffling of feet, voices, whistles. The workday was done.

Finally the colonel stepped back, remarking, "Quite a bird."

"We're proud of it."

"With good reason. Will you be in Florida for the launch?"

"No. As Herb says, I only see this goddamned end of it."

The colonel smiled, and said, "Too bad."

"How long will you be with us, Colonel?"

"A day or so."

"If you're through . . ."

"For now," he acknowledged.

"Perhaps we'd better return. I know Mr. Bergstrom would like to see you before he leaves." He led the way back through the factory, now quiet and almost deserted. Here and there a worker hurried down a lonely aisle or a guard sauntered, prepared for the long night.

As they entered the vice-president's office, Bergstrom rose, extending a cordial smile.

"Have a good look around?" He waved toward some chairs.

"Fine," Hammond assented.

"Visit the labs? Final assembly?"

"Mr. Elliott made quite a complete tour of it."

"How about the mock-up room?"

"We made the circuit," Elliott confirmed.

"Good." The vice-president turned his attention to their visitor. "How does the bird strike you?"

"Favorably from all I've seen." Hammond allowed himself a perfunctory smile. "We'll know better after the initial launching."

"We won't have any trouble there."

"We have full confidence," Hammond said.

"It's a new bird, advanced, and I feel quite safe in saying, a better one," Bergstrom said. "We've been able to cash in on most of the mistakes made in earlier programs. I think you'll find the Monarch will fly like a veteran."

"We sincerely hope so."

Bergstrom nodded, gratified. "We're utilizing advanced fabrication and assembly techniques—all set to swing into operational production." They chatted for a while, then he glanced at his watch. "We'll have lunch with Welkes and Stark tomorrow—hash over our presentation to the Slater committee."

"That would be wise," Hammond acceded.

"Not that we expect any crossed wires. General Barmon has been quite well satisfied with our progress." When the other failed to comment, he continued, "We have prepared considerable material—the facts and figures variety. Elliott here can fix you up."

"I'd appreciate that."

"I had hoped to be able to show you around this evening," Bergstrom pursued, "but unfortunately something rather important has come up."

Hammond observed politely, "That's quite all right."

"However, I do have a few free moments. Suppose we drop by the Sycamore Tree for a drink?"

"That would be fine." Bergstrom rose and the others followed suit. After shaking hands with the colonel and exchanging the appropriate words, Elliott hurried toward his office.

He'd give Carole a call.

Esther Lynn prided herself that she could wrap any man around her finger. Or almost any. Her single reservation was Bergstrom. But, of course, he *was* unusual. Bergstrom. . . . Resentfully, she lifted her eyes and studied Otis Hammond's profile. Oblivious of her, he was watching a torch dancer sway through her midnight routine, twirling two firebrands and from time to time managing to drop a garment. The audience loved it.

Her pique grew. Bergstrom imagined all he had to do was throw someone at her and she'd do the rest. Like tonight. Like all the other nights. He didn't care whether they were fat, thin, young . . . and yet, pondering it, she decided she didn't really mind. That was the damnable part. If she could have planned her life, she would have chosen something very like this. But if only Bergie'd come right out and say what he had in mind instead of the damned indirect way he approached things. Especially after so much time. At least he could mention the job, assure her.

She had always liked older men, like Hammond. They were more interesting, had more—what was the word?—*savoir faire,* that was it. None of the pawing, fumbling, beating around the bush. She looked at the gold eagles on his collar. *Older men, her stepfather* . . . The memory came sharp and clear, poignant yet pleasurable. She pushed it down again, gazing at the dance floor. Pirouetting, the dancer swirled her torches, painting arcs of fire against the dark background. She was down to two scant garments and the crowd shouted encouragement.

"Great, isn't she?" Hammond exclaimed.

"Graceful." She studied him bemusedly. His early formality with Bergstrom had vanished, and she saw he was slightly drunk. Flushed, his eyes bright, he leaned toward her expectantly. She knew the look.

"Been here before?"

"Once or twice," she answered guardedly, wondering what he might know. She had suggested the place as one where Bergstrom had an arrangement for picking up the tabs, as Hammond would discover soon enough.

He leaned closer. "I'm certainly fortunate."

"Oh?"

"Such a pleasant evening. I'd been envisioning a dull trip."

"I . . . hope it's not that."

"Anything but. It's kind of you."

"I'm enjoying myself."

"Like your job?" She glanced quickly at him. He had asked casually, but his face was speculative.

"Shouldn't I?" she parried.

"Of course. Bergstrom seems like a fine man."

"He is."

"Been with him long?".

"Several years."

"Long enough to know, eh?"

She stared directly at him. "Yes, long enough to know."

Hammond was drunk but not, she observed, too drunk. When she came from the bathroom, he was sitting on the edge of the bed. His legs, below his shorts, were thin, almost emaciated, yet his scrawny body held a boyish quality.

"Like me?"

"Take off the bra," he ordered thickly. She removed it slowly without taking her eyes from him. This was a moment she savored; to be desired, the object of someone's total want, lust, to be needed, needed. Pleasure and pain. The figure on the bed could be anyone, anyone at all.

"Yes," he urged. She removed the last garment, conscious of his avid eyes. He reached out and pulled her alongside him, twisting her back on the bed, kissing her and cupping her breast.

"Like it?" she asked fiercely.

"Yes," he gasped.

"Tell me, tell me."

At ten o'clock Wednesday morning, Roland T. Bergstrom held his weekly staff meeting in the small conference room adjoining his office. Present were Elliott, Koepple, Garfield, Henderson and Carole Janek. Vroman, now on his last week, didn't attend, nor did anyone appear to miss him. He usually sat at the opposite end of the table from Bergstrom, tall and gaunt, a rather stern-faced counterbalance to the stolid vice-president. Now Henderson sat in the chair, looking across the expanse of mahogany at Bergstrom. He sat there, crew cut and all, but somehow he didn't fit. Or so Elliott thought.

As soon as they were settled, the vice-president stated abruptly, "From this moment on, until the Monarch is launched, I want every effort directed toward that end. What we do, how well we do it, may have a direct bearing on getting the big contract. I don't have to tell you what that means." He paused, scanning their faces. No one spoke; no one was expected to. "Welkes—and the corporation—expect this to be a memorable day. We don't want any slips. That requires firm plans—every single preparation made in advance."

Garfield broke the silence that followed.

"The responsibility will lie at the other end . . . at Canaveral."

"For handling the actual launching news, yes, but the preparations are being made at this end. That's the purpose of this meeting—to see that those preparations are adequate."

"They're adequate, R. T., at least as far as my department is concerned."

"I want them adequate for all departments, Harry." He looked at Elliott. "How's the press kit coming, Jim?"

"Fine. We'll have it in plenty of time."

"Making it strong?"

"We're hitting it," he assured him.

"History, background, description, personalities?"

"The works."

"I'd like to emphasize plant and corporation capabilities too, show that we're geared to the space age."

"We do that. We have a story on our atomic division—our nuclear engine experiments—and several sidebars on the Guardian."

"Very good. Any human interest angle?"

He nodded. "A profile on the test conductor, key men in the launch, stories and art on the men who made the Monarch possible—Byerkoff, Welkes, Kroeber."

"Factory types?"

"Several interviews. The what-I-do-on-the-Monarch type."

"How about radio and TV?"

"Full coverage," he advised. "CBS is sending down a special crew."

"Good, that'll force the other networks to follow suit," Bergstrom declared. He leaned forward on his elbows. "We should include a downrange map with a dotted line showing the Monarch's trajectory."

"Carole's ahead of you."

"Excellent." The vice-president glanced at her. "Are you showing the locations of the tracking stations?"

"Only Bermuda. No other downrange stations are involved," she explained.

"How about seagoing trackers?"

"Ship positions aren't available yet. If you'd rather . . ."

"No, we'll go with what we have," he decided. "It looks like you've done a pretty thorough job, Jim." The talk became general until he glanced at Garfield, who had been fingering his cigar impatiently. "Something on your mind, Harry?"

"I think we need promotional material as well as this run-of-the-mill publicity."

"I don't want run-of-the-mill publicity, Harry."

"This launching is big. We should make it big."

"That's why we're here," Bergstrom countered. "I'm happy to hear ideas."

"A Monarch tie pin, small plastic models, the Monarch on match covers—that's the kind of things people remember. Tomorrow the general news story is forgotten, buried in the archives."

"Perhaps."

"Every time you light a cigarette you think of the Monarch," Garfield persisted. "That's lasting publicity—a temporal extension in value."

"That's a fancy phrase." Bergstrom's lips curled slightly.

Henderson broke in to suggest small stainless-steel missile models to serve as paperweights for the desks of senior Air Force officers. Koepple wanted Monarch balloons for distribution to all the small fry who would be watching the flight from Cocoa Beach. The talk became animated, and listening, Elliott suddenly realized what it was all about: Vroman's job was up for grabs and everyone was trying to catch Bergstrom's eye. He looked at Carole and let his lid droop in a slow wink. She didn't appear to notice. Garfield dominated the conversation until finally Bergstrom declared: "We haven't time, Harry. Your ideas are too late."

"Late?" Garfield appeared puzzled. "I'm talking about what we're doing. I planned ahead, R. T. I ordered the tie pins and match covers last month. The plastic models too."

Bergstrom said acidly, "You were quite certain of yourself."

"The idea's good."

"All right, Harry, it's your bailiwick." His voice held dismissal as he glanced at Koepple. "What are we doing about advertising, Art?"

"We have a back cover on *Scientific American*. It'll hit the stands the day before the launch."

"That's for the highbrows," the vice-president observed humorously. "What are we doing for Joe Doakes?"

"We have the usual trade mag ads—"

"The usual?"

"But slanted for the launching," Koepple finished.

"We should run a full-page ad in the Washington papers the day of the flight—spice it up with one of Carole's illustrations." He looked at her. "How about it, Carole? Feel up to a masterpiece?"

"Have you anything special in mind?"

"A good lift-off scene, something that gives the impression of size, power. The missile should dwarf everything around it— the pad, tower, background. And we should keep the ad clean, just a simple tag line reading *A Mighty Monarch Roars Aloft*."

Bergstrom shifted his eyes from one to the other. "If there are no questions, I'd like to go on to the next order of business."

In the tense silence that followed, Elliott realized that everyone was waiting for the vice-president to mention Vroman . . . the job. He grew still inside, aware of Carole's eyes. Garfield looked expectant while Koepple seemed to have shrunk inwardly, pulling his frail body deeper into his chair. Henderson hunched forward, watching the vice-president closely. Bergstrom smiled faintly but when he spoke, his voice was brisk.

"Once the bird is launched, I intend to initiate an entire new program, show the Monarch as a superbooster as well as a super-ICBM." Someone sighed audibly and the atmosphere became more relaxed.

"Does that mean we're going to concentrate on NASA?" Garfield asked.

Bergstrom nodded. "NASA and the Air Force both. I don't mind telling you, Welkes is unhappy. We've let a lot of fat contracts slip through our fingers. We intend to remedy that."

"We lose contracts through engineering, not PR."

"Engineering can lose a contract, but PR can sell one. That's a good point to remember, Harry."

"We can sell when we have something to sell—"

"We have something to sell," Bergstrom cut in. "We have a score of designs, for NASA and the military both. But we have to put them across. We need ideas."

"We have plenty of ideas," Garfield countered.

"I hope so. After the launching we want to slant for space . . . get into orbit so to speak."

"The Air Force won't like that."

"Offering our capabilities to NASA? Perhaps not, but we have to look ahead."

"In effect, we'll be concentrating on the launching and structuring a new program at the same time. Is that correct?" Elliott asked.

"That's about the size of it, Jim. Of course, as I indicated, I want primary emphasis on the hot firing."

"We'll have our hands full."

"It can't be helped. For all practical purposes, the Monarch is in the countdown. We haven't much time."

For a while they tossed ideas back and forth, then Bergstrom commented: "I think you get the idea. I want a fresh program, hard-hitting. NASA's dollar is growing and we want to grow with it. At the same time, we want to remember that the Air Force is the bird in hand. We don't want conflict there. So let's consider it and see what we come up with." He looked the length of the table. "Have you any suggestions, Eugene?"

Henderson took the time to place his cigarette in a tray before answering, and when he did, he gazed directly at the vice-president.

"I'm not directly connected with the Monarch but I have generated a few ideas. It's a glamorous bird."

"We'd appreciate hearing them, Eugene."

Henderson smiled, a quick, tailored smile.

"In PR work we have an expression—the Big Picture. I like the term because it donates the overall viewpoint I like to get. One of the things that strikes me about the Big Picture is that we must extrapolate more from it, see what the Big Picture of the future is, how it affects our products and company growth. That's what I've attempted to do."

"You're looking ahead." Bergstrom nodded, satisfied.

"Tomorrow serves as today's guide."

"A good point, Eugene."

Elliott glanced at the speaker. He noted the cut of his suit and the expensive material that went into it. It had not been bought off the peg. He was wearing a soft, off-white shirt and an expensive tie that harmonized with it. He had to admire the way Henderson handled himself. And Bergie. He was saying: "We're absorbed more with the Monarch than in the environment surrounding it, and that's a grave mistake."

"In what way?" Bergstrom encouraged.

"The Monarch is . . . to the rest of the nation . . . just another weapon in a missile arsenal. Quite an extensive arsenal. I believe we should watch the competition more closely, assess its strengths and weaknesses and capitalize on them in our own program. Every dollar that goes to a competitor is a dollar we're deprived of."

"Excellent."

"The Douglas Skybolt is a good example," Henderson explained. "It'll represent around two billion dollars, or will before they're through. In essence, that's two billion dollars less in the pot."

"What the hell can we do about it?" Garfield cut in. His voice and manner displayed his irritation. "You could say the same for Saturn, Nova, the B-70."

"We could." Henderson looked bland.

"Have you anything concrete in mind?" Bergstrom asked.

"Several things. However, I know your time is limited so I'll just mention one—throw it out as food for thought."

"We'd be pleased to hear it."

"I'm thinking in terms of anti-missiles instead of missiles. Now take the Nike-Zeus . . ." Elliott noticed a startled look pass over the vice-president's face and wondered why. "The Army claims that it can be developed into a defensive system that will enable us to knock down almost anything the Russians throw at us. Do you know what such a system would cost? Believe me, it would run into billions—money which might better be spent on ICBMs."

"What's your plan, Eugene?" Bergstrom's face was thoughtful.

"We should stress the invulnerability of the Monarch, play up the fact it carries its own decoys."

"Oh . . ." The exclamation slipped softly from Koepple's lips as he lifted his head to scrutinize the speaker. His querulous expression told Elliott that he understood all right. Henderson had pulled a bear-sized rabbit from the hat.

"If we can sell the idea that the Monarch's invulnerable, the assumption will extend to all ICBMs, Russia's included." Henderson dropped his voice. "It's as easy as that."

"It's a heavily classified system," Koepple said. His protest held a note of surrender.

"Does the Air Force want to see the Army in space?" He looked around the circle of faces. "Sell that and the decision-makers will think twice about where the money's going."

"Good thinking, Eugene." Bergstrom nodded approvingly.

"The Nike-Zeus is built on the principle of being able to discriminate between ICBMs and decoys," Elliott said, directing the remark to the vice-president.

"But it hasn't been proven," Henderson returned. "That's

what's held the system down. We have to sell the idea that our system's foolproof . . . that the Monarch is invulnerable. Let any other idea get around and we'd be dead."

Garfield said bleakly, "Can we claim the Monarch's invulnerable?"

Henderson shrugged. "We should use the money to buy the best system possible. Personally, I'm a Monarch man."

Bergstrom glanced at the chief of publicity. "I think we can assume the Monarch's invulnerable, Harry."

"Lord, you should have seen those people trying to impress me," Roland T. Bergstrom told his wife over dinner. "They're all hot after Vroman's job."

"Who do you think's best?"

"Hard to say. They all have their strong points. It's a matter of experience, performance, deciding who will best fit into the program ahead—a tough one to evaluate." He held his fork poised in the air. "Henderson fooled me today. He's sharp."

"Fooled you . . . how?" Elissa Bergstrom's eyes became inquisitive and he detected the quiet tone she assumed when she grew still inside.

"He threw out an idea on the Nike-Zeus."

Her face relaxed. "What's so magical about that?"

"The Nike-Zeus?"

"His bringing it up."

"Cronkhill shot me a wire on the same subject last week— thought we should be considering a campaign to offset it."

"Why?"

"Because it's ten or twelve billion dollars."

"Perhaps Henderson is your man."

"I don't know."

"Who else is there?"

He disregarded the question, caught with a new thought.

"I can't figure Vroman. I brought him in from the outside, made him."

"I wouldn't worry."

"I trained him for that job," he continued doggedly. "He's tops, and right now I'm not certain he could be replaced."

"But if he's gone . . ."

"I'm hoping he'll change his mind. Perhaps after a few weeks of rest . . ." When she didn't answer, he looked up, catching her eyes.

"Why in hell would a man do that, Elissa?"

Chapter 3

AT FORTY-TWO, Herbert P. Welkes was Midwest Aeronautical Corporation's youngest division president. He had risen through the engineering ranks with phenomenal swiftness, propelled by an unswervable faith in his destiny, as well as that of the corporation. He considered them one and the same. He was, in the parlance of the industry, a corporation man.

Thin, dour, he let his pale blue eyes sweep across the faces of Roland T. Bergstrom and Dr. Otto Kroeber before coming to rest on Paul Gaither, his chief engineer, saying querulously:

"We have a number of overdue items—the Slater hearing, the launching, the matter of contracts. I'd like to get on with them." He paused, doodling for several seconds to let the words sink in. "But first, let me say this. . . ."

Bergstrom listened patiently, recognizing the words as a mere preamble. Kroeber and Gaither apparently felt the same. Relaxed against the red leather couch, they clearly waited for the president to get to the point. Lyman Stark, the executive vice-president, sat to one side, regarding the proceedings woodenly. Tall, lean, ramrod stiff, he gave Bergstrom the impression of still being garbed in his lieutenant general's Air Force uniform. In actuality, he wore a conservative dark brown business suit, slighty tight, Bergstrom thought, in the shoulders. Harsh, austere, Stark puzzled him. In his book of personalities, Bergstrom long since had labeled him a question mark. He returned his attention as Welkes said:

"We can consider this the weeding-out period. The field will be left to the biggest, the fittest, specifications that I intend we meet. We can do it. The corporation is the fulcrum and our brains constitute the lever; used together, they can overcome any obstacles. Do I make myself clear?"

"You're clear, H. P.," Gaither said.

"We're getting lax, Paul. We've come a long way since the Monarch was a blueprint, but we're developing a tendency to lay back on the oars."

"I thought we were doing pretty good." Gaither sat straighter.

"For now, yes, but how about tomorrow? What building blocks are we laying, Paul?"

"We're solid."

"Are we? We're developing the Monarch, yes, and we expect to get a sizable production contract, plus healthy added support for our sea-launch version. We're also producing the Guardian for NASA, and that's all well and good. But we didn't get those contracts through thin air. We earned them by foresight, planning, applied intelligence—by the ability to come up with something better than our competitors. We won them in the marketplace." Welkes rapped out each point. "We were going great guns when we tackled the Monarch, and it was our initiative there, incidentally, that won us the Guardian. But it seems to me that we haven't come up with a productive idea since."

His voice became aggrieved.

"We're not pulling in the contracts, gentlemen."

"Is that what this is about—contracts?" Gaither's voice held a slight edge.

"That's it in a nutshell," Welkes affirmed. "We're not working anywhere near our capabilities. Scores of contracts are to be had and we should be nailing some of them down."

"We've been concentrating on the Monarch, H. P."

"We have to spread our talents, Paul."

"I'm gunning for the big one. That's my responsibility. I can't be bothered with every piddling study contract that comes along."

Welkes said sharply, "Totaled, they represent a lot of money."

"So does the Monarch."

"I know. I know very well." The president let his voice drop, speaking directly to him. "I also know that we have to keep moving ahead—planning for tomorrow. We need money in the bank, Paul, and that's what contracts are—money in the bank."

Bergstrom followed the exchange without too much interest. It was old hat. The push for contracts, an incessant force, occupied a great part of management time. But he could see Gaither's problem too. The Monarch kept the chief engineer's hands full.

"We have plenty of engineers and Ph.D.'s," Welkes said. "I'd think some of them could be put to work."

"Those boys are touchy, H. P. Pile the manure on them and they'll pack up and go home. We're buying degrees, not muscle, and we've got to have at least as many as the next company."

"Oh?" Welkes leaned forward, speaking with asperity, asserting that the bigger the company grew, the fewer contracts it obtained. His reedy voice in the quiet room gave Bergstrom the impression of the high notes of a flute. Stark was watching him, his face expressionless. Kroeber appeared thoughtful. There had been a time when Bergstrom had been perturbed by the empires within empires that blossomed around him almost overnight, but since his ascension to top management, he had learned that this, too, was one of the facts of life. Bigness bred bigness. Bigness *was* power.

Finally Welkes leaned back glowering.

"I might add, parenthetically, that the corporation isn't too happy." He made the statement as if it were the clincher. "Byerkoff mentioned this when I was East. His point, and I think it entirely reasonable, is that as far as dollar value is concerned, we're getting less in the way of research and study contracts than any ICBM contractor in the business. When he's unhappy, I'm unhappy."

"Our first hurdle is the Monarch," Gaither protested. "We haven't sold it yet. We still have to get it off the pad."

"You're the chief engineer."

"I'll get it off the pad, all right."

"I'm happy to hear you say so, Paul."

"I just don't want to have to worry over all this chicken feed."

"It's not chicken feed, not as Byerkoff sees it."

"He doesn't know the problems," Gaither retorted. "Besides, the dough isn't so plush right now."

"We're still not getting our share, Paul. One of our functions is to propose new business—sell ideas, stimulate new contracts. We've done that quite successfully in the past; the Monarch, for example."

"We keep a fairly steady stream of proposals going in," Bergstrom interjected, conscious of being on the defensive.

"Then why aren't we getting the business?"

"We are, but as Paul indicated, the Air Force and NASA are only putting out bids for jobs they consider essential. Neither are buying ideas—not at present. Times are too uncertain."

Welkes raised his head quizzically. "Uncertain?"

"Questions regarding the status of our space program have a holding effect," he explained. "Of course, that applies mainly to NASA."

"What questions? I don't follow you."

"Everyone has a different idea, especially on the moon business. No two brain factories think alike. It's a tug of war, H. P. Add to that the pressure to use solids for bigger boosters and you can see the dilemma."

"I'm still not satisfied."

"We should emphasize space more," Kroeber put in. "We're building a reputation as a weapons manufacturer."

"Aren't we?" Stark asked.

"Yes, but that doesn't sell NASA. We should attempt to establish ourselves as a foremost aerospace firm, not solely ICBMs."

"Doesn't the Guardian do that, Otto?"

"We're still short-cutting space."

"Space is secondary, at least until we get the bird into operational production," Gaither objected.

"We can't look at it that way," Welkes counseled. "We're after markets . . . wherever they are."

"We're going down that road," Bergstrom interceded. "We're giving a big play to space."

"But still not getting contracts," Welkes rejoined. "If Byerkoff thinks we're dragging our heels, then I think we're dragging our heels."

"My main concern is with the Monarch." Gaither was insistent on the point. "That's my prime target. If you're shooting for space and the NASA dollar, that's Otto's concern. He's the director of space projects."

"Not entirely. There are lots of crossed lines. It's a matter of teamwork, Paul."

"I know that. I also know we have to concentrate on the bird, at least until after the launch." It was apparent to Bergstrom that the chief engineer didn't put much stock in Welkes' complaint. His face held a shade of annoyance. Bergstrom watched the president, curious at how he would react. The chief engineer held a unique position in the management hierarchy, for his job exceeded in importance those of at least several higher ranking personnel. And he was a good chief engineer, although inclined to be quite independent and outspoken. Instead of answering, the president picked a paper from his desk and recited what other ICBM contractors were doing, the contracts they were getting. Finished, he let it flutter to his desk, looking quizzically at Gaither.

"Most of that stuff's pretty far out, H. P." The chief engineer appeared unconvinced.

"Far out?" Kroeber asked, amazed. "We should be looking beyond orbit."

"You look beyond orbit. I'm a weapons man, Otto, and my weapon is the Monarch. I can't worry about Alpha Centauri."

"I'm not speaking about Alpha Centauri. I'm speaking about cislunar and lunar space, our immediate future, the types of contracts we need to assure that future."

"The moon." He made it a swear word.

"The Russians find it interesting."

"We're competing for the big dollar," Gaither rejoined, "and that's the defense dollar—one that's being spent to develop systems practicable to our current needs. Right now we're concerned with space this side of orbit—ICBM space. If you don't think I'm right, look at the way the budget dollar's split up. Look at what's going into missiles, then look at NASA's share. That gives the answer."

"For today, yes, but look at the projection."

"To hell with the projection."

"We're committed to getting a man on the moon, and if we're going to participate, we'll have to have contracts," Kroeber stated. "It's that simple."

"My thinking exactly," Welkes cut in. "If we don't keep up, we might as well abandon the field to GD, North American and the others who are smart enough to appreciate tomorrow's dollar as well as today's."

"You can't pull men off the Monarch," Gaither protested heatedly.

"I'm not asking that." It was apparent to Bergstrom that the president's patience was wearing thin. His eyes held an angry glint. "I'm only asking that we put our R & D to work— make proposals and submit bids. Good Lord, Paul, we have engineers and Ph.D.'s hanging from the rafters."

"We need them."

"We need to put them to work, that's what we need. That's our job . . . as of now. I don't care what kind of proposals you submit, or where you submit them, but I do want to see new business. Is that clear?" He ended the words with a snap that spelled finality. Gaither knew it too. He leaned back, tight-lipped, arms folded across his chest. "So much for contracts," Welkes declared. "Now let's discuss the launching—"

"Speaking about the launching," the executive vice-president interrupted. Welkes eyed him, waiting. "We have to make a damned big splash," he finished.

"We certainly do, Lyman."

"We have to go beyond our present plans."

He paused and Welkes said, "Go on."

"We have to show that we're better than Titan II. Their new hypergolic fuel is quite a sensation."

"That we know." Welkes spoke dryly.

"The first Titan II went all the way. I think we should match it."

In the hush that followed, Bergstrom's first startled reaction was: My God! The usual first launch was a limited try, with the bird stripped of all but the booster engines. That was the Monarch plan—a short flight to validate the missile's operational systems and aerodynamic design. But Stark was suggesting a full-scale flight—booster, second stage, trim rockets, nose cone —a six-thousand-mile test instead of the short trajectory now planned. It was ambitious, audacious, dangerous.

Gaither asked incredulously, "You're not serious?"

"Titan II did it."

"Liquid oxygen is a different proposition."

"It's an admission of weakness not to go all the way." Stark's voice overruled the objection.

"It's not sound testing procedure," Gaither stated, tight-lipped.

"But it could be done, Paul?" Welkes fastened his eyes on the chief engineer.

"Is that a question or a statement?"

"Both."

"I suppose it could, if we were lucky—if we didn't have a bug in any of over forty thousand parts. But we'd have to be damned lucky."

Stark smiled curiously. "Isn't it all a gamble?"

"Sure, several hundred million worth, but why risk it all on the turn of a card?"

"Because otherwise we could lose it all."

Welkes nodded. "I agree with Lyman. A full-scale first flight would give us a definite edge."

"If we pulled it off, yes, but I'm opposed to it. It's my neck if the bird flops."

"That's your bailiwick, Paul. See that the bird doesn't flop."

"How can I guarantee that, with what you're demanding?"

"I'm not demanding anything. I'm just suggesting," Welkes replied irritably.

Bergstrom followed the argument closely. Gaither was right, of course. The booster stage should be tested exhaustively before piling on the second stage and nose cone. But the boldness of the scheme caught him, as it would catch others. If they could pull it off, it would lop months from the test schedule—bring the Monarch into operational status that much sooner. That, he reflected, was not to be sneezed at. With the Titan II, the new Series F Atlas and the hotter-than-fire Minuteman searing the skies, time suddenly had become a priceless commodity. He could see Stark's point.

"A booster flight is all that's required," Gaither contended doggedly. "Why push our luck? I'd rather see us follow the schedule. There's plenty of time."

"There's never plenty of time." Welkes' tone held rebuke. "We have more ICBM systems now than we can afford, and that point's going to come up. Believe me, it is. What do you think this Slater hearing's all about, Paul? Someone's apt to get lopped and I want to make damned certain it's not us. We need a system of proven capability as early as we can get it."

"That's my goal," Gaither replied more calmly, "a system of proven capability."

"Just get it off the pad—that's your goal." He turned to Kroeber. "What do you think, Otto?"

The latter eyed him reflectively before speaking. "Paul's right. You have a safety factor in hypergolics that's not present in liquid oxygen. Titan II also has fewer controls, a more simplified system."

"I know all that."

"The probability of failure would rise sharply," he warned. "You're asking for perfection on the first flight. It's extremely risky."

"The Titan people did it."

"With a more simplified system."

Stark raised a hand in gesture. "That's the point. We must prove it's not more simplified; that our system's just as reliable."

"It would be if you'd give us time," Gaither declared.

Welkes spoke sharply: "We have to weigh risk against gain."

"The bigger the risk, the greater the chance of loss," Gaither stated.

"No risk, no gain—that's the way I see it," Welkes rebuked. "How about it, Otto?"

"My reaction is negative."

"Christ, can't we have some positive thinking?" He glared at Bergstrom. "If we could pull it off, and I say if, what would it mean in the way of public relations? I'm thinking of the effect on decision-makers—Congress, the Department of Defense, the high brass."

"Great salesmanship," Bergstrom answered carefully. "The Boeing people did it with the Minuteman—made real PR hay."

"That's a solid-fuel job," Gaither objected.

"If we could claim that capability, it would give real impetus to the pitch we're making to the Slater committee," he finished.

"Exactly." Welkes looked satisfied. "It would certainly indicate how advanced our system is."

Gaither testily asked: "Who are we trying to please, the Slater committee or the Air Force?"

"Both," Welkes replied. "The Air Force is the customer but Slater can affect the purse strings. This tug-of-war among the services for the almighty dollar is going to get a lot grimmer. Throw in NASA and you can see how much grimmer."

"You can't change his thinking."

"Slater's? Perhaps not, but we can influence the press. Even congressmen read. Do you agree, Roland?"

"You'd get a good press."

"I don't like it," Gaither said bluntly.

Welkes declared crossly, "You're too adamant, Paul."

"With good reason."

"We're just exploring the possibility, not making a final decision."

"I'm glad to hear it, H. P."

"Just think it over," Welkes pressed. "Now, let's get to Mr. Slater." He turned to Bergstrom. "Have you talked with Bert Sumner about the hearing?"

"Vroman did," he replied, thinking he should call the congressman himself. "Our Washington office has been in constant touch. He was quite helpful—assured us that Slater's main point would revolve around the Monarch's necessity."

"We're prepared for that."

"As prepared as we'll ever be."

"Did he mention anything else?"

"He'll compare the Monarch with the competition—unfavorably, of course."

"I was thinking of solids."

"He won't miss that."

"No, he won't. Not that bastard."

"He'll give us a rough time," Bergstrom agreed. As another thought struck him, he added, "Our Washington man thinks he might bring up the Skybolt."

"Why Skybolt?" Welkes demanded.

"It's a solid, and in a sense, competitive. There are already a few stories to the effect that it negates ground-launched ICBMs. The Douglas people pull a lot of weight back there."

"I wouldn't worry over Skybolt," Stark interceded.

"Slater might." Bergstrom stared musingly at the executive

vice-president. Skybolt, an air-launched ballistic missile, was also one of the latest additions to the Air Force arsenal. Despite his affiliation with the company, Stark continued to favor all Air Force projects—even competitive ones, he thought.

"Let him." Stark dismissed the subject with a shrug.

"Solids—a nasty word." Welkes eyed his executive vice-president. "Slater will hit us hard in that area."

"He will, but we can't expect Air Force support," Stark advised. "They're committed to both systems." Bergstrom privately considered that as a lieutenant general, Stark's role in the award of the Monarch would likely command Slater's attention. But Welkes could field that.

"I wasn't particularly thinking of Air Force systems," the president explained.

"Nike-Zeus is where the danger lies," Stark advised.

"I'm not so certain, Lyman. It has solid Navy, Air Force and NASA opposition, to say nothing of the Administration. I'd say it was on the downgrade."

"Don't you believe it," he replied emphatically. "It's been dead before, but it always pops back. You're talking about a ten- or twelve-billion-dollar slice of the pie, H. P. That kind of money doesn't die easily. Watch Slater bring it up."

"I didn't say it was dead," Welkes countered.

"It's far from dead." Stark glanced at Bergstrom. "How about it, Roland?"

"I agree, Lyman. We can't write it off." He switched his attention to the president, explaining, "It has strong backing in the House. Aside from that, solids are making big inroads into space. Some of the House members are screaming now over a five-to-one disparity in the money NASA is spending for liquid fuel research as opposed to solids."

"Is that true?"

"Apparently."

"NASA is more familiar with liquids," Kroeber interrupted.

"We hope they stay that way." Welkes looked at Bergstrom again. "Slater bothers me."

"He's solid-minded."

"I know. I'm thinking of the trouble he can cause."

"Yes, considerable."

"We can't win before the committee, Roland."

"No, we can't." He considered it. "We'll have to beat him in the press, muster popular support."

"Well, that's your job."

"I'm prepared."

Welkes fingered his pencil. "The people I've talked with in Washington feel the Nike will get plenty of publicity but damned little money."

Stark's face took on a quizzical expression. "That's what they said about the Polaris, and look at it now."

"I'm not so certain that the Army has that kind of salesmanship, Lyman."

"Don't you believe it," he asserted forcefully. "The propaganda buildup is tremendous."

"I agree," Bergstrom interrupted. "To my way of thinking, solid fuels are getting attention out of all proportion to their value. I know Cronkhill's concerned."

The president turned to Kroeber. "You know something about them, Otto. What do you think?"

"About Nike-Zeus or solids in general?"

"Both."

Kroeber held his gaze for a moment before answering. "About Nike-Zeus, I'm not prepared to say. I have a feeling the system's feasible but, as Lyman indicated, it would require billions to perfect. The idea of shooting down oncoming ICBMs is quite ambitious."

"It's been done," Stark warned ominously.

"Staged," Kroeber objected. "They knew the Atlas flight profile."

"I don't like it."

Kroeber appeared not to hear him. "There's the problem of radar discrimination, distinguishing between ICBMs and decoys. Still, I believe it should be explored."

"At that cost?" Welkes snorted.

"I believe so," he answered. "I can also see how solid propellants could contribute far more to the space program than they do. And to weaponry too. Minuteman and Polaris are prime examples. You can't overlook their simplicity and reliability."

Welkes eyed him caustically. "We're not trying to sell solids, Otto."

"You asked for an assessment of their value."

"So I did." His lip curled slightly. "No doubt we'll have to answer such questions."

"Sumner mentioned that as a gun in the arsenal," Bergstrom commented.

"We have to consider this anti-ICBM problem," Kroeber pursued.

"Why?" Welkes shot back.

"The Russians are tackling it."

"To hell with the Russians."

"Slater will dwell on the point," Bergstrom warned.

"Let him."

"It's worth thinking about, H. P., if for no other reason than that it strikes right at the core of our own program. The system is dangerous."

"I can see that," Welkes acceded, "but it's more probable that Slater will try to show we're pushing ICBMs to the detriment of space. We should be prepared on that question."

"He will," Bergstrom agreed, "but until we get an operational

Saturn, our liquid ICBMs offer the only big space boosters we have. He can't discount that."

"Saturn's coming along fast." Welkes looked at his director for space projects for confirmation.

"Yes, it's moving," Kroeber confirmed, "but its use will be limited to large loads. It wouldn't be economically feasible for the everyday programs. We'll still have to depend on present boosters."

"Then that's what we'll stress, the Monarch as a booster," Welkes decided.

"I'd soft-pedal it," Stark cautioned. "The Air Force doesn't cotton to this buttering up to NASA."

"Goddamn, doesn't the Air Force use boosters?"

"For Air Force projects, yes."

"Okay, we won't talk about NASA. We'll talk about our boost capabilities."

"If you're thinking about Slater, you'll have to be specific —show in what way liquids are superior," Bergstrom advised. "He's certain to try to show otherwise."

"That's Otto's baby," the president replied. "He's our space expert." He doodled a crosshatch before continuing: "I have the feeling we're in for some surprises."

"Are you referring to Slater?"

He nodded. "We know him only in generalities, Roland. It's a fuzzy profile."

"We have plenty of personal data—religion, marital status, lodges, politics, business interests. They give us a clue."

"Even to sweet little what's-her-name you were telling me about, but that doesn't tell how he thinks."

"I've gone through the hearing transcripts, and past hearings." Bergstrom paused. "He's pro-Zeus, solids, Army and the corporations backing those interests. He's for space and against ICBMs in general, and he's against liquids in all forms. That seems to sum him up."

"It's not much to go on," Welkes said tentatively.

"It's a theme," he persisted. "I believe he'll follow the same pattern. Have you talked with General Barmon?"

"Lyman has. The Air Force sees it about as we do, but they can't be too perturbed over the Monarch. They have the rest of the weapon systems to worry over."

"True." He looked musingly at the president. "We'll stay with it. I'll keep the Washington office on the job."

"Do that." Welkes glanced around. "We might as well wind this up." As the others rose to leave, he turned to Bergstrom. "By the way, I'd like to compliment you on the way you handled Colonel Hammond. He went out of his way to remark how cooperative you'd been." The president looked pleased.

"We gave him the full VIP treatment."

"Evidently. I understand this is John Vroman's last day. I hate to see him go."

"So do I," he admitted.

"What are we doing about his spot?"

"I've been considering a man but I don't want to rush it. I want to make certain I have the right man."

"Why did he quit? I never understood that."

"It's not final." He hesitated. "That's another reason I'm not rushing to fill the job."

"Not final?"

"He has a health problem, but if it clears . . ." He didn't finish. He'd talk with Vroman again. If he knew what was biting him, he'd know how to handle him. If he knew . . . He edged a faint suspicion from his mind.

"I hope it comes out all right," Welkes said. "John's a good man. We can't afford to lose him."

"I'm trying to see that we don't." As the president nodded dismissal, Bergstrom rose.

James Elliott brought Carole Janek to the party at the Bergstrom house with some misgivings. It was true that the vice-president regularly gave a Christmas party for his section chiefs and their wives; but this wasn't Christmas. He dismissed as fantastic the idea that Bergstrom might use the occasion to announce Vroman's successor, reflecting that more probably it was to decide on one. That it was a command performance, he found the more galling.

"He's using the situation to size us up," he complained as they drove through the rolling Palos Verdes Hills toward the vice-president's house.

"Not we, you. You're the candidate."

"You'll be the candidate's wife."

"Will I, Jim?"

"You know it, honey." He patted her knee affectionately.

"You haven't asked me."

"Well, I haven't gotten down on my knees, if that's what you mean."

"You seem quite certain of the answer."

"Shouldn't I be?" Alert to the touchiness in her voice, he didn't push the question, not wanting to break her mood when she didn't respond. She had been happy when he picked her up, and he intended to keep her that way. He glanced sideways at her, feeling the ungovernable urge to stop and kiss her. Instead he stepped harder on the accelerator.

Roland T. Bergstrom's house was located on a winding street on the western slope of the hills, overlooking the sea. They arrived a little late, although not as late as Garfield, who entered with his wife, Madge, a good hour after the others, and now was explaining to Bergstrom the rush job that had held him at the plant.

"We haven't seen you since I don't know when," Madge Garfield said to Carole and Elliott, trying to overhear what her husband was telling the vice-president. "We'll have to get together soon."

"We'd love to," Carole murmured. Elliott smiled politely.

"Oh, hello, Madge . . ." Elissa Bergstrom came toward them from the other room, wearing a black sheath adorned with a single rope of pearls. Smiling the correct, perfunctory smile of a hostess not too well acquainted with her guests, she continued: "We were beginning to think you wouldn't make it. Here, let me take your wraps."

"Harry had to work late," Madge explained.

"Poof, these men." She raised her eyebrows at Elliott. "I'm always suspicious of that excuse."

"I'm certain you have no reason to be," he replied gallantly. At first sight he had found her attractive, now he wasn't so sure. She had evenly chiseled features, gray eyes, and a voice on the sexy side, but her smile was brittle, giving her face a set, artificial quality.

"We're never sure, that's our strength," she explained.

Madge wrinkled her brow enigmatically. "Perhaps we delude ourselves."

"A distinct possibility." She glanced toward the buffet, where Eugene Henderson was talking with the Koepples over highballs.

"You have a lovely home," Carole observed. "I've been admiring your prints."

"A decorator," she confessed. "Have you seen Roland's den? He has several of your Monarch and Guardian drawings on the wall. I think he steals them."

As she went to put the wraps on the bed, Bergstrom asked, "What are you drinking?"

"Scotch on the rocks," Garfield promptly replied.

"A martini," Madge added. Bergstrom chuckled as they moved toward the bar in the next room. Koepple looked around, his thin face warming.

"Hello, Madge . . . Harry."

"Hi, Art," Garfield boomed. "Thought we'd never make it."

"You've met Eugene, haven't you?" Koepple asked Madge. "Eugene Henderson . . . Madge Garfield."

"Of course, the Christmas party," she exclaimed. "It's been ages." She turned to Koepple's wife, appraising her swiftly. "It's been a long time, Dorothy. You're looking well. I like the dress."

"I'm afraid we don't get out much." Plump, with vestiges of prettiness in her serene face and several inches taller than her husband, she reminded Elliott of a hen brooding over a chick. They exchanged chitchat while Bergstrom mixed the drinks.

"Our boy will graduate from high school next year," Dorothy Koepple confided to Garfield. "My, where do the years go?"

"They've been kind to you, Dorothy."

"Fiddlesticks."

"Would you want to be a girl again, start over?"

"I don't know. No, I don't think so. Once is enough."

"Madge would. She'd start over in a minute. She's always trying to make herself look younger."

"I suppose we all are, at least subconsciously."

"Consciously," he corrected.

Next to them Madge Garfield exclaimed to Eugene Henderson, "I feel as if I work at the plant myself. It's all Harry ever talks about. I'll be glad when they get the bird launched. See, I even say bird."

"We all feel that way."

"I feel positively antisocial when I talk of anything else."

"What would you rather talk about?" he asked, watching her eyes.

She winked.

"We love California," Elissa said to Elliott. "When I think of all the years we spent in the East . . ."

He gazed at her gray eyes. "I notice you're close to the sea."

"Cliffs—sheer, towering cliffs. The nearest bathing beach is miles away."

"But you have a pool."

"It's not the same."

"I'd settle for it," he answered, wondering how much younger she was than her husband. Slender, but shapely, he placed her in the middle thirties. "You have a beautiful home."

"It's so big we rattle around in it. We used to live in a walk-up," she confessed, "a long time ago, when we first were married."

"Nothing wrong with a walk-up."

"At times I wish we had it back, or at least something smaller."

"This is very nice."

"Not at tax time." She pouted. "All men are alike. You need a mansion to prove your importance."

"Not me." He smiled at her. "I live in a bachelor apartment— a walk-up."

"Oh, I didn't know." She roguishly flicked her eyes. "Etchings?"

"I show them my rejected manuscripts."

"Does it work?"

"As well as etchings, I believe."

"Then it works," she affirmed. "I'm certain they're not all rejected."

"Most of them," he admitted ruefully.

"What do you write?"

"Rejected manuscripts." She laughed, turning away to say something to Henderson, and Madge corralled him, chatting lightly about nothing in particular. Petite and vivacious, she appeared in odd contrast to her husband, yet in some way he couldn't fathom he realized they complemented each other. He became aware, too, that beneath the light talk, she was sizing him up. Casually he glanced around. Bergstrom and Carole were talking in the corner, their faces animated.

Garfield and Elissa Bergstrom sat on the living room couch. She balanced her cocktail glass between her fingers, listening politely.

"Roland works too hard," he was saying. "A man shouldn't have to work that hard. You must feel like a widow."

"At times," she confessed.

"He gives too much."

"Won't things slacken after the launching?"

"Not at all, Elissa. You know that."

"I suppose not. Roland's the kind of man who isn't happy unless he is working."

"Sure, I'm the same way. It's habit. You know what habit is; it's like smoking, or anything else." He paused, watching her. "Does that make sense?"

"Yes, of course."

"Sometimes I think: Slow down, Harry, but I really can't. The job gets in your blood."

"Roland's viewpoint exactly."

"He influences people, Elissa. We see him work and we drive to keep up. He instills the drive. It's a vicious circle. Madge tells me it's even harder on the wives. Do you find that?"

"You should know, Harry."

"Yes, I'm seldom home."

"What's the answer?" She held his eyes.

"He should relax," he promptly replied, "take some of the fruits of life."

"You can't change him."

"He should delegate responsibility," he insisted, leaning toward her to take her into his confidence, "let us carry the load, especially now that Vroman's gone."

"As burdened as you already are?"

"That's what we're there for, Elissa." He gave a sacrificial smile. "We should take the weight from his shoulders, free him for the big problems. He should leave the routine tasks—like Vroman's job—for us. Lord, I've been with the company over twenty-two years. I know the ins and outs." He let his eyes drift over her face. She had a rather narrow nose but the rest of her features were good, and when she smiled, her teeth were white and even. He looked at the long neck and slender body, calculating how much younger she was than her husband. "Taking that load's the least I can do for him," he finished.

"No one can tell him, Harry. He has to be convinced."

"That's what I'm trying to do—convince him."

"I hope you have more success than I've had."

"I hope so too, Elissa. I really hope so."

Across from them Madge Garfield, looking into Eugene Henderson's cleanly shaved face, said, "You single men have an advantage."

"Is that an advantage?"

"Definitely."

"Why?"

"You know why." She lifted her eyes archly.

"Marriage is safer, or so they tell me."

"But not so exciting."

"It could be."
"Ummmm."

Sipping his drink, Elliott opened the double doors and went out onto a cabaña that overlooked the pool. It had, he cynically noted, the usual clump of banana trees in one corner, and the usual clutter of deck chairs and umbrellas. A striped beach ball and plastic raft floated on the water. California living. It looked, he reflected, like a scene from a travel advertisement.

Glancing back toward the room, he decided it wasn't a party at all, at least not in the sense of a group of individuals gathered in shared conversation and conviviality. It was more a gathering of strangers, each sparring, each seeking his niche— Bergstrom the granite monolith to which each made obeisance. He scanned the party slowly. Garfield, stocky, with thick iron-gray hair, a strong, swarthy face, the sharp look of a predator; the birdlike Koepple, a scarcely fleshed skeleton in loose clothing, moving around nervously as if never quite certain of his reception; Henderson, suave, slightly disdainful, at the moment playing it close to Madge Garfield; Dorothy, plump and motherly; Elissa, brittle and blond and quite certain of herself, fingering the rope of pearls as she moved among her guests; Carole, lovely in a low-cut gown of pale blue. And Bergstrom. The man perturbed him. At times he was quite understandable, like the large type in an ad, and yet . . . At other times quiet, almost aloof, he possessed an unfathomable quality that he'd never been quite able to decipher. He gave the impression of force, a man fully in command of himself, and others, and yet there was that part of him that resided behind a curtain. But tonight he was the genial host, talking and smiling, sipping his drink as he mingled with his guests. It was as if he had removed his stolid exterior and laid it aside for the night.

He gazed at the pool.

Approaching the house, he'd been struck by the broad expanse of lawn and the nonchalant landscaping carefully planned to enhance its simple lines. Of contemporary style, it featured heavy plank siding, ample red brick and glass, a low, heavy shake-shingle roof, and a high rear fence that set off the garden and gave privacy to the cabaña. The house spelled success; at first sight he believed it gave him a clue to the vice-president. Solid, impressive, the structure held a commanding air. For a brief moment he felt he understood Bergstrom—his hopes, dreams, ambitions. It was all here around him, from the tiled pool to the private den tucked off the main room. Bergstrom was just another human with human strengths, frailties, foibles. Yet he held the key to his future. But did the house tell him all these things? Did anyone really know Bergstrom? Did Garfield, or Henderson? Elissa, she knew him, but even of that he wasn't certain. Bergstrom was not a surface phenomenon. And perhaps the house was not a mirror, but just another façade. He couldn't make that mistake.

Why was he here? Because it was a command performance? Because of the job, that's why. That's why they all were here—Garfield, Koepple, Henderson, the wives. Damn the job. He cursed silently, knowing he wanted it more than anything he'd ever wanted. Not the pay, not the prestige, but the job itself. James Elliott, director of PR . . . With a few drinks under his belt he could admit how much he wanted it. And why not? It was a good job, essential, several cuts above the expectations to which a man might reasonably aspire. A word from Bergstrom would do it. Just one word.

He looked moodily through the glass doors. Elissa and Henderson were gabbing by the fireside. The PR man, half a head taller, wore an intent, serious expression, and occasionally she replied to something he was saying with a scarcely noticeable movement of her lips. Bergstrom stood near the bar, his hand on Garfield's shoulder, directing his conversation to Carole. She raised her head, laughing. Koepple, his wife and Madge . . . The scene depressed him. After a while Carole detached herself from the group, glanced around and came toward the cabaña. He moved from the shadows to meet her. She caught sight of him and quickened her step.

"I was wondering where you'd gone."

"Escaping," he explained.

"It isn't that bad," she reproached, "not nearly as bad as I thought it might be."

"What did you expect?"

"A stuffy evening, perhaps. I really don't know." She looked reflectively at the pool. "It's delightful here."

"We should have brought suits."

"Can't you see it?"

"It's an idea." He caught her hand, tugging her toward the shadows and kissed her. She accepted it without response. The scent of liquor on her breath increased his ardor and he held her close, brushing her ear with his lips, whispering, "You're lovely tonight, more lovely all the time." He moved his hand slowly over her back.

"Don't, Jim."

"Can't resist."

"You can and will," she said definitely, pushing herself away. He caught her hand.

"I wish we could leave."

"But we can't."

He held the hand, looking wonderingly at her. For most of his adult life he had sought this woman, and now that he had found her, he didn't want to relinquish a single moment of it.

She was deep and full and tremulous, and yet she was withdrawing too, at times fleeing altogether. She couldn't know how badly he wanted her, not even after all these months. They had scarcely scratched the surface.

"Maybe it'll break up before long," he murmured, drawing her close again. He kissed her long and tenderly, then more passionately, aware that her hands resisted him.

She stepped back, urging: "We'd better go in."

"Why?" His eyes pleaded with her.

"You know why."

"You do things to me."

"I don't want to, Jim."

"That's not true."

"You very well know what I mean."

"I know I love you." He stepped closer, pressing his lips against her neck.

"Stop it, Jim."

"Don't be angry."

"This is no time or place." She broke away and moved to the side of the pool, gazing at the water.

"You don't give me a chance," he protested.

"Jim—"

"I know," he went on, forestalling her words, "but I can't help it." Caught by her loveliness, the slow surge of desire quickened and he forced himself to take a deep breath. In the splay of light, her face held a taut and yet wistful expression. He came behind her, encircling the soft breasts with his arms, and kissed her honey-yellow hair, whispering, "You're lovely."

"Am I?" There was no vanity in the question.

"And strange."

She revolved slowly, facing him. "In what way?"

"At times you're so close, so dear."

"And at other times?"

"You're a stranger."

"I could say the same, Jim."

"I don't keep my thoughts from you." The light from the room gave her skin the texture of pale marble and her face was lonely. He resisted the impulse to gather her into his arms, reassure her.

"It's not that," she finally answered.

"What then?"

"We're different, Jim."

"We're drawing closer."

"In ways that count?"

"We are," he said gravely. He searched the shadow pools hiding her eyes. "It's not me you're fighting, Carole. It's yourself."

"You understand that?"

"Yes, and you're wonderful."

"Please, Jim."

"At times you want to hear it and at times you don't."

"Yes, but it's more than that."

She turned, facing the room. He saw the party had changed patterns again. Madge and Bergstrom were engrossed in conversation just inside the patio doors. Beyond, Henderson was smiling politely at something Garfield was telling Elissa. The Koepples were off by themselves, carefully balancing their glasses as they talked. His mood changing, he asked, "Like Elissa?"

"She's . . . all right."

"A lot younger than Bergie."

"Somewhat."

"Lord, I wish this were over."

"Hush."

"Well, I do."

"Let's go in."

"All right." He sighed deeply, following her into the room.

"The GD, Martin and Boeing people are getting a lot more in the way of national publicity than we are," Bergstrom explained. He spoke slowly, so that each word had the succinct quality of being conceived and analyzed as a separate entity. "That not only goes for the ICBM programs but for space as well." He leaned back in the big leather chair, watching the four men who faced him from a couch near the fireplace. The women were gathered in the other room and occasionally Elliott heard a silvery laugh.

"They're going concerns . . . have hardware in space." Garfield spoke with authority. "We'll be right in there with them when we get the bird launched."

"We'd better be." Bergstrom responded with a wry humor that was new to Elliott, and he thought he was seeing another facet of the man.

"Besides, it's the punch that counts," Garfield insisted. "We punch harder."

"It's space that counts."

"You have to have space to punch in," Henderson interjected.

"If the punch is good, you'll get the space," Bergstrom amended.

Garfield leaned forward. "How are we missing the boat? If it's my department, I want to know."

"I'm not pointing a finger, Harry. I'm merely suggesting that we're not getting the maximum space for our efforts."

"It's the same thing."

"I think we've chosen to confine ourselves to too narrow a niche—looking at the forest and forgetting the trees," the vice-president explained. "Take propulsion systems, existing and potential, for example. We have solids, liquid bipropellants and monopropellants, nuclear, ion, photon, and I don't know how many others."

"We're liquid people."

"Not for the purposes of publicity."

"Go ahead," Garfield said contentiously.

"It's the unique type of article that commands the most space, and systems like those I mentioned point up our diversification—show that we're not a single-contract manufacturer as some people seem to think." Bergstrom paused, then added emphatically: "We don't want Western Aerospace regarded as an ICBM company but as a company with roots deeply imbedded in the space technology. We have to shoot for tomorrow, Harry."

"Photon . . . ion drives?"

"We're researching them."

"That's up to engineering—the eggheads. If they generate the information, we'll polish it and sell it, but we can't pull it out of a hat. Personally, I'm not up on my photons, and I suspect no one else here is."

"We have to dig the information from engineering," Bergstrom remonstrated. Elliott suddenly realized the vice-president was enjoying the exchange with his chief of publicity. His eyes held an ironic gleam. "If we didn't, we'd never get anywhere. Those slipstick boys simply aren't oriented in that direction. We have to generate material as well as sell it. What do you think, Eugene?"

"I agree." Henderson contemplated him thoughtfully. "But the biggest problem is in planting material—selecting markets on the basis of relative merit, gearing our publicity to the highest return."

"Exactly."

"That's how we operate at Space Electronics."

"You're doing a good job, Eugene." Bergstrom nodded, satisfied, and Elliott shot him a puzzled look. Usually sparse with his praise, the vice-president certainly accorded Henderson far more than his share. The wonder boy, the golden-haired boy . . . He'd heard the whispers. Garfield's face held a studied look. Koepple broke the brief silence:

"Good publicity—like the good ad—is a matter of planning."

"A good analogy, Art."

"You have to plan the market as well as the ad—match the two for the best effect," he pursued.

"That's important, Art." Bergstrom glanced at Elliott. "What does the voice of the news bureau say?"

"We haven't reached all markets," he agreed, "not nearly all, but manpower keeps us selective."

"We should do better, Jim."

"Yes, we should."

"Then why aren't we?"

"We tend to fall into a rut," he answered honestly. "Perhaps it's inherent in the system, but we tend to become mechanical, use yesterday's success as a criterion for today." Hesitating, he continued: "We select proven markets rather than trying for better ones."

"That's an honest appraisal, Jim." The vice-president nodded approvingly. "What do we do about it?"

"More thought and less motion." He sat back, waiting.

"Yes, I believe that sums it up." His expression told Elliott he had passed a test.

"We all know what could be done but, as Jim stated, there's that old bogey manpower," Garfield interceded. "It seems to me I work twelve hours a day, planning and grinding out material. The only way I can increase output is to increase my staff. Do that and I'll even sell photons."

"It's not a matter of more staff but how we use the staff we already have," the vice-president returned pointedly.

"I'm listening." His voice held a bite that evoked Elliott's admiration. Garfield was a battler, every inch of the way.

"Let's look at it another way," Bergstrom suggested. "Most of our publicity is slanted toward the people, mass man"—he lingered on the phrase, one he was fond of—"and that was all right for a start. We didn't have anything but a dream, a bushel of plans, and we had to sell Monarch's necessity, create a public image. But we're big boys now, fighting in the major leagues. Times have changed and I don't believe we're keeping pace."

"We should be reaching the decision-makers," Elliott interposed, catching the reference to mass man. "People are conditioned to going along with a heavy-budget dollar, so perhaps we should concentrate more on the people who spend it."

"Precisely, Jim. That adds up to think pieces planted in the right spots. We should hit for the key military men, scientific consultants, the NASA people."

"We do," Garfield interjected, grinning. "Last week I fixed up an Air Force VIP. The only way I could have improved it was to have had a Monarch tattoo on the gal's belly."

When the general laugh subsided, Henderson asked, "How come you overlooked that?"

"She wouldn't buy it . . . said she represents other contractors, too."

Bergstrom chuckled. "I wasn't thinking of that kind of influence."

"It's potent, R. T."

"Yes." Abruptly his mood changed, becoming serious. "Neither are we hitting the engineering market hard enough. Personnel spends a fortune on recruiting. It's fantastic the amount we shell out for each man hired. Welkes brought it to my attention just the other day."

"They're migratory," Henderson declared. "Summers in Denver, winters in Southern California."

"It's more than that, Eugene. A good engineer—one worth his salt—is attracted by a company's capabilities, his chances for recognition and promotion. We should stress those aspects in our ads." He gazed shrewdly at Koepple.

The latter looked unhappy. "Personnel goes right along with us," he protested.

"They look to us for guidance, Art, but the market's changing. Last year we hired anyone who could add two and two and called him an engineer. Now we can be more selective, hit for the best. Let's introduce more think into our ads."

Koepple frowned. "I'll take a good look at it."

"Do that, Art. We're also missing bets on the Monarch—"

"I feel as if I live and breathe that goddamned tin bird," Garfield cut in caustically.

A cold gleam sprang to Bergstrom's eyes.

"We're expected to, Harry. The Monarch's our bread and butter, the reason for the company, the key to its future. I live with it, too, twenty-four hours a day. That, I think, is the least that's expected of us." He waved aside the other's protest. "Even so we haven't told the whole story. Let's forget the exotic aspects of space for the moment and concentrate on the Monarch, as I think we should, with the hot firing coming up . . . the contract."

He eyed his chief of publicity. "What do we tell the world about it, Harry?"

Garfield removed his cigar, furrowing his brow before answering. "We give 'em the works—thrust, range, size, what it can do, its advantages over other ICBMs, its future as a space booster, its role as a prime deterrent to war. Hell, we cover the ground, and along with it we sell the corporation and the men who make it. We're doing a damned good job," he asserted.

"So we are," Bergstrom agreed, "and yet there's much we haven't told. We should wring the story for every inch we can get; this is a critical time."

"What haven't we told?"

"Consider the Monarch," he continued, as if he hadn't heard. "It literally starts life as so many rolls of stainless steel. Every inch of this steel is inspected for gage, surface finish, flatness, camber; it is wrapped around mandrels, cut to form sections, and one by one these sections are welded together to make the tanks. We test them, move them to the assembly docks—install the upper stage engine, the booster engines, all the miles of pressure lines, cables, hundreds of pieces of bracketry. We install the electronics, pods, guidance and destruct systems, and with all this we keep the product under constant test—individual systems, subsystems, entire systems, then static tests of the completed missile. To accomplish this we've evolved new tools, new systems, new methods of welding and fabrication. By the time we've finished we've put some forty of fifty thousand parts together—created an artifact so complicated that no hundred men in the plant together understand all there is to know about it." He looked slowly at each man in turn.

"Have we told this story?"

"Yes," Garfield affirmed. "Of course a lot of the material is classified."

No, we haven't told it, Elliott mentally contradicted. He felt a quiet excitement. The long, complex fabrication of the Monarch was just part of the story, meaningless unless one went to the human equation. The engineer bent over his drawing board, the masked welders staring at the blue heliarc flame, the computer operator following the slow curve of an automatic writer, chemists peering through microscopes or watching metals vaporize—this was the stuff of which the Monarch was made. But more, it was a story of long hours, heartbreak, rugged working conditions, frustration, kids who forgot what the old man looked like and wives too lonely to wait. Dedication, that was part of it, the men to whom the missile had become a thing of life: a creature of bone, muscle, a vascular system, a brain—and they were its creators. More than that, it was dedication to the thing the missile represented—the security of the American way of life, an insurance policy that guaranteed mother and apple pie and the freedom to fornicate in just about any old motel of your choice. No, they hadn't told the story, not by a long shot. He grew conscious of Bergstrom's eyes.

"You might consider that as an article, Jim." The vice-president glanced around leisurely. "Let's put it this way: I want to hit hard from now until the hot firing—exploit the Monarch to the fullest, every single detail. And let's give particular attention to the decision-makers."

"Back to the mill," someone said.

"Another thing," he went on. "What are we doing about the static test at Desert Center?"

"I plan to cover it," Elliott answered.

"Good. Anyone care for a drink?"

"A quick one," Garfield accepted. "I have a rough day ahead."

"Enjoy yourself?" Elliott asked, winding down through the Palos Verdes hills toward the coast highway.

"Interesting." Carole's voice lacked enthusiasm.

"Bergie was human tonight—let his hair down." As she remained silent, he continued, "He's hard to figure."

"I can't see that he's complicated."

"Not complicated exactly."

"I like him."

"Sure, nothing personal. Harry certainly put on the pressure."

"I hadn't noticed."

"Cornered him every chance he got." He peered through the windshield, conscious both of her presence and her increasingly pensive mood. They were sparring—he knew it in her flat, toneless answers, the tense way she sat, and the desire that had been with him all evening came flooding back. It came as a quickened pulse, a slow throbbing at the temples, a sense of urgency. In her withdrawal she was overpowering. He reached over and squeezed her hand. "I want to kiss you, hug you. I've been thinking of it all evening."

"Have you?" she asked dully.

"Yes, you're lovely." She didn't answer, letting her hand lie inert in his, but he felt her stiffen. That was part of the strangeness of her, the magic, the moods which he'd never deciphered, yet knew so well. He wondered if her conflict were in part rationalization, as if it somehow absolved her from guilt, and decided not. Her fight was too genuine, a tossed mixture of emotion, reason, values—roots extending back through the years.

"Feel all right?" he asked.

"Yes." She uttered the word in a monotone.

"Carole . . . ?" When she appeared not to hear, he stared ahead, hearing the rush of wind past the car, knowing he was driving too fast, yet unable to slow down. He wanted to race at the tempo of his body, his mind, match the speed of the car with his desires. Once he glanced sidelong at her. She sat against the back of the seat, eyes closed, lost to him.

When they reached the apartment where she lived, he escorted her to the door, waiting. Opening it, she said in a strained voice, "It's late."

"Yes, it's late."

"Jim . . . ?"

"Go in," he urged.

She went in wordlessly and he followed, waiting in the center of the room while she snapped on a corner lamp. She turned slowly, saying listlessly, "You'd better go."

"No."

"Jim . . ." He took a step forward and she waited, standing straight, her face taut and unyielding. He grasped her shoulders, giving way to the craving inside him, whispering, kissing her face and ears, absorbing her with all his senses.

"I love you, love you." She said nothing and he kissed her more passionately. "I love you."

"Jim . . ." He pulled her close, his lips on her eyes, her mouth. She placed her hands flat against his shoulders, pushing away from him, saying, "No."

"Carole . . ." He breathed the name with suppressed breath, fighting to break her will, wanting her with a fire that flamed with growing intensity. His hands found the zipper at the back of her dress and lowered it.

"No," she repeated numbly. He slid the dress down over her shoulders and hips, letting it fall to the floor. She stood absolutely still, neither helping nor hindering. He removed her slip, and then the brassiere, running his hands gently over her breasts while she said, "No, no, no." Feeling the pounding in his body, he sought her lips savagely, his hands cupping her, then lowered his head and kissed her nipples, the soft white of her throat, caressing her body, feeling the violent trembling within her as she said, "No, no, no." She gasped brokenly and tore herself free. "No, Jim."

He stepped forward, gathering her in, pressing his mouth to her breast, his hands moving slowly over her body. When she was naked, he stepped back. "God, you're lovely."

He picked her up, marveling at her lightness, and carried her to the bed, lowering her gently. She uttered no word of protest, watching him in the darkness. He lay beside her, embracing her, his hands and lips caressing her for long minutes before he moved over her. For the barest instant she resisted, holding herself rigid, then let the air expel from her lungs as she sank back, and he entered her.

"Yes, yes, yes," she whispered, "God, yes." Her arms, her lips, her hard breasts thrust against him, her fingers like steel talons in his back, her legs entwined with his, her body alive—all else was swept into oblivion. "Yes, yes, yes . . ." There was no world, no people, no room, nothing except the two of them. She moaned, tossing her head, clenching his flesh, bruising him. "Please, please . . ." He felt the beginning of the spasm in her body, the sudden clashing of her hips against his, the sharp intake of her breath. "Don't stop, don't stop, please, please, please." His head whirling, he met her ferocity, overwhelmed by what was happening. "Ah . . ." she gasped. "Ah . . ." He felt the rush to meet her, the surge, heard the sharp exclamation torn from his own lips.

"Jim, Jim, Jim," she whispered.

Later, lying across her bed, her eyes closed, her face flushed and her lips moist, she whispered, "I could hate you."

"But you don't, Carole."

"No . . ."

"I want you to love me."

"You think you possessed me?"

"Not in a way that matters."

"No, not in any way that matters."

"You're very lovely, Carole, very precious."

"Jim, don't say that, not now."

"Lovely and glorious."

"Jim . . . ?"

"I love you, Carole."

"I don't want to hear it."

"I love you."

"I've never said that to you, Jim."

"You will . . . someday. I can wait."

"Perhaps . . ." The word sounded distant and lonely.

"I could have made you say it tonight."

"Yes, but it wouldn't have been the same as my meaning it."

"No, it wouldn't be the same."

"Garfield can be plenty outspoken at times," Bergstrom remarked. He removed a shoe and dropped it to the floor, leaning back on the bed. Elissa sat in front of a mirror, dabbing cream on her face.

"Those horrid cigars," she said distastefully.

"He's a good PR man," he reflected, "though perhaps a bit offensive at times."

"Then why consider him?"

"Because he knows his job . . . the company."

"So he told me."

"Harry's not backward."

"He certainly isn't."

"That can be good, Elissa."

"Can it? I wouldn't think so, not with the entertaining he'd have to do."

"Perhaps not there." He could see her point. Garfield certainly wouldn't be the best representative in that respect. Some of the Air Force brass, in particular, had to be handled with finesse.

"Elliott's a handsome man."

"Elliott . . . handsome?"

"I wonder how he got the scar?"

"I wouldn't know."

"Is he going to marry Carole?"

"How should I know?" he asked, thinking it would be very fortunate for Elliott if he should. Carole was a beaut, and what's more she had a good head on her shoulders. "I understand they're keeping rather steady company."

"She's pretty." She paused, watching his reflection in the mirror.

"A knockout."

"Well, he should," she said with finality. He couldn't exactly follow her logic, but it pleased him that Elliott was revealing considerable depth. Although inclined to hold his counsel, he wasn't a bit backward about presenting his ideas.

"He's easygoing," he said musingly, "has a real knack for getting along with people."

"You don't sound too certain."

"Whether he's best for the job? No, I can't say that I am."

"If you're not certain, then I wouldn't consider him," she advised. "You can't afford another Vroman." He didn't answer, wondering at the train of thought that allowed her to couple the two. Not that she was being entirely fair to the latter, either. Vroman probably had his reasons. Besides, he wouldn't write him off yet. He decided against mentioning that. She turned, facing him.

"Henderson appears the brightest of the lot."

"He's young."

"Age never stopped you, Roland."

"True." He debated the point; she was right. The qualities he wanted had to do with dedication, ability and loyalty, not years. Cronkhill had pushed him ahead of many older men for those very reasons. He contemplated his wife without appearing to do so. Her perceptiveness startled him at times, her knack of going straight to the core. Her eyes held a sharp, expectant glint that perturbed him. There was something about her that he'd never quite understood, a certain hardness, if he could call it that.

"He's much the kind of person you're looking for," she pressed.

"Perhaps."

"I think he is, Roland."

"In what way?" he asked sharply.

"He's the sort of man who wouldn't let anything stand in his way." She deliberately held his eyes.

"Do you mean ambitious or selfish?"

"Both. If the Monarch represented his future, he'd sell it, even if it were powered by flashlight batteries."

He weighed the observation.

"Yes, I can see that. There's more to Eugene than meets the eye."

"Much more, Roland."

"Still, I've got to know. I don't want to be swayed by personalities or words or promises. When I decide, I want to know the decision is right, even if it turns out to be Koepple."

"Even?"

"He's unobtrusive," he explained, "perhaps too quiet for the job, but he's sharp. I'd never make the mistake of underestimating him. At any rate," he continued, "I'll hold off until after the launching. By that time I'll know."

"I'm sure you will, dear."

He leaned forward to pull off his socks. "I wish to hell I didn't have to fly East this week."

"Something important?"

"Briefing Cronkhill on the Slater material."

"It'll do you good."

"You must think I enjoy it."

"I know you do. You're just a traveling salesman at heart."

"Sometimes I feel I ought to quit, go into some other kind of business. This is a damned madhouse," he stated, realizing the words were utter nonsense. He wouldn't leave—couldn't. The corporation needed him, and he needed it. The latter came as a surprise, but it was true; he did need it. Without it, his life would be void, utterly meaningless. Elissa put the cover on the cold cream jar and reached for a piece of facial tissue.

"You wouldn't change for anything, and you know it. It's in your blood—like printer's ink."

"Let me tell you something," he came back defensively. "You think because I have a big office, a big desk and a fat salary that I've got it made, that I don't have to do anything but sit on my duff and ogle my secretary's can. You ought to sit behind that big desk sometime, see the problems I have to contend with, the decision-a-minute schedule. Public relations and advertising, ha! Half the decisions I make aren't even related to my department. Welkes, Kroeber and that chief engineer, Gaither—I do the brainwork for all of them."

"You wouldn't miss it," she accused.

"No, I suppose not," he conceded. "I swear I'll quit every time my ulcer kicks up, but I guess that's part of it. What drives me is the knowledge that there wouldn't be a missile if it weren't for public relations. The engineers believe they created it; hell, we created it—built it with words, made the people who could pay for it want it. You think that's easy?" he challenged.

"You're doing a big job, Roland."

"You're telling me. Just about the time I get one problem whipped, another comes along. If it isn't Congress yapping about a tougher budget, it's a competitor getting the jump with some new technological twist, or some screwball idea like the Nike-Zeus. Solids," he grumbled.

Elissa swung around on the bench to face him.

"If you want my advice, just go ahead and appoint someone and get if off your mind. Let him worry for you."

"Yeah, but who?"

She examined a broken nail. "Henderson—I think he's best."

"Maybe I should," he assented, looking at his wife's legs. "Let's go to bed."

4

Chapter 4

THE Monarch intercontinental ballistic missile was born of the same force that gave rise to its predecessors—a Red tide lapping ever more hungrily at the shores of the free world. It came upon the scene at a time when conventional weapons of the past were fast disappearing, replaced by rockets of all sizes, shapes, and degrees of destruction, each designed to accomplish a given mission in the war men hoped would never occur, even as they prepared to join in global conflict. It came at a time when the first of the large atom-powered submarines was prowling the seas, when men spoke in whispered terms of "orbital bombardment" and "manned space interceptors," and when the criterion of a scientific discipline was measured by its contribution to the art of weaponry.

Unlike its predecessors—the liquid-fuel Atlas and Titan and the solid fuel Minuteman—the Monarch was a relative latecomer in the mushrooming field of politics by missile numbers, and this proved advantageous in many ways. It allowed Midwest Aeronautical Corporation's management and designers to profit by hard lessons already learned—to use parts, components and systems proved reliable, to select materials found suitable for the tremendous shifting forces and variable temperatures which make up an operational missile's natural environment, to shelve concepts proved impractical through experiment and actual flight. It also afforded a reservoir of manpower already trained in the arts of missilery, and the opportunity to acquire scientists and engineers whose names were bywords, this by the simple expedient of bidding above the salary ranges of established competitors, or by furnishing better offices or more impressive titles, or all three.

There was truth in the Western Aerospace claim that the Monarch possessed ". . . an improved airframe, more efficient engines, more accurate guidance," for these had been developed in the crucible of countless tests and hot firings since the Red tide had commenced its surge toward flood proportions. Lamentable failures of the past—the devastated launching sites, the missiles destroyed while barely clear of the pad—added up to clear profit in the eyes of the Monarch's designers. The short, accelerated history of space also gave them the advantage of established missile ranges, existing tracking systems, and a host of nose cone recovery techniques developed for the benefit of earlier missileers.

It was not by chance alone that the Monarch progressed from a state of mental imagery to a weapon of awesome power in a shorter time than any missile of its type. Although its wings were yet untried, the voice of this new bird already was heard in the subsummits of government, where international policy is planned. Today it offered a potential deterrent to the warmakers of the world; tomorrow it would still those voices. Or so men hoped.

The Monarch had its own just claims to birthright. Uniquely designed, it could be fired from several different types of launchers with but minor modifications. It could join its Atlas or Titan cousins in fixed burrows in the earth, to belch forth when needed, when the diplomacy of threat no longer sufficed. But perhaps its outstanding feature, the one that had opened the military purse strings to the Midwest Aeronautical Corporation's obstetricians—its Western Aerospace Division still unborn—was its promised capability of being launched from the sea, a system derived from the Navy's spar buoy concept. Unfortunately, this aspect of the weapon system immediately became so heavily classified that no mention of it could be made. As the PR men knew, it was a public relation man's dream—a vividly colorful capability shared by no other ICBM—but the merest hint was taboo.

The operation's claimed simplicity and the fact that any body of water in the world offered a potential launching site acted as spurs to the Monarch's development. Unlike the Polaris, no submarine was necessary. A special barge was designed to handle a deck-adapted launcher and to provide the necessary fuel and parts storage. It could be serviced at sea, just as tankers serviced the surface fleets. Following the spar buoy concept, the barge would bob like a cork in the sea until the missile, brought into erect position just before firing, reached a point of alignment perpendicular in all planes with respect to the surface, when it could be fired by radio ignition from a nearby ship or hovering helicopter. This was considered of critical advantage in that but a single aircraft or surface vessel could fire a large number of such missiles synchronously from a dispersed fleet of barges, thus assuring the simultaneous destruction of over half the globe.

Once airborne, such a missile's inertial guidance system and complex brain would relieve mankind of any further responsibility concerning the bird's goal, or what would transpire after it arrived there, for an automatic brain has no conscience. The Monarch's promised versatility first interested the Air Force while the Monarch was still a paper dream.

Since then the money had been unending.

The missile blew.

One moment it stood erect in its gantry at the Desert Center static test site, awaiting the firing of its giant liquid oxygen/hydrocarbon fuel engines; the next it had exploded into a flaming mass of twisted debris in which missile and gantry were indistinguishable, lost in a pall of gray-black smoke topped by an orange fire cloud.

The catastrophe had occurred so suddenly that from his post in the blockhouse, where he was watching the test over closed-circuit TV, Elliott glimpsed little more than a winking flame where no flame should be before a black mushroom of smoke surged upward and a brilliant flash lanced the sky. A roll of thunder, scarcely more than a muted roar in the depths of the steel and concrete command post, rolled over the desert hills, echoing like a dying drumbeat. He stared disbelievingly at the inferno until the shrill scream of a siren broke the momentary tableau around him.

"Emergency water . . ." Cursing and shouting orders, the men of the test crew sprang to action. Elliott swung toward one of the technicians who stood spellbound at the television screen, as if awed by what he saw.

"What happened?" The words seemed to shake him from his trance.

"How the hell should I know?" A glance at the screen told Elliott the destruction was total—flames engulfed the missile, tower, and a large part of the nearby ground support equipment. It was as if the mighty tank had collapsed, spewing out the flammable fuel in all directions. His mind transferred the scene from Desert Center to Cape Canaveral. Christ, if the bird did that on the pad . . . Silly, damned silly. He jerked his eyes from the screen. The first moment of pandemonium had passed, and Charlie Haygood, the test conductor, was barking sharp orders to the men around him. They moved quickly, efficiently. Glancing at him, Elliott slipped into Haygood's small office at the rear of the blockhouse and closing the door, leaned against it, conscious that his heart was thudding against his chest wall. He stood there for a moment, forcing himself to think clearly. With Bergstrom East, he'd have to depend on Koepple or Garfield. Deciding on the latter, he put through a call, waiting impatiently until the voice of the publicity chief came on.

"Elliott . . . Desert Center." He spoke tersely. "We just lost a bird."

"Oh, how bad?" Garfield didn't sound perturbed.

"The whole thing went."

"Explosion?"

"I'm not sure. I haven't talked to Haygood, but I doubt if anyone will know until they go over the data, examine the wreckage. The tapes might tell the story."

"I doubt it. When those birds go, they go. We're damned lucky it happened in the middle of nowhere instead of at the Cape."

"The same thought struck me." The words sobered him.

"Doesn't surprise me." Garfield spoke matter-of-factly. "That's one bird we can scratch."

"You'll be deluged by calls from the news services."

"It sounds like a 'No Comment' to me."

"We can't get away with it," he declared. "That blast was heard halfway to Nevada."

"There's not much we can say. The Air Force would scalp us. As a matter of fact, we can't say anything. Period."

"The press would murder us, Harry."

"Let them," he cut in. "It wouldn't be the first, or the last, time."

Elliott considered it. Garfield was right, of course. But they'd have to say something. The mushroom of smoke would be visible for fifty miles. Deny everything and the press would make a holiday of it. He knew that from his own experience. He tried again.

"With Bergie away, we'll have to play it on our own. Just say you had a report of a small fire—nothing official."

"No go," Garfield snapped. "I don't want any part of this potato. If anyone asks me, I'm blank. I haven't even heard of Desert Center." Elliott gritted his teeth, considered asking for Koepple, then decided against it. "That's the way you'd better play it, too," Garfield finished.

"Okay, I'll handle it."

"Don't go too far."

"Just say you haven't had a report," Elliott decided. "Let them call me."

"It's your baby." Garfield sounded relieved.

"You'd better inform Welkes, or someone in top management."

"Welkes," Garfield agreed. "Give me what you have."

"There's not much." He hesitated, probing his memory. "I saw a small flame near the base of the missile an instant before the main engines fired . . . or I think it was before. It might have been at the same instant. Charlie Haygood—that's the test conductor—tried to shut her down but it was too late."

"Like May Day at the Kremlin, eh?"

"Something like that."

"Sounds like a fuel leak to me."

"I wouldn't hazard a guess."

"Neither would I. Tower gone?"

"Everything."

"Any casualties?"

"No, the pad was clear."

"Okay, I'll tell Welkes," Garfield said briskly. "Better let me know what happens."

"Okay." He hung up, remaining at the phone while he contemplated his next action. He had to say something, yet nothing. He couldn't afford a conflict with whatever statement the Air Force might decide to release, nor could he afford to run counter to company policy. Bergstrom would react the same as Garfield, admitting nothing but in a more suave manner. He couldn't blame Garfield for wriggling off the hook. Returning to the main room, he found the initial excitement had passed, and managed to snag Haygood.

"We'll probably be hearing from Welkes," he stated. "Do we know the trouble?"

"Christ, does he know already?"

"I had to put through a call."

"We don't know the cause, won't until we run an autopsy, and perhaps not then," he snapped irritably. "I hope you can keep Welkes off my back."

"I'll try."

"Damned if I want to be the one to hang."

"Can you give an estimate of the damage?"

"Hell, you can see it." Haygood waved a hand toward the screen.

"I was thinking of a dollar loss—a round figure."

"Whatever it costs to build a new tower," he answered sourly. "Throw in a beat-up missile and some ground-support equipment and you have it."

Elliott plucked at the straw.

"A beat-up missile?"

"A pile of junk. We've tested it a jillion times."

"One of the men thought it might be a fuel leak."

Haygood's eyes weighed him. "Anything special in mind?"

"It might raise some questions . . . with the hot firing coming up."

"No connection," Haygood growled. "This was an old tank —tested to death. There's no structural defect in the missile, if that's what you mean."

"I didn't think so, but the point might come up."

"Hell, yes, it'll come up," he snarled bitterly. "I'll probably be answering questions for the next umpteen years."

"We'll try to play it down."

"I hope to God you can." He glanced around. "I'd better get to it."

Elliott returned to the office, found some typing paper and, inserting a sheet in the roller, paused reflectively. Some outside cause? Human error? No good, it wouldn't wash—the press no longer was that naïve. Although a cover-up could raise a real clamor, he realized he was dedicated to that course. Policy dictated it. He was working for the company now, not the press. Though the thought discomfited him, it would end with a whitewash no matter how he felt, and with Jim Elliott handling the brush. Strange, he'd never contemplated such a thing happening to the Monarch. Titans blew and Atlases blew but they seemed in another world, a different kind of missile. The Monarch—a symbol of reliability. Koepple had carried that in an ad, and somehow he felt it was true. The Monarch was engineered for integrity. He'd said so himself. Recalling the scene the instant before the explosion, his mind's eye clearly visualized the small blue flame near the base of the missile and he realized that Garfield was right—there had been a fuel leak. But that didn't necessarily imply an inherent weakness in the missile itself. Like Haygood said, the bird had been tested to the high heavens. As he pushed the image of the blue flame aside, the phone rang.

It was Welkes.

"I hear you had some trouble," he stated briskly.

"We lost the test missile and tower."

Elliott started to explain the details when he cut in, "Garfield mentioned a fuel leak."

"A possible leak," he corrected. "I saw a small flame at the base of the missile just before she went."

"I wouldn't say that," Welkes interjected sharply. "We have the Slater hearing next week. We have to soft-pedal this."

"I'm not saying anything. I'm just reporting to you," Elliott replied, feeling a slight anger.

"I don't want to hear any mention of a leak. That makes it sound as if we have structural problems, and that's not the case at all. We don't want any of those rumors floating around."

"They won't come from me."

"I don't want them to come from anyone." Welkes' voice rose. "What does Charlie Haygood say?"

"Nothing, he doesn't know."

"No ideas?"

"He was quite certain there are no inherent structural defects—"

"Exactly," he cut in. "We can't afford anything that might bring the launching into question."

"This was an old missile—"

"Old and shopworn," Welkes caught up briskly. "It had outlived its usefulness."

"How do you want us to handle the story? The wire services will probably call us direct."

"Don't tell 'em a damn thing," he shot back. "This will be forgotten by tomorrow."

"We created enough noise and smoke to raise a lot of questions."

"Questions can't harm us, Elliott, unless we answer them."

"If we clam up, they'll really hit us."

"What can they say? They're not there."

"They can guess."

"Let them."

"I was thinking about the Slater hearing."

"What about it?" Welkes rasped.

"We should explain this thing, not leave it up to him."

"He'll crucify us anyway, Elliott. We can't afford to give any ammunition."

"I don't think we can afford to let him guess," he countered, feeling his way. The president had an uncertain temper. "Feed them a tidbit and they might be satisfied."

"Perhaps." He could sense the other's hesitancy. "Any ideas?"

"I'd play it down."

"Away down. As far as we're concerned, the damage is minor."

"The word will get out that we lost a missile," Elliott objected.

"An expendable one. That makes it minor. Don't give a cause."

"I won't."

"I'd rather assign the trouble to test equipment," Welkes pursued. "That seems more reasonable." His tone suggested that he thought it entirely reasonable.

Elliott dodged the issue, saying, "I'll minimize the damage."

"All right, just don't volunteer anything."

"Supposing the Air Force calls?"

"I'll handle that end."

"Okay." He felt relieved. "Anything else?"

"That should do it."

"We'll try to keep it under control . . ." Welkes had hung up. For a long moment he glowered at the typewriter.

A Monarch missile was reported damaged today as result of a small fire followed by an explosion. He studied the lead, then x'd out the reference to the fire and explosion, and continued: *. . . as a result of a malfunction in part of the equipment during a static test of the huge ICBM engines. Damage was light. The Monarch is being developed for the Air Force . . .*

Scanning the copy, he added the usual blurb giving the manufacturer and the missile's capabilities, then added:

A spokesman for the company stated that the first Monarch ICBM would be launched from Cape Canaveral, Florida, in the near future. He said that the missile, well ahead of schedule, is expected to be operational at least three months early.

That was enough. He reread the copy, sighed and rolled it out of the machine, thankful that Welkes had assumed responsibility for handling the Air Force. The Ballistic Systems Division of the Air Force Systems Command formed an intricate complex which exerted management control over the Nation's ICBM programs. It also controlled public information with an unspoken motto: SAY NOTHING. Elliott was preparing to seek out Haygood again when a call came from Jack Embry on the city desk of the *Bulletin-News*.

"We heard a rumble about some trouble with one of your missiles," Embry began questioningly.

"Oh, where'd you pick up that?"

"Come off it, Jim. We put out a daily paper here, or had you forgotten?"

"We had a bit of difficulty," Elliott admitted.

"Check, only that's not the way we heard it. Eyewitnesses in Mojave said it looked as if an atom bomb had exploded, and that's thirty miles away."

He laughed dutifully. "Christ, Jack, if anything big happened, we wouldn't sit on it. You know that."

"Sure, absolutely," Embry replied. "Suppose you tell Uncle Jack all about it."

"As a matter of fact, we did have a flurry of excitement, but it was a long way from an atom bomb. Here, let me read you the release."

He reached for the copy.

Elliott sat at the bar in the Sycamore Tree, idly sipping a drink. Although he felt drained and let down, he found himself unwilling to go home. The press, radio and television had given him a rough afternoon, sensing a major story behind the black mushroom that had climbed into the still desert air; but he had stuck to his guns.

Before he'd finished, he'd gotten calls from Paul Gaither, the chief engineer, Lyman Stark, the taciturn executive vice-president, and, finally, from Bergstrom, in the East. Behind the mask of questions he had perceived a common worry—a fear that the disaster might raise questions regarding the Monarch's structural integrity. Obliquely, each had conjectured the trouble as originating with the test equipment or human error rather than with the Monarch itself.

The *Herald-Examiner* had headlined the story, MONARCH MISSILE IN MYSTERY EXPLOSION, with a drop head reading, BLAST SHATTERS SECRET TEST SITE. But the information hadn't come from him. He knew it represented the careful craftsmanship of putting together isolated facts and, in the process, coming dangerously near the truth. The *Times* and *Bulletin-News* hadn't played the story quite so hard, but the wires had picked it up, relaying it to the nation. Welkes would fret, but that couldn't be helped.

Once, he mused whimsically, he had been on the other side

of the fence. He knew exactly how Embry and the others felt, but neither could that be helped. Someday he'd tell Embry all about it—after the big bird flew. Then, contemplating the launching, he felt a nagging doubt. The explosion had shaken him more than he cared to admit, for he perceived that the Monarch *was* fallible. Not that he had expected perfection, yet that was the way he had come to think of the big bird—as a rocket vastly superior to the ICBMs against which it competed. Suppose it did have a structural defect? Chances were it was nothing serious. A slight modification—perhaps as simple as reinforcing a weld. That was all part of developing a missile. But it hurt. Coming when it did, it hurt badly. Fuel for Slater —for all those shouting against the missile. No matter how handled, it was certain to cast a gray shadow over the launching.

He ordered another drink, wishing Carole were with him. She had avoided him since the night of the party. Part of her conscience, he decided, part of the conflict. She thought on a high plane, followed certain standards, and when they crashed around her . . . That was one thing. Another was the job. She didn't consider what it meant—the salary, the future. She saw only the bad aspects, none of the good. Doing what you wanted was one thing; making a living was something quite else. Besides, he had an investment in the Monarch—a couple of years and a lot of faith. She never considered that.

His eyes lighted on Jane Cooper, sitting with one of Garfield's men. Leaning over the piano bar, they moved their cocktail glasses to the rhythm of the music. Her mask of powder and platinum hair gave her a jaded, dissipated appearance, and in the dim light her skin reflected a waxen pallor. He knew her partner to be but one in a long succession of conquests. A hell of a life. Everyone racing, speeding to escape, trying to drown reality in the false bliss of bars and beds, creating a harsher reality in the process. Why couldn't people take life as it came?

LeRoy Parsons, the hollow-cheeked art director, sat at a nearby table discoursing with a thin, dark girl. Burton, Hackleberg, Eggert of photos, Dorothy Baker of art . . . the same old crowd. They worked together by day, played together by night, almost as if they moved as a unit from the crate-shaped home of the Monarch to the palm-shaded motel so conveniently located across the way. Hackleberg would get drunk, make a fool of himself, Dorothy Baker would find a playmate, Parsons and the thin dark girl would vanish. He knew exactly how the night would end. But why was he here? Not for the drinks. Not for the crowd. Because a bird had exploded somewhere on the desert? No, not that, either. Why then? And again, why not?

He caught sight of Harry Garfield chatting with a couple in the foyer. The chief of publicity held his cigar a few inches from his mouth, head cocked as he listened to something the woman was saying. Occasionally he nodded. Elliott studied him sourly, recalling how he had wriggled out of the explosion story. Garfield knew a hot potato when he saw one. Not that he blamed him. It wasn't his story. And it was hot. One wrong word and a head would roll. He caught sight of Elliott and waved casually, and a few moments later sauntered over and took the empty stool alongside him.

"One to settle the nerves, eh?" He spoke airily.

"Helps," Elliott replied shortly.

"Hear from Welkes?" As he nodded reluctantly, Garfield continued: "I called him immediately—thought he might take you off the hook."

"Or put me on one."

"Oh?"

"He ordered me to sit on it."

"You did, didn't you?"

"As much as possible."

"That's what they have us for," Garfield asserted breezily. He rapped on the bar and ordered a Scotch on the rocks before continuing. "Hell, it's just a tin bird. We have a barn full of them. By tomorrow it'll all be forgotten."

"I hope."

"These boo-boos are old hat."

"Not with the Monarch," he corrected.

"Monarch, Atlas, Titan . . ." Garfield shrugged. "They're all the same. You gotta lose a certain number of these birds before you get 'em ticking right."

"It could cost us."

"If you're thinking of the contract, that's the least of our worries."

"How do you figure that?"

"Sheer economics," Garfield explained. "Did you ever stop to think how many people that missile's feeding? Cancel that bird and you'd have a first-class depression on your hands."

"L. A. could absorb it."

"It's not just L. A.," Garfield remonstrated. "Hell, we must have a couple of thousand subcontractors spread around the country. That's a lot of gravy they're siphoning off. Plenty of them—the smaller ones—would fold if it weren't for us. You're talking about a helluva lot of jobs, Jim. Hell, no, they won't cancel the Monarch. They can't."

"I wouldn't say can't."

He listened, amused, as Garfield explained the philosophy underlying the arms race. According to him, the big weapon systems were vast artifacts to keep the national economy alive. Without it, the structure would topple and there would be chaos, anarchy, communism. The contracts, he said, were distributed on the basis of need, both economic and political. But there was more. The big corporations had formed alliances with the military services to effect a vast centralization of the industrial effort. It was the centralization of money, power, the growth of the garrison state . . . the submergence of individual man. The survival of small business increasingly depended upon association with big business and, ultimately, upon control by the latter. It was an old argument, one that filled editorials, lecture halls, shabby rooms in Washington. A score of columnists made a living from the theme in one variation or another.

"What it boils down to," Garfield continued, "is a battle for power—the services pitted against one another, each with its battalions of corporations and political power blocs." As he saw it, the Air Force's big gambit was the ICBM, the Army's the Nike-Zeus, the Navy's the Polaris. That's why he had no worries over cancellation of the Monarch. "We talk about a hundred-million-buck production contract but what we mean are several billion bucks. That's what these things always wind up costing. It's in the bag, signed, sealed and delivered," he concluded.

"Not delivered," Elliott corrected.

"No? Wait and see. We can blow that baby up on the pad and we'll still get it."

"How do you account for big contracts that have been canceled—the F-105, for instance?"

Garfield shrugged. "The Navy beat the Air Force, that's all. That's just one of the skirmishes. Did you ever look at where McDonnell's sitting . . . the political power ringing it? Symington, Cannon and God knows who else. Christ, it's right in their back yard. And I'll tell you something else. Big cutbacks are rare. The effects show they're disastrous. They're politically and economically unacceptable. The government can't take it, Jim."

"So the Monarch's safe?" He smiled dubiously.

"Safe as they come."

"You sound like quite a booster."

"Sure, the bird of freedom, the bird of paradise." Garfield wore a smirk. "The Monarch's a 430,000-pound thrust fourth generation super-duper wonder. I tell people that all the time." The dark eyes mocked him. "Don't you follow my publicity?"

"It's still a good bird, Harry."

"Sure it's good—as good as the others. I'm not apologizing on that score."

"It's got to be more than that," he replied seriously.

"We'll make it more than that. We'll dust off the old typewriters, Jim." Elliott saw Esther Lynn threading her way among the tables. She sat next to Dorothy Baker. Garfield's eyes followed her. "A nice piece," he observed.

"I wouldn't know."

"We're in the same boat, but I wouldn't turn her down," Garfield confided. "That's the nicest pair of knockers in the plant. I wish she were my secretary."

"Jane wouldn't like that." He studied the object of Garfield's attention. In truth, she was extremely attractive. Dark hair and slanting eyebrows gave her an Oriental look. Tonight she wore glasses with colored rims that matched her sleeveless blue dress. She was exquisitely made. He wondered if she worried over her job. A new director might very well replace her. That was standard practice. She was rumored to have some special drag with Bergie and he thought it might be true, for he had sensed that Vroman hadn't particularly cared for her, yet had made no move to replace her. Certainly there had been none of the affinity so often found between boss and secretary.

For a while they chatted, then Garfield excused himself to speak with someone at the far end of the bar. Elliott nursed his drink, watching the ebb and flow of the crowd. Stover of graphics entered. Eggert of photos left. LeRoy Parsons and the dark girl followed. Esther Lynn and Dorothy Baker sat alone, toying with their glasses.

Morosely he finished his drink.

Esther Lynn crushed her cigarette in a tray, and watching as Elliott left the bar, wished she knew him better.

"Interested?" Dorothy Baker asked, following her gaze.

"Not particularly."

"He's a hunk of a man and, besides, he might turn up as the new director."

"I've thought of that."

"It's worth a try."

"Anything's worth a try." They measured each other over their glasses.

After a while, Dorothy asked, "Hear anything?"

"Nothing."

"See Bergie?"

"Not lately."

"He's funny. I can't figure him out."

"Neither can I," she admitted. "At one time I thought I knew him pretty well."

"Nobody knows him," Dorothy said. "I'll bet even his wife doesn't know him. Are you worried?"

"No, but I wish he'd say something."

"It must be a relief to be rid of Vroman."

"Yeah, he gave me a spooky feeling."

"Do you think he knew the score?"

"He knew, all right, but he'd never say anything."

"How could he?" Dorothy asked. "Who do you think will get the job?"

"If I knew that," she said slowly, "I'd know what to do."

Dorothy reached over and patted her hand. "I know you would, darling."

Her brief qualms had gone.

The waiting was delicious, the more so because this time it was her own home, her own room. She studied herself in the mirror, sensing only the urgency, discovering a freedom in what had heretofore been a monotonous cell, at times monotonous almost beyond endurance. The mockery heightened her anticipation. The first time had been in a cottage at Manhattan Beach; she remembered it had been set atop a dune overlooking the sea. Later there had been motels, his apartment, once in a car. Now, waiting, she thought: *Here, in my room* . . . It was something she had to do.

Sitting, she looked taller than she really was, and younger—far younger than her thirty-six years. Her ash-blond hair, combed in a halo to soften her features, enhanced the gray of her eyes and gave her cheeks a slightly hollow look. Carefully inspecting herself, she added a touch of eye shadow and rouge, a dab of powder to erase the thin lines which lately had become etched into the corners of her eyes, then studied herself approvingly. The nylon tricot, an autumn beige, was enchantingly feminine; she had selected it with care. Painting her lips, she heard the door chimes and quickly lifted her head, smiling in secret amusement. Taking the time to add a few deft touches and casting a backward glance at herself in the mirror, she went to answer the door.

She opened it and Eugene Henderson walked in.

"Am I early?"

"No, no . . . not early." She stepped back and the words tumbled from her lips: "I've been waiting."

Chapter 5

OTTO KROEBER was a dedicated man.

During the nearly two decades since he'd worked on the airframe of the German V-2 rocket at Peenemünde, from which the United States Army had rescued him in its famous "Operation Paperclip," almost his every waking hour had been spent delving into some phase of space flight. Indeed, the German "Vengeance" rocket had been part of his dream of conquest, but one which had nothing to do with war. Long before the V-2 he had belonged to the *Verein für Raumaschiffahrt,* the Association for Space Travel, founded by ardent young space enthusiasts before Hitler's rise to power. Obtaining a Ph.D. in aeronautical engineering from the University of Goettingen in 1926, he applied his knowledge to commercial aviation while pursuing his own studies on mechanical designs for space and avidly devouring the works of his countryman, Oberth, and Goddard in America, for in them he saw the seeds of the future.

Kroeber's presence at Peenemünde had been by command, although truthfully, he had welcomed the opportunity. His interest in the V-2 had been not in its use as a weapon but as a first step toward projecting mankind into a newer and better era, by which he meant space flight, for he believed the earth symbolized the link between man and his barbaric past. He saw the V-2 as the first tentative step in the pre-dawn of a new technology. Although a weapon, and quite crude, he perceived in it a machine that would grow in size, speed and range until, ultimately, its makers would realize that its greatest potential was not as a weapon, but as a vehicle which could accomplish that beyond the capability of any previous human artifact— the capability to pierce the high realms of space. The dream lay in his mind through all the grim days that followed until, finally, the Third Reich toppled, and with it an epoch.

Leaving Germany, he carried the dream with him.

In America he instructed Army and civilian personnel in the development and flight-testing of long-range rockets. Within several years, it taking him that long to master the English language, learned treatises on subjects ranging from rocket propulsion to celestial mechanics began appearing in scientific journals under his name. Within a few more years these had grown to a torrent of technical and popular articles, books, and talks before both academic bodies and amateur rocket enthusiasts, for he had learned that, in America, publicity paved the way to success.

Gaunt, with sparse gray hair, perpetually melancholy features, and arms that dangled from always too short sleeves, he was in constant demand as a speaker because of his ebullient dedication to the principle that man's true future lay beyond the earth. Listeners quickly forgot his rather drab exterior, the luminous, myopic eyes that peered from behind old-fashioned gold-rimmed spectacles, the schoolmaster trick of tilting up his head to look down his nose, and remembered only his vibrant words. Vroman once had described him as "a disembodied voice."

Somehow Otto Kroeber, who came out of the ruins of Peenemünde, had caught the eye of Martin L. Byerkoff, chairman of the board of Midwest Aeronautical Corporation, who saw in him a reservoir of publicity for his own company, which belatedly had turned to missiles as the demand for military aircraft lessened. Byerkoff had found Kroeber willing. A satisfactory agreement was quickly reached and the German scientist joined the then declining aeronautical empire, not, as Byerkoff suspected, for the lucrative salary, but for working conditions which gave him wide authority in a space program that was as yet but a paper dream. When Western Aerospace was formed as a division of the parent company, he came West as its technical director.

Possessing a marked antipathy toward weapons, he seldom referred to the Monarch as an ICBM, but as a space booster, for to him the giant missile represented a tool with which to propel other vehicles into space. The earth was a giant launching platform, the planets stepping-stones, the stars the ultimate goal. The dream transcended centuries. He interpreted the deep-swirling, ever-continuing battle of missiles versus spacecraft as one of war versus progress, in which each of the opposing forces, deeply integrated into the national economy, had fabricated its own power center. No one openly admitted such power centers or placed names to them, for in the early days the battle lines were loosely drawn, shifting, often changing altogether. But gradually the Air Force had tightened its hold over ICBM and IRBM space, emerging supreme among the services, then turned its attention to the National Aeronautics and Space Administration, which in turn had ballooned into a giant of formidable proportions. Kroeber saw that the ultimate control of space lay between a growing military juggernaut and an unstable civilian bureaucracy, and between those purposeful opponents he must tread, seeking the favor of each in order that the cause of progress be served.

The aerospace world had become enmeshed in administrative red tape, a complex of confusing and unwieldy offices with crisscrossing lines of authority, no single voice of command. Committee meetings, budgetary jockeying, crash programs, wasted billions of dollars, useful designs and completed systems junked because they did not fit into the grand strategy— in such things he found himself involved. He learned to think and plan in new terms—allocations, economics, power complexes, politics—and yet he was optimistic: man had a way of forging ahead despite himself. It was almost as if the Creator had built in obstacles to force his creatures to ever higher hurdles. Kroeber tried to keep his thoughts above the jungle, dedicating his life that generations yet unborn might realize the purpose for which the first cells spawned in the warm seas of a primeval planet had been ordained. Or so he believed.

A practical man, he understood before most that the key to space lay in the magic word *thrust*, which to a missileman is reaction force produced by expelling hot particles at high velocity through nozzle openings. The airframe, guidance, controls, upper stages and payload formed integral parts of the rocket, but its heart and soul lay in its engines. The expelled particles might be liquid, solid, gaseous, or even take the form of radiant energy, but thrust could endure only so long as material remained available to expel. Hence the problem to a large extent was reduced to fuel. The leading liquid propellant available when the Monarch was designed brought together a kerosene-like hydrocarbon and liquid oxygen, the latter forming the oxidizer without which the liquid fuel could not burn in the airless regions above the earth. This represented the fist that drove the Atlas and Titan I, and would drive the Monarch. Although an advancement over previous fuels, it imposed severe limitations, for its use required engineering and weight factors which largely negated its value for space exploration. Kroeber thought of the fuel as a stone ax in the technology of propulsion, yet he realized that the giant boosters must be designed around such propellants at least for the present years.

Thrust, power, the gigantic sledgehammer needed to drive man beyond the earth, spelled engines of gargantuan size. He early began exhorting the need of such an engine, or cluster of engines, capable of boosting huge weights above the air ocean; he watched, baffled, as those same engines were produced, not by his adopted country but by Russia. It was not until the heavens became filled with "beeps" that his words were harkened; by then he was called prophetic.

Although variously thought of as a dreamer, a genius, a madman, those who knew him best considered him a blend of the three. His workday usually extended far into the night, and more often than not into weekends as well. Humped over his desk in the small hours after midnight, he was a familiar sight to the janitors who came to wax and polish, and to the guards and firemen making their security rounds.

Periodically he liked to roam through the big, noisy factory, stopping to watch the welders, the drop hammers, the huge explosive forming machines in which shock waves forced metal blanks against dies to produce large hemispheres and other complex shapes that went into the making of the Monarch and its peaceful cousin, the Guardian. At times he wandered to the machine rooms where the various cutting, bending, grinding, drilling and punching operations were performed; or he followed a specific unit through assembly from the warehouse to the time when it formed part of a complex system within the missile or Guardian space vehicle. Occasionally he asked questions; more often he merely watched. Paul Gaither declared that Kroeber could improve any operation in the plant merely by observing it for five minutes. Regardless of the truth or falsity of the statement, Kroeber enjoyed such visits, for he considered the factory the true cradle of the future.

As the years passed he drove himself faster and faster, often working to the point of sheer exhaustion, when he would collapse at his desk, sleeping with head in arms. Unknown to others, he had a single dream: to live to see the first human foot touch the moon.

The dream had become a drive, for Kroeber had passed his sixtieth year, and the moon was very far away.

Elliott wasn't considering Otto Kroeber's alleged eccentricities as he approached the latter's office, but rather the job vacated by Vroman, and his own possibilities of getting it. Although he had come to gather information for an article, the thought lay in his mind that Kroeber could well be a power in the naming of a new director. His status and prestige were indubitable. More to the point, he felt Kroeber liked him.

He found the scientist bent over his desk, deep in a graph, and he lingered at the threshold. Kroeber sat hunched as if consciously pulling together his shoulders. His gray hair was thinning badly, the hand holding one corner of the graph was veined, gnarled. On the wall before him hung a large drawing of the Guardian space vehicle.

"May I interrupt?" Kroeber lifted his head without changing his position. "I'd like to get some information for an article."

"All right." Kroeber sounded reluctant.

"Thanks." Elliott sat across from him, explaining, "We're doing another article on the Monarch's booster capabilities."

"What's it boosting this time?" Elliott detected a mocking gleam in his eyes.

"Communication satellites."

"Where'd you hear that?"

"Welkes. It's in his prepared statement for the Slater committee."

"It's not designed for that purpose, Elliott."

"No, but it's a capability, isn't it?"

"Yes, using a Guardian second stage, but there'd have to be modifications."

"To the Monarch?"

"The Guardian," he corrected.

"That's all we're claiming," Elliott explained. "Bergstrom wants to push the idea."

"I don't like it."

"The article?"

"Giving the Slater committee that type of information," Kroeber explained. "The Guardian has a specific mission. We can't make it all things to all people."

"That's Welkes' baby."

"Yes, it is," he replied disapprovingly.

In the pause that followed, Elliott said, "Too bad about the test missile . . . coming at this time."

"Those things happen." His voice closed the subject.

"About the article . . . ?" Elliott pushed.

Kroeber regarded him owlishly. "What do you wish to know?"

"How such a system works."

"Like any booster system, Elliott, it's a problem of injecting mass into space—power, correct programming—"

"My concern is the satellites."

"There are several types of systems, if that's what you're asking—high and low orbit, passive and active vehicles."

"I'm not up on them," he confessed.

"The high orbit is the more sophisticated system," Kroeber went on. "Three such satellites placed above the equator could blanket most of the habitable earth, all but the Polar regions."

"Isn't such a system in the mill now?" As Kroeber nodded, he added: "It sounds glamorous."

"Glamorous?"

"Isn't it?"

"A symphony in mathematics . . . engineering," he said simply.

"Could you explain it"—he smiled—"from the glamour point of view?"

Kroeber eyed him bemusedly, then began talking while balancing a pencil between his fingertips. After the first few sentences Elliott became aware that he no longer was the audience, at least as far as Kroeber was concerned. Curiously, Kroeber's voice was low, monosyllabic, yet with each word clipped and precise, conveying exactly what he wished it to convey. Elliott forgot the tired face with its myopic eyes entranced by the picture he was drawing.

He spoke of satellites located at the apexes of an equilateral triangle, over 22,000 miles above the earth. If he closed his eyes, Elliott felt he would see them there—small, bulbous bodies with weird antennae speeding among the stars, tying the world together with mysterious electromagnetic wave-trains. A unit called a transponder would receive a signal, feed it to an amplifier, thence to a transmitter which would beam it to earth, or to another active transmitter at another point of the triangle, from whence it could be sent to receivers on the opposite side of the globe. Kroeber dropped the pencil, occasionally gesturing to paint in the relationship of the earth and its far-flung communication points.

The satellites would appear stationary, for each followed a path directly over the equator, orbiting in the same direction, completing each revolution at a time coincident with an earth rotation. Kroeber's hands shaped a cone; gnarled and aged, they suddenly became graceful. A directive antenna array would radiate such a cone of energy to the earth, covering an area from 81 degrees north to 81 degrees south and 162 degrees along the equator.

He spoke of the variety of receiving and transmitting equipment, antennae and solar power generators each satellite would need—the necessity of developing long-range radio measuring equipment to track the satellites with minute precision. He's thinking aloud, Elliott thought. He's building the system now, in his mind. He doesn't even know I'm here. And finally the thought: He's like Vroman, or like Vroman had been in the early days. There was the same enthusiasm, the same dedication and intensity. Kroeber caught and held him now, as Vroman once had done. Finally he began speaking of the design of the satellite itself; his language became technical as he absently jotted figures on a pad at his side. Elliott stirred and abruptly the voice stopped.

"You're losing me," Elliott admitted. "However, I catch the general idea."

"There's nothing mysterious about it," Kroeber observed. "Nature is symmetry, a matter of balance, perfect proportions expressed in such factors as thrust, mass-ratio, gravity, time—precise engineering formulated on precise mathematics. We have the technical knowledge now. These aren't new systems. They're under development and test."

"I've read about them," he admitted. Kroeber didn't reply immediately, and watching him, he was caught by the fatigue mirrored in the other's face. The lines etching the corners of the dark eyes and the grayish skin pulled taut over the cheekbones reminded him of a death's head.

"Nothing is impossible except the will to do it," Kroeber resumed, "and except for the misdirection of our energies."

"You're speaking of this system?"

"A general comment."

"You're probably right."

"We waste energy, time, money." A note of irritation crept into Kroeber's voice. "Scientific programs don't have much dollar-pulling power, Elliott, unless they're related to the military."

"It seems to me we spend quite a bit."

"On the wrong things," he said. "We're going in all directions. We're too concerned with megatons . . . warheads. How many articles have you put out on the Guardian?"

Caught by surprise, Elliott answered, "Quite a few."

"Let's say as compared with the Monarch?"

"The Guardian represents a much smaller contract," he replied, feeling on the defensive.

"But a less important one?"

"That's a matter of judgment."

"Precisely. The amount of time you give to each is roughly proportionate to the value you place on each."

"Probably." He debated it. "But the Monarch's our bread and butter."

"That's what I've been saying."

"It's not a matter of choice."

"I understand that."

"The Monarch is important to space," Elliott insisted. "It's a damned good booster, or will be."

"I'm glad you're not trying to sell it on the basis of a weapon." Kroeber gave one of his rare smiles. When Elliott didn't reply, he continued, "You don't create a rocket like this overnight." Kroeber looked past him into space and Elliott conjectured at his thoughts. The gaunt face told nothing.

"Maybe I can do more for you in the way of space," Elliott suggested. He hesitated, and encouraged by a quizzical look, went on: "I've got some time on my hands. Vroman left us, or hadn't you heard?"

"Yes, I know."

"I'll be on my own until they appoint a successor."

"Have they mentioned a name?"

"Not that I know of." He paused, seeking some clue from the other, but found none. "The policy of promotion-from-within indicates one of our men—Garfield, Koepple, possibly Henderson of Space Electronics."

"How about yourself?"

"I have the least seniority."

"That shouldn't be a point."

"Perhaps not, I don't know."

"Isn't ability a factor, Elliott?"

"It should be."

Kroeber nodded. "Yes, it should. How old are you?"

"Thirty-two."

"Alexander conquered most of the known world by that age."

"But I'm not Alexander," Elliott said dryly.

Kroeber went on as if he hadn't heard. "I was designing my first rockets by then. It's not young, not young at all. But it's a period of time when life seems endless, when vistas stretch on and on. Youth, Elliott, it's wonderful, a golden age. There are years to throw away. It's like sowing grain. Then suddenly you realize you have to hurry to catch up. That's when you begin to feel old. Time is relative . . . relative in our minds. It shrinks. It's like an hourglass; you don't realize how fast the grains are dropping until but a few remain. Too fast. It's a macabre dance. There's no brake on the world, Elliott. We go faster and faster."

"We have to go faster to keep up."

"I suppose." Kroeber sighed. "You want the job?"

"Yes, of course."

"It's thankless."

"Someone has to do it."

"I don't imagine there's a lack of volunteers," he remarked.

"Not in this case," Elliott admitted. "But you can't stand still. You have to keep moving. When you stand still, you're sliding backward." He spoke quickly, aware he was on the defensive, yet he felt Kroeber understood.

"There's nothing wrong with standing still, Elliott. Some people are born to stand still."

"I'm not," he shot back.

"I surmised that."

"If we all stood still, we'd never get anywhere."

"I wasn't arguing in favor of it, I was just commenting," Kroeber explained. "But at times I think the people who stand still are more at peace with themselves, and with the world. They don't burn the energy."

"I'm willing to burn the energy," he said pointedly.

"I'm sure you are." Elliott was uncertain if he detected a note of mockery when the other continued: "Perhaps things will work out for you."

"I hope so."

"So do I, Elliott." He dropped his eyes to the graph again, and thanking him, Elliott withdrew. Returning to his office, he felt inwardly disquieted. While he hadn't actually solicited Kroeber's help, what he had done amounted to the same thing.

The thought made him vaguely uncomfortable.

Carole Janek had been sitting at her drawing board the first time she saw him. Working on a sketch of the Monarch, she had become aware of someone standing over her, and had looked up. Her first impression was of a flat brow, a strong, slightly bent nose, dark eyes under heavy ridges. The white scar running from temple to hollow cheek came next, then the short dark hair.

The face smiled.

"I'm Jim Elliott from the news bureau. You the new artist?"

"Carole . . . Carole Janek," she said, unable to take her eyes from his face. She thought it the strongest face she'd ever seen, and yet it wasn't handsome.

He looked at the sketch she was doing. "The skirt's too high. It should end here, near the top of the booster stage." His finger jabbed the spot.

"Oh, I drew it from another sketch."

"I'll get you a photo, then you can scale it off."

"I'd appreciate that . . ." She hesitated.

"How'd you like to go out in the factory, see the bird?"

"I'd like to."

"Now?"

"I'm afraid not. I have some work."

"Tomorrow?"

"I . . . don't know."

"Okay, any time. I'll be glad to show you around."

"That would be fine."

"Just give me a call . . . the news bureau."

"I will, and thanks." She watched him leave—his size, the brief moment he filled the doorway, his easy walk—and when he was gone, continued staring after him.

The next morning she found a portfolio of Monarch and Guardian photographs and line drawings on her desk. No name or note was attached.

She saw him a number of times after that—in the halls, the cafeteria, occasionally in the art department—brief encounters with seldom more than a "Hi, Carole" on his part and a quick, nervous nod on hers. Yet she felt he was watching her, appraising her, that the dark eyes took in far more than the casual glances revealed.

Occasionally in the evening she set her easel up on the beach near her small apartment and sketched, but more often she walked along the shore, setting herself no goal, taking pleasure in the spray-laden winds that whipped her hair and clothes and at times bit like a sharp knife into her body. Again, driven by a strange restlessness, deep-rooted yet unidentifiable, she walked swiftly, heedless of wind and sea until long after the sun dropped below the rim of the sea. At such times his face was apt to pop into her mind, the dark eyes scrutinizing her, and she sensed a great void in her life, a something-that-was-missing that was as formless as the winds which brushed the sands.

Then, entering the plant one morning, she had noticed him coming from the parking lot and had unconsciously slowed her step to allow him to overtake her. In the ensuing conversation he had pressed her to meet him for lunch and, moved by a curiously pleasant quickening sensation, she had agreed.

He appeared at her office promptly at twelve.

"Ready?"

"A moment." She straightened her desk, conscious of his scrutiny, then rose determinedly to join him.

"How's the job coming?" he asked over lunch.

"I'm catching on."

"Like it?"

"I like my work."

"That's not the same thing."

"No, it's not," she agreed, surprised at his perspicacity.

"What don't you like about it?"

She hesitated, drawing together her impressions. "It's organized chaos. Every little task assumes gigantic proportions. Even a simple illustration eventually involves a dozen people. I seem to spend most of my time on paper work." He nodded understandingly and she continued, compelled by a curious need to talk: "I have the feeling of losing my identity, that I'm not really a person but just some sort of a machine. Sometimes

I have to tell myself who I am. Have you ever felt that way? I can't imagine people working here for years."

"Why'd you come here?"

"Economic necessity."

They laughed and he said encouragingly, "It's not as confusing as you think. After a while you'll get the hang of it . . . see where the different lines go. Most of it turns out fairly logical."

"Perhaps," she said dubiously.

"What do you want to do?"

"Illustrate children's books."

"Why aren't you doing it?"

"I'm trying, Jim." She used the name deliberately, testing the sound, and decided she liked it. The name fitted him, just as the white scar fitted his face.

He inclined his head. "Doing anything tonight?" The question caught her unprepared and as she hesitated, he went on, "I'd like to take you out—supper, a show or dance. Or we could drive, spin down to Malibu."

"I don't know." She wanted to call the words back, say yes, yet felt a strange reluctance. She hoped he would insist.

"Boy friend?"

"No." She flushed.

"Then why not?"

"I . . . have some work to finish." She wondered at her lie.

"Here?"

"At home. I work there too," she explained.

"Tomorrow night?" He leaned forward engagingly.

"Well . . ."

"We'll decide tomorrow. Okay?"

"Yes."

"Over lunch?"

"All right."

"Why don't we decide now and have lunch together anyway?" She laughed at his persistence and he bent closer, his elbows on the table. "Tomorrow night?"

She felt the odd stirring come again, and said, "Yes."

They had dinner in Beverly Hills and later drove along the winding coast highway to Zuma Beach. He got her home by eleven and escorted her to the door, where they chatted a moment before he left.

That was all.

She had remained standing, watching until the taillights of his car disappeared before she went in. Afterward she lay in bed, unable to sleep, remembering his closeness as he sat beside her in the car. Once their thighs accidentally touched; it had been like an electric shock. She heard the dull boom of the surf, the sibilant, gurgling water streaming over the sand slopes, and felt as if it were caressing her flesh. Later she slept.

There were other dates.

"Hi, Carole. How about dinner?"

"Doing anything tonight, Carole?"

"Let's take in a movie, okay?"

He didn't change. He didn't push her or press her. After the second or third date he kissed her casually at the door before leaving. Yet she felt a change, a slow, surging emotion within her, punctuated by sharp desires and mental imagery which she sought to banish, but which always returned. It was worse at night when she was lying alone in bed. At such times her solitude imprisoned her completely, and she found herself wishing he were there, with her. She could not force the thoughts away. Did he feel the same? Or was it just herself?

Occasionally, when he brought her home from a date, she felt positively weak; it crystallized her resolve to surrender no part of herself. It was as if she were preparing for a battle that had no tangible form save what was within her. She had her life mapped, planned, if not in detail, at least in a broad outline of desires, ambitions, goals—the freedom to express one's self and be free, to use one's talents to the utmost, without restriction. In retrospect she thought her world had been created without consideration of Jim Elliott. His entry on the scene fortified her resolve not to compromise with life, in any form.

But when she was with him, the restlessness flooded back, and often she withdrew, her shield against him. It revealed itself in her flat toneless voice, the uttered monosyllables that were bare skeletal answers to his questions. He knew. Although they never spoke of it, she knew he knew, and when she did, she raged inwardly at him, as if he were a spectator viewing the decline and fall of Carole Janek. Where would it end? At night, alone, the question ran through her mind.

"Let's go down." He had caught her hand, and laughing, had led her along a twisting path to the beach. At the bottom they removed their shoes and stockings. She finished first and darted over the sand toward a rock ledge, and reaching it, looked back. He stood, legs apart, hands on hips, watching her, then laughed and raced toward her. She ran lightly between the rocks and tideline, mocking his efforts to catch her. With the wind whipping her hair and brushing her skin, she dodged this way and that. Just as he thought he had her cornered, she sprang away again.

Finally, breathless, they began exploring the beach. Gathering seaweed and shells, they clambered between the rocks and splashed through the tide pools, laughing as the wet spray stung their faces. Getting a stick, he drew a large heart on the beach and she etched an arrow through it; a wave rolled over it and receding, left only the sand. As the water flooded back over their ankles, she said, "We should have brought suits."

"Next time." He studied the waves. "Now if it were dark . . ." She caught his meaning, flushing, and he grinned. "We used to."

"Swim . . . naked?" She forced herself to say the word, conscious of a sharp intake of breath.

"At night . . . summers." He spoke casually. "We used to come down on picnics, build bonfires, ride the breakers and swim."

"We?"

"When I was a kid, and later, during college."

Realizing he hadn't answered her question, she said, "I used to come here."

"Picnics?"

She nodded. "And swimming."

"College?"

"Yes." She caught his expression and exclaimed, "Not what you're thinking."

"Oh, was I thinking something?"

"About the suits."

He threw back his head, laughing. "It never entered my mind."

"What would you think if . . . ?" She left the question dangling, wondering why she had asked. It had been almost a compulsion.

"If you swam naked?"

"Yes."

"Nothing."

"Nothing?"

"Lots of people swim naked."

"Mixed?"

"Certainly, you know that."

"Yes." She felt his eyes mocking her and hurriedly explained, "I guess I said it badly."

"Said what badly?"

"About . . . being naked." There, he had made her say it again. She felt a sudden jolt inside her and forced herself to look at his face, wanting to see his expression. He appeared unchanged except for the eyes: they held amusement.

"What's wrong with the word?" he asked.

"Naked?"

"Yes."

"Nothing."

"You look like I bit you."

"Do I?"

"Yes," he said gravely.

She tore her eyes away, gazing at the tide pools. "There are anemones, starfish, sea urchins . . ." She talked to break the moment, the curious agitation within her.

"Crabs too," he said. "Let's explore." He clasped her hand, drawing her to one of the tide pools, then relinquished it and waded in. She followed, picking her way over the mossy bottom. He discovered a sea cucumber, then moved deeper searching for abalone while she gathered the small, colorful scallop shells. Emerging from the pool, she stepped on a loose boulder and would have fallen had he not caught her, holding her tight until she regained her balance. The laugh died on his lips as their eyes met, and lowering his head, he kissed her, drawing her close. When he released her she stepped back, looking away quickly, the pressure of his body against her sharp in her mind.

That had been the beginning.

The thoughts came tumbling back as she stared at the woman in the mirror. Why did everything have to be so wrong? She liked him enormously, and yet . . .

What do I want from life?

She saw the lips of the woman in the mirror move. I want to be happy, but so does everyone. Happiness is just a word, a mask to explain human wants and experiences. A person who speaks of happiness is really speaking of drives, emotions, pleasurable occurrences. That's reasonable, so what do I want?

I want identity.

I want to be free.

I want to create.

I want Jim.

I want him now, tomorrow, always. But how much do I want him? Enough to change the course of dreams?

He had taken one course; he had sacrificed—was sacrificing —a better one, and inevitably he must be embittered. She couldn't stand to see that, would crumple in the process. She had two choices: Jim or not Jim. How would they weigh if placed in the balance?

At times there seemed to be two Caroles. One was the Carole she'd known for almost all of her life—the certain Carole who had moved with assurance, saying of life: *This is what I want.* The other was the new Carole, the alter ego born of the tides within her. She had been the sculptor, remodeling the clay of the old image. This was the Carole who trembled at his touch, who said "yes" when the other Carole said "no." If the second Carole were the true Carole, then the first had been nothing— a sham, a façade, a cardboard self. But if the first Carole were true, then what she was doing was vastly wrong. Was she a wanton? She looked steadily at the face in the mirror. I am me, she said. I will not surrender me.

The telephone rang.

She looked at herself again, then rose from the dressing table and went to answer it.

6

Chapter 6

GENERAL," said Representative Stafford C. Slater, "I think we are going around in circles."

The piercing dark eyes under the shaggy brows fixed on Major General Alexander Barmon, United States Air Force Ballistic Systems Division, who for the greater part of an hour had been testifying as a witness for the Air Force before Slater's House Appropriations subcommittee inquiring into missile and space systems economics. Cool and apparently at ease, Barmon remained silent, for the words required no answer; Slater was merely talking while he formulated another assault.

Herbert P. Welkes followed the testimony closely, for he considered that each *riposte* and nuance afforded an insight into Slater's complex makeup. Although ostensibly a hearing before a subcommittee of the Appropriations Committee, the proceedings had thus far proved a one-man show; the other five committee members were present merely as window dressing, or so Welkes thought. Dr. Otto Kroeber, looking haggard and bent, sat next to him. Occasionally they conversed in low tones, but mainly they watched, and listened.

Slater cleared his throat and observed, "We have heard testimony regarding the billions heaped upon billions which these weapon systems of deterrency have cost. I would like to state right now that this committee is not so much interested in questioning costs—at least at this time—as it is in determining the value received for the tremendous amounts of money that Congress is being asked to appropriate. But I don't seem to be getting that information, General. Now, as I understand it, the Air Force has four ICBM weapon systems either operational or nearly operational. Is that correct?"

"That is correct, sir."

"That includes the Monarch?"

"That would fall under the 'nearly operational' category, yes, sir."

"I understand this system is being developed by concurrency; that is, the missile, its bases and all of its logistics and maintenance aspects are being developed simultaneously so that, in effect, everything will be completed at once."

"That is correct," Barmon replied. "If we didn't start the bases until the Monarch became operational, we would lose years. Concurrency ensures against that."

"Yes, I can see that," Slater affirmed. "Let's put it another way: If we canceled one of these systems—say the Monarch— we would lose not only the vast amount of money invested in the missile, but also the tremendous sums invested in the bases and associated hardware. Is that correct?"

"Yes, sir."

"So in effect, concurrency might be considered a device to prevent the cancellation of a missile."

"No, sir, I do not believe that to be the case," Barmon protested. "Concurrency is a means toward shortening the time to operational status, and that's all it is."

"Well, well, I'm glad to hear that. Indeed I am." Slater adjusted his glasses while glancing at his notes. *Sonuvabitch,* Welkes thought, he's been over that ground a dozen times. He glanced irritably around. Thin-faced and several decades the junior of the chairman, Representative Sumner, sitting at the far end of the committee table, caught his frown and dropped an eyelid suggestively. "I understand the Monarch is a liquid fuel missile like the Atlas and Titan," Slater continued, looking at Barmon again.

"Yes, sir."

"In what way does it differ from those two missiles?"

"Well, as a later missile, it is more advanced, more sophisticated, which is the reason we refer to it as a fourth-generation ICBM. Technically, such changes affect the propulsion and guidance systems, and the airframe; in fact, almost all aspects of the missile. I believe we can truthfully state that it represents a further step on the evolutionary ladder of weaponry."

Slater queried sharply, "Does it serve the same purpose as the Atlas and Titan?"

"If you mean as a weapon of deterrency and retaliation, yes, sir, it serves the same purpose."

"Then could you please tell this committee exactly why three liquid fuel ICBM systems are necessary? It seems to me we have some sort of duplication here."

"No, sir, I don't believe that to be the case." Barmon's voice was patient. "Each ICBM, or any weapon system for that matter, must be evaluated in terms of the mission for which it is designed."

"Then their missions differ?"

"Yes, sir."

"In what way?"

Barmon hesitated. "Well, some missiles are designed for precision bombardment, others for saturation bombardment, and of course there are differences in range and payload. The choice of missile and payload depend upon the target."

"Could you give us an example?"

"I'm afraid I don't quite follow the question."

"What is the Atlas designed for?"

"Precision bombardment. It is a powerful, highly accurate ICBM."

Slater leaned forward. "From what you have said, I would understand that the Titan is designed for saturation bombardment. Is that correct?"

"No, sir, the Titan is highly accurate too."

"If I understood your testimony the first time, you indicated there was a difference in mission assignment between these two ICBM systems, and you spelled out this difference as saturation versus pinpoint bombardment. Is that correct, or isn't it?"

"I'm afraid this case falls in a slightly different category, sir." General Barmon's voice took on an edge that didn't escape Welkes' attention. "The Titan was designed as a back-up system in case the Atlas failed. The latter was a completely new design—what we call a stage-and-a-half missile. At that time we considered the Titan an insurance policy."

"The Atlas didn't fail?"

"No, sir."

"But we retained the Titan?"

"Yes, sir."

"So we really have two missiles that are very much alike?"

"Not exactly," Barmon said quickly. "There are differences, quite a number of them. These differences are structural and operational and, of course, affect the entire mission concept of each. In addition, the Titan—Titan II—has uprated thrust. They aren't the same system at all, although superficially they might seem so. For one thing, all of the Atlas engines are fired on the ground before launch, thus making this particular missile especially high in reliability."

"The Titan hasn't this asset?" Slater asked.

"It's a different concept, sir."

"How different?"

"In the Titan, the second stage engine doesn't ignite until after the booster stage shuts down and separates."

"Does this make it less reliable?"

"There are other advantages," Barmon maintained. "A complete explanation would involve considerable technical detail."

"I can see that," Slater acquiesced. "Indeed I can." He looked knowingly at the Air Force officer. "By the way, you mentioned Titan II. Isn't that a completely new missile?"

"It's an extension of the Titan I program, sir."

"I understand it operates on"—Slater glanced at his notes —"nitrogen tetroxide and UDMH."

"Yes, sir."

"I take it that this fuel has advantages?"

"It can be stored in the missile for long periods at room temperature," Barmon explained. "It's what we call a hypergolic fuel."

"A simpler system?"

"The fuel starts burning when the nitrogen tetroxide and UDMH come in contact. That does away with an ignition system and, of course, increases the missile's reliability."

"Then, in essence, it is a completely new system?" Slater queried.

"You . . . might call it that."

"So that makes five ICBM systems?"

"No, sir, Titan I and Titan II really represent a single system. One is just an extension of the other."

"But Titan II is the better system?"

"Yes, sir."

"Let's see, if my memory is correct, we have around six hundred million dollars committed in the Titan I. Is that correct?"

"I believe that's a fair figure, sir."

"And now the system is obsolete?"

"No, sir, I don't regard it as such."

"Does the Air Force?"

"No, sir."

"Well, we'll let that pass . . . for the time being," Slater said. He looked up suddenly. "By the way, aren't they having some trouble with the Monarch?"

"Trouble?" Barmon inquired. Welkes stiffened, knowing what was coming.

Slater asked pleasantly, "One exploded recently, didn't it?"

"Oh, the test missile."

"Test missile, or whatever it was."

"We lost one during a static test at Desert Center," Barmon affirmed. "It was an old missile, used for all types of tests—a test workhorse, you might say."

"I understand there was considerable damage. Is that correct?"

"It's still too early to get the figures, sir."

"But they lost the tower . . . the test stand?"

"Yes, sir."

"And some quite valuable ground-support equipment?"

"I believe they lost some liquid oxygen tanking equipment, sir."

"Will that set the program back, General?"

"No, sir, the company has other static test facilities and, of course, the facilities at Edwards Rocket Base are available. No, it won't affect the program time-wise, sir."

"Well, I'm not so concerned with that, even though it means a considerable loss, but I am concerned over the possibility of a structural flaw."

"It wasn't a matter of a structural flaw," Barmon said emphatically.

"The report I received stated it was a fuel leak."

"Possibly."

"Wouldn't that indicate a weakness in the tanks?"

"Not necessarily. It's completely understandable that such a leak might occur in a missile tested for as long and as hard as this one was."

"You say possibly?" Slater's eyes fixed him closely.

"We can't be certain exactly what did happen until after we study all the data, sir."

"If you can't be certain, how can you rule out an inherent structural weakness?" Slater demanded.

"Each missile is thoroughly tested, both during and following fabrication," Barmon explained. "Each is exposed to maximum internal pressures many times. This particular missile had been used in a number of vibration tests—was being used in such a test, as a matter of fact, when the accident happened."

"I'm willing to accept that explanation, General, at least for the time being, and I certainly hope that nothing similar occurs."

"We sincerely hope not, sir."

"That brings up the question of the Minuteman. Would you tell us, General, how this ICBM differs from the others?"

"The Minuteman is quite dfifferent, sir. It is a solid fuel ICBM, designed for saturation bombardment."

"Will you yield right there please, Mr. Chairman?" Representative Hansen asked, from the end of the table.

"Yes."

"The Minuteman is a more advanced system, is it not, General?" Hansen asked. Welkes eyed him quizzically. Like the chairman, he was known as a spokesman for the solid fuel lobby.

"Yes, sir, it is," Barmon agreed.

"I understand it's also a more economical system?"

"There are many advantages."

"I was referring to economics, General. Money."

"Yes, sir, it is more economical."

"I hear the Air Force is very happy with the Minuteman, General."

"Yes, it's an excellent weapon."

"You see an expansion of this program, do you not?"

"That is the plan, sir."

Hansen rubbed his hands. "I am very happy to hear it. That is all, Mr. Chairman."

"Ah, now we're getting somewhere," Slater commented. "So there is a difference in ICBMs?"

"Yes, sir, a very great difference."

"And in their missions?"

"Yes, sir."

"I understand the Minuteman is a later missile than either the Atlas or the Titan. That is, the Titan I. Am I correct in that assumption, General?"

"That is correct, sir."

"How did the Minuteman come into being?"

"I'm afraid I don't quite understand the question, sir."

"What gave impetus to the Minuteman?" Slater asked. "You've explained the target differences, but it would appear to me that this factor alone would not justify an added program. As long as we already had two ICBM systems, what particular situation arose that demanded a third?"

Welkes noted the question sourly, thinking that this had been Slater's goal all along. Regardless of whether or not he was owned by the solid fuel people, it was a fact that members of the press had dubbed him "Mr. Solids," and indeed he had proved a strong proponent of such power sources. Welkes watched Barmon, who was saying:

"Advances in the state of the art, sir. Certain technological breakthroughs occurred which made the use of solid propellants particularly feasible for certain mission requirements."

"Do I understand from this that solid propellant missiles represent a forward step in weaponry?" Slater asked.

"Yes, sir."

"The committee would be pleased to hear some of these advantages, General. I am thinking of specific points which would justify a weapon system of this magnitude."

"Well, of course, a solid fuel missile is of much simpler design," Barmon explained. "We attain a greater ease and speed of fabrication—produce a missile which requires less maintenance while at the same time providing increased reliability. More to the point, the missile can be fired in anger in a shorter period of time inasmuch as it is always in a state of readiness. The Air Force considers this a very great advantage."

"This is all quite interesting," Slater observed.

"There are, of course, advantages in transporting and storing such a missile, and in the training of missile-handling personnel," Barmon continued. "I would like to add that the Air Force considers this concept an economic breakthrough." Welkes winced, wondering why Barmon went to such great lengths.

"The committee is certainly happy to hear that," Slater exclaimed. "This subject of money is becoming quite critical, and it is always pleasant to hear of a savings. Then you believe the Minuteman represents a definite step forward?"

Something in the way he put it alerted Welkes, and he leaned forward on the edge of his chair.

"Yes, sir, I do," Barmon assented.

Slater let his pencil tilt toward Barmon.

"Then, General, why did the Air Force select as its fourth ICBM another liquid-fueled missile?"

"As I said before, there are advantages in each type."

"And disadvantages?"

"Yes, sir, but each weapon is selected only after a careful tactical and scientific evaluation. Here, of course, we weigh such factors as cost, availability, mission requirements, payload and a great many other things. I think it fair to state that each of these systems has a job to do, a specific job, and no other system can perform that job quite as well."

"Possibly, possibly . . ." Slater glanced around the table and continued: "I would like to touch on the Monarch again, if the committee is agreeable. I know we have been over this ground before, but I think there is one point we haven't covered, General. I understand the Monarch can be launched from the sea. Is that correct?"

"That is a capability, yes, sir."

"Would you care to comment on it?"

"This is classified and should be discussed off the record, sir."

"Well, that's certainly agreeable." While they conversed, Welkes, realizing that the subject could only add to the Monarch's stature, leaned toward Kroeber.

"What do you suppose he's driving at?"

"Hard to say, but I think we're going to hear much more about solid fuels."

"I gathered that."

"He seems to be biding his time."

"Probably waiting for us," Welkes observed cynically. A stir came from the table and he saw the meeting was back on the record.

"That type of mobility sounds like a Navy function to me," Slater was saying. So that's it, Welkes thought. He's going to snipe at the Air Force.

"No, sir, it's merely a launcher at sea—what you might term an extension of our land-launch capability."

Slater arched his brows. "Isn't that what any warship is—an extension of land power?"

"This isn't a warship, sir. It's a floating launcher."

"So is a cruiser."

"This hasn't any of the attributes of a conventional naval vessel," Barmon explained.

"Except that it goes to sea." Slater allowed himself a slight chuckle. "Well, it's interesting. Indeed it is interesting. I hope you don't mind if I go off on a tangent for a moment, General?"

"I am at your pleasure," he replied politely.

"Several of the committee members have been curious over increasing expenditures being put into these ICBM systems in view of counter-missile designs. Frankly, I am too. Would you care to comment?"

"There are a number of such systems—"

"The Nike-Zeus," Slater cut in. "The Army has testified that this system is capable of shooting down hostile ICBMs. If this is true, it would seem to me that we might be pouring billions into weapon systems which already are on the road to obsolescence."

"As I understand it, the Nike-Zeus is largely a theoretical system, sir. A paper system."

"Like the B-70? Or is it the RS-70?"

"Well, we have prototypes of the RS-70 ready for flight test," Barmon explained.

"There are prototypes of the Nike-Zeus, too. In fact, they've had a number of very successful firings."

"They can launch such a missile, of course, but knocking out an oncoming ICBM is something quite different, sir, when the trajectory is an unknown."

"An Atlas was shot down."

"It's trajectory was known."

"We could argue this all day," Slater remarked dryly.

"It's a critical point, sir. In war we would have no way of knowing where such launchings might originate. Besides, we couldn't protect the entire nation. There simply wouldn't be the time or money. So which flanks would we protect? How much good would partial protection do? That's assuming such a system is feasible, and that has yet to be proved."

"The Air Force feels the B-70 would work, would perform the missions for which it was designed if the funds were available. Is that correct, General?"

"Yes, sir."

"But you don't have the same faith in another paper system —the Nike-Zeus?"

"Let me answer it another way," Barmon proposed. "War might come tomorrow, or next year—we don't know. But we do know that a defensive system, however commendable it might appear, has little deterrency value and no obliteration value. We need the best possible weapons in hand—attack weapons."

"I've heard it claimed that all our missiles, bombers and nuclear submarines could not stop a single attacking ICBM," the chairman observed. "Isn't that true, General?"

"The chairman is speaking of attack forces," Barmon replied pointedly. "The weapons mentioned could totally crush an aggressor, but a defense weapon such as the Nike-Zeus couldn't kill a single enemy."

"I'm afraid you're engaging in semantics, General."

"Not intentionally, sir."

"Isn't it true that if we had an anti-ICBM—say a weapon like the Nike-Zeus—we would automatically invalidate the principle of peace through parity?"

"If such a weapon were feasible, yes, sir. And if it could be developed within our financial structure and within the time of its need."

"Not everyone believes those to be serious limitations, General. Do you?"

"Yes, sir, very serious."

"As I understand your background, you are primarily a soldier. Is that not true?"

"I'm afraid I don't follow you, sir."

"You are not a scientist."

"No, sir."

"Yet you are passing technical judgments on the merits of the Nike-Zeus."

"The Air Force has a strong task force of competent scientists," Barmon replied.

"Your think factories?"

"If you wish. I prefer to consider them as scientific advisors, and highly qualified."

"But they think as the Air Force wishes. Isn't that true?"

"No, sir. Our scientists have independence. We seek only the truth."

"It seems odd to me that these so-called think factories are always in such perfect agreement with the Air Force," Slater commented.

Barmon said quickly, "That's because there is no alternative to the truth, sir." Welkes restrained a smile, thinking that the General was indeed a worthy opponent for the slow-speaking, deliberate committee chairman. The latter eyed the Air Force officer intently.

"Isn't it true that many equally eminent scientists believe such a weapon as the Nike-Zeus to be feasible, General?"

"I believe some do."

"Would you say these scientists are less qualified than those in the Air Force think factories?"

"I'm certain I can't pass on their merits, sir."

"But you can pass on the merits of your own scientists, is that right?"

"The Air Force has faith in them, sir."

"Well, it's interesting. Indeed it is interesting." Slater glanced at the clock and continued, "But I see we're running behind time. We still have the representatives from industry to hear, and I'm looking forward to that. I am very much. So I want to take this opportunity on behalf of the committee and myself to thank you, General Barmon. If there are no questions . . ." He glanced around. "I think we should recess until after lunch, if that is agreeable."

"All these hearings are the same," Ralph Palmer, the company's Washington man, assured Welkes and Kroeber over lunch. "It's yak-yak-yak."

"It's yakking I don't like," Welkes declared.

"It's for effect."

"Certainly, and we're the goats. Business should have some protection against these people."

"It's part of the game, H. P. Today they're at bat. Tomorrow, when we launch the bird, our turn comes."

"We'll stuff that damned missile down his throat," Welkes said. "By the way, Sumner sat there like a wooden Indian, didn't do a damn thing to help out." His eyes challenged the Washington man. "I thought we had him in the bag."

"Don't worry about Bert Sumner. He does his work where it counts," Palmer said. "This is Slater's committee and he's willing to let the old boy have his glory, but believe me, Sumner's got access to the right ears."

"He ought to have, at least if your expense accounts are any criterion."

Palmer grinned. "They are. As Slater would say, indeed they

are. Partying comes high in this town. At that, we don't run close to what the competition spends. Good Lord, Ed Noble— he's with the solids bunch—runs 'em down to the islands by the planeloads. His girlie bill alone would buy a couple of Monarchs. That ain't hay, H. P."

"I can't say that we're putting out hay either. Did Sumner indicate the line of questioning Slater might pursue with us?"

"Only what I already told Bergstrom. He'll probably pound away on the question of necessity. Sumner's really interested in this. He's getting some pressure."

"Pressure?"

"The rumors about the Monarch contract being canceled," Palmer explained. "You know how those damned things start."

"What's that got to do with Sumner?"

"Hell, he's getting letters and telegrams from every damned union member in town, let alone their wives and grandparents. But it's good, it works out in our favor."

"A crackpot rumor."

"Well, it keeps Sumner on his toes. He knows it's a lot of malarky but he's got to make the folks back home think that he's doing something. Then, when it blows over, he gets the credit."

"Christ, we donate enough to elect him ourselves—"

"Sure, but don't worry. Like I said, it's just a rumor."

"Did he mention anything else about Slater?"

"He might hound us on our Guardian program."

"I can't see the profit in that."

Palmer shrugged. "The Guardian's just another liquid-fueled white elephant as far as he's concerned."

"Well, Otto can take care of that."

"Solids have their usefulness," Kroeber asserted, "but they still have some shortcomings for space work."

"Don't be too honest," Palmer counseled.

"Not honest, just factual. You can't deny scientific facts. I think we should admit them, but show the superiority of our system, especially in the matter of guidance and controls."

"Superiority has nothing to do with it," Palmer asserted. "It's what you can sell, Otto."

"We sold the Guardian."

"Sure, and we want to keep on selling it. It's just a developmental vehicle now. We want to see those babies buzzing all over the solar system."

Kroeber glanced speculatively at him, saying, "They weren't designed for that."

"See, you're too damned practical," Palmer declared.

Listening to the byplay, Welkes realized that he'd never been too sure of Otto, at least of his political *savoir faire*. A topflight technical man, and one of the nation's ranking space geniuses, he was far too much the naive scientist to play at politics. Still, Welkes had primed Kroeber for this one, and reflecting on it, he thought grimly: Otto better not slip this time.

"These committee hearings are often extremely tiring, to both members and the witnesses," Representative Slater said slowly, "but the quest for truth is never easy. There are labyrinthine channels to be followed, facts to be sorted, weighed, viewed in perspective, and it is often necessary . . ."

Outwardly at least, Welkes kept his eyes on the chairman. Slater's meandering failed to lull him, for he knew that each statement had a calculated effect. After being sworn in, at his own request Welkes had read a prepared statement which summarized events leading to the award of the Monarch contract, cited the progress of the program to date, and emphasized the missile's necessity and the rapid development program which had cut months from the original schedule. He had also managed to insert a plug for the forthcoming launching as well as a solid boost for the Guardian space vehicle. But still he felt uneasy; Slater was no patsy.

"Mr. Welkes, I understand that in addition to the Monarch, your company produces space vehicles, military aircraft, naval landing boats, army tanks, and a great variety of electronic equipment, arms and armaments. Is that correct?"

"If you consider the corporation as a whole, yes, sir. Western Aerospace itself produces the Monarch and, of course, the Guardian space vehicle. We also hold several minor contracts."

"That sounds like quite an industrial complex," Slater observed.

"It is . . . one of the larger corporations."

"It certainly seems to be. Personally, I've never put much stock in the military-industrial power bloc concept we hear so much about from time to time—this garrison state, as it is called —but I'll have to admit that a few of these larger companies certainly monopolize the defense dollar. Don't you believe that to be true, Mr. Welkes?"

"A product like an ICBM requires a large manufacturing organization," he replied carefully.

"So it does, so it does," Slater agreed. "But at this point the committee is primarily interested in the Monarch itself; or, more bluntly, a justification for its inclusion in the nation's weapon systems complex. Would you care to comment?"

"I think that has been answered in my prepared statement, sir. However, if you'd like me to repeat—"

"That won't be necessary," Slater cut in. "I just want your statement that you, personally, believe the Monarch to be a necessary missile. Such a statement, of course, would consider the vast amounts of money which such a weapon system entails."

"Sir, I have no doubt concerning the Monarch's necessity,"

Welkes replied in a firm voice. Behind the glasses he saw Slater's eyes brighten as he asked:

"Mr. Welkes, just how did your company acquire the Monarch contract?"

"We won it on the basis of good design—a design that best fulfilled the Air Force's mission requirements."

"Ah, yes, of course. The Monarch was won in the marketplace."

"Yes, sir."

"An exemplification of free enterprise."

"It could be stated that way, yes, sir."

"Tell me, Mr. Welkes, isn't it true that an Air Force lieutenant general named Lyman Stark had considerable to do with the award of that contract?"

"The award was made as a result of a technical evaluation of the designs submitted," Welkes retorted, careful to keep his voice and manner unchanged. "Ours proved to be the best."

"I am speaking from a matter of record," Slater said.

"So am I."

"The record shows, at that time, that General Stark strongly advised—insisted, perhaps I should say—that the contract be awarded to Midwest Aeronautical Corporation."

"On the basis of its design, yes, sir."

"And it just so happened that upon retirement, General Stark became the executive vice-president of this selfsame company. Is that not correct?"

"Of Western Aerospace, not Midwest Aeronautical Corporation."

"But Western Aerospace was created by Midwest Aeronautical Corporation especially to handle the Monarch contract, or so I understand. Am I in error?"

"That is correct, sir."

"That I am in error?"

"That Western Aerospace was created as a division of Midwest Aeronautical Corporation."

"To handle the Monarch contract?"

"Yes, sir."

"Mr. Welkes, would you call this a happenstance?"

"To what are you referring?"

"To the fact that General Stark, who so strongly espoused the cause of Midwest Aeronautical Corporation in this particular contract, should become a high management official in the same company."

"Not entirely." The reply brought a startled look. "When a corporation hires a man for a high-level job, it hires the best man it can get—the most technically knowledgeable, the most competent. In our case, Lyman Stark just happened to be that man."

"Just happened to be . . ." A faint smile touched Slater's lips. "It seems to me there is altogether too much of this kind of thing. I was reviewing the old findings of the Hébert committee the other day, and do you know what I discovered? Over fourteen hundred retired officers of high rank were employed by the top one hundred corporations which, in fiscal year 1959, split up a fifteen-billion-dollar armament plum. That list included over two hundred and sixty officers of flag rank, Mr. Welkes. Would you care to comment?"

"Only to express my personal view that the corporations are hiring good men. If you're dealing in mathematics, you hire a mathematician. If you're dealing in weapons, you hire military men."

"I take it that General Stark is a valuable management asset?"

"Very valuable, sir."

"From the standpoint of his technical competence?"

"His technical and managerial competence," Welkes answered firmly. "General Stark is extremely capable."

"Of that I have no doubts, Mr. Welkes. What are his main duties?"

"Exactly what his job title implies—executive management, administration, decision-making."

"Could you please be more explicit? I don't know much about an aerospace plant myself and I'm frankly curious over what sort of contribution a retired general might make . . . at forty thousand dollars a year."

The sonuvabitch. Inwardly cursing, Welkes began enumerating Stark's duties—his areas of jurisdiction, committee responsibilities, management details, liaison functions—purposely including the trivia, conscious as he spoke that the committee members were dawdling over papers or conversing in low asides. Slater alone stared at him, his face set and expressionless.

When he had finished, the chairman said, "He sounds like a very busy man."

"A very busy man," Welkes agreed.

Slater poured a drink from a blue carafe.

"Why does he spend so much time in Washington?" he suddenly demanded.

"His duties require it."

"Does your company conduct its business from Washington?" The chairman cocked his head inquiringly.

"No, sir, but our executives spend a great deal of time there. I do myself. After all, our customer is the government and this is the seat of government."

"Indeed it is. But I was under the impression that our ICBM programs were under the jurisdiction of the Air Force Ballistic Systems Division. Is that not correct?"

"Yes, sir, BSD has technical and managerial authority."

"BSD is located in California," Slater observed.

"We maintain liaison there also."

"But General Stark is more concerned with the Washington end."

"Not necessarily," Welkes replied, wishing the chairman would get to the next topic.

"Hobnobbing with the Pentagon crowd . . ."

"I would expect a man who spent the greater part of his life in the service of his country to have friends in the military services," Welkes said stiffly.

"Apparently, apparently," Slater affirmed. He looked sharply at the president of Western Aerospace. "You place a great amount of confidence in General Stark."

"I do personally, and so does the company," he acknowledged. "General Stark is extremely capable."

"So it appears. Indeed I am happy to hear that. But it does seem strange to this committee that the dollar value of contracts awarded these large companies appears in proportion to the number of retired officers they employ. Wouldn't you say that was strange?"

"I have no information on the point, sir."

"No, but this committee has, Mr. Welkes. How many retired generals and admirals does your company employ?"

"I have not those figures with me, sir."

"No, I didn't imagine you would, but seventeen is the figure. Yes, sir, fourteen generals and three admirals. It would almost make one believe that generals were more important than admirals, wouldn't it, Mr. Welkes?"

"I see no difference, sir."

"I was thinking of the value to a company which primarily builds Air Force aircraft and missiles—an aerospace company such as yours."

"We hire men for their capabilities, not their military rank."

"I am certain you do," Slater acceded. "As I mentioned earlier, the quest for truth is often long and difficult, and somewhat painful at times, but this is a matter of concern to this committee, Mr. Welkes. Are contracts for very costly weapon systems being awarded on the basis of competence, or are they awarded on the basis of influence? Are we in the process of building a gigantic military-industrial complex for the sake of bigness and power, as some people claim, or are we pursuing a necessary course? We might go a step further and ponder if all these weapon systems are even necessary. Indeed we might. These are the kind of questions this committee is concerned with. Don't you believe it should be, Mr. Welkes?"

"I am certain it is a very commendable endeavor, sir."

"Indeed it is," the chairman said. "At times it seems as if committees such as this go on and on, gathering ream after ream of testimony in what might appear to be the casual pursuit of empty goals. But occasionally there are little rays of light, Mr. Welkes. And when there are, let me assure you that they do not go unheeded."

"I am very certain of that, sir."

"There are fundamental truths we are trying to get at, Mr. Welkes. This Congress has repeatedly urged one kind of weapon only to have the military select quite another weapon. It is the constitutional duty of Congress to raise and support armies. Yes, sir, that's the very wording, and this member of Congress intends to do just that. It's time we decided just who does run the military, Mr. Welkes, and that includes the weapons employed by the military."

"Yes, sir," Welkes said as the chairman paused.

"But we have been digressing. Indeed we have." Slater rubbed his hands. "I believe you stated that the Monarch developed over 430,000 pounds of thrust. Is that correct?"

"That is its rated capability," Welkes affirmed, thankful to be on a new subject.

"In other words, we are not gaining anything?"

"I'm afraid I don't follow the question, sir."

"Isn't that the thrust capability of the Titan II?"

"I believe it is. However, the Monarch possesses considerably more thrust than the Atlas or Titan I."

"But not more than Titan II?"

"No, sir, but thrust is only one capability."

"An important one?"

"Yes, sir, but so are reliability and guidance."

"You feel you have an extremely reliable missile, Mr. Welkes?"

"Yes, sir."

"You lost one recently," Slater observed.

"That was a static test missile—never intended for launching."

"But it was a Monarch, the same model as the one which I understand is to be launched from Cape Canaveral in the very near future. Is that not correct?"

"Yes, sir, but our static test missile was tested exhaustively . . . over long periods."

"General Barmon was kind enough to explain that," Slater remarked. "Let me assure you that this committee is not concerned with the loss of a single missile. Indeed, that happens quite frequently, quite frequently. But it *is* concerned with the implications of such a loss."

"I'm afraid I don't follow you."

"To be blunt, did this loss occur as a result of a structural weakness in the Monarch? I'm not referring to the test missile but to the design of the Monarch itself. Or I could phrase it this way: Could this same weakness exist in the missile which your company is preparing to launch from Cape Canaveral?"

"No, sir, there is no structural weakness in the Monarch." He realized he was speaking too loud and lowered his voice. "The test missile was old . . . shopworn."

"That has been stated."

"And it's true, sir."

"We hope so. Indeed we do, but questions like these are extremely critical, Mr. Welkes. This nation is finding itself overburdened financially, and somewhere we have to start paring down. For that reason, we have to make our assessments carefully. Wouldn't you say that was right?"

"Yes, sir."

"As a patriotic American, you wouldn't want to see an inferior missile in the field, would you?"

"No, sir."

"Nor an unnecessary one?"

"No, sir."

"But you don't place the Monarch in that category . . . in either of them?"

"No, sir, I do not."

"You stated that the Monarch was extremely accurate—that is, it possessed a superior guidance system. Is that correct, Mr. Welkes?"

"Yes, sir."

"General Barmon testified that the Atlas was also extremely accurate. Do you agree?"

"Yes, sir," he said reluctantly.

"So then the Monarch contributes nothing in this respect—that is, nothing that the Atlas doesn't contribute. Is that correct?"

"No, sir. That is, there are degrees of accuracy."

"As I understand it, a thermonuclear warhead has a large radius of destruction. Is that not correct, Mr. Welkes?"

"I'm not an authority on nuclear weapons, sir."

"Let's put it this way. If that were not true, then the Nation is investing considerable money in weapons that fail to meet the purpose for which they are designed. I believe your company has claimed the Monarch has this destructive capability —or can't it deliver a warhead of adequate size, Mr. Welkes?"

"Yes, sir, it can."

"Then pinpoint accuracy is not absolutely essential? I am thinking of radius of destruction again."

"The more accurate, the better, sir."

"How much more accurate is the Monarch than the Atlas?"

"We can't put a number on it, sir."

"Miles? Yards?"

"I couldn't say, sir."

"But you feel it is more accurate?"

"Yes, sir."

"Without being able to put a number on it?"

"Yes, sir."

"Then this added accuracy could be guesswork?"

"No, sir, it is basic to the guidance system."

"Do you know exactly how accurate the Atlas is, Mr. Welkes?"

"Well, not the exact figures."

"Well it appears to me that the Monarch and Atlas are very close in this respect, and the Titan too, if I understood the Air Force testimony correctly. But you believe the Monarch to be a superior weapon?"

"Yes, sir."

"Well, that is heartening. Indeed it is, coming from a knowledgeable man." Welkes didn't answer, but kept his eyes warily on the chairman as the latter continued, "But back to the matter of thrust. I am not speaking of the Monarch as a weapon now, but as a space booster. It is intended for that use also, isn't it?"

"Yes, sir."

"I can't see that this amount of thrust adds anything to our space capabilities. It seems to me we need more thrust, not a duplication of the same amount of thrust. I can't see that we are getting anywhere."

"I believe we are, sir."

"How? In what way?"

"Only the Monarch can boost the Guardian, which we regard as one of the Nation's most promising space vehicles."

"We?"

"Our company and NASA."

"Is the Monarch unique in this capability?"

"Insofar as the Guardian is concerned, yes, sir."

"Would you explain that, Mr. Welkes? Why couldn't another booster be used just as well?"

"It's a matter of engineering," Welkes explained. "As General Barmon testified earlier, each military mission requires a specific type of weapon. In the same sense, each space mission requires a certain type of space vehicle, which in turn requires a certain type of booster."

"That sounds somewhat like a manufacturer who puts out a product which can only be repaired using his own tools," Slater observed. "I would like to pose a hypothetical question, Mr. Welkes. If the Monarch were canceled, would we lose the Guardian as well?"

"That's about the size of it, although it perhaps could be modified for service with other boosters."

"How much of a loss would that incur?"

"Somewhat over a hundred million dollars, sir, but I would like to point out to the members of this committee that the monetary amount would be but the smallest part of the loss."

"The committee would appreciate your comments," the chairman said.

"Aside from the loss to science itself—not an inconsiderable loss, in my estimation—there would be, of course, a rather severe economic chain reaction, and there it's generally the small businessman who suffers. I might recall to the committee's attention the severe economic dislocation resulting from cancellation of the Navaho, to mention but a single instance."

"That was quite a while ago," Slater remarked.

"But the principle is the same, even though the potential loss is perhaps now far greater." As Slater nodded, he continued: "I have a number of slides showing our company's subcontractor structure, if the committee would care to see them."

"That is thoughtful of you, Mr. Welkes, but we're a little pressed for time. Could you leave them with the committee?"

"Yes, sir, I would be happy to."

"Perhaps you could give us the figures."

"In essence, these slides show that we do business with some two thousand subcontractors distributed throughout thirty-seven states."

"On just the Guardian?"

"And the Monarch."

"That seems like quite a number."

"We attempt to benefit small business; that is corporation policy."

"How much of this business does California get?"

"Quite a bit, but it's economical to favor plants in close proximity to ours," Welkes explained.

"Could you express California's share on a percentage basis?"

"Around seventy-five percent."

"That seems quite large," Slater commented.

"Would you yield, Mr. Chairman?" Representative Sumner interceded.

"Yes."

"I don't think it's large, not large at all. California is a tremendous state—in size, population and national importance. California has attracted the most capable businesses. Those contracts have been earned, Mr. Chairman—earned on the basic principle of private enterprise. That is all I wanted to say, Mr. Chairman."

"Indeed that is interesting. Very interesting. What was that figure again—seventy-five percent, Mr. Welkes?"

"Yes, sir, but I would like to add a remark, if I may."

"Certainly."

"We were speaking of subcontractors for the Monarch and Guardian. However, when you consider base construction, you can see that there are many more subcontractors involved, and of course those are out-of-state firms. There are also tens of thousands of jobs at stake."

"There are times when such sacrifices must be made to a greater cause," Slater said.

Welkes debated whether he should cite the company's fifteen subcontractors in the chairman's congressional district, but decided against it as too bald a plea. Instead, he said, "However, that is not the most important thing."

"Please continue," Slater urged.

"I firmly believe that the Guardian represents one of the nation's foremost assets in its whole space effort, and I am certain that many responsible scientists, engineers and others share this view. In a manner of speaking, the Guardian is designed to carry forward our national prestige. We're in an all-out race with Russia and I believe the Guardian represents a valuable runner in that race."

"We have many runners. Can you assign more prestige to the Guardian than to, say, the Gemini, or Centaur?"

"Each serves a different purpose."

"We have to select our purposes. We can't serve them all."

"There has been a high degree of selection," Welkes argued. "The Guardian represents a step forward—'The space ship with the space look,' we call it."

"A catchy slogan. Then you believe the Guardian might help us overcome any lead the Russians might happen to have? I am thinking now of thrust. We have it on good authority that they have space engines developing almost three times as much thrust as the figures you quoted for the Monarch."

"The chairman is speaking of booster-type vehicles," Welkes pointed out. "The Guardian is an upper-stage vehicle."

"But small compared with the Sputnik. I understand they average over five tons each. How does the Guardian help us overcome that kind of lead?"

"It doesn't, but neither was it designed for that purpose. The Guardian was developed for a specific mission—to land instrumented packages on the moon."

"You could justify any space vehicle on those grounds," Slater retorted crossly. He pointed a pencil at Welkes. "Do you mean to say that for every mission we require a special upper stage? Is that what you mean? Couldn't some of these vehicles be designed for general purposes?"

"Some are," Welkes admitted. "As a matter of record, the Guardian could prove quite useful in placing communication satellites into high earth-orbit. I believe I developed that point in my prepared statement."

"So you did." Slater leaned toward him. "But we already have upper stages for that purpose."

"Yes, sir."

"So that would be another duplication?"

"I mentioned it merely as a capability."

"But the Guardian's main purpose is to land payloads on the moon. Is that correct?"

"Yes, sir."

"And wasn't Centaur designed for that purpose, Mr. Welkes?"

"Yes, sir."

"Aren't there others?" Without pausing, Slater answered his own question: "Yes, there are, quite a few others." He sighed. "It looks like we're out to fill the craters, wouldn't you say, Mr. Welkes?"

"Their missions differ, sir."

"Then the Guardian has a unique mission?"

"Yes, sir."

"Unique in what way, Mr. Welkes?"

"We land a different kind of package."

"Then, it's the package that's unique."

"Yes, sir."

"I find this quite perplexing," Slater said. "First the missions are different, then they are the same and it's the payloads that differ. Just what does differ, Mr. Welkes?"

"Both mission and payload, sir."

"Can you see now, Mr. Welkes, why it is that we build up reams of paper in hearings such as this? It is extremely confusing. Indeed it is." Slater glanced at his notes, then looked up again."But you admit the Guardian is limited in scope?"

"No, sir, I do not." Welkes replied quickly, suppressing his anger. Slater regarded him equably.

"You seem quite satisfied with our space program, Mr. Welkes."

"I believe it to be a very good program considering funding limitations," he replied.

"Funding limitations?"

"Money buys progress. The more we have, the faster we move."

"Money is a very interesting subject," Slater said, peering at him. "I have the feeling myself that it's not a matter of more money, but of how we use the money we do have. Don't you believe that to be true?"

"We should use our money wisely and I think, in the main, we do."

"Would you say that perhaps we should put less into defense and more into space, Mr. Welkes?"

"No, sir, the defense dollar is too small as it is."

"Do you believe that we could economize without sacrificing, Mr. Welkes?"

"I don't quite follow that, sir."

"I was thinking of standardization, say fewer types of missiles and space vehicles—the same number but fewer types. Don't you believe that would result in a considerable economy, Mr. Welkes?"

"I don't believe it to be feasible, sir."

"Trying to economize?"

"No, sir, trying to standardize."

"I would appreciate your comments, Mr. Welkes."

"We can't standardize the missions, sir."

"I know." Slater smiled slightly. "It's the old story, Mr. Welkes. We have different missions, hence we must have different space vehicles, and the same applies to missiles. Did you ever consider the number of different space systems we have now? The number of different weapon systems? We have only so much money. We have to be extremely selective, Mr. Welkes. Does that make sense?"

"Will you yield right there please, Mr. Chairman?" Representative Hansen asked.

"Yes."

Hansen looked the length of the table. "I understand the Guardian is a liquid fuel vehicle, Mr. Welkes. Why don't we use solids for this kind of work?"

"Liquid fuels are better, sir."

"In what way, may I ask?"

"They are of proven practicality, sir. Liquid fuels possess certain characteristics which make them more applicable to space missions."

"I would be pleased to hear what they are, Mr. Welkes."

"I would rather defer that question to Dr. Kroeber," he answered. "He is our space authority."

"Will you yield to me a minute?" Bert Sumner cut in.

"I yield," Hansen said reluctantly.

Sumner looked at the witness.

"I have read your prepared statement very carefully, Mr. Welkes. In addition, because these questions we have before us are extremely vital, I have made a thorough study of the whole situation, have talked with a great number of people. As a result, I find myself highly enthused with your program. With both programs—the Monarch and the Guardian. I believe your company has performed a magnificent job."

"I am pleased to hear that," Welkes replied, recognizing Sumner's intercession as a move to end the hearing.

"You have an outstanding safety record."

"We are proud of it."

"And cost figures that are quite low."

"We are proud of that, too."

"I am impressed with the speed with which the Monarch has been developed," Sumner continued. "You are certainly ahead of other ICBM manufacturers in that respect."

"We are three to six months ahead of schedule, sir."

"A great saving," Sumner agreed. "I intend to be present at the Cape when you launch that magnificent missile. I am greatly impressed by the uniqueness of its design. I believe the Monarch will make a great contribution to the Nation's defenses."

"That is our goal, sir."

"That's all I wanted to say. I just wanted to assure you, Mr. Welkes, that the great work of Western Aerospace has not gone unnoticed."

"Well, I thank you, Mr. Sumner," Welkes responded. "It's most gratifying to be appreciated."

"Your company has earned it," Sumner declared warmly. "That is all, Mr. Chairman."

"I am certainly happy to hear such warm praise from our colleague," Slater said. "Indeed I am. It instills a great feeling of confidence in those of us who must pass judgment on the fiscal merits of these great programs. But time is running short and I think we must get along. We have been very glad to have had you with us, Mr. Welkes. You have been most cooperative."

The room stirred to life as Welkes exchanged seats with Kroeber, then sat back to light a cigarette and relax. Bert Sumner, he noticed, had disappeared, and one of his colleagues appeared to be asleep. Welkes let his eyes wander around the room, hoping that the chairman would stick to technical questions with Kroeber and not wander into fields of political opinion. As Palmer had observed, the director for space projects was too damned honest.

Slater began with a verbal dissertation, ending with: "Your name is a very famous one, Dr. Kroeber. Indeed it is. We are fortunate in having you with us today, and we will try to be brief. Are there any questions on my left?"

"Mr. Chairman . . ."

"Ah, yes, Mr. Hansen," Slater acknowledged.

"Taking advantage of your kind offer, Mr. Chairman, I would like to ask the witness several questions regarding the merits of solid fuels."

Something about the speaker's voice and manner alerted Welkes and he frowned worriedly. Hansen's face wore an utterly disarming look, and yet he sensed in it a sudden eagerness, like that of a runner poised for the starting gun.

"Earlier in the day," Hansen explained, turning toward Kroeber, "General Barmon gave certain testimony regarding solid fuels, and I am just trying to clarify in my mind several of his points. In the interests of simplicity, let's assume these questions pertain to solid fuels versus liquid fuels—that is, we are weighing the merits of one against the other. Is that agreeable?"

"It sounds agreeable." Welkes detected a dubious note in Kroeber's voice which he took as a good sign.

"Do you regard the solid fuel missile as of simpler design than the liquid fuel missile?" Hansen asked.

"Are you referring to just the power plant?"

"Yes, just the power plant."

"It definitely is."

"Hence more reliable?"

"Yes."

"More economical?"

"Yes, but . . ."

"Do you believe that a solid fuel missile could be fired on shorter notice, Dr. Kroeber? Fired in anger, as General Barmon put it."

"Yes, I do."

"I understand solid fuels are easier to store?" Hansen asked. Welkes flushed, clenching his jaws savagely. Christ, couldn't Otto see the trap?

"That is true," Kroeber affirmed.

"Do you consider the Minuteman a good missile, Dr. Kroeber?"

"For what is was designed to do, yes."

"And the Polaris?"

"Yes . . ."

"Both these are solid fuel missiles, are they not?"

"Yes, sir."

"So in essence we have said that in economy, reliability, simplicity of design, safety, ease of handling and superior storage characteristics as well as in quicker firing capabilities, the solid fuel missile is superior to the liquid fuel missile. Is that not correct?"

"Yes, but . . ."

"That is all, Mr. Chairman."

"This has been most interesting," Slater exclaimed, "but I see that our time has run out. On behalf of the committee I would like to thank you, Dr. Kroeber. You have been most co-operative. This committee will stand adjourned until tomorrow morning at ten o'clock."

7

Chapter 7

THE decision was due.

The thought plagued Garfield as he drove toward town to keep an appointment with Alex Witek, a free-lance publicity agent. He'd seen it in the vice-president's eyes and manner, knew it by the testy way he spoke. He licked his lips fretfully. How long had it been? Three, nearly four weeks, with the job still hanging. Christ, if he could only read Bergie's black polished eyes . . . He came to a red light and stopped.

He could handle it. Damn right he could. He was the only one who really knew all the ins and outs of the game. More important, he alone understood the big Picture—the total socio-economic and political stew in which the gigantic weapon systems had emerged as the prime ingredients. The missile existed simply because of the need for a venture of sufficient scope and complexity to require the pooling of the nation's economic, industrial and scientific strength. Earlier men had built their economies and societal patterns around grotesque gods, and men still did; but now the gods were hypersonic and needle-nosed—gods competing with gods for men's attentions. Paper gods like the RS-70, power gods like the Atlas, gods-to-be like Saturn, like the Monarch.

And what counted was the image created in the public mind. The Monarch might or might not be better than other ICBMs, but the fact in itself was immaterial. The adroit manipulation of *mass man*, that was it. Bergie's *mass man*. Modern troglodytes who crouched in their stucco and chicken-wire caves, blank-eyed, waiting to be stirred. He was pleased by the analogy, by what he regarded as his own peculiarly unique insight into this phase of human existence. Did Bergie know it? Probably. He had to give the old boy his due. He was sharp, far sharper than he appeared.

As he drove east on Olympic, the gray pall hanging over the city began to thicken and his eyes became blurred and watery. He hated the downtown section with its hydrocarbon sky and noxious exhaust fumes. Off to one side a great freeway arched above the drab buildings, spilling cars and trucks down its exits to clog the narrow midtown canyons. Finally he reached Broadway and, parking near the old *Examiner building,* walked to the Half Moon, a small cocktail lounge where Witek liked to conduct business. Just now Witek handled the Citizens Committee for Civic Improvement, which was engaged in an all-out campaign to sell metropolitan Los Angeles as the nation's hub of science and culture, and in it, Garfield saw a good chance to publicize the company and, incidentally, enhance his own position.

He found Witek at the bar.

"Am I late?"

"You're always late." Witek's voice was thick. "What'll it be?"

"Scotch on the rocks." He eyed his companion dispassionately. Sloppily dressed, he had a fleshy, moon-shaped face netted by purple veins, a short, rotund body, and skin that appeared drab white. Garfield had the momentary impression of staring at a fungus.

"What's going on at that goddamned tin bird factory?" Witek asked.

"The usual."

"Except that you lose one now and then, huh?" He grinned confidingly.

"They all do."

"You made it sound like two dollars and sixty cents worth of damage," the publicity man said. "What really happened?"

"A little worse. It'll run close to five bucks."

"Sure, and the test stand?"

"I understand it was scratched a bit."

"Are they still going to try and fly that damned bird on schedule?"

"Sure, why not?"

"They say you got a bum tank."

"A goddamn rumor," Garfield assured him.

"I wouldn't take any bets that you'd make it."

"I think we will. It's as good as the next bird."

"You hope." Witek paused until the bartender brought their drinks. "The papers really raked you over the coals on that congressional hearing."

"It'll blow over."

"Jesus, Kroeber plumping for solids. What the hell was he thinking of? I'll bet Welkes is sizzling."

"Probably." Garfield eyed him speculatively. "I've got a hot idea—thought you might be able to use it in your campaign."

"Here it comes . . ."

"No, seriously."

"Promise not to sell me the corporation and I'll listen."

"To hell with the corporation." He explained his idea briefly.

"I kind of like it . . . relating the roles of the major sciences to missiles and space. It shows why so many scientists are here."

"Different kinds of scientists." He leaned closer. "That's the keynote of your campaign, Alex. You can ballyhoo this as the space center of the world—call it an academy for the future."

"The Academy for the Future . . ." Witek tested it for effect. "That's a pretty good angle."

"Damned good. You can work it different ways: 'Los Angeles, the University of Tomorrow—The City That Looks Ahead'; or something like 'Where Tomorrow Lives Today,' or 'The Cradle of the Future.' But hell, I don't have to tell you the business."

"Pretty good." Witek paused dubiously. "If it's not too much of a company pitch. Taper that down . . ."

"It's not. Of course we have the most scientists, a stockpile of Ph.D.'s that makes the competition look like hurdy-gurdy operations. Kroeber, for example, the nation's top spaceman; Slotkin, the mathematician; Kelser, the aerodynamics wonder boy."

"I can't be partial to one company."

"No one's asking you to be," Garfield replied. "We're contributing the idea as a community service."

"Sure. Any slides?"

"The whole package—everything."

"Well, it might be worth thinking about."

"Thinking about, hell. It can't miss," Garfield exclaimed. "We even stress the cultural benefits."

"Sure, the fur-lined sewers." The publicity man sniggered. Garfield leaned back, satisfied. Witek would get a pat on the back from his committee and he'd get one from Bergie.

Witek plumped down his glass, looking at him inquiringly. "I hear you're in line for Vroman's job."

"Oh?" He was startled until the other's quizzical expression told him it had been a shot in the dark. "Hadn't heard. Where'd you pick it up?"

Witek shrugged. "The grapevine. You know how those things go. But I hope it's true. I'm all for you."

"I'm glad to hear it, Alex."

"Besides, you haven't much competition."

Garfield weighed the remark, wondering if the compliment were double-edged. "Isn't Lee Brownlee, our vice-president for administration, on your committee?" he asked, knowing full well he was.

"Sure, want me to put in a plug?"

"How well do you know him?"

"Like the back of my hand."

Garfield doubted it, but said, "If you can put in a word . . ."

"I'll do that." Witek's voice became confidential. "How do you figure you stand?"

He shrugged. "I'm in the running."

"I know that. Who else?"

"Elliott, maybe Art Koepple. Henderson," he added reluctantly.

"Henderson?"

"He's Bergie's fair-haired boy."

"Oh?" An odd quality in Witek's voice caused Garfield to look up sharply. "Man, what I know about that guy."

Garfield felt a tremor of anticipation. Watching the moonish face, he tried to keep his voice casual. "Sounds interesting."

"It's nuclear."

"Well?"

"A woman. I got that right from the horse's mouth."

"Oh, that." He felt let down.

"Yeah, that. It wouldn't amount to a damn except for the woman."

"I take it you know her?"

"I sure as hell know who she is." Garfield watched him closely, but Witek's face held a smug expression. "I'm half looped but not that looped. Do your own bird-dogging." He let his eye droop in a wink.

"It really doesn't make much difference." Garfield raised his glass to conceal his disappointment. "Well, here's to it."

Elliott was *it*.

The whisper spread quickly through the department. Someone told Al Rossini, Koepple's chief assistant, who promptly told his boss. Someone told Elliott's secretary, Harriett Miller. Esther Lynn heard it from Dorothy Baker. Startled, she quickly tried to confirm the rumor by calling Joan Wesley, perplexed when the latter denied any knowledge of it. Joan, in turn, received discreet inquiries from Stover of graphics and Eggert of photos.

She called Eugene Henderson.

Elliott had been in a heated argument over the Slater hearing with his old *Bulletin-News* friend Barry Walsh, the special features editor, when the conversation turned to John Vroman.

"He looks like a million," Walsh informed him. "Quitting WAD was the best thing he ever did."

Elliott stifled his surprise. "I thought he was having health problems."

"He was, of a sort."

"What do you mean . . . of a sort?"

"There were psychological factors."

"I won't buy that," Elliott said firmly. "You don't toss away a career for nothing. He was just a step from Bergie's job."

"Is that good?"

"Isn't it?"

"If you had Vroman's job, Jim—salary, prestige and all—you'd hang on to it?"

"I sure would." Elliott grinned. "Just give me the chance."

"Even if you weren't happy?"

"That's the point—I would be happy."

"Then it's the salary and prestige that would make you happy."

"You're twisting my words," he accused. "Anyway, what's that got to do with Vroman?"

"John was under a lot of pressure, Jim. I think he was having a conflict in belief—that he had sold himself a bill of goods."

"I'm not certain that I follow you."

"I'm not certain that I'm putting it very well." Walsh held his eyes. "Do you believe in the Monarch, Jim?"

"Certainly."

"Everything you say about it, claim for it?"

"Well . . ." Elliott debated the point. "Yes, I think that's a fair statement. Look at the state of the world, Barry—Berlin, Southeast Asia, Africa, ready to explode. This isn't a cold war; it's a hot one, and it's apt to get a hell of a lot hotter. You have only to glance at the headlines to know that. We're sitting on a dynamite keg, and if war comes, it won't be like the old wars. We're talking about thermonuclear weapons now."

"Unfortunately."

"But true. This is a battle of ideologies in a world shrinking so fast that only one will be allowed to exist—theirs or ours. Ideology isn't a meaningless word. It stands for a way of life —in our case, our culture, religion, freedom. It's babies like the Monarch that protect those things, and we'd better by a damn sight have enough of them."

Walsh agreed that the ICBM did indeed augur the type of conflict which might ensue, but he saw the holocaust forecast in nuclear shadows simply because the military was neither prepared for, nor wanted, any other kind of war. "If you have but one kind of weapon," he said, "that presupposes one kind of war. But it's not black or white—a Tellerian war or nothing. It's a multi-faced situation. It might blaze hot with fireballs crisping cities, or it might be fought in the march of inches. It could be another Hundred Years War, Jim. Perhaps the prime weapon is an ICBM, but it could just as well be a radio transmitter . . . or a schoolbook."

"Perhaps."

"We might be winning the battle of the ICBMs and losing the peace," he continued, developing his thesis. "The point is, every boondoggle we sponsor subtracts from the potential we require."

"So now I'm on a boondoggle?"

"I didn't say that." The newsman's eyes twinkled. "But it's worth considering."

"Come back in a week or so"—Elliott smiled—"after we get the Monarch launched."

"What difference will that make?"

"We'll know what we have," he replied equably. "You'll know too."

"It won't prove a thing, Jim."

"Oh?"

"What will it prove? Only that it can perform as well as the Atlas . . . the Titan. That's what Slater was getting at."

"He's just pushing his own gravy train."

"Do you know that absolutely? How much of that is propaganda?"

"He's causing enough damn trouble."

"Supposing he's sincere?"

"It's a possibility," he admitted.

"Only a possibility? At any rate, you can't discount him, Jim. He's got a solid phalanx behind him."

Elliott paused. "Did Vroman feel that way?"

"About the boondoggle or too many ICBMs?"

"Both."

"I can't say."

"But you've been saying."

"I've been speaking for myself, Jim. That's the way I feel. Believe me, I've been watching the arena for a long time, long enough to know that everything's not Hoyle."

"I don't know, Barry."

"You're too close to the picture."

"That should help," he objected.

"Not necessarily. You get blinded by your own words. So do I, Jim. It's a human weakness."

Elliott sat at his desk trying to muster enthusiasm for the work at hand, but somehow he couldn't put his mind to it. For one thing, no sooner had Walsh left than Joe Stone, his assistant, confronted him with the rumor he was slated for the job. Although caught by surprise, he failed to be elated, for he knew the plant to be rife with whispers. They raced through the corridors in unending chains, borne on the feet of such messengers as Jane Cooper. He voiced his disbelief.

"It could be true," Stone mused.

"I don't believe it is." He didn't know why he rejected the idea, unless it was that he feared to build his hopes too high. Now, pondering it, he was at the same time aware of Barry Walsh's probing eyes—the uncomfortable questions regarding values. Well, what were his values? He wasn't sure, nor was he certain that it made much difference. Values differed with age, sex, status, experience, intelligence—with the multitude of variables which made each individual unique. And, within the same individual, they came and went, like dust devils before a wind. Considered in that light, why weigh his ambitions against intangibles which constantly changed color and form, or vanished altogether? Yet he had to cling to certain things—

his faith in himself, in his work, the Monarch. He had to take a stand, be willing to be counted. In effect, that's what Walsh said Vroman had done. If it were true, when had the self-questioning started which finally had driven him from his job? Certainly it hadn't been there two years ago. A year? Six months? He didn't know. He had seen the man's growing fatigue; yet, if anything, his drive had increased, right down to the final day. Had it been energy without spirit? Drive but not enthusiasm, he reflected, at least not in the final months. What did that signify?

Himself a former *Bulletin-News* editor, Vroman in offering Elliott the news bureau job had talked of the Monarch's necessity, its growth potential, its deterrency capabilities. He saw it as a shield for the free world. It would, he said, provide the most complex technological challenge ever flung at an engineer . . . or a PR man. The words had fired him. But now Vroman was gone.

And yet he wasn't Vroman.

Sure, the job wasn't all roses and whiskey, but it *was* a necessary one. Of course there were platitudes, slogans, meaningless claims—paeans to the company as the big teat that nurtured the economy; but these were only the trimmings. Beyond them lay the deadly message: *This missile represents survival.* If the missile were essential, it followed that it had to be sold. Barry had a right to his opinion, just as did Carole. By the same token, so did he. If he were a panderer for a metal bird, it was at least a bird in which he believed.

Happiness was something else again. Had he been happy? That was what Walsh had been getting at. Someone had once called happiness an inner peace, but if peace were the main ingredient of happiness, then he had rarely experienced it. The road to a goal seldom proved placid. Goal-seeking implied drive, fervor, aggression, the very antithesis of peace. But how could a man exist without a goal? Life itself implied an objective, if only death. Happiness . . . ?

Moodily he returned to work.

They drove toward Malibu for dinner.

He'd insisted on the date, their first in a week, even though Carole had tried to beg off. Sensing her reluctance as part of the strain between them, he'd been all the more adamant. It had been growing, slowly but inexorably, an intangible wall that separated them as surely as if it had been built brick by brick. The damn job was the cause of it. Bitterly he wished for the good days when they had laughed and played, when her face had been a radiant smile. He wanted to say, "Look, honey, I love you." And: "Trust me. It'll be all right." And: "We've a whole life in front of us." But the wall restrained him.

A cluster of neons came into view and he dropped his speed, swinging into a parking lot alongside a weather-beaten café. They found a booth by a window and peered out at the breakers. A frail splinter moon hung in the west, all but lost among the stars, and the waves held a spectral, phosphorescent quality, sparkling with a cold green light as they crested and broke.

They ate in virtual silence, but when the coffee had been served and they had lighted cigarettes, Carole spoke tensely: "I heard the rumor about the job."

He looked up quickly, surprised that she should mention it. "I don't believe it."

"Neither do I."

"Because you don't want to?" He immediately suppressed his pique, wanting to avoid an argument.

She eyed him calmly. "On logical grounds, Jim. When Bergstrom decides, the man he chooses will be the first to know."

"Yes, I suppose." She was right, of course. He studied her tentatively, then plunged ahead. "How do you think it got started?"

She shrugged. "How does any rumor start? Someone with imagination."

"You're just as glad?"

"That it's a rumor? Yes, I am. You know how I feel."

Her voice moved him to solicitude. "Is that why you're unhappy?"

"In part, Jim." She glanced covertly at him, fingering her cigarette.

"You don't try to understand it from my viewpoint," he objected. When she didn't answer, he continued: "I feel that I'm doing something, Carole. I feel that helping sell the Monarch might be one of the most important things I'll ever do. It's like building a big dam, or a skyscraper, only more so. The Monarch's not a toy, or an icebox. It's a missile, a damn important one. You get"—he hesitated, trying to give the thought focus —"sort of a sense of destiny. Does that strike you as corny?"

"You sound like Bergstrom."

He caught the bitterness in her voice. "Do I? Someone has to feel that way."

"If that's your viewpoint."

"It's that kind of a world, Carole. It's tough, and you have to be tough to survive."

"We don't want the same things, Jim." Her voice was low, almost husky, and he knew it had come to a head, the estrangement between them. And, curiously, he felt a sense of relief.

"It's up to the individual to control his own life," she went on, "to make of it what he can. He can't allow circumstances to control it. Here your life is ruled by the missile, by shells of men like Bergstrom. Stay at it much longer and there'll be nothing left of you. Look at Koepple. Do you think I want you to end that way? Do you think I want it for myself? It's all wrong, Jim. Believe me, it is."

"I don't see it that way, Carole."

"You used to write . . ."

"Sure, a regular Hemingway."

"Don't scoff. You were selling."

"Making peanuts." He laughed harshly, partly at the memory, but more because she had struck a sensitive chord. Sure, he wanted to write, but there were only so many hours in a day. Now the dreams lay in a bottom drawer gathering dust.

She dwelt on his face. "Lots of people do the things they want, refuse to compromise their values . . ."

"Not many. The point is: writing's a dream but this *is* my profession, and right now I've got a chance to get to the top. I can't throw it away. Do that and I'd have to start over. You should understand that."

"It's not worth the price. Not when you sell your soul to a tin balloon. For God's sake, Jim, look at Kroeber, Bergstrom, any of them."

"All right," he said angrily, frustration welling inside him, "look at them. To them it's what your art is to you. It's their satisfaction, their creativity, their future. Can you imagine Bergie quitting, for *any* reason?"

"And their wives? Their families?"

"Elissa Bergstrom lives high enough off the hog."

"You don't know what's inside a woman, Jim."

"You don't know what's inside me, either," he retorted bitterly.

She glanced away, her face clearly revealing that he had hurt her. He felt immediately contrite, and with it a sense of bafflement. Lord, it *was* a good job; it *did* represent a future; it *was* vital. What more could she ask? He shifted uneasily, and as he did he spotted a familiar face and paused to look closer.

Henderson—what was he doing here? Then the girl sitting across from him turned her head and he got his second surprise. Joan Wesley! So, Henderson was dating Bergstrom's secretary! Carole caught his look.

"Henderson . . . with Joan Wesley." He nodded toward the far side of the restaurant.

"What's so strange about that?"

"Well"—he felt taken aback—"nothing, I suppose. It just surprised me."

"I can't see why."

"Bergie's secretary?"

"What difference does that make? It's no different than our being together."

"You're not Bergie's secretary," he said emphatically. "That gives him a toehold in his empire."

"Does it bother you?"

"It might Bergie," he replied, dodging the question.

"You're assuming she tells him things she shouldn't."

"Sure, I'm just suspicious."

"It's just possible he might have some other motive."

Taunted by her sarcasm, he fell silent once more.

When they reached her apartment, he followed her inside without invitation and put on the hi-fi while she busied herself in the kitchen. Relaxing on the divan, he felt, despite the tension between them, the odd stirring that always came when they were alone. It was a comfortable room. The chairs were covered with white leather, complementing yet contrasting with the red shag rugs. Reed shades covered the windows. A well-filled bookcase extended along one wall; the opposite was decorated with sketches from childhood wonderland—Alice romped with Tweedledum and Tweedledee, Wynken, Blynken and Nod sailed on their river of crystal light, and off in a corner, Jack busily climbed his beanstalk. Several seascapes and a charcoal sketch of a woman peddling supplies leaned against the front wall, as if she weren't quite sure what to do with them. Then Carole returned, bringing coffee, and sat in the chair opposite him.

"Jim, it's more than that." The intensity in her voice brought his eyes up guardedly.

"More than what?"

"Than the job." She watched him steadily. "Our whole relationship is wrong."

He set down his cup.

"What are you trying to tell me?"

"Our . . . being together."

"Our making love?" he asked deliberately.

"Yes. It's my fault, what I wanted," she said dully. "I rationalized, told myself that it was right for us. No . . . I'm losing myself."

"No," he denied, "you're not losing yourself. What is there between a man and woman but give and take? This isn't just an affair. It's, it's . . ."

"What is it, Jim?"

"We love each other."

"You don't know how many times I've told myself that," she said bitterly. "You don't know how many times, here, alone. Now I feel like a fool."

"Just because . . ."

"Because we've gone to bed? Go ahead, say it. Yes, because we've gone to bed. Doesn't it mean anything to you?"

"Sure it does."

"What—that I'm good in bed?"

"For Christ's sake, Carole . . ."

"Answer me."

"You know how I feel, every bit of it."

"I know how you feel about the job."

"Certainly, I can't marry you without one. How the hell do you think I'd support you?" He lashed out, knowing it was the wrong thing to say, unable to stop himself. "If you'd let me get squared away, I could give you what you want."

"Are you asking me to marry you, Jim?"

"Yes, I'm asking. I've been asking ever since I knew you. Of course I'm asking. I love you."

"More than the job?"

"Hell, you can't . . ."

"I have no intention of being Mrs. Western Aerospace. I told you that before."

"So you did," he said stiffly.

"You don't believe me."

"You might mean it, yes."

"I do mean it. I've got my life to live."

"I'm not going to plead with you."

"Go home," she cried, "go home. I don't want to see you."

"All right, I will." He rose uncertainly, looking at her, unable to comprehend her sudden, bitter outburst.

"You think just because I . . ."

"Carole, listen . . ."

"Go," she cried brokenly, "go home."

"Carole, I . . ."

Still he paused, looking at her tear-streaked face until she turned away. Then he left, closing the door softly behind him.

Madge Garfield was watching television when her husband arrived home.

"Hello, sweet," she called without getting up.

"You still awake?" He asked the question automatically as he hung his jacket in the closet, conscious it was after midnight.

"Hard day?" she asked solicitously.

"The usual." He watched a young woman on the screen sing platitudes about a popular brand of dog food.

"Anything new?" she asked as the commercial ended. She pulled her nylon robe more closely around her. The question was routine, but this time he took pleasure in answering it.

"Yes, as a matter of fact, there is." He patted her knee. "According to the grapevine, Elliott has the job sewed up."

Her face showed instant concern.

"It's probably just a rumor," she said encouragingly. "I wouldn't worry."

He smiled. "I'm not."

"I wonder who started a thing like that?"

"I did."

8

Chapter 8

WELKES was furious.

Bergstrom knew it by the way he stood with his back toward them, staring through the window while they settled down for the sudden conference he had called. Hands clenched behind his back, he ignored them. Paul Gaither, the chief engineer, knew it too. Winking, he drew a finger slowly across his throat.

Annoyed, Bergstrom turned away, trying to assign a reason for the president's anger. Welkes had been irked over the adverse publicity which had followed the Slater hearing, but this was something new. He wondered what had precipitated it. His eyes settled on Otto Kroeber, who sat at one end of the sectional couch talking with Lyman Stark, and he mused at the irony that these two men had supplied Slater with much of his ammunition—handed it to him on a platter, so to speak. Kroeber had been nicely boxed. Simply too damned naïve to compete in the political arena. As for Stark, the company knowingly bore the cross. "The general who gave the Monarch to Midwest Aeronautical Corporation," he was fair game for any

225

congressional investigator beating the woods. Still, he was well worth the price.

At last Welkes turned and glared at them for eight or ten seconds before rasping, "I'm damned mad, gentlemen, and I don't care who knows it." He walked stiffly to his chair and sat, leaning toward them. "We have a damned good bird, one we can be proud of, and I think it's time we quit apologizing for it and sell it."

"Apologizing?" One part of Bergstrom's mind placed the voice as Gaither's as he tried to fathom the president's reasoning.

"Apologizing." Welkes reiterated the word harshly. "We're not defending it and that amounts to the same thing."

"Oh!" The exclamation slipped from Bergstrom's lips.

"All sorts of rumors are making the rounds—the Monarch is in trouble, is facing a cutback, will be canceled. Byerkoff just called me and I can tell you, he's burning."

"We'll issue denials," Bergstrom said quickly, thinking it was not the rumors which had aroused the president's ire, but the call from Byerkoff.

"Damn right we'll issue denials. The press has been taking all sorts of potshots at us since the hearing. I intend to squelch these irresponsible rumors."

"I think we should."

"I know we should." The president nodded. "They're being systematically planted. As such, they're dangerous. Allow a rumor to gain credence and it'll end by influencing a decision. I sense a concerted drive here, Roland."

"We'll spike it," Bergstrom said decisively.

"A lot of it's coming from the Army people," Stark cut in. "They're paving the way for an organized Nike-Zeus drive."

"It's more than that," Welkes said forcefully. "Every competitor in the field would like to see us shot down. These programs are growing . . . faster than the dollar. Something's got to give. I don't believe a single one of us appreciates how serious the situation is."

"We have to defend ourselves."

Welkes nodded quick agreement.

"Damn right we do, Lyman. I have a transcript of testimony given the House Space Committee and, believe me, it's something to think about. Listen to this." He rustled in his desk for some papers and began to read. The assistant chief of the Bureau of Naval Weapons urged the development of a seaborne satellite defense system; the commander of the Air Force Air Research Development Command wanted its own orbital anti-missile system; the Army director of Research and Development was pushing the Nike-Zeus. "And that's just part of it. Throw in a few items like the Skybolt, the F-4H and a few of those NASA bubbles and you can see where we stand. There's going to be one hell of a battle for control of the budget dollar, and I don't intend to get lost in the squeeze."

"We're Air Force," Stark said decisively.

"We're where the money is, Lyman. We're Air Force where the Monarch is concerned, or any Air Force contract we happen to handle, but we're not Air Force when it comes to pipe dreams like the B-70. That's what siphons off the money."

"We can't hit the Air Force or any part of it," Stark countered. "We have plenty of other opposition to hit, like Nike-Zeus. That's where I'd start."

"We have to think this through carefully," Bergstrom interceded. "Our Texas division carries a hefty Army tank contract."

"To hell with the Texas division." Welkes glared angrily at him. "I'm interested in this plant. We rise or fall on our own."

"I'm looking at it from Byerkoff's point of view."

"My interest is right here, Roland. We sell Monarchs, not tanks."

"I agree, but we can't slap the Army. Not openly."

"Wait and we'll be crucified," Stark cut in.

"I'm still thinking of the corporation," Bergstrom said firmly. He looked from one to the other, knowing Welkes would agree when he thought twice about it. He continued, "I'll talk with the Air Force, see if we can't work out some sort of mutual program."

"On what?" Welkes asked.

"Protecting the Monarch."

The president eyed him. "Normally, that's in your empire, Roland, but I'd like to make a suggestion."

"Certainly."

"I'd like to have Lyman talk with General Broadmire again." Welkes glanced at his executive vice-president, adding, "He seems to have considerable influence in that area."

Stark chuckled. "According to Slater, yes. I wish to hell I had half the influence he credits me with."

"You do all right, Lyman."

"That's all right with me," Bergstrom acceded, recognizing the truth in the president's statement. Stark could indeed work miracles. "Just so I'm plugged in."

"You will be." Welkes turned his attention to Stark. "While you're at it, Lyman, you might talk to him about the orbital weapon system bid that's coming up. It'll be lucrative."

"I've broken ground on that."

"Ahead of me, eh? Good. I'll leave it in your bailiwick."

"I'll handle it." Stark nodded smugly.

"But back to this rumor thing." Bergstrom noted that Welkes' voice had dropped a notch; his eyes dwelt coldly on the chief engineer's face. "The Chicago papers stated that we have structural problems with the Monarch, and I can tell you, Byerkoff is hopping mad."

"I'm not responsible for what people write," Gaither said.

"According to Byerkoff, the story was leaked by your people."

"How did he determine that—a ouija board?"

Bergstrom interceded. "What did the story say?"

"That one of the bulkheads in the liquid oxygen tank had sprung a leak."

"Guesswork," Gaither snapped.

"It quoted our data," Welkes said coldly. "There was no guesswork involved."

"That doesn't prove it came from my people."

"Where else?"

"It could have come from anywhere."

"I want the source of the leak, Paul."

"You won't get it," he said bluntly.

"No?"

"A hundred people have had access to the data."

"Start with Haygood, work down. There must be some way of finding who peddled it."

"We'll deny the rumor," Stark interjected.

"Damn tootin' we'll deny it. We can't have that kind of talk floating around." Bergstrom remained quiet, holding his peace, waiting for the president to cool down. Good public relations weren't formulated in the heat of passion. Welkes tapped a finger against the desk. "What about that bulkhead, Paul?"

"The leak apparently occurred in one of the weld seams. Under sustained operation, the load was too much for it."

"Something inherent?"

"We don't know. We gave that bird a helluva beating before we had trouble." His voice reflected uncertainty. "We'll beef it up."

"Will that do it?"

"Yes, but it's not that that worries me."

"Oh?" Welkes eyed him sharply.

"It's the bird at Canaveral."

"It's too late for the bird at Canaveral."

"I'd feel better if we worked it over."

"We can't afford it. A delay now would be an admission of trouble."

"Loss of the bird would be a bigger admission."

"The schedule has to stand, Paul. I don't want any slippage."

"I'm just giving you my opinion."

"The odds against similar trouble are in our favor, aren't they?"

"Yes," he admitted reluctantly.

"Then we won't borrow trouble." The president's voice dismissed the subject, and in the pause that followed, he regarded Kroeber fixedly before saying, "We'll also have to do something about your testimony, Otto. They're billing you as a proponent for solid fuels."

Kroeber gazed back imperturbably. "Do you know any way I could have avoided it?"

"I know, you were mouse-trapped. It's not that, Otto."

"Then why single it out?" The scientist spoke quietly, without emotion, yet Bergstrom detected a cutting edge in the words more powerful than if he had shouted the answer, or cursed. But then, Kroeber had nothing to fear. He could walk into any aerospace plant, name his salary and title, get them. Especially with the growing emphasis on space—the growing NASA dollar.

Welkes regarded him carefully. "It's just that it's a damned awkward situation, Otto. We want to be more careful in the future."

"These stories that are being leaked," Bergstrom broke in. "They also mentioned Lyman." He glanced apologetically at the executive vice-president, who retorted:

"To hell with them. I've weathered worse."

"Byerkoff mentioned the same thing," Welkes said. "In fact, there was damn little he didn't mention."

"I've hesitated to issue denials on everything," Bergstrom said. "At times it's better to let an issue die than to risk fanning it into a real conflagration."

"I want a categorical denial on the cancellation rumor," Welkes ordered.

"Agreed. But on Lyman, I think we should let the issue die. It's come up before and it'll come up again."

"I'd rather refute it."

"How?" He soberly regarded the president, curious how one could refute what amounted to a public record. Welkes drummed his fingers against the desk.

"I'll leave it up to you. You're the PR expert."

"I also think we should let the structural problems story die."

"But will it? The people in back of this will keep pushing it, Roland."

"Let them. The press won't buy it—not unless we start a controversy."

"They are buying it."

"It'll die."

"It's not just a question of negating the story, Roland. It's giving the Monarch a positive pitch, especially in Washington. How about Bert Sumner? He should be able to do us some good."

"He is."

"Not that I've seen in print."

"He's reaching people, H. P."

"I want action I can see . . . hear."

"I'll call Palmer, get our Washington office to work," Bergstrom conceded.

"Do that. Give him carte blanche. I don't care what he does but I want results—some damned strong pro-Monarch sentiment. He sure muffed the ball at the hearing," Welkes added crossly.

"He's doing a good job." Bergstrom made the rebuttal without hesitation. Palmer was his man, a good one. "You can't cover all the angles."

"He could have pried more out of Sumner, given us a better chance to prepare."

"It was Slater's show."

"Sumner's on the committee, isn't he?"

"It's a one-man committee, H. P. You know that."

"Why don't we run a full-page ad in the Washington papers, list all our subcontractors and show the dollar share each is getting," Stark broke in. "We're shoring up the national economy, quite extensively in some areas. I think we should show it."

Bergstrom regarded him sourly.

"That's putting pressure on Congress," he warned. "They'll think we're trying to influence the award of the production contract."

"Aren't we?" Welkes eyed him cynically.

"It could have repercussions."

"To hell with repercussions," Stark said. "We're after a contract, not opinion."

Welkes nodded approval. "Monarch money is keeping plenty of those congressmen's voters happy. They should know it— see it in print."

"They know it. We gave Slater the whole picture," Bergstrom replied, thinking the president naïve when it came to the more delicate aspects of public relations. Stark too. Opinion made contracts.

"I still think it would be a good idea," Welkes persisted.

"I'd go slow. That's a real pressure tactic."

"That's what I want—pressure."

"You can generate adverse pressure."

"That's your problem, Roland. I also want to hit the local picture. This rumor of a possible cutback or cancellation has a lot of people jittery. The union's getting nervous, and so are some of the businessmen. We want to put the town straight— we're in business, we're going to remain in business, and we're going to ship Monarchs from this factory from here on out."

"I'll talk with the papers, see if we can't get a few well-placed editorials," Bergstrom promised.

"Editorials?"

"And a good splash in the news."

"I don't care how you get it, but get it."

"We'll get it."

"Good." Welkes swung back toward Gaither. "We're still considering a full-scale flight, Paul. Byerkoff feels it would clinch the contract."

"There isn't time." Gaither edged forward on the couch. "That baby's set up for a booster-only flight. It's too late to change. We have less than two weeks. We'd have to rig the upper stage, get it flight-ready, set up the down-range tracking."

"There's time if we work around the clock."

"I doubt it."

"Then create time!" Welkes' voice rose in pitch. "We have the booster and the upper stage, and if the Air Force is willing—"

"I'm against it, H. P. It's damned risky."

"I know the risk. So does Byerkoff. But we can overcome it by close engineering surveillance."

"I can't guarantee that."

"You can guarantee to give it your best effort, Paul."

"I do that anyway."

"You can give the missile a last-minute shakedown."

"I don't want to over-test it."

"No, but we can take all reasonable precautions."

"All reasonable precautions are being taken," Gaither stated emphatically, "but I can't promise miracles. You're demanding an unqualified warranty to over forty thousand different parts on the first flight, H. P."

"I'm not demanding anything." Welkes' voice grew testy. "I'm just asking that we take all reasonable precautions."

"I'm still opposed."

"Titan II did it. The Minuteman did it."

"Minuteman is solid-fueled."

"If a solid fuel missile can do it, we can."

"They weren't so lucky on later shots," Gaither reminded.

"Later shots don't count. It's the initial shot that gets the spotlight."

"And if we're not lucky?"

Welkes eyed him coldly. "We hope to be."

"You can explain away failures," Bergstrom said. "It's done all the time."

Welkes nodded. "Byerkoff feels—and I feel—that we need something extra right now. We have a lot at stake and somewhere along the line we have to take a bit of a risk."

"A *bit* of risk?" Gaither asked.

"Jesus Christ, Paul, do you know what we're talking about in the ultimate? A few billion dollars, that's all. And no one's going to give it to us. We have to compete." He swung angrily toward the executive vice-president. "How do you feel about it, Lyman?"

Stark smiled faintly. "If I remember correctly, I suggested it."

"I'm speaking about the risk."

"There have been first-flight failures before. I can't say they hurt anyone."

"You can't call a failure a help," Gaither said.

"I don't like this word 'failure.'" Welkes glared at his audience. "We seem to assume that any first flight is doomed to disaster. It smacks of a defeatist attitude."

"We have to consider it," Kroeber interrupted.

"We *have* considered it, Otto. Now I'm trying to get reactions."

"I'm opposed."

"And I," Gaither added.

"I'm for it. I think it's a good gamble." Stark looked at the others coldly. He sat stiff, uncompromising.

Welkes inclined his head. "I'm certainly happy to get some support. How do you feel, Roland?"

"You know my views, H. P. I can answer only for public relations, but in that area, it would pay off handsomely. You can't very well argue against a missile that proves its capabilities in the initial flight."

"Exactly."

Kroeber said decisively, "The mathematics of probability are against us."

"I know all about the mathematics of probability," Welkes snapped. "Don't you people ever think in terms of success? It seems to me we undersell ourselves—an attitude I intend to change."

"You can't order changes in mathematics," Kroeber replied calmly.

"And just what have I got a staff for?"

"You want the truth," Gaither said.

"The truth is this," Welkes replied. "We are merchants of missile power. That's our stock in trade. We don't sell shoes. We don't sell cars. We don't sell yo-yos. We sell missiles, and it's our job to sell them—whenever we can, however we can, as many as we can. It's that simple. Lyman understands that, and Roland too. If we have to take shortcuts, we take shortcuts. If we have to take calculated risks, we take calculated risks. Right now we need a shortcut and a calculated risk."

Gaither sat straighter. "Is this thing firm? Has a decision been reached?"

"I'm hoping for a decision today."

"I want to put my opposition on record, in writing." The chief engineer's voice was sharp, his eyes angry.

"Put it in writing," the president said bluntly. "Now let's get on with the next problem. Byerkoff feels we should take measures to counter this flood of solid fuel propaganda." He looked at Bergstrom.

"I've been in touch with Cronkhill about it. Are you still thinking of the Nike-Zeus?"

"Solids in general," he explained. "Byerkoff feels the Zeus will never get off the pad, not with the Secretary of Defense dead against it."

"You can't count on that," Stark cut in. "There's too much power behind it. Hell, it's been dead a dozen times, now look at it."

"I'm inclined to agree with you, Lyman. Have you seen the Douglas ads?"

"It's a hard sell," Stark affirmed.

"Cronkhill mentioned something of the sort," Bergstrom revealed. "He says the Pentagon has a couple of hush-hush systems on the fire."

"Army?" Welkes queried.

"And Air Force."

"Did he have any suggestions?"

"He pretty much left that up to us."

"What steps are we taking?"

"We're laying out a program."

"We can't wait too long, Roland."

"We'll be ready to go as soon as we get over the hot firing."

"Why not before?"

"We can't rush it. This is ticklish business."

Welkes poured a drink of water.

"We want to take positive steps, determine the best way to sell the superiority of liquids, then sell them. There's a lot at stake here. Not just the present but the future."

"We plan a positive program, H. P."

"I'm particularly concerned about space," Welkes continued, as if he hadn't heard him. "Solids are getting a foot in the door. We should do our part to shut it."

"We're looking at the total picture," he assured.

"We want to hit hard. The best defense is an offense." Welkes spoke savagely. "Those bastards can do the defense effort a lot of harm. The space effort too."

"They can do *us* a lot of harm," Stark said pointedly.

Welkes' face grew angry. "Why is it that liquid fuels dominate the big missile and space programs?" He leaned toward Kroeber. "Isn't it because they're better, Otto?"

"Definitely better for manned space flights. They have superior acceleration characteristics."

"We should bring that out, hammer away at it."

"An anti-missile weapon—say like Nike-Zeus—is a different proposition," Kroeber pursued.

"How different?"

"Solid fuels are better for that type of mission."

Welkes said with veiled sarcasm, "We want to exploit their weak points, Otto, not their strong ones. We've done too much of that already." In the discussion that followed, Bergstrom listened idly. It was the old argument—Kroeber's technical logic against Welkes' political considerations. Both were right, he reflected, and both wrong. The sun, climbing in the east, had brought with it a flat desert heat, and Welkes' secretary had lowered the Venetian blinds; now the light splayed zebra stripes across the deep rug and furniture. He noticed that the flower she had placed in the small vase at the corner of the president's desk was the same kind Joan had placed in his that morning, and he wondered where they came from. He smiled slightly; he knew very little about the mysterious workings engaged in by the executive secretaries. They moved in a different orbit—a world in itself, he mused. He—the top executives—saw only the pleasant smiles, heard only the genial voices, knew little beyond the surface manifestations. He became vaguely aware that the president was complaining about the poor publicity once more.

"What do you think, Roland?"

"I'll take care of everything," he answered, not quite sure of the question.

"I'd like to see a draft on our denial of the cancellation."

"Today," he promised.

Welkes continued, "We know what we have to do. Now let's do it. Lyman, you'd better get with the Air Force immediately."

"I'll fly East tomorrow."

"Good, and I'd like you to consider the possibility of a full-range flight, Paul." He looked at Bergstrom. "You know what I want."

"I'll get right at it."

"Make it a positive statement. We're here to stay. Period." He glanced around. "If everyone's satisfied, we'll wind this up." As the others rose to leave, he said conversationally to Bergstrom: "By the way, what's the story on the director?"

"The status is the same," he replied candidly.

"Still trying to get Vroman back?"

"I have hopes."

"How's his health?"

"I'm not certain." Again the lingering suspicion ran through his mind. "I'll give him another call."

"I'd still like to fill the position, Roland. Why don't you call him, lay down the cards, and if he says no . . ." The president paused, waiting.

"I have another candidate."

Kroeber, who had paused to listen, asked, "How about your man Elliott? I've been quite impressed with what he's done for me."

"He's good," Bergstrom said.

"Well, it's your baby," Welkes concluded, turning toward the window.

Frowning, Bergstrom returned to his office. It was bad enough to have Welkes hounding him, but he was getting it from all sides. Friends of Garfield, friends of Elliott—subtle remarks, gentle boosts, a word here, a hint there. Just the other day he'd received a friendly note from an Air Force colonel to express his appreciation for a tour of the plant arranged by public relations and, quite incidentally, to give Harry Garfield a hefty pat on the shoulder. Pressure—they were all applying it. Even Koepple had his boosters.

Why not appoint Henderson, be done with it? He could placate Garfield with the spot at Space Electronics, transfer a chunk of the publicity chief's empire to Koepple, give Elliott more money. That would take the monkey off his back. Henderson? The move would please Elissa. Faintly disturbed, he switched his thoughts to Vroman. Regardless of the merits of the others—and they were good—he owed it to the company to get him back if he could. He couldn't expect someone else to step in, take over and perform so capably, especially at such a critical time. That was the problem. In truth, he was more disturbed over the Monarch's prospects than he cared to admit. The Slater hearing had opened a veritable Pandora's box of wild rumors, but with enough factual substance to give credence in the ears of the uninitiated. On such rumors the Monarch could rise, or fall. Regardless of its merits, the ultimate responsibility for its success lay with him. The sell. He decided to try Vroman again. Perhaps if the offer were right . . .

He entered the office, pausing. "Any messages?"

Joan looked up, not quite meeting his eyes. "Mr. Clark called. I told him you were away for the day."

"Good." He hesitated, sensing something amiss. She appeared distraught. "Anything else?"

"No, Mr. Bergstrom." The dubious note in her voice confirmed his belief. When she dropped her eyes to the typewriter, he went to the inner office, glancing distastefully at the pile of mail. He was going through it when he became aware she was standing just inside his door, watching him uncertainly, her tongue nervously edging her upper lip.

"Yes?"

"There is something I think you ought to know, Mr. Bergstrom. Of course, it isn't any of my business but, well . . ." She hesitated.

"Go ahead." He spoke kindly, aware of a curious paternal feeling. Seeming to take courage, she returned his gaze.

"There's a rumor that Mr. Elliott will get the director's job."

"Oh?" He leaned back. "Where'd you hear that?"

"Everyone's talking about it."

"Yes, but who specifically?"

"Esther called me first, trying to confirm it. Then I had calls from Eggert and Stover. All the girls are talking about it."

"What did you tell them?"

"Nothing—just that I didn't know."

He kept his face expressionless, wondering if he should bother to deny it. Instead he said, "Thanks, Joan. If anyone else gets curious, tell them to ask me."

"Yes, Mr. Bergstrom." He caught her disappointment as she turned away, and puzzled over it. Of course, such a rumor could prove quite disturbing, especially to the other section chiefs. Each had his heart set on the job; he discerned that clearly enough, even relished their competition. It showed they valued the job, the company. Besides, competition weeded out the unfit; it was an instrument of selection. He had competed, was competing all the time. But how had such a rumor started? It was impossible to know all the chains of interaction. Then he recalled the plug Kroeber had made for the man. And in front of Welkes! Could Elliott have started it? He immediately rejected the idea. He had become increasingly pleased with the chief of the news bureau since Vroman's departure. Elliott had handled the test missile loss in good fashion, had done a magnificent job preparing Welkes for the Slater hearing. Perhaps a friend of Elliott's? Well, he'd be damned if he'd let himself be stampeded. No matter whom he appointed, morale would sag like a ruptured udder. Vroman, he thought, that would solve everything. He reached for the phone and dialed, waiting until the familiar voice came on.

"Hello, John." He spoke heartily. "This is Roland Bergstrom . . ."

"Hello, Esther."

Esther Lynn glanced up from her magazine and seeing Bergstrom framed in the doorway, let it slide to her lap. She smiled.

"Won't you come in, Mr. Bergstrom?"

"Thanks. Just for a moment." He crossed over and sat alongside the wall, nonchalantly extending his legs. She waited, aware of a breathless sensation, a tightening of the nerves.

"You must feel like a recluse," he observed.

"Oh, no, there's lots to do. I help the others." She felt herself floundering and managed to add, "Mr. Koepple, Mr. Garfield."

"That's fine."

"I'm as busy as ever."

"No use overdoing it. Take it easy while you can."

"I like to keep busy." She gave him her most charming smile, her unease sparked by the trace of cynicism she detected in his voice. His eyes, dark and blank, yet somehow penetrating, were fixed on her face, and she had the disagreeable feeling of being weighed. What did he want? It wasn't . . . another visitor. She instinctively knew that. The job? The rumor that Elliott would get it rushed back and she felt a slight panic, nonetheless unable to avert her gaze. Perhaps Elliott wouldn't want her! With the thought came an icy hopelessness.

Bergstrom asked casually, "Growing impatient?"

"I . . . don't know what you mean."

"Being without a boss."

"But I'm not." She forced her eyes to his and even managed a smile. "I have a boss."

"Yes, of course." He regarded her jovially and she felt her tension wane, thinking she had handled it just right. "I was referring to a departmental boss," he added.

"Well, it would be nice . . ."

"We'll have one before long."

"Oh?" She held her breath.

"I wouldn't mention it."

"How could I?" She attempted to make a joke of it. "I don't even know who it is."

"No, of course not." To her disappointment, he didn't enlighten her, but she felt positive it was Elliott. His visit had come too soon on the heels of the rumor for it to be otherwise. She knew a quick chagrin that she hadn't taken the opportunity to get better acquainted with the chief of the news bureau. Perhaps it wasn't too late.

"I just wanted to check, make certain you were getting along all right."

"Everything's fine, Mr. Bergstrom."

"You seem to manage."

"I try."

"You do very well, Esther." He rose to leave, tall and wide and as inscrutable as ever. She waited hopefully. "Let me know if you need anything."

"Thank you, I will." He paused in the doorway, scanning the outer office. After a while he moved away, and watching him retreat, she wondered why he'd dropped in and what he really had in mind. Perhaps his caution to remain silent meant that he actually hadn't informed Elliott yet. That made sense. Supposing it wasn't Elliott, but someone else? No, that was silly. Everyone knew it was Elliott.

Let me know if you need anything. Sure, she needed something; she needed the job. It was a choice plum, one of the choicest, and she didn't intend to lose it. Besides, she had done so much . . Damn him, with one word he could have relieved her anxiety, let her know that everything was all right.

"Tired?" Elissa Bergstrom inquired as her husband removed his topcoat and hung it in the hall closet.

"A little. I think I'll have a drink."

"Mix one for me too," she called.

He got the glasses and ice. "Have a good day?" he asked, measuring out the whiskey.

"The usual. I swam at the club."

Making his drink stronger than usual, he replaced the bottle, his mind on the Welkes conference. The old boy had been plenty burned, and he couldn't say that he blamed him. Questions regarding the Monarch's structural integrity and all that loose talk of canceling one of the ICBM programs were damn dangerous, and the way Kroeber had allowed himself to be mouse-trapped at the hearing . . . It would be easier if they could tackle the sea-launch angle. But of course they couldn't; they'd have to hold off until they got the go-ahead from the Air Force, which could happen almost any time now. That was one good thing that had come of the hearing, he decided with satisfaction; the line of questioning had made the Air Force jittery enough so that it would counter with an all-out PR drive.

He returned with the drinks and sat beside her. Absently, she asked, "Anything new?"

"Welkes was raising hell," he said, explaining what had happened. "I think he's getting jittery over the hot firing."

"He'll be there?"

"All the brass will."

"I wish I could go with you."

"It won't be a picnic. I'll be stuck at the Cape. I'll have to leave a few days early," he added.

"Oh, why?"

"Check the press arrangements . . . set up a party for the boys. We don't want any hitches."

"Anyone going with you . . . from your office, I mean?"

"No need for it," he told her. "Henderson put in a request but I shot it down."

She watched him carefully. "Have you decided about the job yet?"

"That's one of the things Welkes needled me about."

"What did you tell him?"

"That I had a man lined up if I can't get Vroman back."

"I wouldn't take him back!" she exclaimed.

"He's a good man—a very good man."

"You'd lose face."

"Perhaps . . ." He fingered his glass. "It's not my feelings that count, Elissa. It's what's best for the missile, the company. With tens of millions of dollars at stake, you don't make evaluations or decisions on the basis of personal feelings. I learned that long ago."

"John Vroman wasn't that important."

"No one is, but if he could nudge the decision even a quarter of an inch in our favor . . ."

She changed the subject. "Who did you say you had lined up?"

"I didn't say. Just mentioned that I had a candidate."

"Have you?"

"Not exactly. I'll know better by the time we get the Monarch launched."

"What has that got to do with it?"

"The launching? Only that the tempo of our program will pick up, change as we get into the home stretch for the production contract. It'll be time for fresh blood to step in, get things rolling."

"But you know?"

"I've got it boiled down," he admitted, "but it's a little hard to figure. Just today somebody started a rumor that I was going to appoint Elliott. It's all over the plant."

"Oh? Who do you think started it?"

"I wouldn't know."

"Perhaps Elliott," she offered tentatively.

"He's got more savvy than that."

She sucked her lip vexedly. "That leaves . . ."

"I really don't know," he replied honestly. "It's a job where you meet a lot of people, have to influence diverse types. That calls for a bit of finesse at times, especially when it comes to entertainment. Personality is damned important."

"That should make it easier," she asserted. "I can't see Koepple in that role."

"I can't see him pimping a girl for a customer," he said humorously, "but I can't discount him."

"That sounds horrid. You wouldn't do that, would you?"

"Who do you think signs the tabs?"

"But that's different. I mean actually getting the girl."

"Well, I suppose I've done that too." He toyed with his glass.

"I agree with you that Koepple's not the right man," she stated decisively.

"He's a good worker—a good company man. And he's loyal. That's a priceless virtue, Elissa."

She disregarded the comment. "Just from what you've told me, especially about the importance of entertainment, I can't see Garfield either. He's not smooth enough."

"Well, he's no Lyman Stark, but he has his points. It all depends on what kind of customer you're dealing with."

"I still don't like him."

"I have to give him full consideration." Suddenly he realized they were sparring. She was trying to tell him something that he was just as cagily avoiding. It was a technique she had, introducing a topic and then using it as a wedge to get something across, but usually she camouflaged the point so carefully he had difficulty discerning it. The soft sell, he thought whimsically—she put across her ideas with few rough edges. Now, at least on the idea level, she had steered him toward eliminating all but one. She had taken the same tack, he realized, when she sold him on appointing Henderson to his present position. Why? At times she possessed a strangeness that he found almost frightening. Or was it a hardness? Her eyes held that look now, bright and calculating. He switched his thoughts to avoid something nibbling at the border of his mind.

"I won't eliminate any of them."

"But if entertainment's important?"

"What about entertainment?"

"I can't imagine Koepple or Garfield, well, pimping, as you call it. Or Elliott, either."

He weighed her words and said deliberately, "Can you imagine Henderson doing it?"

"Yes," she answered slowly, "I can."

"Is a man like that repellent to you?"

"No"—her gaze was level—"not if a woman knows what she wants."

9

Chapter 9

It was not Arthur Koepple's habit to stop by the Sycamore Tree, although infrequently he took advantage of a pleasant hour or two in the dark grotto so conveniently located across from the plant's main gate. In more honest moments, he admitted it was a relief to be rid of his wife occasionally and all the yakking about George's adolescent problems and the horrible children with whom he had to associate, simply because none were around who met her standards.

On this particular evening he found himself gazing into the dim bar mirror at the reflection of a thin strained face, sparse gray hair above and narrow shoulders below. It had been a hard week, shattered by the rumor that Elliott had been tabbed for John Vroman's job. As the rumor grew without denial, he had accepted it as a certainty, seeking only to conceal his bitter disappointment.

Sipping his drink, he pondered over the effect the change would have. Probably none, he reflected, except that Elliott would move up, take over Vroman's secretary and polished desk. Joe Stone, his assistant, undoubtedly would slip in as chief of the news bureau and everything would go on as before. He would go on, too, endlessly, watching the younger men scramble to the top. The picture depressed him. He saw Paul Gaither approaching, shirt collar open and tie hanging loose. Sight of the engineer's harried face momentarily dispelled his own troubles.

"Hi, Paul," he greeted. "Tough day?"

"They're all tough." Gaither sat alongside him and fished a pack of cigarettes from his pocket before ordering a drink.

Koepple asked speculatively, "I hear you pinned down the trouble on the test missile?"

"Yeah, a fuel leak."

"Will it affect the launch schedule?"

"No." He shrugged, a gesture that held eloquent meaning.

"I'm glad to hear that." Koepple glanced obliquely at the other. "Some of the rumors . . ."

"It's that damned Slater committee."

"It'll pass over."

"That, or get a lot worse."

"I doubt it. They did a lot of fishing but there was nothing factual."

"The loss of the test missile was factual," Gaither replied significantly. "It's the kind of thing that gets blown out of all proportion, and the damnable part is, people believe it."

"Some people."

The chief engineer swung toward him. "Welkes wants to go all the way on the first shot . . . try the full range. How's that for a damned fool idea?"

"Nice if you could do it," he reflected.

"Anything's nice if you can do it."

"The Titan II—"

"I know all about the Titan, and the Minuteman too," Gaither interrupted. "Welkes and Stark gave me that song and dance.

But we're not talking about the same missiles, Art. We have some damned tricky fuel problems. Welkes should know that. He's an engineer."

"It's a gamble," he agreed.

"I don't want a gamble, Art. I want certainty. Who catches it in the neck if something goes wrong? Paul Gaither, that's who. Welkes, the corporation, the Air Force—everybody and his mother would be after my scalp. No thanks."

"It'll go okay," he encouraged.

"It better." The chief engineer contemplated his glass. "Muff it and we're cooked."

"Not really?" He felt sudden alarm. "It couldn't hurt us that much, not with what's been sunk into the program."

"Couldn't it?" Gaither smiled faintly. "They're just waiting to chop us, Art. Look at the howl since the Slater hearing, and all because of a lousy test missile. What do you think would happen if we lost the flight missile? They'd nail us to the cross, Art."

"They?"

"Politicians, power blocs, the segment of the Air Force that wants the dough sunk into the B-70, or RS-70, or whatever they decide to call it." Gaither shrugged. "How the hell should I know? I'm just an engineer. But I do know that one flopperoo could be fatal."

"I can't believe it."

"Nike-Zeus, Polaris, Minuteman . . . It's all power politics, Art." As he spoke, Koepple detected a trepidation in the other that he hadn't known before. The insight shook him. It was not that Gaither didn't have confidence in the bird, nothing like that. Rather, it was a feeling of impending forces too vague to define, too vast to combat—"the unpredictables," as Gaither put it.

"That's what they have us for," he said, when the other had finished. "Selling is our job."

"Sure, I know, I get it from Bergie all the time," the chief engineer said. "To hear him tell it, the hardware's just an incidental feature of the program. But the fact remains, nothing counts but demonstrated success. If the bird flies, we're in; if it doesn't we're kaput."

"You think so?"

"They could cut us down to a couple of squadrons. Compared with the Atlas and Titan, we'd look like a weed patch in a forest."

"It won't happen if it flies."

"If it flies," Gaither reiterated slowly. "No, not if it flies."

"It'll fly," Koepple asserted.

Gaither set down his glass with a thump.

"Sure it'll fly. Basically it's the best-designed goddamned ICBM yet. They'll know that if we get a chance to prove that baby can be adapted to the sea as well as some multimillion-buck cave; but there are too many unpredictables. It's like human error. People jazz us up. If it isn't someone goofing in the factory, it's someone goofing in top management. A political goof is as bad as a mechanical goof."

"Part of the fault's our public relations." As he spoke he noted that the profile of Gaither's face appeared fuzzy, as if he were rocking his head gently. It gave him a dizzy feeling.

"You can say that again."

"Believe me, it would be different if I were running things."

"Yeah." Gaither looked at his watch, then slid from his stool. "Gotta be going . . ."

"Good luck." He forced a cheerful countenance, then pensively watched the chief engineer's back. *If I were running things.* If. The world was full of ifs. What if it didn't fly? No, that was crazy. It would fly—it had to fly.

His hand tightened on the glass.

How many had he had? Four . . . five?

I'm a goddamned anachronism, he thought fitfully. *I come from a different time and place.* How had it happened? Sure, he'd been in step once. He was no stuffed shirt; he'd danced and played with the rest of them, yet somehow that hadn't been enough—he hadn't kept pace. But it was more than just the social life; it was a speeding up that permeated every facet of existence, from cradle to grave. Schools, the church, business and industry—everything had been slammed into a terrifying high gear to create a Mach 3 age. Men whirling around the earth, probes seeking the moon, billions upon billions being spent to reshape the universe . . . Since the war the neons were brighter, the cars faster, salaries higher and faces more wanton until the world resembled a grotesque caricature of the one he had known in days past. The world of the Monarch. . . .

Reflecting on it, he wondered if the whole rotten structure wasn't crumbling. Twenty-three thousand for a house that was falling apart, just like his shoes a couple of weeks after he bought them—shirts that didn't fit and socks that shrunk. It was a speed-up, wear-out-sooner philosophy that went hand-in-hand with a live-faster age. Live faster, live harder, try more things—sample everything and take your choice. Only he hadn't been able to sustain the pace. It showed in the way others regarded him, a deference he found exasperating. Brooding, he caught snatches of conversation amid the laughter.

"Man, you should hear that clarinet. Sweet . . ."

"So I told this yahoo, listen, I said . . ."

Gay voices, raucous voices, masculine and feminine voices, laughter, the drop of music from the piano bar filling the cave of night. Run, run, run, run, run . . . *Who's that not running? It's Koepple—Koepple's not running. He's standing still.*

He shook his head to clear his thoughts and ordered another drink, trying to concentrate on his career. *You'll be a big man, someday, dear. I just know you will.* That was Dorothy . . . years ago. Years, the speeding years. . . .

Somehow, since coming to WAD, the huge ICBM took all his waking hours. *It's the challenge of your lifetime,* they'd told him at MAC, before he'd transferred to the Coast. At first the giant forms taking shape in the factory were quite incidental in the scheme of things, just another product such as might be fabricated by almost any large company. But as knowledge of the missile's tremendous potential seeped into his mind, it came to dominate every facet of his life while, strangely enough, the corporation appeared to recede until, finally, it formed merely the backdrop against which the Monarch pirouetted across the stage of his life. *The metal bird, the monstrous bird . . . Tomorrow the bird would fly.*

He remembered—it seemed long ago—he'd had pangs of guilt about contributing to a weapon system which, in turn, might contribute to the obliteration of the human kind. Not that he was creating the missile, but he was eulogizing it. Later the pangs diminished, replaced by the rationalization that he was working for the good of mankind. Far from being a destroyer, he pictured the Monarch as a gigantic shield erected against a godless foe bent on destroying every value in which he had been raised to believe. The benevolent bird, the provider of food, shelter, clothing—shaper of economic and political beliefs. Lord, why those thoughts? He thumped his glass against the bar.

"Another, Mr. Koepple?"

He nodded, studying the lounge with bleary eyes. The room oscillated gently.

Run, run, run. Hey Koepple, you're dragging your feet. Voices, laughter, the world spinning. *I'm an anachronism,* he repeated dully. Not that he wanted to change things; the others were the mixed-up ones. He liked his life with Dorothy, even if she did run around the house in a sloppy bathrobe and spend half the time watching TV. And their boy. Yes, sir, George would grow up to amount to something, have a sense of responsibility and a sense of . . . honor. The thought of how much he owed his family brought another pang. He couldn't afford to stand still; he'd been in the same job at nearly the same salary for three years. He had to move on . . . move up.

He fingered the glass, aware of an increasing giddiness. Ability was no good in a missile plant. No good at all. Management was afraid of the bright ones. The password was mediocrity, a protective coloration which enabled a man to edge upward inconspicuously. The criterion pleased him. Hacks, the world was full of hacks. Hack writers like Elliott and Stone, hack publicity men like Garfield and, yes, hack advertising men like himself. Even Bergstrom was a hack, a division-level hack striving for corporation status. Make it and he'd be a corporation hack. He had little doubt but that he'd make it.

God, his spinning head.

Elliott later thought it strange that in over two years at Western Aerospace, he had scarcely noticed Esther Lynn other than as John Vroman's secretary and, of course, as a girl more attractive than most.

He had met her a few nights before, quite incidentally, and they had had a drink.

He had met her again last night.

And now tonight. Nor did he wonder why he was there, sharing a table with her in a darkened corner of the Sycamore Tree lounge. It had been a harrowing day, with Bergstrom at his shoulder the entire time, creating and slanting a flow of news. In a cool, driving, purposeful manner, he had painted the giant ICBM as the nation's foremost weapon, its most advanced space booster. *Ready for launch. Successful beyond all design expectations. Slated for full-scale production*—such had been his message to the world. Wondering at the vice-president's sudden counterattack, Elliott concluded the order must have emanated from above—Welkes, perhaps Byerkoff. Certainly the facts had been distorted beyond all proportion, and editing them, he had felt slightly discomfited.

He looked at Esther. She had eyes as dark as her hair, a manner of pursing the full lips that gave her a sulky appearance. Her features were good. Holding her glass musingly, she was gazing across the room. He started to speak when she said:

"There's Koepple. He looks swacked." Turning around, he spotted the ad chief hunched over the bar, eyes down as if squinting at the polished surface.

"I can't imagine it."

"His getting swacked?"

"It's not like him."

"Maybe he's worried."

"Could be." He caught the reference to the job. She spoke in innuendos; everything she said seemed calculated, just as her body movements, if not provocative, certainly were suggestive. But she was interesting company. When he let it pass, she fell silent. He felt a slight headiness, momentarily wishing Carole were with him. No, he didn't wish that either. Regarding his glass morosely, he felt a slow anger at memory of their quarrel, and all over the damned job. No matter what she said, that was it. She was a fool. Or was he? But he'd be damned if he'd crawl . . . chase her. He'd sit back, let her come to terms. He wished she could see him now, with Esther. That would pull her off her high horse. Whose high horse? Use your head, Jim Elliott. What a hell of a life. Moodily he lifted the glass.

"I don't think he has a chance," Esther said suddenly.

"Chance?" He brought back his attention.

"Koepple . . . for the job."

"I don't see why not." He withheld his amusement. She spoke of Koepple but her real concern was herself. Not that he blamed her. She wanted her job as much as he wanted Vroman's, and she was realist enough to know that it could very well depend on the whims of Bergstrom's appointee. That's why she was with him now. He didn't flatter himself she could have another motive. She eyed him coolly.

"There are others."

"Such as?"

"You."

"You've been listening to the rumor."

"Supposing it's not a rumor?"

"Then I'd be your boss."

"I know.' She gave the words a special inflection. He returned her look. There was no denying her attractiveness; she was loaded with it. Her face was expectant.

"Would that be good?"

"It could be."

"You never know."

"I think I do."

"I might disappoint you."

"I doubt it." She watched, gauging his reaction.

This time he let it pass. Taking a slow swallow from his glass, he let the liquor roll over his tongue, savoring the taste. Although he'd had several, the effect was delayed, not much more than a slow warming at the pit of his stomach, a sensation of well-being. He didn't give a damn if Carole saw him. In fact, he rather hoped she would. It felt good to be with Esther. It helped him forget the plant—Bergie and his goddamned job.

But if he lived to be ninety, he'd never forget the Monarch. The steel balloon, the metal bird—by any name it was the same. At times he felt like a barker in a sideshow.

Step right in, folks. Step right in and see the fabulous Monarch, the only 430,000-pound thrust, 8,500-mile range, liquid-propelled thermonuclear missile in captivity, presented through the courtesy of Western Aerospace Division of Midwest Aeronautical Corporation. Step right in. Except that it wasn't the only such bird in captivity. Atlas, Titan, Minuteman —the woods were full of them. They differed only in detail. That's what Walsh had been trying to tell him. But the Monarch was the newest, the best bird. Was it? Welkes said it was. So did Bergstrom. And himself? He felt less certain than before, but it was not an unanswerable question. The answer lay locked in a great steel gantry in Florida. When they lit the candle . . .

He glanced around. The dark lounge reminded him of all the bars he'd ever known, right down to the same faces, the same drinks, the same bartenders polishing the same glasses. The same people. The lush, the gilded laugh. Bars were memories, sometimes happy and sometimes poignant—crypts where one resurrected the past while trying to escape the present. But the past was often a mockery. Damn Carole. Dorothy Baker came in, hesitating to accustom her eyes to the darkness before coming toward them. A slender blonde, she wore a blue blouse with a full skirt that emphasized her hips. Watching her approach, he recalled some of the rumors he'd heard. But he'd heard the same of Esther, of others. She paused by the table.

"Enjoying yourselves?"

"Hello, Dee." Esther looked up lazily, but it seemed to him that they exchanged swift glances.

He invited, "Have a drink?"

"Not tonight, thanks. I have a date." They exchanged a few meaningless words before she moved away.

For a while they chatted, and suddenly he realized they were sparring, Esther carrying the assault, he assiduously avoiding the bridge she sought to build between them. He wondered at his reaction. Once she shifted and he felt the pressure of her thigh. Why not? There had been girls before Carole. He let the names and faces drift through his mind. If she wanted to be so damned obstinate . . . He knew it was the liquor talking, yet the question remained. Tomorrow he might think differently, but now . . .

He glanced at her again, thinking there was nothing subtle about her. Perhaps she wasn't as blatant as Jane Cooper or some of the others, but she left little to question. He saw Koepple stumble from the stool and lean against the bar, head drooped as if sick.

"Stoned," Esther said. He didn't reply.

Suddenly Koepple pushed himself erect and started toward the door, stumbling as he groped with an arm half extended. He reached the entrance and leaned against the side of the door before straightening his body and stepping out into the night. Keeping his eyes on the empty doorway, Elliott said, "I'd better drive him home."

"I think you'd better."

He looked at her, pleased. "If you don't mind . . . ?"

"No."

"It's been pleasant."

"Real pleasant."

"I hate like hell . . ."

"It's all right," she interrupted. "You'd better hurry."

He got up, looking down at her. "Good night."

Outside he paused, seeing Koepple standing under the glare

of a floodlight. The scene recalled a picture he'd seen once of the Babe, head bowed, standing alone in the immensity of the Yankee Stadium. Koepple looked that way now—a thin wisp of a figure dwarfed by the night. Lurching, he started across the parking lot. When Elliott reached him, he was leaning against the door of his car.

"A rough night for driving, Art." Koepple turned, rocking as he blinked to bring his eyes into focus. "I'll drive you home," he finished.

"Home, sure, gotta go home." Koepple's voice was thick and slurred. "I'm sick, Jim."

"I'll drive."

"Sick, sick . . ."

"Got the keys?" Koepple looked down, patting his pockets uncertainly before he fished them out, and holding them, peered owlishly at him.

"I'm jush sick."

"I'll drive."

"Stuffy, a stuffy night."

"Damned stuffy, Art. Better give me the keys."

"Why?"

"I don't want you to drive."

He appeared to debate it. "Yes, you better." He surrendered and Elliott helped him into the car, afraid he was going to be sick. Koepple slumped against the seat, holding his hands to his face. Elliott was starting around to the other side when he heard his name called softly. Turning, he saw Esther coming across the lot. He moved a few steps to meet her.

"I'll follow you," she offered.

"No need to."

"How'll you get home?" Before he could answer, she said, "I'll pick you up."

"I can get a cab."

"I don't mind." She placed a hand on his arm and squeezed gently. For a moment their eyes locked.

"All right." He went around to the driver's side and slid in, waiting for the lights of her car before starting the engine.

"I'm sick," Koepple mumbled.

"That's all right, Art. We all take a holiday once in a while."

"Holiday . . ."

"You'll feel better in a bit." He glanced into the rearview mirror, watching Esther swing in behind him. The lights of her car burned a message in his brain. *I'm following you,* they said. *I'll meet you.* So what was wrong with that? It was no one's damned business.

Koepple pulled himself erect, mumbling, " 'Scape, thas what it is."

"We all need that occasionally."

" 'Scape."

"You're okay, Art."

Koepple peered at him. "You know what I'm 'scaping from? The job."

"It's a damned grind, Art."

"I'm 'scaping and you're shel'brating."

"Celebrating?" He glanced around, surprised.

Koepple nodded. "Shel'brating—the new director. You know? I'm glad's not Henderson."

"You're wrong, Art." The turn in the conversation startled him. So, that's why Koepple had got drunk. Lord, how he must have wanted the job. He had known it, but he hadn't suspected how much, nor had he considered him as a serious contender. The ad chief had always seemed to typify the faithful standby —the man who did the work but seldom reaped the rewards.

"Wrong?" Koepple uttered the word incredulously.

"It's just a rumor, Art."

"You mean . . . the job's open?"

"Still open," he replied gently. Koepple riveted his eyes straight ahead, peering through the windshield. Elliott felt a quick stab of sympathy. Koepple was a man at the end of a trail. He wasn't old, not as age is measured, but old for the environment. Strange, he hadn't considered that before, but he knew it to be true. Koepple hadn't managed to adapt as Garfield had. He belonged in a different world, a more gentle one, and momentarily he wondered what twist in fate had brought him to a missile plant. Somewhere, long ago, he had taken the wrong turn. He should get out, as Vroman had. *As Vroman had?* He repeated the words, sensing the opening of a small lock in his mind. But it wasn't the same. Not the same at all. Why had Vroman quit? Once more he found the question disturbing. As he turned down the street where the ad chief lived, the lights of Esther's car reflected in the rearview mirror. Koepple struggled erect.

"I wish it had been the other way, Jim." He seemed to muster quiet dignity. "It would have been a good decision."

"I don't know," he answered, thinking that he really didn't know. The picture he had held so tightly seemed to be shifting, like sand draining away beneath a foundation. Spotting the neat gray house with its red brick flower boxes, he began slowing to swing into the driveway.

Koepple spoke again. "An age has passed, Jim."

"You're home, Art."

"An age," Koepple said. "It's gone."

"Witek, we've been friends a long time." Garfield pronounced the words slowly, keeping his eyes on the other's face. Sitting in his office, they had just finished reviewing the publicity kit he had prepared for Witek's civic committee, and now he wondered how to approach the real purpose he had in mind.

"A couple of years," the publicity man agreed. "You've only been here three."

"Seems like a decade."

Witek smirked. "What are you buttering me for?"

"I'm not, I'm just stating a fact."

"All right, so what's on your mind?" As the other wriggled more comfortably into his seat, Garfield eyed him speculatively, then decided to take the plunge.

"It's Vroman's job," he confessed. "I want it."

"So?"

"I need your help."

Witek avoided the plea, asking, "How's she stacking up?"

"Normally I'd say I was in line for it, at least on the basis of experience and ability."

"Sure."

"No, I'm serious." The other's attitude nettled him. "All we have here are hacks."

"Then what's the trouble?"

"Henderson—I can't shake the feeling that he has it taped."

"If he had it cinched, he would have had it by now," Witek pointed out.

"Not necessarily. Bergie's in no hurry, but I have a damned good idea he's sold on him."

"A hunch?"

"More than that. Dammit, I've got twenty-two years sunk in this corporation and I don't want to get beat again."

"Again?" Witek looked inquiringly at him.

"When Vroman was hired," he explained.

"I didn't know that."

"Bergie went outside to get him. Damned if I know why. Maybe someone pushed Vroman off on him."

"He was pretty good."

"Yes, he was." He eyed the other shrewdly. "Now it's Henderson."

"But you're not sure?"

He ignored the question. "I've got to sink that boy."

"Don't look at me." Witek smiled foolishly. "I just came here to look over a publicity handout, remember? I can't help you there."

"But you can," he interjected sharply. "You know damned well you can. You unbuttoned your lip enough last time to tell me that much."

"It's buttoned again," Witek said defensively.

"Let's unbutton it." He pushed the point, striving for an advantage. "You mentioned a woman—said it was enough to blow Henderson out of town. Or were you just talking?"

"I wasn't just talking." The publicity man wore a hurt expression.

"But you know it's true?"

"Yes, I know that."

"How?"

"Jesus, you can't keep that kind of thing under cover. You go places, and there's always people . . ."

"Someone saw them?"

"Yeah."

"Someone dependable?"

"I know him like an uncle."

"Witek"—he leaned forward, fixing the other intently—"I've got to have the name of that woman."

"No soap. I live in this town too."

"Look, you're not doing me a favor," he said smoothly. "We both can benefit."

"Baloney on that plural stuff. I don't want any part of it."

"I'm serious, Witek. I'm a trader. You help me and I'll help you. That's the way people get along in this world, or at least the smart ones. This is one time your knowledge can pay off—a jackpot. If I get the job, you're in. You can't do anything but win." He leaned back and stared at the fleshy face, trying to discern a reaction.

The eyes watching him from behind the puffy lids wavered uncertainly before the publicity man licked his lips, asking, "What's the proposition?"

"A job—one that's right up your alley."

"No go," Witek replied firmly. "I'm a free-lance PR man and I intend to stay that way. I sure wouldn't work in this tin can factory."

"I'm not talking about a job here."

"Oh?"

"What are you planning to do when your committee folds?" Garfield pressed.

"Find another account."

"That's what I'm talking about—an account."

Witek arched his brows. "Tell me about it."

"You know the polls we run?" Without waiting for an answer, he continued, "A couple of times a year we run a poll to determine the company's status in the community—questions about how people think we stack up against other companies, our value to the community, how favorably we're regarded, WAD as a place to work and things like that."

"Christ, I'm a PR man, not a pollster," Witek objected. "I don't know beans about it."

"Get wise to yourself, boy. That's the big thing. Everybody needs polls. We can't do without them. I'm offering you an easy way into the racket."

"I still don't know beans about it."

"That's the good part, you don't have to. It's just another phony empire, and the best thing about it, you're God. No one knows whether you're right or wrong."

"Witek and Gallup." The fat man snickered. "We might merge."

"For Christ's sake, be serious," he snapped irritably. "I'm offering you a chance in a million. It's a damned good account."

"Yeah, and how much staff would I need? The few polling outfits I've seen were plush-lined. It sounds to me like a lot of overhead."

"Practically none," he assured him. "That's why it pays off. We give you an idea what we're after—I can show you some of the past questionnaires—then you jot down the questions, crank 'em out on a mimeo, and hire some two-buck-an-hour slob to get them filled out. That's all there is to it. Do that and you're in like Flynn."

"I dunno . . ."

"It's a sweet racket, Witek. You just sit back and count the money."

"You make it sound like a cinch."

"It is a cinch," Garfield said, with sudden relief. Fat boy was caving in nicely. He could read it in his words, see it in the clenched hand and the thin film of perspiration that clotted his brow. Money talked and Witek was getting the message. "It falls in Vroman's empire. If I get the job, it's my decision."

"Who handles it now?"

"Some jerk outfit that operates from a garage. There won't be any trouble."

"So after I give you the info?" Witek pursed his lips, his small eyes searching Garfield's face.

"You know damned well you can trust me," he answered, knowing he'd won. Vroman's job seemed infinitely closer.

"Sure, I know I can trust you. You know why?" Garfield stirred uneasily under his gaze. "Because you're like me." He chuckled and leaned back. "A man of principles."

Dynamite—pure dynamite.

Garfield sat alone, considering the information he'd obtained, half wishing he'd never pressed the question. A little knowledge was a dangerous thing, or could be if mishandled. Witek was right. The information could blow Henderson out of town; it could also blow everyone associated with it out of town. Twenty-two years . . . He'd hate to have to start over, but it could happen. One slip—it would take no more. But on the other hand, the big chip—the blue chip—lay on the table, awaiting only the fall of the cards. Strictly a gamble, but with the deck stacked.

Chewing his cigar, he drew satisfaction from the knowledge that he held Eugene Henderson squarely in the palm of his hand. A whisper in the right ear. Yeah, a whisper. He frowned. Muff it and he'd wind up hacking the copy right back where he started, on some flea-bitten publication on the back streets of Chicago. He knitted his brow at the memory, glad those days were far behind. Now just ghosts, they had nothing to do with the future. Despite his misgivings, he knew he'd use the information. *Harry the gambler,* he told himself cynically. It wasn't whether he'd use it, but how.

Elliott was not *it.*

Unlike what had happened after the rumor that he would succeed Vroman, no one rushed to tell him he was *out.* Rather, the knowledge came in the form of vague glances and subtle nuances which, in the absence of words, served as an equally effective medium of communication.

Just when the knowledge penetrated that he was low man on the totem pole, he couldn't say; but he *knew.* It came like a voice whispering: *You're out—someone else is in.* That was the substance of his impressions, but he felt they were accurate. Later, as the atmosphere of the office switched to business-as-usual, he realized it was because he *did know*. His secretary brought some letters to sign, Hackleberg wanted an okay on a news release, Garfield popped in to chat over the launch.

Later in the day Joe Stone, his assistant, dropped in, busying himself with a cigarette before saying, "I heard the rumor."

Elliott smiled. Stone was blunt but he liked him, and felt grateful that he had brought the situation into the open.

"It's about what I expected," Elliott told him.

"I'm not surprised."

"Oh?" He raised his eyes, curious.

"I never believed the other rumor—that you'd get it," Stone explained. "You're not a company man. Neither am I."

"I never thought of it that way."

"That's the only way to think of it. You have to be all company to crash the upper hierarchy."

"Vroman wasn't a company man."

"No." Stone thought about it. "But neither did he stay."

"You could be right," he replied doubtfully.

"I don't think you lost a damn thing," Stone said cheerfully.

"How do you figure that?"

He shrugged. "What is it, except a bigger headache?"

"If you call responsibility a headache."

"What responsibility, Jim? We're all yes-men. The director's just a bigger one."

"He still has responsibility, Joe."

"I suppose, but he has to follow a damned tight party line."

"Would you turn the job down?"

"I don't know." He studied Elliott gravely. "I'd sure give it one hell of a hard think."

"Do you expect to stay in your present position forever?"

"Hell, no," he exploded.

"What then?"

"This is just a stepping-stone. You know that."

"To what?"

"Damned if I know," he confessed. "I'm like a lot of others, just riding along looking for a way out. This isn't my future, Jim."

"What's wrong with it?"

"It's a carnival."

"I'm serious, Joe."

"What is there to look forward to? Half the people here are sweating out the Monarch. Hell, this is a paper house. Look at the Douglas Skybolt that's coming along . . . a plane-launched ballistic missile. Next thing you know, they'll decide that's the ultimate weapon, then we'll be back in planes again."

"Don't tell me you're worried about security," he said disbelievingly.

"It's not security," Stone protested. "It's just the damned rat race."

"You could get up there in time . . ."

"Sure, the goddamned treadmill would carry me there, but it hasn't anything to do with ability, as you damn well know. You just coast, play the right politics, butter the right people and, if you're lucky, coast into middle management on sheer momentum."

"It doesn't seem to work that way for me," he replied wryly.

Stone grinned. "You're new here, Jim. You have to invest fifteen or twenty years. You're trying to move too fast."

"God forbid."

"That's what I'm saying." His face grew serious. "You have to have satisfaction too. What satisfaction is there in promoting this goddamned tin balloon?"

"Someone has to do it."

"Why?"

"It has to be sold."

"Jesus, you sound brainwashed."

"Brainwashed?"

"It's not that important."

"The bird? I think it is."

"You have to look at your own life," Stone insisted.

"You can rest easy." It was Elliott's turn to smile. "I know what I want, Joe."

"Damned few people do."

"Sounds like you're advising against the job," he said dryly.

"Yeah, I guess I'm getting sour."

"Would you give Garfield or Koepple the same advice?"

"Not Garfield. He's a natural for it. I suppose Art would do okay too."

"They have something that I haven't?"

"It's the other way around, Jim." There was more of the same, and Elliott clearly got the message. As far as Stone was concerned, WAD was a trap, and the director's job was just part of the floss.

He sat quietly after the writer had gone, aware of mixed feelings. What did it take to get the job? He had banked on ability, but was it enough? No, he wasn't a company man; he'd never thought he was. Not as he understood the term. The company man was one for whom the company served as surrogate for God and family; its policies and its future, his future—a blind adherence to a system. Garfield fitted the specifications. And to a lesser extent, so did Art Koepple. In the case of Midwest Aeronautical Corporation, even such towering figures as Arnold Northcott Whitestone and Martin L. Byerkoff, president and chairman of the board respectively, were merely higher symbols representing the same cause. Man was mortal but the company was immortal. Long after the Whitestones and Byerkoffs departed this earthly realm the company would remain, still expanding, fed on the blood of crushed competition, headed by other grim-faced but transient men. Sure, those were the facts of life, but they didn't affect him. He was his own man.

Without consciously considering it, he had associated the company man philosophy with much of the evil he detected in the system. It erased the profile of individualism until it blended harmoniously with all the other profiles, an insidious abrasive that smoothed away resourcefulness, initiative, determination—wore them down until the end product resembled an elite robot. Garfield might be sharp and aggressive, but he was sharp and aggressive within confines, hewing to one narrow path. "The doctrine of unchallenged leadership"—that's how Vroman had once described it. He sure as hell didn't fit that picture. Yet . . .

He forced himself to let the idea unfold.

He believed the Nation's ICBM program absolutely essential, yet he realized that management was prone to regard a mishap or setback in a competing program as grounds for quiet rejoicing. Such an occasion was regarded as strengthening the company's own position, a viewpoint which he knew derived from the missile as an economic rather than a military symbol. And he'd gone along with such thinking! More, he'd stated half-truths as truths, explained weaknesses as strengths, buried failures. Why? He'd denied being brainwashed. But was he?

The company was accepted as animate and sentient—the company *thought* but individuals didn't *think*. Total conformity demanded that individual ideas and personal convictions be stifled, that decision-making be held to a minimum, for ideas and decisions had become the group province. He'd recognized the philosophy from the first, but he'd never bought it. At least not consciously. While such a system allowed the individual to operate undisturbed and protected him from the consequence of inept work, it also deprived him of the authorship of his creations. He had recognized the basic mechanisms, but he certainly hadn't approved them, at least in relation to himself. The basic tenets went hand-in-hand with the job considered as just a job, the company as a bountiful provider. Stone had called it a "treadmill," a term often used with overtones of pride, as if the Western Aerospace treadmill were something quite novel. He suspected the Martin and Boeing people felt much the same about theirs.

But this, too, was vital and necessary . . . to others. The treadmill was considered a giant conveyor belt that carried its riders to their destinations with but scant effort on their part, a view which discarded the fact that something had to make the belt move. The basis of this acceptance, he suspected, was that few expected to rise far in the hierarchy—a managerial or supervisory plum would be the ultimate expectation, and the belt could carry them that far. In that respect, it was the great leveler.

How did all this apply to him? He'd never regarded the company as a vehicle for automatic advancement, but rather as a vehicle to further his own advancement. There was a difference. He was willing to rise or fall under his own steam. More important, he attached responsibility to his job. Human motivations and questions regarding the Monarch weren't related. People could ride the Monarch; but the Monarch in itself *was* important. The Monarch—that was the real question. Welkes said and Bergstrom said and Barry Walsh said and he said . . . But what the hell was it really? A shining sword? A tin balloon?

That, he had to think about.

"I thought the story clever," Garfield said, flicking the ash from his cigar.

"Cute." Esther Lynn watched him speculatively. They had been quite friendly of late. Now, with Elliott out, he could very well be the new director. She discerned he had something in mind and deliberately allowed him several openings, to no avail. But he'd get to it. They all did in time.

"How's the job coming?" He asked the question casually but she saw his eyes brighten, fixing her a bit too intently.

"Okay, I guess."

"You don't sound too enthusiastic."

"I'm not." She kept her face expressionless. "I heard a rumor."

"About Elliott?"

"No."

"Who?"

"John Vroman."

"What about him?"

"Bergie's trying to get him back." The words brought a startled look and he leaned forward, scrutinizing her closely.

"Where'd you hear that?"

"One of the girls." She didn't mention that Joan Wesley had told her during lunch. Joan had appeared quite distraught, and at the time she wondered why.

He leaned back, his face thoughtful, and finally said, "I don't believe it."

"Why not?"

"I can see Bergie trying . . ." He spoke musingly, his brow furrowed.

"I don't see . . ."

"Vroman wouldn't come back," he said decisively.

"What makes you say that?"

"I don't know. I just think it."

"I hope it's not wishful thinking," she said, hoping he was right. She'd hate to have to put up with Vroman again.

"I don't feel it is."

"I hope not."

"Don't like Vroman, eh?"

"He's . . . kind of a stick."

"I know what you mean." She caught his appraising glance before he added briskly, "But I'm not going to worry. There are other things to worry about."

"Such as?" She returned his gaze, impatient for him to get to the point. He hadn't just dropped in.

"Such as who might really get the job."

"Yes, that makes a difference."

"Quite a difference."

"Have you any ideas?" she murmured.

"Some." He let the silence build up before adding, "However, I don't think you have to worry . . . unless Henderson gets it."

"Why?" The word tumbled from her lips. He knew something!

"He probably has a girl lined up."

"You don't know that," she said sharply.

"I've heard it. You know how those things get around." As she struggled to regain her composure, he added, "It's worth thinking about."

"Yes." Their eyes met. He was trying to give her a message, pave the way for something. "Have you heard anything . . . I mean about the job?"

"Nothing definite."

"You sound doubtful."

"Well . . . you know." He gestured. "However, I've got an idea."

"About the job?"

He nodded. "Why don't we get together for a drink? Perhaps if we put our heads together . . ."

"I can't tonight," she said reluctantly. "I have a dinner date."

"Later this week. It doesn't matter."

"That would be fine."

"I'll keep in touch." He got up, a quizzical half-smile on his face. "It should be interesting."

"The talk?"

"That too."

She contemplated his departure with smug satisfaction. Their conversation, if short, had been quite illuminating, especially in what had been left unsaid. But she would correct that. For a while, after Vroman left, she had dangled in a vacuum. When people did drop in, their voices and looks managed to convey just the right amount of sympathy, as if her transfer or termination were a foregone conclusion. Nor had her past relationship with Bergstrom eased her mind. She knew so much and should he . . .

She pushed the thought from her mind. Yes, things were looking up. She was in solid with Elliott, or could be if she chose to beckon. She savored the memory. If only he hadn't lost out. She was in with Garfield too, or soon would be. She discounted Koepple.

That left Henderson.

That's what Garfield had been driving at. In his mind, Henderson was the threat. But he had a plan. Well, she didn't give a damn what it was, as long as it got her what she wanted. Besides, Garfield could prove quite interesting. They should get along together.

That decided, she opened her purse and began powdering her nose.

10

Chapter 10

AT AGE fifty-five, John Vroman was tall, slightly stooped, his face lined; yet his eyes, as gray as his thinning hair, remained sharp and clear. A crinkling at the corners broke his otherwise austere features. A closer look revealed a sensitivity in the wide forehead and narrow nose not apparent at first sight. Today he had selected a gay brown and gold tie to enliven his tan summer-weight suit.

Across from him at Ferdinand's, Elliott was struck by the changes which had occurred in the short time since he'd left his job. The possessor of an ulcer and cardiac symptoms, he had looked sixty-five, hollow-eyed, with a tired, drawn face that held lines where no lines should be. Seldom missing a day, he rarely had worked less than twelve hours and often longer, a record embellished in a habitual mask of fatigue. No longer pallid, his face clear and alert, if he looked his fifty-five years, certainly he appeared no older.

Elliott had called him the previous night, pleased when he readily accepted his invitation for lunch. Regarding him as a friend, he hoped for advice and counsel. At the moment

Vroman was explaining a job he was considering with one of the city's advertising agencies, a substantial firm with roots firmly embedded in the local economy. As he spoke, the thought crossed Elliott's mind that the firm was much like the man himself, solid and respectable.

"So I'm not retired by a long shot," Vroman stated. "It's just a change of pasture."

"Does Bergstrom know?"

"I haven't mentioned it." Vroman's eyes twinkled. "Should I?"

"According to rumor, he's trying to get you back."

"He called several times."

Elliott let it pass, declaring, "You look ten years younger."

"I feel ten years younger."

"I can see why you quit."

"You can?"

As Vroman raised his cup, Elliott caught the wisp of a smile tugging at his lips and said defensively, "From a health standpoint, yes."

"But you're not certain?"

"No, I can't honestly say that I am. You had a top spot at WAD."

"I'm better off, Jim."

"I can understand that. The pressure's terrible, especially with the hot firing coming up."

"I've been following it in the papers," Vroman assented. "Looks like Slater gave you the hotfoot."

"More rumor than fact, John."

"Is the launch date still firm?"

He nodded. "Next week. I wish to hell it were past."

"Sounds like you're feeling it."

"We all are, from Bergie on down. We lost a static test missile and it has everyone jittery."

"Did you locate the trouble?"

"A fuel leak."

"Design defect?"

"Welkes says not."

"Of course," Vroman stated dryly.

"Gaither says not also," he replied defensively.

"Paul's an honest boy."

"No major weapon system ever was developed without bugs," he protested.

"I suppose not."

"Anyway, we need a good first firing. After that we have the big contract to worry over."

"You have to learn to take it easy, budget your time," Vroman counseled. "But I should preach."

"How can you? There's just so much that has to be done."

Vroman took a bite of steak before answering.

"That I know all too well, but I also know that we make part of our hell. Ambition—everyone struggling like mad. Now, I imagine, it's worse." He gazed shrewdly at him. "Garfield, Koepple, Henderson, yourself—all breeding ulcers, wondering how you can outmaneuver the other for the job. Right?"

"I suppose so," he sheepishly admitted, "but everyone has to look out for himself. No one will do it for you." He realized the words sounded trite but that's the way he felt. No one ever claimed that society wasn't a dog-eat-dog proposition.

Vroman didn't appear to notice, observing, "That's why I left."

"I don't follow you."

"I was looking out for myself." Catching Elliott's inquisitive look, he continued: "It starts early. The wreck at sixty is the result of not applying the brakes at thirty. The long hours are only part of it, Jim. It's the environment, demands, the constant rushing from pillar to post. Some people adapt to it and grow hardened, or else fall into a rut and coast, propelled by habit; others are ground down, but I think we all pay the piper in the end."

"I can see it," he agreed, picturing Koepple's harried face, "but I still have to get ahead. I can't stand still. Do that and I might as well be reading copy on some farm monthly." As he spoke, he thought this something he shouldn't have to explain. The First Commandment of Management stood as hard and firm as if chiseled on Mt. Sinai by Moses himself: *Thou shalt not stand still.*

"There are worse jobs, Jim."

"Sure, but any job worth its salt is work."

"I'm not disputing that."

"Then what's the argument?" he replied vexedly. The other laid aside his fork.

"No argument. Work, that's all right. No one ever died from work. It's the other pressures—internal politics, mental conflicts, your own feelings about the value of the job. I just happen to believe they're not part of every job."

"I don't know, John. People are people, with the same drives and motives."

"The same kind of people but in a different atmosphere," Vroman corrected. "Environment modifies people, Jim."

"I'll grant that."

"A missile plant's rugged, whether you're welding or punching typewriter keys, and people react accordingly. It's part of the defense picture, Jim. The worker has seen the plants empty before and the vision's there—one of the intangible pressures that keeps him scrambling, trying to make it before the roof caves in. He's got that bungalow and TV set and the kids' shoes to think of. Put him under that kind of pressure and he changes."

"Why just a missile plant?" he challenged.

"They're newer, growing giants. The competition within them is keener. Within them and among them," he amended. "They've sprung from the earth, sprouting in the short span of a decade, but already they're in a life-and-death struggle for survival. The shield against extinction is contracts, and there are only so many to go around—certainly not enough for all."

"I'll agree to that."

"The fight's a dual one—to expand the contract base while whittling down the competition . . . battalions of corporations against battalions of corporations."

"It's part of it," he grudgingly admitted, "but there are other considerations."

"Let me go on," Vroman said, "and we'll come back to them. Defense plants haven't the stability of established industries. People working for them recognize the fact. That's why they're so restless, so insecure. Tomorrow we sign a peace treaty and the next day they're all out on the street, like after the war. Feast or famine, all dependent on international affairs. Defense is a future pegged to war. No war, no future. How the hell can a man plan in that atmosphere?" he exclaimed.

"You didn't think that way before," he challenged.

"I did, but I considered that an occupational hazard. I was more interested in the job to be done—believed it necessary. I imagine you feel the same."

"I wouldn't be there otherwise, John. But even so, I can't see missile plants going down the drain like aircraft. The aircraft factories are victims of technological change, just like the carriage-makers lost out to the automobile-makers; but now we're at the final stage. There's no technology to replace space; it's the final step."

"Missiles and space vehicles aren't quite the same."

"Perhaps not, but I don't think you'll see the day when plants like WAD lie empty. When missiles go—if they go—space technology will take over. We'll be turning out space vehicles like Carter turns out liver pills."

Vroman's face creased. "I'll modify my statement. Our space program is booming as part of defense. It's one and the same, Jim—different parts of the same picture. Our spy-in-the-sky and interceptor satellite designs are another phase of NASA's man-in-orbit. The latter is the low Fahrenheit phase of the war—the so-called cold war."

"Perhaps."

"Why do you think we spend umpteen million dollars to get a man into orbit, Jim? To tell us what the stars look like?"

"Of course not."

"Explorer, Surveyor, Gemini—name a program and I'll show you an ultimate military use for it. The same goes for Sputniks and Luniks. Those *are* front-line efforts." He waited until the klaxon blast of a passing truck subsided before resuming. "Every space program we have represents a contest against Russia . . . the Red world. You know that. You can't separate space from defense, and neither can the man in the street. The taxpayer wouldn't put up peanuts if he didn't have to. He's interested in Mars like I'm interested in King Tut. He's paying because he's scared, knows it means survival, if not for him, for his children. Pull that away and your popular support would melt like snow on a hot griddle. The government is your only customer, and that for as long as space can be justified on Military grounds. So you see, Jim, everything does depend on war. It keeps the wheels turning."

"Does Kroeber think that way?" he asked shrewdly.

"He's different," Vroman responded easily. "He's certainly not a militarist, nor would I even say he's a scientist, at least in the sense that his prime drive is scientific in objective. With him, space is a religion."

"I've thought that."

"He views a space vehicle as merely a mechanical contraption to carry mankind to whatever gods he sees out there. He's mystical in purpose, Jim."

"He's not alone."

"Thank God."

Elliott musingly sipped his coffee. Kroeber was more than a creator of space systems. His eyes looked beyond any horizon yet known to man. Not with dreams or vague hopes, but with certainty, as if he were following a genealogical chart of the future which scaled both time and distance. He suspected the chart contemplated wars, interregnums, vacillating economies, the passage of governments and gross human failure—but that somehow all of these were but detours on the road to a goal which he believed as certain as the stars. "Tomorrow is made inevitable by what we do today"—Kroeber had told him that once. One could almost consider it a philosophy of predestination, although Kroeber insisted it arose from the logical nature of science, in which each small step created the inevitability of the step to follow.

He caught Vroman's eyes on him and said, "This is an odd conversation, in view of the fact that you sold me on the Monarch."

"So I did." Vroman grew pensive. "At that time I was new to the game, much like you are now. I found myself caught by the fear of war, the urgency of our time."

"You're not now?" he asked disbelievingly.

"Very much so. You can't look at the world and blind yourself to stark reality. The five-ton Sputniks whizzing overhead underline that. This is a grim time in history, Jim, the more so because of the subtle and insidious nature of the attack. I feel like a man standing under a snow cliff awaiting an avalanche. The danger is very great." He paused reflectively before continuing: "I was a crusader and my crusade died. It's that simple."

"Why?" Perplexed, Elliott thought Vroman had wandered from the path of logic.

"Conflict. My doc called me a man fighting myself. I started out fully sold on the bird, saw it as a better weapon in a superweapon arsenal. Deterrency held real meaning. The word 'war' meant 'nuclear,' with anything less unthinkable. That's why deterrency became the hope. The psychology of the atom, Jim—once such destructive power emerged, we assumed the automatic obsolescence of all other weapons; they became mere stopgaps while we swung to heftier and heftier atoms. My own thinking followed right along, oriented by the necessity of arming rather than how we should arm."

"Who sold you? Bergie?"

"In part. But it's not just a matter of being sold, Jim. It's also seeing things . . . from a viewpoint other than your own. We get prejudiced in favor of ourselves."

"I can see that."

"I glimpsed the Monarch's destructive power and clung to it. Later, as I got a clearer insight, I began to take stock of my thinking. Or perhaps it was a growing awareness of the reality of war, I don't know. But I do know that a thousand Monarchs on their pads, nuclear-nosed and all, wouldn't have saved Cuba. Finally I came to the conclusion that I was just another huckster for another missile. After that the end came fast."

"I can't see it," he countered. "You can't downgrade the Monarch, at least not until after it's flight-tested, if then."

"You'll know shortly."

"We will," he responded firmly.

"However, I didn't state that the Monarch wasn't a good

missile. I said it wasn't a necessary one. There's a difference."

"I don't think we're in a position to judge that, John."

Vroman's eyes crinkled. "A few moments ago you stated you were working because you believed your job necessary . . . the missile necessary."

"You're more like Barry Walsh than ever," he declared. "I can't win an argument. Looks like I trapped myself."

"Much as I did."

"There's an assumption of necessity," he insisted.

"Let's look at it another way," Vroman suggested. "Do you believe the ICBMs we're stockpiling now could blow Russia off the map?"

"I'd say so," he admitted, recognizing the trap.

"So why the Monarch?"

"It's more advanced."

"How many times can you kill a man, Jim?" When he didn't answer, Vroman continued: "I grew tired of the battle. I began to see the greed . . . the power drives. Suddenly it seemed pointless, worse when I began to question the job."

"I won't argue that there's not a battle for power."

"A battle of corporations as well as among the military, Jim. Our fences need mending. Have you ever felt you were just a unit in a vast economic struggle for survival in which defense formed merely a convenient backdrop?"

"You're arguing several sides of the question," he accused.

"It has several sides, but answer me."

"If I thought that, I wouldn't be here, John. But you have to consider a corporation like an individual—it's got to move ahead."

"We need weapons, not power complexes."

"That's what we're producing."

"The best weapons, Jim? Assess the battlefield before you

answer. How much territory have we lost since the age of ICBMs? Considerable, wouldn't you say? Now we're adding still another ICBM. We have to have the means to fight the many faces of this war—Army and Navy weapons, Marine Corps raider battalions, arms for psychological warfare." He drummed the table. "Weapons should be chosen on the basis of need, not economics or politics. If the Monarch were clearly a superior system that would replace the others, I could see it, but it's not in the cards, Jim. More and more it looks like another duplication."

"Then you didn't quit for health reasons." He made it a statement.

"Physical *and* mental health. When I realized I was doing something I had come not to believe in, it kicked the psychological props from under me. A man has to live with his conscience, Jim. One day my thinking crystallized and I quit. Now I know something was restored to me that day. That might be hard to understand."

"I think I can, John."

"I'm not giving you a hard sell. These are the kind of things a man has to work out for himself."

"I'll agree that the Monarch's not perfect, but if it represents an advance over other ICBMs . . . ?"

"That's the crux of the problem. Does it?"

They fell silent. Finishing his meal, Elliott felt he understood his companion. A man of integrity, he had been compelled to follow his conscience, and for that he could respect him. And what if he had erred in his major premise? At least the move had been good for him. If his battle had been personal, he had won it. Not that his observations were new. He himself had seen many duplicative programs among the services, senseless cutbacks, contracts that waxed and waned with shifts in military, economic and political thought: the Navaho, Vega, nuclear aircraft—the rise and fall and rise again of the B-70 turned RS-70. Nike. Was it a big pork barrel? Or did such things reflect shifting requirements as the face of battle changed?

When he considered it, he recognized the ever-present fear that the Monarch would prove somewhat less than perfect, that it might lose out in the struggle among power blocs, be negated by the thunderclap of a technological breakthrough, or simply be eliminated. He'd heard such worries, had seen them mirrored in Bergstrom's solid claims to the contrary. He suspected the vice-president's concern far exceeded what his stolid countenance reflected. Cutbacks in other programs sent small tremors of apprehension throughout the plant, accompanied by hasty rationalizations which demonstrated why such a thing could not happen to the Monarch. But if the shadow of fear lay over the plant, it certainly hadn't affected him personally. He worked for the bird because he believed it represented a good sound program. Or was that a rationalization?

"How's Carole?" Vroman asked suddenly.

Startled, he brought back his thoughts. "Fine."

"Only fine?" The other eyed him bemusedly.

"Well"—he grinned ruefully—"she's a bit irked just now."

"The job?"

"She doesn't like the idea of my trying for your spot," he confessed.

"Not because it was my job," Vroman replied dryly.

"No." He hesitated, wondering how much to say.

"Wants you out, eh?"

"She thinks I'm a potential Hemingway."

"That's not the case, Jim."

"No?"

"She's looking toward the future. She's a topflight girl, Jim." His eyes grew merry. "Now if I were twenty years younger . . ."

"Yeah," he agreed, not noticing. "She's plenty determined, too."

"What's the status?" Vroman asked frankly.

"We're not dating. Says she won't until I make a decision."

"On quitting?" As he nodded, Vroman pursued: "I'd give it serious thought. You don't find girls like her every day."

"I know."

"You certainly wouldn't have a job problem."

"I'm trying to get a job, not give one up," Elliott exclaimed.

"So I gather. But supposing it's a decision between Carole or the job?" Vroman watched him closely.

"If I get it, she'll come around," he said without confidence.

"You don't believe that, Jim."

"I'm not giving up," he said doggedly.

Vroman sighed. "It's no good preaching. You'll have to learn by experience, as I did."

"I know about the experience. I thought you might give me some advice—a few pointers."

"I have."

"I mean about the job," Elliott corrected. "I'd like to know how I stand. I'm too close to assess it myself."

"I'll probably disappoint you. All I can advise is that you do the best you can, keep your nose clean, and see what happens."

Let down, he asked, "Have you any feel for how it might go?"

"Yes, I think I have." Vroman uttered the words slowly. Leaning against the edge of the table, Elliott waited as the other set down his cup. "Do you want encouragement or my honest opinion?"

"Your honest opinion, of course."

"I think Henderson will get it," he answered. "I think he has it cinched."

Elliott returned to the office feeling morose. Vroman's words about Henderson had the ring of an irrefutable statement; yet he found Vroman's reasons for quitting even more disturbing. The Monarch—a boondoggle? That was but one man's opinion; Vroman's stacked against Welkes', Gaither's, Bergstrom's and, yes, his own. How much did the opinion of a non-engineer weigh against those of engineers and scientists? Against those of the military? Yet, in cold logic, what did he really know about the Monarch? Nothing, really, except the glittering generalities of his own claims. Beyond that he recognized in Vroman's words an echo of what Walsh had said, and Carole. Some of the trade journals had made the same claims editorially; so had Congressman Slater. Were they right?

Settling back in his chair, he fingered the papers on his desk, seeking some objectivity in the claims and counterclaims that constantly rocked the industry. How many thousands of words had he poured out glorifying the Monarch, a missile that had yet to fly as far as an inch?

The Monarch missile, developed for the Air Force by Midwest Aeronautical Corporation's Western Aerospace Division, adds a terrifying punch to the nation's ICBM arsenal. But does it? A standard lead, it had gone into a thousand news releases with but scant variation. Name the missile, name the corporation, then add the weak excuse for running the names. If there were no excuse, invent one. Sucker the editors in.

A fourth generation intercontinental ballistic missile, the Monarch possesses the dual capabilities of boosting manned vehicles into orbit or deep space, or delivering a thermonuclear warhead to any part of an enemy nation. . . . Fourth generation. What did he mean by that? What generation was the

Atlas? The Titan? The Minuteman? Not the fourth, certainly, but the Monarch was—the fourth because it came later, was more sophisticated, whatever that meant. Why not the fifth generation, or sixth? Hell, why not have a really sophisticated missile and call it the twentieth generation, or simply Monarch XX? That would prove its superiority. Auxiliary thought: Sprinkle in a few personal names. Byerkoff, Whitestone, Welkes—Kroeber the spaceman, late of Peenemünde. Let the public know the guiding geniuses behind this fourth generation, liquid fueled, 430,000-pound thrust, 8,500-mile range super-duper wonder, now practically ready to begin scheduled deliveries to Mars. Or Moscow. Pour on the hot air. Sell the Monarch. Sell the corporation. Don't let the American people forget for one moment that their survival depends on the Monarch, a way of life preserved for them by the grace of Midwest Aeronautical Corporation under the auspices of its benevolent offspring, the Western Aerospace Division. Launched from land, launched from sea, the Monarch was all things to all men. Except the taxpayer. Don't mention the cost. Don't think of it.

But after the Monarch gets into full-scale production, the cost is expected to drop below two million dollars per missile (the stripped-down model, less the nuclear warhead, ground-support equipment and all the fancy extras). Cheap, a dinger of a bargain. Missiles by the dozen. At that price you could plaster them all over the landscape, fill the seas. Except you couldn't mention price. Only indirectly. It was good policy to let the community know how greatly its economic security depended on Western Aerospace. Yes, sir, fifteen thousand people pumped umpteen million bucks per year into the community's lifeblood, kept it from stagnating, kept the wolf away —the yearly guarantee of a new car, a new TV, a new mistress. No bread lines with good old WAD. Millions in salaries, millions to subcontractors—the money moved from hand-to-hand and everyone got a share. (So actually the Monarch didn't cost a dime. The money started with the people and ended with the people; the Monarch was simply a phenomenon born of the process.)

In effect, those were the messages he'd sent out. They sounded good, sounded wonderful, told a waiting world what it wanted to know. The reassuring voice. He was a man with a message—he, James Elliott, the bell ringer. Well, that was all right too. But there was only one thing:

Was it true? Was it?

He became aware that Harriett had entered, and glanced up.

"Mr. Bergstrom's secretary called."

"Well?" he asked brusquely.

"Mr. Bergstrom would like to see you."

Scanning some papers when Elliott arrived, Bergstrom nodded curtly.

"Sit down, Jim." His heavy face, seldom expressive, held a tired look; the black eyes were more sunken and the flesh beneath them hung in puffy folds. He's feeling the pressure, Elliott thought. Like all of them, his metabolism was attuned to the countdown, burning more furiously as time zero for the Monarch drew nearer. He stacked the papers and pushed them to one side.

"I'll be leaving for Florida Tuesday—want to get there a few days early to make certain everything's at go."

"The press material's ready," he offered.

"Good." The older man eyed him reflectively. "A smooth launching will put us over the top."

"I'd like to see it," he exclaimed impulsively.

"Unfortunately, we need you here. Maybe on a later firing . . ." He pursed his lips, speaking again. The gist of it was that they couldn't afford to slacken off. "Right now we must keep the publicity flowing—build up strong local support."

"Anything in particular?" he asked, sensing that the vice-president was driving toward a specific goal.

"I'd like to stress the theme of the city and the company as an economic partnership," Bergstrom replied.

"In what respect?"

"The dollar volume we dispense."

"We've done that."

"Not hard enough. Drive it home, stress our payroll, what we spend as a local buyer, the extent of our subcontract commitments." He spoke incisively. "I want big business, small business and labor to know what the stakes are, Jim. This is one of the most populous areas of the country; those are forces of influence."

"It'll take some researching."

Bergstrom disregarded the comment.

"You might slant some of the stories for the labor press."

"I'll see what I can do."

"I'll be away, so it's in your hands."

"I'll take care of it," he promised.

"I intend to hold a staff meeting before I leave—iron out our thinking on the launching, Jim." He weighed him for a long moment. "We have to start thinking about the future . . . the new look we discussed earlier."

"I've been gathering ideas along the line."

"Good."

The vice-president's voice held a note of finality and Elliott rose, asking, "Anything else?"

"Not at the moment. Oh, by the way, I've looked over your article on the Monarch fabrication. It was done very well."

"Thank you. I was planning on giving it to Barry Walsh."

Bergstrom leaned back and something in his face warned Elliott before he said, "Unfortunately, we can't use it."

"Why?" he demanded, surprised. "You asked for it."

"So I did."

"It's cleared for security."

Bergstrom looked somewhat ruffled. "Unfortunately, Koepple tackled the same thing, got it in first."

"It was clearly understood that I do it." He tried to suppress his resentment.

"I don't know about that, but it points up one thing"—Bergstrom folded his hands into a steeple and spoke disapprovingly—"this matter of duplication. You'll recall that I mentioned it earlier."

"You assigned the article to me," he repeated pointedly.

"Perhaps Art didn't understand."

"He understood all right."

Bergstrom appeared not to hear. "I realize the turmoil we've been in, but I hope to correct that soon."

"When?" He found the indirect reference to Vroman's job irritating, and didn't take pains to hide his feelings. A flicker of annoyance crossed Bergstrom's face.

"I expect to make a suitable appointment immediately following the hot firing."

"Anything else?" he asked bluntly.

"That should do it, Jim."

Elliott rose and started toward the door, then turned to ask, "By the way, how did Koepple handle his lead?"

Bergstrom raised his head questioningly. "Why, the same way you did—about the Monarch beginning its life as a roll of steel. I thought it quite a coincidence."

"You shouldn't." He spoke dryly. "You wrote it." He passed through the doorway before the vice-president could reply.

Sure, Koepple would start it that way; the chief of advertising was a brain-picker.

"Bergie's primed to make a decision," Harry Garfield confided to Esther Lynn over cocktails in a Beverly Hills lounge. "Right after the hot firing, I hear."

"Where'd you hear that?" she asked sharply.

"A friend . . . close to Bergie."

"Any idea who?" She watched him intently.

"No."

"You sound doubtful."

"Do I?"

"It would be a relief to know," she pouted.

"Yes." He felt his way cautiously, unhurriedly, aware that after tonight he'd be committed. But he had to go all the way. The dark girl across from him represented his hole card. Leaning toward her, he said, "Confidentially, we'd have it made if it weren't for one thing." He took care to emphasize the *we*. Resting his elbows on the table, he kept his eyes on her face, noting the compressed lips and sullen way she returned his gaze. It struck him that she was an angry girl, not with him but rather a life-directed anger that placed her in perpetual hostility to the world. The immediate corollary thought was that she neither recognized her hostility nor knew the wellsprings of its genesis. But he knew her, just as assuredly as he knew that tomorrow morning would come.

Deliberately he let the silence build until he forced her to ask: "Henderson?"

"You think that too?"

"It's possible."

He nodded. "He has an in, a solid one. He's gold-plated. If it weren't for him we'd be a cinch." She moved her head in agreement, leaning back as if to consider the statement, but her wary look told him that in reality she had paused to consider her own position—how much she should say and not say. So far she'd been picking her way cautiously, avoiding the pitfalls of outright commitment. That she was here with him now because he appeared a likely candidate, he had no doubt. It was the sort of cat-and-mouse game that he enjoyed.

She arched her eyes. "How about Elliott?" He shook his head negatively. "Why?" she persisted.

"Too new, not enough experience. His work's all right but when it comes to corporate policy, well . . ." He shrugged off-handedly; he couldn't worry over Elliott. Henderson had the drag, the ultimate, final drag that could outweigh all else. Unless . . .

"Henderson's just as new," she objected.

"Yes, but he knows someone."

"Bergie?"

"He's close."

"Do you know anything definite?"

"How close he is? No, but he certainly zoomed to the top in a hurry."

"Yes."

"That's just part of it," he added. Words, they were sparring. But he needed time.

"What's the other part?" she asked irritably.

"Henderson's weakness."

"What weakness?" she asked in a perplexed tone.

"Everyone has a weakness," he pointed out. "It's just a matter of finding it, then knowing what to do."

"You've found it?" She spoke softly, leaning toward him, scrutinizing his face as if hopeful of detecting the answer.

"Perhaps."

"You have or you haven't," she said logically. Her face portrayed her disappointment.

"It's a matter of how to use it."

"Use what?"

"His weakness."

"What is it?" she exclaimed impatiently.

He went on as if he hadn't heard her. "If we handled it right, we'd be as snug as two bugs in a rug."

"That would be sweet."

"It would be, and if we were willing to work a bit, we could cinch it."

"How?" she asked guardedly.

Deliberating the answer, he took refuge in another evasion. "How would you like to be private secretary to H. Garfield, director for public relations and advertising?"

"I'd like that very much."

"So would I. It could be quite pleasant."

"Quite pleasant." She stressed the words.

"It's a distinct possibility. And someday we'd move upstairs. Bergie won't be there forever."

She forced a quick smile. "That's planning ahead."

"So it is. But it's this first step we have to get over—the big one." The speculation in her face encouraged him. "It can be done."

"If I knew . . ."

"We're getting to it," he assured her.

"You make it sound easy."

"I have some ideas." He glanced at the ceiling, deciding there was no use in sparring. They had talked enough that each knew exactly where the other stood. In effect, he was committed. More, she had prepared herself to pull all stops, do whatever she had to do, regardless of any bruised feelings or risk. More than that, he had her, had her in the palm of his hand, just as he had Henderson. The time had come to go all out.

"Well?" she asked edgily.

"It's risky."

"What isn't?"

"But if we're careful . . ." He let the words trail, his eyes fixed on her face.

"It's my job too." She displayed a slight petulance.

"That's right, it's your job too." He emphasized the words, sensing both relief and victory in her admission. It was, in effect, a declaration of intent—she would do whatever she had to do to assure her own position. That she would be feathering his nest in the process was irrelevant. The cards were on the table, in plain sight—all but the hole card. "If Henderson gets it, he'll bring along his own girl," he added as a clincher.

"You said that before."

"So I did, and it's true. I have it on good authority that he has some doll over there lined up." Her quick, startled glance told him his words had scored. Dropping his voice, he said, "But he won't get it. Not unless we let him."

She returned his look expectantly, moving her tongue slowly over the curve of her lip in a manner he found both sensual and disturbing. He'd come to know her quite well; yet many things about her he didn't know, such as how close she might be to Bergie. A tug of caution made him debate how he might use the information he'd wrung from Witek without implicating himself too deeply. If only he had time. But he didn't, and that was the crux of the whole thing. The dark, shapely girl sitting across from him represented his last chance for the top of the blue badges, for Tuesday Bergstrom would leave for the Cape, and when he returned . . . ? *Harry the gambler*—the phrase ran through his mind. *Put your money on the line and take the plunge. You know the hole card.*

She broke the silence. "We've agreed, we're both working for the same thing . . . together." He caught the way she had injected meaning into the word and nodded. "You might as well tell me," she ended.

"I'm not holding back."

"Then what is it?"

"Maybe you'd rather not know."

"We're in this together," she impatiently reminded him.

"Bedmates," he agreed. Picking up his cigar he took a drag and replaced it in the ash tray, saying, "Sometimes it pays to be a bastard. It's about the only way one can get along any more."

"It seems that way." Her eyes were steady.

"So do we want to be bastards?"

"We want the jobs."

"It's a nice payoff."

She said crossly, "What is it?"

"I'm coming to it," he replied imperturbably, wishing she wouldn't push quite so hard. "Henderson's got a woman."

"I don't follow you." She arched her eyes.

"A woman, a horizontal playmate."

"So what? He's of age."

"Certainly, but this is different." He waited, watching the comprehension grow in her face. At the moment her dark eyes held a feline look, carnal and alert. She leaned closer.

"Who is she?"

"Like I said, this is dynamite."

"We're committed." She licked her lips.

"So we are." Weighing the next step, he decided to kibitz, tell her only as much as she had to know. He could attain the same end. He added, "I don't know."

Her face fell. "Then what good does it do?"

"My informant"—he emphasized the words—"tells me it's an executive's wife." As she sucked in her breath sharply, he continued, "That's one thing Bergie won't go for. He'd sack the man in a second."

"Yes, he would," she agreed. "But how could you find out?" She paused, showing a trace of uncertainty.

"We don't have to. That's the good part," he quickly assured her. "If Bergie knew that much, he'd investigate . . . and that would be the end of Mr. Eugene Henderson. He couldn't risk letting a scandal like that ride. He'd have a private eye on him so fast it'd make your head swim."

She tilted her head inquisitively. "The wife of one of the Space Electronics executives?"

He hesitated. "One of ours—quite high up, I understand." She tossed her head, her face sullen.

"Do you expect me to tell him?"

"Hell no, but if we played it right . . ."

"How?"

The single word told him he could stop worrying, and he asked, "How well do you know Joan?"

She looked thoughtful. "Pretty well. We have lunch together quite often, shop together once in a while. We're friendly enough."

"If . . . in the course of chatting . . . you dropped a hint, merely as a rumor, of course . . ." He spoke casually, trying not to say too much. She didn't answer immediately and he felt the quiet close in.

"That's risky," she finally stated.

"It shouldn't be. Do you think she'd pass it along to Bergie?"

"I don't know. Yes, I believe she would," she declared, changing her mind.

"Why?"

"Well, she's his private secretary. In a way, something like that would be her responsibility—to keep the boss informed. I would if I were in her place."

"They're that close, eh?"

"If you mean what I think you mean, I don't think so. Bergie's a pretty cold fish."

"No, I didn't mean that. I meant were they close enough for her to pass along that kind of rumor?"

"I'd say yes." Her eyes played over him speculatively.

"Think you could manage it?" Seeing the sudden caution in her face, he hastily added, "Just offhandedly, as a rumor. Don't make a point of it."

"Perhaps."

He added the clincher. "It's bound to come out anyway. Bergie'll hear it sooner or later, but later might be too late for us."

"I can do it," she decided.

"For God's sake, don't give the source." Suddenly he felt jittery, and wondered if he'd gone too far. She seemed to read his mind.

"Don't worry, I know how to handle it."

11

Chapter 11

THIS is a big week in the life of the corporation," Roland T. Bergstrom told his section heads. They were gathered in his small conference room for a kickoff talk prior to his departure for Florida. "We stand at the threshold of all that we've worked for, and while I feel that we have done a commendable job, I know that our most trying days lie ahead."

"A never-ending battle," Eugene Henderson asserted.

"A never-ending battle," he agreed, "but the prize is well worth the effort. Today our job is the Monarch countdown, tomorrow the big production contract. After that . . ."

As he paused, Henderson spoke again: "We'll be on our way."

"The GM of space," Garfield cut in.

"It depends on us, how well we sell," Bergstrom cautioned.

"We're salesmen, R. T."

The thought struck Elliott they were wrong—it depended on the Monarch, how well the bird proved itself in the crucible of fire.

"Don't get too cocky," Bergstrom rebutted. "We have a rocky road ahead."

"Are you speaking of the Monarch?"

"And the contracts beyond the Monarch. In the future we're going to have to be more malleable, shape our public relations and advertising to meet the exigencies of changing times and keep abreast of technological and policy change—"

"I think we do," Garfield interrupted.

The vice-president didn't answer, but let his eyes dwell on each person in turn, ending with Eugene Henderson. The latter had arrived at the conference with Bergstrom, and Elliott's immediate reaction had been: *Vroman was right. He has it wired.* Koepple appeared equally perturbed, but Garfield wore an odd smirk, and at the time he wondered why.

Bergstrom hunched forward, saying, "I can tell you, in confidence of course, that when that bird leaves the pad, we're suddenly going to find ourselves heading public relations for the nation's foremost weapon system. Not just another ICBM, gentlemen, but *the* ICBM."

Elliott lifted his eyes, surprised. Bergstrom obviously savored the moment. Resting on an elbow, he shook a cigarette from a pack, taking his time about lighting it. A twitching muscle in Koepple's jaw revealed his strain. Elliott felt sorry for him. The ad chief was tired. He switched his gaze to Carole, then back to Bergstrom, who continued:

"The usual procedure for a first missile launch—the one followed by the Atlas people, for example—is a limited try, using only the booster engines. We feel we've passed that stage."

"We're going all the way?" Garfield exclaimed incredulously. Elliott felt a sense of shock.

"All the way," Bergstrom affirmed. "Booster, staging, second stage engine, payload—we're hitting for the full operation. We're going to place a dummy nose cone smack in the middle of the Atlantic splash net. It's not full range—we'd need the Indian Ocean for that—but it's well over five thousand miles. I don't have to tell you what that means."

"Isn't that risky?"

"Risky?"

"It's betting a lot on the first shot, R. T."

"Is it, Harry?" Bergstrom narrowed his eyes and Elliott realized he had interpreted the query as a reflection on company policy. Henderson smirked and he felt his dislike kindle anew. Harry was right, it was risky. A good six or eight seconds passed before Bergstrom continued:

"Our engineers and scientists don't believe so. Neither do Welkes or Byerkoff, and the Air Force has bought it. The launch stand, blockhouse, ground-support equipment, missile . . . everything has been tested and retested, thoroughly and many times, so I believe we are on safe ground. Does that answer your question?" He smiled acidly.

Garfield flushed, and setting his jaw in a hard line, said, "I'm still surprised."

"I think it's a great idea," Henderson cut in. His words implied that he had already known of the plan. "They pulled that stunt with the Minuteman and they've been using it to sell solids ever since. This will pull the spotlight back to liquids."

"Exactly," Bergstrom agreed.

"There's no doubt but that it would move us into operational status sooner," Garfield conceded.

Bergstrom nodded. "That's the point. This can tip the scales in our favor, influence the decision-makers. We're well ahead of schedule on our base activation; now the problem is to overcome our own lead, push an operational missile into the field at the earliest possible moment. Believe me, time's at a premium."

"We need the full-range flight," Henderson explained, looking at the chief of publicity. "It has glamour you'd never get using just the booster. We have to assess some of these things in terms of public relations rather than engineering."

As Garfield flushed angrily, Bergstrom said, "That was Welkes' point."

"Aside from that, I have full confidence in the bird."

"So do I, Eugene. We can be proud of it."

For some reason Elliott thought of Tweedledum and Tweedledee. Bergie and Henderson were like the drawings on Carole's wall: whatever one said, the other agreed to. Or was he sour? Reflecting on it, he decided it was the latter. In all truth, Bergstrom hadn't shown any particular favors. But Elliott realized he felt differently of late—less certain, more skeptical. When had it started? The loss of the test missile? With Carole? Walsh? Vroman? Tension, he mused. They had waited too long for this day. They had put everything they had into the bird, and now it was the bird's turn. He'd be glad when they lit the candle.

He returned his attention to Bergstrom, who was saying, "I expect this to establish a landmark in our own operations. That's why I mentioned malleability. You'll remember, I spoke of a new program earlier."

"I've been thinking a great deal about it," Garfield cut in.

"I hope we all have." The vice-president let his eyes wander around the table. "I consider the launching as the kickoff for a new look. We're going on the offensive, moving into the marketplace with an aggressive program. We have a product to market, and we're going to market it."

Someone asked quietly, "What kind of a new look?"

"A forward look, the look of confidence."

"The Monarch look—that's what we should call it," Garfield asserted.

"I'm using that," Koepple complained.

Bergstrom raised his eyes. "The Monarch look?"

"The Monarch—a new look in weapon systems," he explained. "Carole did the artwork for it."

"I rather like that, Art." Bergstrom inclined his head approvingly. "It has a catchy ring."

"I'm trying to plant the idea of the future—show that we're ahead of the game."

"And we are." Bergstrom glanced at his notes. "I'd like to acquaint you with the general outlines of what we propose so you can give it some thought. But first I'd like to say this. I know we've been working under a handicap lately—some strain and uncertainty—but I can promise that everything will be ironed out once we get the bird in the air."

"Is that firm?" Garfield asked contentiously. Hunched forward, his eyes fixed the vice-president aggressively. Elliott had to admire him. Garfield wouldn't drop the offensive until the final count, if then.

"Immediately on my return," Bergstrom responded promptly. "I intend to make that the first item of business." In the silence that followed, Garfield cast a swift glance at Henderson. It struck Elliott that the chief of publicity saw the handwriting on the wall—that he had pegged Henderson as the future director. The fleeting smirk came again, puzzling him. But Henderson didn't have it yet, wouldn't have until the small blue memo came around. As for himself, he'd hang to the fact that the job remained open, that technically, at least, he was very much in the running. Briefly he wondered what he would do if the decision were adverse.

Bergstrom straightened briskly.

"In the future, we'll delve more heavily into psychology, politics, the socio-economics of the day—in short, the Big Picture. We'll be dealing with a missile which, we're certain, will occupy a favored niche in the hierarchy of free-world weapon systems. It's our responsibility to place us in that favored position." He paused, slowly moving his head, holding his body in the expectant attitude of one seeking agreement. One hand, square and stubby-fingered, rested on the table.

"The big, big time." It was Henderson who broke the silence. Koepple nodded with a slight, birdlike movement, his lips tight. It occurred to Elliott that his career had been a succession of big pictures, a term used to describe almost any publicity structure, or the market to which it applied.

The vice-president said abruptly, "We're moving out of low gear."

"I don't follow this," Garfield challenged. "We've created an image of the Monarch that's nationally accepted, or at least everyone knows what it is and what it looks like. Take our slogans, *The Space Master, The Bird of Freedom,* for instance. Anyone hearing either of them would immediately think of the Monarch, know it's an ICBM, realize what it means to our defense and space programs; yet you tell us we're in low gear. Frankly, I don't get it."

"I meant low gear in another sense," Bergstrom said. "We've been approaching the market with a soft sell, as if unaware of competition. Now we're going to recognize that we have competition, stack our bird against it and battle for the number one position. That's Welkes' decision, and Byerkoff concurs. We'll consider the Monarch not as an ICBM but as *the* ICBM. In the Nation's ICBM program, we represent the end product—the ultimate weapon. That's our message."

"That will take some selling, R. T." Garfield appeared skeptical.

"It will, Harry, but we can do it."

They discussed ways and means. Henderson wanted to push for declassification of the Monarch's decoy system, plug its invulnerability, downgrade Nike-Zeus. He argued that making the Zeus the goat would arouse a controversy which would keep the Monarch in the spotlight, thus overshadowing the Atlas and Titan. It was, he said, self-generating publicity. Koepple warned against it. He didn't believe they should mention another system by name. He preferred to upgrade the Monarch. Garfield favored building a program around the sea-launch capability, stressing this as a step beyond Polaris.

"That'll give us Air Force support," he contended.

"So will putting the skids to the Zeus," Henderson rejoined. "Zeus is half dead."

"We should finish it off," he reasoned. Elliott listened quietly, aware he had no stomach for the argument. All he wanted was to get the bird launched, get on with it. But he noted that Bergstrom followed the exchange with interest.

"We want an assumption of power," Henderson stated. "If we assume the Monarch's the top bird, others will assume it. That's pure psychology."

"Good thinking," Bergstrom interceded. "I want that assumption reflected in all our media—news, audio-visual, advertising."

"I do that anyway," Koepple answered querulously.

Bergstrom appeared not to hear him. "During the Monarch's development, we fought at the fringes of the ICBM industry. Western Aerospace was a stepchild battling for the fringe dollar. That's past. I want our program to reflect that. Now we're battling for the big dollar. It's a dollar that can only be split so many ways; that's the corporation's problem. That and the fact that we can't produce the kind of weapon system the Nation requires and deserves while we're dealing with pennies." He paused, looking around, and the echo of Vroman's words rang in Elliott's mind like a distant bell—the big dollar, the fought-over dollar. The vice-president was talking pure economics, not missiles, even though he equated the two. Garfield's lips framed a question, leaving it unasked as Bergstrom continued:

"There are strong indications that the Nation can't continue to support both a growing defense structure and an expanding space program. Something has to give. Mr. Slater, if nothing else, alerted us to that danger. The corporation expects it to be a prime issue at the next budget session."

"We're just getting under the wire," Hendersom commented.

"We are. The launching comes none too soon. Aside from that, we face expanded Minuteman and Polaris programs, a hefty chunk for Skybolt—a drive to increase solid propellants. The danger signals are in the air. We have to recognize the fact that the difficulty at Desert Center raised awkward questions."

"Everyone's lost test missiles," Garfield objected.

"The questions are still there, Harry."

"We'll answer them."

"We are answering them. The full-range flight is an answer, but we can't erase the fact of the loss, or the damage caused by the rumors. Some people have long memories."

"When it serves them."

Bergstrom straightened thoughtfully and Garfield fell silent.

"What I have to tell you now is corporation confidential information and I'd like you to treat it as such." In the hush that followed, all eyes were riveted to the vice-president's face. He let the silence prevail for a number of seconds before continuing. "One of the ICBM systems might be pared drastically, conceivably eliminated. Corporation policy is to favor that view, but to plant ourselves so solidly that we won't be the one chopped. There are, of course, certain advantages in a pared-down field."

"Are we that solid?" Elliott asked, wondering why he bothered. This kind of thing would be determined at a White House-

DOD-USAF summit. Even the contemplation of it here seemed ridiculous.

Bergstrom said quietly, "We will be. The Department of Defense is excited over our sea-launch capability. Stark's been doing some talking in Washington, and I can tell you, we're getting an excellent reception. It'll be the biggest innovation in weaponry since the V-2. I don't have to tell you what that means in the way of contracts. All we need is a successful flight. After that, our stance will be aggressive. We have a good, marketable ICBM and we're not going to be backward about selling it."

"How do you propose to go about this?" Elliott pursued, aware of Carole's eyes.

"We have to convince the Nation that we have the best product, not the second best," the vice-president explained. "We must treat competing programs as if they were stopgap systems, a means of plugging the dike until the Monarch gets into full-scale production. It'll take clever wording."

"Then we are going to mention names . . . the competition?" Koepple asked, wonderingly.

"We are, Art, when necessary."

"It'll be a dogfight," Garfield interrupted.

"It already is, below the surface."

"Those babies will fight back."

"We're in the marketplace," Bergstrom replied pointedly. "We'll do what we have to do to sell our wares. You know the techniques."

"I'm not objecting, R.T."

"I didn't think you would, Harry." Bergstrom favored him with a nod. "At the same time, we want to take a firm stand against solids—show the superiority of our system."

"The full-range flight will do that," Henderson stated.

"It would be extremely helpful. I don't mind saying we have some strong friends in Washington, and in the Air Force and NASA too, but we have to supply the ammunition."

"We're striking out in a lot of directions," Garfield warned.

"We have to, Harry."

"The solids people can muster a lot of strength."

"We're in the process of identifying that."

"The opposition?"

"And strength." Bergstrom paused musingly. "We have to establish public empathy—sell the idea that the Monarch is *your* missile, it protects *you*."

"Like investing in a war bond," Koepple reflected.

"A good analogy, Art."

"The Monarch—the people's friend." Garfield snickered.

Bergstrom disregarded him. "Our prime endeavor should be to make each person feel like a shareholder. I recognize that there are certain canons of ethics and techniques to which we must adhere, but I have every faith that our product is fully as good as we believe it to be and will claim it to be. We have to establish that knowledge in the public mind."

"Rapport," Henderson asserted.

"Yes, rapport." Listening, Elliott realized Bergstrom had echoed Vroman's main indictment—that the missile had to be sold regardless of its merits. But that didn't reflect on the Monarch itself, only on the people selling it. It had nothing to do with the question of necessity.

"Let's not forget the space picture," Bergstrom cautioned. "We want to hold the Guardian in the limelight along with the Monarch. The corporation expects a hefty increase in the space budget. The politics are touchy but I believe we can find our way. Again we have a share at stake."

"How about the orbital weapon system and Space Scanner contracts?" Garfield asked.

"We're bidding them."

"It's a cream pot, R. T."

"It is, Harry. Stark's been talking with the Air Force people and we stand a good chance for a bite, perhaps even the military satellite."

"What's the dollar value?"

"Around two hundred million . . . as a starter."

"A nice plum."

"Very nice." Bergstrom glanced around. "But let's go on with our plans for the Monarch. We should start by stressing its unique capabilities—things the competition lacks, such as its sea-launch potential."

"I'd love to break that in an ad," Koepple observed wistfully.

"Perhaps you can, Art."

"Is it being declassified?"

"Stark talked with General Broadmire . . . set the wheels in motion. The Air Force is highly perturbed since the hearing. They're as eager to break it as we are. It'll only be a limited go-ahead, but once we plant a wedge . . ."

"A neat angle to offset the Polaris," Henderson observed, as if unaware he had argued against it a short time before. It gave Elliott a new insight into his makeup.

"Definitely, but we still have worries. Between anti-missiles, solids and liquid competitors, we haven't a tailored path. If it's not our enemies, it's our friends." Bergstrom smiled without humor. "We have our work cut out."

"We'll get a good, bang-up program going," Garfield promised. "Perhaps the competition's good. I know it keeps me on my toes."

As the talk became general, the vice-president turned to Elliott: "You did an excellent job on the local economic picture, Jim. I'd like you to follow that up. Welkes was pleased. He wants to hit it hard—show exactly what our dollar is doing for the town."

They discussed it briefly, then Bergstrom swung back, waiting until the room quieted, and said, "Welkes made a statement that clings to my mind, and before closing, I'd like to repeat it. 'Our job is to sell missiles.' I believe that sums our position pretty well. Bear it in mind and build a program around it. If there are no questions, that should do it."

"Negative," someone answered. Elliott straightened, glad to see the session end.

As they were rising, the vice-president said to Henderson, "I'd like to have you stop by a moment, Eugene."

Elliott timed his exit to intercept Carole at the door, and said sheepishly, "Hi."

"Hello, Jim." She answered without looking at him, the cool kind of "hello" he might get from almost anyone. He fell into step alongside her as they walked toward the elevator.

"Look," he said, "isn't it time we stopped playing games? I'll admit, I was mad, but so were you. It's silly to keep on this way."

"I'm not angry, Jim."

"You're not?"

"Disappointed." Before he could reply, she continued, "This should answer some of your questions."

"Bergstrom's pitch?"

"The big sell."

"You can't blame him," he argued defensively. "It's his job."

"And yours."

"Yes, mine too," he replied stiffly.

In the silence that followed, he felt his last chance slipping by, and with it a sense of desperation. He was wrong and she was wrong—both were utterly wrong. A word on his part could make everything right again. Or a word on hers. But she wouldn't say the word. Her compressed lips, the tight set of her face, told him that. He glanced at her, seeking the right thing to say without complete capitulation. She held her eyes straight ahead, her expression immutable, and walked down the long corridor of Kingdom Hall as if alone.

"Carole," he began, "we have . . ."

"We've said it all, haven't we, Jim?" she interrupted. He set his lips firmly.

They walked the rest of the way in silence.

Esther Lynn was having lunch with Joan Wesley when the talk turned to the subject of their work, and seeing her chance she asked, "Who do you think will take Vroman's place?"

"I don't know," Joan answered cautiously.

"It would be nice to know who I'll be working for," she murmured.

"It shouldn't be long."

"After the launching, I hear." Joan's eyes were noncommittal. "For a while I thought it would be Elliott."

"Oh . . . ?"

"The rumor," she explained.

"There's nothing to it."

"The rumor, or his getting the job?"

"Both," Joan replied.

Watching her, Esther felt certain she knew more than she admitted, else why was she so positive? Pondering how to pursue the opening, she said, "I can't imagine Koepple."

"Neither can I."

"That leaves Garfield and Henderson." She gazed fixedly at her companion.

"Garfield?" Joan uttered the name distastefully.

"Don't you think . . . ?"

Joan returned her look. "I couldn't say, Esther. I really couldn't, but . . ."

Esther felt a quick stab of panic. Joan wouldn't say, wouldn't betray a confidence from Bergstrom, but that *but* . . . It revealed her friend's thoughts completely, told her everything she wanted to know. Her mind raced. If Garfield were out, that left only Henderson, in which event she, too, was out. Or so he had claimed.

Almost without thinking, she said, "He's certainly more eligible than Henderson."

In the shocked hush following her words, she glimpsed the quick, startled expression that flashed across the other's face before she managed to ask, "Why do you say that?"

The tone of her voice should have warned her, but it didn't, and she blurted, "Why it's common knowledge he's having an affair with some executive's wife."

"I don't believe it," Joan snapped.

"That's what I heard."

She didn't answer, but glanced quickly away, her face distraught. Esther watched her uneasily, wanting to undo the blunder. Damn, she thought bitterly, leave it to me to bitch it up. Joan's reaction—the shock, sudden withdrawal, hurt—told her more than any number of words. The young fool had a crush on Henderson, and she had little doubt but that it was reciprocated. Strange, she had never suspected the involvement, but she should have. Things like that usually got around. So that was the source of Henderson's drag. He'd been using Bergstrom's secretary. And who else? Looking at Joan now, she felt as if they were two strangers sharing a table.

They finished lunch in silence, and when they parted in the hall, it was with scarcely more than a strained nod on Joan's part. Esther felt dead inside. She had killed herself with Henderson—Joan would see to that. She would be absolutely vitriolic, and so would he. At the same time, she saw in Joan's statement a death knell for Garfield's hopes, since she could only have revealed Bergstrom's views. It was that simple.

Trying to assess the situation logically, she brought the disordered facts together. If Garfield were out, three candidates were left. But Henderson *was* out too. Garfield had been right. A secret as big as the one involving the Space Electronics man couldn't be kept, and once it became known . . . And it would become known. Garfield would see to that. His urgency to solicit her assistance and the lengths to which he already had gone were too great to imagine that he would have any scruples when it came to spreading the story.

That left Elliott and Koepple.

Between the two, she decided it most certainly would be Elliott. Koepple puttered around like an old lady, habitually worried or fussing, not seeming at all like the kind of man the vice-president would choose. He'd want someone like himself —big, with assurance, someone who could meet people, convince them. That described Elliott perfectly.

Sitting at her desk, she felt suddenly quiet inside. Elliott would get the job. All the signs pointed that way. But he didn't know it. That was the thing. He didn't, and she did. He probably considered Henderson his chief competition, and if she gave him the ammunition to dispose of that threat . . .

She examined the point. He didn't act as hard or as aggressive as Garfield, but she sensed a drive in him that told her he could be ruthless if the price were right. Well, the price was right, for them both. She found herself appalled at how little she actually knew of him—almost nothing when she tabulated it. Large, better-looking than most despite the scarred face, he possessed a quiet easiness and humorous smile that she found in sharp contrast with the others. Even the night she had picked him up at Koepple's . . . She purposefully had avoided him after that, to force him to come running. Only he hadn't come. But it wasn't too late . . . she had to cling to that.

She let the thoughts run through her mind.

She found him at his desk, leaning on an elbow while he read some copy. The quitting whistle had blown a few moments earlier, and with the exception of Joe Stone, bent over his typewriter in the outer office, everyone else had gone. She paused uncertainly in the doorway. Deep of chest, husky, he dwarfed the desk, but she scarcely noticed that, more concerned with how to approach him. She'd have to play it by ear— She stirred and he glanced up.

"Hello, Esther."

"I . . ." Her tongue touched her lip nervously.

"Sit down," he invited. "Something on your mind?"

She nodded. "If I'm not interrupting."

"Not at all."

She sat across from him, probing for words, and finally blurted, "It's about the job."

"Worried?" he asked softly.

"No." She tried to pull her thoughts into some semblance of order. "I liked working for Mr. Vroman."

"He was tops."

"Yes, he was." She pursed her lips. "I don't know who will get it next."

"Neither do I, but I wouldn't worry." Knowing he meant to reassure her, she inclined her head in assent, uncertain how to proceed. "I doubt the change will affect you," he finished.

She forced a smile. "I feel that too. In fact, Mr. Bergstrom practically said as much."

"Then why worry?"

"I'm not sure I'd want the job." She hesitated deliberately.

"Not under certain circumstances." When he failed to respond, she continued: "I don't know that I could work for the man who might get it."

"Oh?"

"Henderson," she finished lamely.

"He wouldn't be bad to work for, Esther. Eugene's all right when you know him."

"Well, I like Mr. Bergstrom . . ."

"What's that got to do with it?"

"Everything." She leaned forward, saying quickly, "He's doing something Mr. Bergstrom wouldn't approve. It would cost him any chance he might have for the job if he knew and, well, I couldn't work for him under the circumstances."

"You want advice?"

"Yes, of course." She felt the silence well between them and managed to add, "Mr. Henderson is mixed up with some executive's wife. So you see . . ."

He straightened perceptibly. "I don't want to know the name."

"I don't know who it is," she confessed, hiding her disappointment. He didn't look like a man trying to get a job, not like Garfield. He had grabbed the ball, but quick.

He asked soberly, "If you don't know the name, how do you know it's true?"

"Everyone knows it," she said defensively.

"Does Bergstrom?"

"Everyone except him."

"I doubt it. At any rate, you could be doing him an injustice. Supposing it isn't true?"

"Well . . ." She compressed her lips, thinking she was getting into deep water. "I hope it's not true. I sincerely hope so, but I'd hate to work for him if it were. That's why I wanted advice. I had to talk to someone."

"I wouldn't mention it," he cautioned. "It's probably just another rumor."

"I hope so."

"So do I. Now do you want my advice?" His eyes held her and she hesitated, struggling for the right words. Finally she just nodded. "Forget about it," he advised. "You'll feel better if you do."

If Elissa Bergstrom had been asked "What is the dominating theme of your life?" she most assuredly would have answered, "Boredom."

That condition, except for a few prized occasions, had been with her for almost as long as she could remember. It was, she mused, as if she had been born into a timeless world which unerringly ran in one direction, where each event and each day shadowed some previous event or day, so that life took on the aspects of the second reading of a book. Whatever enjoyment she found was dimmed by the knowledge that the stimulus could never be as sharp or as satisfying as the original.

At age seventeen, a quietly conducted campaign to escape the tedium of her surroundings terminated with surprising suddenness in the room of a college student she had chanced to meet through a girl friend. She was left with some discomfort and considerable awe at the ease with which she had managed the transition from girlhood to womanhood. Mingled with it were seeds of contempt, not toward herself but toward the now all-but-forgotten student, although she never quite understood why.

But it was not until her junior year in college that she envisioned the possibility of complete escape. It came in the form of Roland T. Bergstrom, who at age thirty she saw as a tall, ruggedly handsome figure with a commanding position in public relations at Midwest Aeronautical Corporation, one of the

Nation's industrial giants. That he was nine years older than she only added to her desire, for in her eyes he was mature, suave, a man-of-the-world, and while he didn't ride a white charger, he did possess a late-model Plymouth convertible with red leather upholstery, he did speak knowingly of famous personages. Apparently the fascination had been mutual, for they were married within a month of the day they first met.

Before a year had passed, she bitterly recognized her mature, suave, man-of-the-world for what he really was—in her eyes, a slow-moving, big-shouldered, rather handsome man who had chosen to dedicate his life to the corporation with the same earnestness with which another man might embrace the priesthood. She perceived that he had married simply because that was the respectable thing to do, but that he considered marriage secondary to his work. The corporation represented his real home and school and church. In it, or so she judged, he had found a personal trinity composed of board chairman, president, and the senior vice-president for public relations and advertising. Not for several years did she realize that in his eyes the trinity merely symbolized the exposed face of the corporation, which was an entity in itself. With that knowledge came the awareness that people who composed or ran it, from Byerkoff down to the lowliest janitor, the huge buildings which housed its tens of thousands of workers, the voracious machines which consumed vast amounts of raw materials and disgorged finished parts or the products themselves, whether dime-sized diodes or ninety-six-foot-long Monarchs, were important only to the degree to which each contributed. A creature of insatiable appetite, it consumed men, raw products, such intangible things as ideas and dreams, and on such fare, thrived and grew.

This, however, she found not half so maddening as her husband's attitude toward marriage. Although far from the patriarch her own father had been, he held a disconcertingly similar view: a woman's place was in the home. He expected little of her other than that she should mirror other corporation wives who, to her, formed an ornamental clique of tea-pourers and purveyors of meaningless chatter. As such, she would speak from the script of habit, and always say and do exactly the right thing. Worse, she came to believe that he considered her incapable of thought, other than as it related to the trivialities of wifely and domestic duties. Her old existence had been recreated, with only the promise changed; the material aspects were on a grander scale.

She could never quite reconcile the air of decorum which enshrouded their lives with his job, or its undercurrent of after-work liaisons, and she found it exasperating that he regarded his profession as a man's work, just as he regarded matters pertaining to money and love as peculiarly male provinces. Eventually, however, he perceived her perspicacity, especially with regard to people, even to the point of occasionally seeking her advice. Over the years, when no children came of the marriage, he included various clubs and other places of social gatherings as falling under the province of the home, or at least as an extension of it; later he even encouraged her toward such activities. Still, she had failed to find the freedom which she so ardently sought.

She was moodily considering the past when Henderson called from the kitchen, "Ready for another drink?"

"I still have this," she answered tonelessly.

"You'll never get stiff that way."

"Do I have to get stiff?" He didn't answer immediately and she heard the clink of ice cubes.

"Everything all right?" he finally asked.

"Yes, of course."

"You sound tired."

"I am tired." It was the truth. She was tired—damnably so,

filled with a weariness that nagged her mind but left her body strangely untouched. Listening to him move around the kitchen, she brooded. In all fairness she had tried to fit the picture her husband had created of her, or was it for her? She had been the perfect wife and hostess, charming and witty, with just the right amount of giddiness to appeal to his friends and, more important, to his superiors. She had been one of Hamilton Cronkhill's favorites. But with all that she had tried to carve a bit of existence of her own.

Now, sitting on the couch in front of the television set in Eugene Henderson's apartment, she felt unutterably bored. A handsome blue satin negligee flowed elegantly around her, both covering and revealing, and she sipped a martini and pondered why she was there. The flame which had taken her to him had glimmered and died, suddenly, just as other flames, had died. Or did the flame actually consist of nothing more then the risk, the elements of the chase, the moment of exposure when her husband would stand in the light of the life he had created for them and see its results?

She found the idea intriguing.

Henderson was not the empty façade in an expensive suit that some people believed. She had early perceived his ambition, ability, and selfishness, a trio of qualities which fascinated her. He had much the same drive as her own husband, but with one notable difference: Bergstrom labored, devoting his energies and sacrificing others that he might enhance the corporation; Henderson also labored, but he sought only to enhance his own position. She defined it as the difference between working for the corporation and having the corporation work for you, although oddly enough, the company benefited in both instances. He had few ideas of his own, but served as a funnel through which ideas flowed; he gathered them in and dispersed them, putting each to work to perform a given task. As her husband often reminded, this function constituted the essence of PR administration.

Realistically, she realized that Henderson had but one genuine interest in her—what she could do for him. That, in itself, she had found exciting. In the beginning, it had seemed a fair trade; he had gained the post at Space Electronics, and she had maintained the privilege of enjoying the horns which her husband unknowingly wore. She liked to think of them as gigantic antlers displayed above a very small mantel. But Henderson, too, had palled, and the affair had become a diversion which no longer diverted.

She heard the tinkle of ice cubes again as he came from the kitchen and, stopping behind her, leaned down and pressed his face into her hair. She waited, eyes closed, enduring the moment. Walking around the couch, he sat on a hassock facing her.

"You know, I keep thinking about that damned job," he said.

She knew the affair was finished, and now he knew it. She hadn't told him in so many words, it hadn't been necessary. He had fought against it, assaulting her coldness with an ardor which served only to increase her resolve. She had found a cruel satisfaction in the unspoken desperation in which he beheld not only the end of the affair, but also the end of his hopes. The battle was unspoken—her withdrawal against his aggression, her determination to leave and his attempts to persuade her to remain. In leaving, she had won. Oddly enough, he hadn't reacted to defeat at all as she thought he might, but had merely smiled, almost boyishly, saying ,"It was a good try."

They both knew exactly what he meant. Momentarily she wondered if she had underestimated him. Certainly he had lost with grace, and she resolved, in any case, not to stand in his way.

She failed to notice the car parked a short distance behind her as she drove away, or the girl at the wheel who watched her with large, pain-filled eyes.

On the eve of his departure for Florida, Herbert P. Welkes had a confidential chat with Lyman Stark.

"We have to cinch that production contract," Welkes was saying. "We can't gamble."

"We shouldn't have trouble," Stark counseled.

"We have to be certain."

"I'm pushing it."

"General Rylander?"

"He's the key man," Stark assented. He fixed the president sharply. "Why the sudden concern?"

"Byerkoff called," Welkes admitted. "He has a feeling that the Air Force might be reluctant to push the Monarch too hard at this time."

"Did he give a reason?"

"It might detract from their chances to sell a full-blown program in intermediate range missiles."

"An Air Force fear or his own?"

"Apparently the Air Force."

"Bad if true," Stark mused, "but I'm inclined to doubt it."

"Why?"

"Our sea-launch, H. P. It's a damned potent sales capability and the Air Force knows it."

"We can't bank on it, Lyman." Welkes observed him attentively. "Has Rylander ever mentioned this point?"

"That the Air Force might balk? No."

"Ask him, put it to him bluntly," Welkes ordered. "Byerkoff expects an answer."

"I'll do that," Stark promised, "and I'll call Alex Barmon, see what he knows."

"Good." The president leaned back thoughtfully. "Rylander's near retirement, isn't he?"

"Quite close, I believe."

"Has he ever discussed it?"

"Not directly."

"You might sound him out—offhandedly, as a conversational piece, of course."

Stark looked interested. "What are the table stakes?"

"We're growing, Lyman. Perhaps a v.p.?"

"That's not the biggest plum."

"With a stock option?"

"That helps."

"I'll leave it in your hands," Welkes decided. "The only thing I'm interested in right now is the contract. We have to cinch it. Whatever Rylander has in mind, we can top. Put that in your portfolio of facts, Lyman."

"I'll do that."

They discussed it for a while, and when Stark rose to leave, Welkes urged, "Better check the status of the orbital weapon system contract while you're East."

"It's on my list."

"Good." His lips wreathed curiously as he watched the tall figure of his executive vice-president make his exit. Stark was a good man.

A very good man.

He sat in a corner of the room under the sharp cone of a floor lamp with parts of a manuscript scattered around him, occasionally making notes as he sought to review and piece together the forgotten parts of the story, grasping at the lean straws of memory.

The rest of the apartment was dark.

When he heard the light rap on the door, he said, "Come in," without rising.

Carole entered, walking to the edge of the cone of light before she halted. She wore a plain blue dress with a high white collar and a simple dark jacket that served to make her features pale in contrast. He pushed aside the manuscript, watching her curiously. Her face was cold and composed. Finally she said, "You didn't expect me?"

"No."

"You know why I'm here?"

"I believe so."

"I want to be free of you, Jim. I want to be as I was before I met you. If there's nothing between us but the physical, then there's nothing." She spoke in a low flat voice without moving her eyes. She kept them on his face, absolutely expressionless.

"Carole," he began.

"Hear me, Jim. I told you I felt like a fool, and I do. I believed in you, and what we had, and when I did, I didn't deny you, Jim. I gave myself freely. But when it came to sharing our lives, there was nothing to share, nothing but our bodies. I want you, Jim. From the first time I saw you I wanted you. But I hate you too—for being what you are, for wanting you, for making me as I am." She caught her breath, touching her lips with her tongue, then continued: "I want to be free of you—your hands, your lips, your claim on my body. I want to rid myself of the tension, the torment of needing you. I want to be myself— clean, released from the doubt and uncertainty and arguments and rationalizations over a future which doesn't exist. I want to end your claim on me, Jim. Now. I can't change the person I was and I can't live with the person I am." She stood resolutely, her face controlled.

Silence filled the room. He sat relaxed, and yet taut; a muscle twitched in his cheek.

"I can't hold you, Carole," he said. "Either I'm sufficient, or I'm not. Only you can decide.

"I came to you as one kind of a person," he went on, "and I am still that kind of person, unchanged. I didn't cheat you or lie to you, Carole. I made no pretensions. I offered you what I was, not what you expected I might be. Nor did I make any demands of you. I accepted you as you were, gladly. I offered you my love and I was grateful for yours."

"You say you have no claim . . ." She eyed him numbly. "Do you know the torment I'm in?"

"Do you think you're alone, Carole?"

"You say you love me."

"I love you very dearly. I told you that, even though you've never told me."

"Jim . . ."

"Hear me out, Carole. You know what I am. Think back. You've always known it. You told me as much when you said you'd never surrender any part of yourself."

"But I did."

"And I did. We accepted each other as we were, or at least I did. I didn't ask anything except what you offered. Can you deny that?"

"It's my fault," she said dully. "I haven't come here to fight with you, Jim, but only to free myself."

"It's no one's fault," he gently contradicted. "You were looking at one person and seeing another, but I can't be that other person. I am myself, just like you are yourself, and putting me in a different environment wouldn't change me, Carole."

"Jim . . ." She looked away, clasping her hands nervously, and he continued:

"I love you, want you for what you are. Do you believe I would have you different? Yet you demand that I be different, that I conform to some picture you hold of me. I can't do it, Carole. I can only offer what I am. You'll have to decide."

"Jim, I came here . . ."

"I know why you came. You're very lovely."

"Don't say that."

"I love you."

"No."

"You can't deny how I feel. You can only deny your own feelings. You're not fighting me, you're fighting yourself. I told you that before. The job's just a pretext, an excuse erected in your mind to justify not surrendering all the way, Carole. That's why you'd never admit to loving me, not even with what we've had. You know why? Because true love is total surrender. It can't be a halfway measure. Can you deny any of that? Can you? I love you, Carole. Look at me." She raised her eyes slowly.

"Jim . . . Jim . . ." Tears brimmed her eyes and she began to sob brokenly.

12

Chapter 12

ELLIOTT felt the bustle, like a wind permeating the big plant, sifting through the administration and engineering buildings, the complexes of laboratories and shops, mingling with the factory noises. Present in the subdued atmosphere of Kingdom Hall, from which most of the lords of the missile had gone to Florida to witness its launching, it also penetrated the basement of the administration building, where the janitors had their headquarters, the stock and storage warehouses, pump chambers, the hush of the large temperature-controlled analogue and digital computer rooms in which giant machines busily plotted man's future.

The excitement had been building all morning; suppressed in the earlier hours, it took on more restless forms as time for the launching grew near, so that people's faces, if not their voices, proclaimed: *The bird is on the pad—ready, ready, ready.* . . .

Yes, the bird was on the pad, still locked in its great trussed-steel gantry under a blue Florida sky, listening to the tolling of time, waiting. It mattered not that men had been hurled into orbits, that probes had sought the moon from this selfsame place, for today was its day. The bird built from dreams and blueprints, from great sheets of steel, plastic, and electronic, electrical, mechanical, hydraulic and pneumatic parts, now awaiting the lighting of the torch that would give it life—send it spanning the earth in a great trajectory to land its nose cone at a spot designated "X" somewhere in the emptiness of the South Atlantic.

The bird was ready, ready, ready. Everyone knew it. The welder, the pattern-maker, the electrician and the chemist knew it; the engineer, the scientist and the computer man knew it; so did the gardeners who cared for Byerkoff's green parks, the chefs and cashiers in the glass-walled cafeteria, the guards at the gates. The bird was ready.

In the plant's two great empires—one of hardware and one of paper—anticipation lay like a heavy hand, stifling all but the excitement felt over the bird. The mood was one of ebullience and tenseness mingled, an exhilaration tinged with fear. In the empire of hardware the great machines sounded less loud, the welding torches appeared less bright, the movements of cranes and tugs and people more subdued, as if the green badges had paused, awaiting a voice from Florida. In the paper empire of typewriters, duplicating and addressing machines, calculators, dictaphones, computers and drafting machines, the slackening off was even more noticeable.

People walked through the hallways, nodding and whispering to one another as if engaged in a giant conspiracy. Green, striped and blue badges mingled indiscriminately. Voices on the telephones spoke more briskly, smiles came more spontaneously, the small groups of talkers grew more numerous and the coffee machines busier as somewhere in Florida time was tolled off, a knell which would resound in the corridors of aerospace history. Or so it was hoped.

The bird is going all the way.

The secret spread in the form of whispers, guarded conversations. Jobs were left undone, appointments postponed, schedules fell by the wayside, for today nothing mattered except what happened at the other side of the continent where the bird waited. *T minus X minutes.*

Due to the time difference between the two coasts, Elliott had arrived early, wanting to be on hand well before launch. He felt the growing stir of the plant, and with it his own excitement grew. He could see it, too, in the faces of the others, detect it in their speech and manner, the air of confidence each exuded.

Bergstrom phoned early.

"The Air Force has released an announcement that the Monarch will go all the way," he stated.

"We heard it."

"We should have a sidebar story explaining its significance."

"I have one . . . ready to go."

"Excellent. You'd better have everyone standing by, available for a long-distance conference immediately the bird is fired. We want to wring every bit of publicity we can from this one."

"Everyone's here."

"Fine, I'll call you." Elliott heard the click and replaced the phone in the cradle, wishing he were in Florida. He'd like to see the Monarch go.

The morning TWX wire from Florida, usually sober, terse and factual, began: TODAY A NEW BIRD WILL CRY. . . . He liked that, and planned to use it in his lead. The stuff of which publicity was made. If the bird was a creature of fire and fury, it was also a symbol of hope, a messenger charged with changing the course of history. How could he put that into words?

The TWX message likened the Monarch in its gantry to "a

hawk in a metal cage, savagely impatient for the freedom of the skies"; nor did he think the teletype operator had gone overboard. His words mirrored the sense of expectancy which had pervaded the plant since the beginning of the countdown, some hours before. The giant metal bird had changed subtly from *the* bird to *our* bird, so that the enthusiasm generated in reality reflected the pride of creation in which the lowliest factory worker had as great a stake as Byerkoff. *Today our bird will fly.* . . .

The countdown for the first hot firing of the Monarch Intercontinental Ballistic Missile from its pad at Cape Canaveral, Florida, had started in the small hours of the morning, with T minus zero seconds scheduled for 10:30 A.M., EST. A brief sprinkle had occurred in the pre-dawn hours, but the rising sun found the broken clouds scurrying eastward, leaving clearing skies behind. Meteorological predictions were good.

A malfunction in one of the electrical systems caused a hold at T minus 57 minutes while the trouble was located and repaired, with the result that the countdown was recycled to T minus 85 minutes, and picked up again. Oddly enough, Elliott sensed the hold as a reprieve—a period in which to take a second breath and fortify himself against the resumption of the count. The faces around him told that others felt the same.

A faulty reading on a propellant utilization console brought another hold at T minus 7 minutes, the loss of over 30 minutes and recycling of the countdown to T minus 72 minutes. Now, at T minus 55 minutes, it looked like a late morning firing.

He masked his impatience, fretting at the total dependence on the TWX wire for progress reports. Earlier they had come through with maddening slowness, increasing only as the missile approached its final hour. Someone brought cakes and coffee and, later, Carole came down from the art department.

"Mind if I join you, Jim?" she asked quietly. Their eyes

locked, and for an instant he felt an absolute stillness as if they were alone in the room.

"I'd like that, Carole." His face held understanding. He brought her a cup of coffee before being called to the phone. The news from Florida was good and he felt his spirits rise.

The department grew more crowded in the final hour of the countdown. Parsons of art and Eggert of photos joined Elliott and Carole around one of the desks, chatting as they waited for reports. Jane Cooper, Claire Abbott and Harriett formed a group next to them, while off in a corner, Esther Lynn and Dorothy Baker had their heads together in guarded conversation. Waiting, conversing, from time to time glancing at their watches, they mentally followed the countdown, half fearful of another hold.

Elliott rested his eyes on Koepple, who sat with a small group of men around Garfield. The ad chief fidgeted, his face apprehensive, and occasionally uttered an odd chuckle at something one of the others said. Garfield was expansive. Speaking volubly, he explained to Stover of graphics just why they had no worries over the big contract. His face reflected wise assurance. His curly iron-gray hair and big features combined to produce the solid look of a man who failed to admit the existence of obstacles. Pausing, he glanced at the clock, then consulted his countdown sheet. Peering from behind shaggy brows, he took a bite of cake and said, "When that baby goes, we're on our way."

"It's a long road," Henderson countered.

"Long road, short road"—Garfield shrugged—"if this one doesn't go, the next one will."

"You don't sound overly optimistic," Henderson commented pointedly.

"Sure I'm optimistic, but it's damned easy to flub."

"Worried?"

"Not over the contract." He winked at Koepple.

Watching, Elliott had the impression that Henderson was uneasy, or troubled—he couldn't decide which. The smooth face appeared less suave, his smile artificial, and something had gone from his cockiness. Had it to do with Esther's story? He wondered. That kind of thing was dynamite. If it were true, and should Bergie hear . . . He switched his eyes back to Carole, striking in a gold suit that matched her hair. Contemplating her, he felt a stir of excitement. He switched his attention to the hours ahead.

Today would open a new horizon, or close one. The bird rested on the pad now, staring at the Florida sky, while hundreds of feet away men in a steel and concrete blockhouse lived a thousand years. Bergstrom, Welkes, Kroeber, Gaither, Byerkoff—they'd all be there, eyes glued to the closed-circuit television screens or fastened on the test conductor, who suddenly had become the most important figure in the missile world. The scores of test engineers and technicians, the vast blockhouse with its rows of gray-paneled machines, and even the missile standing in solitary splendor on its distant pad seemed merely a backdrop against which he performed. Now, at this moment, he sat at his small launch console, earphones clamped to his head, eyes riveted to a myriad of flashing panel lights, methodically checking off the flight readiness of each system and each step of each system, waiting for an affirmation before proceeding to the next. Working from a checklist, he resembled the director of some huge Hollywood production. To hold or fire . . . The decision was his. Tomorrow he'd be forgotten, his brief moment of trial past; but today, hunched on his lonely island in the midst of the blockhouse, he held the center of the stage. To hold or fire . . . An ineffably lonely man, Elliott mused.

A second lonely man on another island, the range safety officer, held a similar vigil. Once the bird became airborne, he would take up where the test conductor left off, follow its flight by electromagnetic wave-trains, computers, visual scopes —watch as the bird soared, his finger on the DESTRUCT button. Should the bird waver . . .

The big wheels of the military were there also—star-studded generals and colonels mingling with civilian scientists, all watching the play of lights and the small figure at the center of the stage—listening to the terse commands, the sharp click of solenoids, the soft whir of machinery. Helpless, they waited.

He wished he were there with them, had the freedom to write the story, tell the people all about the bird—what it would do today and what it meant. Not the usual mishmash of size, weight, thrust, range or the uniqueness of its design, but the real story behind the story—like those of which he used to dream, in the days when he'd wanted to be a war correspondent; but this was bigger. The Battle of the Bulge, Marines storming the death beaches of Tarawa, the terrifying scream of fire bombs plunging into the entrails of doomed Berlin—such stories became minor in comparison. It was not what the bird did, but the significance of what it stood for. The voice of diplomacy in a mailed fist. A promise. A dove with teeth. The small wavering nations would find fresh hope as the bird soared; the Red tide would diminish and the hand in the Kremlin would grow more fearful, less likely to reach for the black button of extinction.

Yes, this was bigger, so much bigger that he found himself baffled by the small corners at which he nibbled, praising the bird when he should be crying its vast political implications. Not that he could. Not that anyone could. It wasn't like a battle that came to a sharp decision, followed by brief trumpets of peace. The ultimate ramifications lay in the shadowy guess-world of opinion heaped upon opinion, in which reality and unreality appeared inseparable. In truth, he reflected, a statement of the missile's value resembled the extrapolation of a curve from a complex scatter of points; its true worth could be substantiated only when history overran the prediction line. Such terms as *value* and *significance* were unreal; only the bird was real.

Over in Florida it now held the center of the stage, watched by the eyes of America, by African, Japanese, German, Turkish eyes—by dark eyes peering from behind the forbidding walls of the Kremlin. *The Bird of Freedom*—the new-age dove of peace which, instead of a twig of holly, offered a thermonuclear warhead as a token of the tranquillity it sought. The Monarch ICBM: *Yet shall ye be as the wings of a dove, covered with silver, and her feathers with yellow gold.* Today he was proud to be where he was, to serve the bird and to serve America. The bird was part of him and he was part of the bird, and together they were creating a new freedom for the peoples of the earth.

Hackleberg popped his head in the door. "T minus twenty-five minutes and counting," he called, and withdrew.

"They'll be closing and locking the blockhouse doors," Koepple remarked, his voice strained and unnaturally high.

Garfield consulted his countdown sheet. "Not yet—they're getting final weather reports from downrange—checking the positions of ships and planes."

The warning horn, the wail of LOX pumps filling the great silvered tanks with liquid oxygen at minus 297 degrees F., green lights winking across control panels . . . Those were the things that counted now. The Big Day. Elliott capitalized the words in his mind, nodding as he caught Carole's strained look. Florida—everyone would be on edge. They chatted aimlessly, feeling the minutes steal by—long minutes as if some magical hand had put a brake on time. Inwardly fretting, he wished he could teleport himself across the nation, be there to see the bird go instead of following it through the impersonal medium of a teletype machine.

Kroeber, who had worked on the airframe for the German V-2, would be peering with his dark, analytical eyes to see how the missile responded as it drove upward through the dense masses of the air ocean. Gaither, also, would be watching the aerodynamics. Designers would watch to see if the airframe, power plants and flight-control units functioned together properly under the heavy stresses of acceleration; autopilot men sought to know how the missile responded to the electronic black box that constituted its brain; other engineers were concerned with propellant flow, the action of hydraulic and pneumatic systems, internal temperatures, pressures and vibration.

What did they think, these watchers? Each saw the bird differently, he conjectured. Kroeber would visualize a space booster; Gaither would consider it as simply the carrier of a thermonuclear warhead. What did Bergstrom think? He would be waiting, his heavy face expressionless, his opaque eyes fixed on the test conductor, perhaps his mind already on the next step. What did they think now—Byerkoff, Whitestone, Welkes? The phone jangled and he picked up the receiver, conscious the others had paused to listen.

"T minus fifteen minutes and counting," Joe Stone reported from the TWX room. "She's hotter than a two-dollar pistol."

Elliott sensed the excitement in his voice, and ordered, "Good, keep me plugged in."

"The Cape's jammed. Everybody in Florida's watching from Cocoa Beach."

"We'll give 'em a show." He replaced the phone and looked at Carole. "T minus fifteen minutes; looks like we'll go this time."

"They're over the hump," Garfield stated authoritatively,

scanning the countdown sheet. "A few more minutes and they'll be pouring the water over the flame deflectors." He laid the sheet aside and leaned back in his chair, rolling his cigar slowly between his fingers. Elliott watched the blue smoke curl upward, and the silence came again. A whistle blew in the factory, resounding faintly through the walls, and he heard the passage of feet in the outer corridor.

"We should be hearing," Henderson commented. Koepple nodded and Garfield whirled his cigar a little faster. A short time later the phone rang again and Stone reported the countdown at T minus ten minutes.

Elliott relayed the information, saying, "I'd better mosey over." He looked at Carole. "Want to see the excitement?"

"Yes," she said simply.

"Somebody better cover the phones," he suggested. "We might be getting some rush calls from Florida." Henderson and Koepple volunteered.

"Good, then I'll go with Elliott and watch the big bird fly," Garfield announced. He stared at his mutilated cigar a moment before dropping it in an ashtray.

The TWX room was jammed despite the presence of two security guards and a sign above the door which read SECRET. Although most of the top brass were at the Cape, the supervising design and test engineers and second-tier management personnel had crowded inside, or waited in the outer hall for word to be relayed. Smoking, speaking in subdued voices, they switched their eyes in quick glances or cocked their heads in listening attitudes, nodding in wise, veteran fashion. Click-click-click-click. The steady drone of the teletype resounded against the babble of voices.

Elliott led Carole through the crowd, his eyes smarting from the thick tobacco smoke as he sought Stone. Finally spotting him a few yards from the machine, he pushed through to his side and asked, "Where is she?"

"T minus three minutes and counting," Stone replied. "They've just turned on the water . . . to douse the flame bucket," he added.

Elliott glanced toward the machine. "Thank God for no more holds. I was beginning to worry."

"So was everyone," Stone admitted. He said cheerfully to Carole, "This won't take long."

"I don't mind. We've waited a long time for this day."

"You can say that again."

Elliott crowded closer to the machine and a short, bald man barring his path glanced fretfully at his badge before grudgingly making way. Click-click-click-click. The teletype beat a steady din, pounding above the babble of voices. Glancing back to catch Carole's eye, he smiled encouragement and pushed forward to see the carriage, aware that Garfield had elbowed his way next to him. Despite the excitement and air of expectancy filling the room, he felt a tiny worry nag at the corners of his mind. He watched the keys.

POWER TO INTERNAL
FUEL LEVEL CHECK ROGER XXXX
TELEMETRY IN LAUNCH CONDITION
SECURE LOX TANKING XXXX
T-2 AND COUNTING

"T minus two," a voice rang out, followed by a cheer. The bald man jostled Elliott, trying to read the message.

ENGINE PREP COM LIGHT ON
STATUS CK
ALL SYSTEMS XXXX HOLD HOLD XXXX

"A hold," someone yelled.

"*Hold . . . Hold . . . Hold . . .*" The word ran through the crowd, accompanied by exclamations of disappointment. Elliott stared at the machine, catching his breath. Click, click, click, click.

ROGER ALL SYSTEMS GO

"No hold!" a jubilant voice next to him proclaimed.

No hold . . . No hold . . . Roger on the bird . . . The bird's at go . . . A quick, nervous cheer started, and as abruptly stopped as a sense of the impending moment swept back. Elliott glanced at Carole and nodded vigorously, feeling a sudden sweep of confidence. It was going, he knew it was going.

T-60 AND COUNTING

RANGE SAFETY LIGHTS ON XXX

RANGE READY

WATER SYSTEM READY XXXX

"T minus sixty," the bald man yelled.

"T minus sixty . . ." The call was taken up, relayed outside and a cheer came from the hall, followed by the quick hubbub of voices.

Man, I'd like to be there.

. . . Saw an Atlas go once.

This baby'll beat 'em all.

Despite his earlier qualms, Elliott's excitement grew and he suppressed a desire to study his hands, see if they trembled. Garfield slowly removed his cigar and blew a puff of smoke toward the carriage of the machine. He appeared unnaturally calm.

T-50 AND COUNTING XXX

"Come on, you baby," a voice prayed.

"Come on . . ."

"Come on . . ."

The chant rose and fell. *Come on, baby.*

The Monarch would make it. He knew it. The knowledge came in a flash of insight. She was perched, ready to go, a bird bearing dreams. The words he'd pounded out month after month were coming to life. For some reason an image of Kroeber's gaunt face with its myopic eyes flashed through his mind, to be swept away as the excitement filling the room welled, pulsated, rising and falling like the life movements of a gigantic blob of protoplasm.

He caught Garfield's eyes riveted on the teletype as if hypnotized by the falling keys. Strained voices, strained faces. Click, click, click, click. John Vroman should be here. He'd love it. The bird was on the pad, ready to go. Light the candle, free the bird—send it winging on its way! Something caught high in his throat and he imagined he could feel the thump of his heart against the chest wall. How could Garfield stand there like a rock? Click, click, click, click. Each click a heartbeat, a marker in eternity, a sign post spelling the end of one era and the beginning of another. Time clicking, history clicking, each click a toll of the bell of hope. Click, click, click, click. The bird was ready.

"Come on, you beautiful bastard," someone breathed aloud, and the blasphemy in the smoke-filled room was like a prayer.

T-40 AND COUNTING
LOX LEVEL ROGER XXX
TLM RECORDERS ON
T-35 AND COUNTING
T-30 AND COUNTING
XXX ALL SYSTEMS GO XXX
T-25 COUNTING
ENGINE START XXX

The murmur stopped, the breathing stopped and except for the click of the teletype, all movement and sound ceased. Elliott cast a fast backward glance at Carole and nodded reassuringly; she gave no sign of having seen him. Her face wore a tight, expectant look. Click, click, click, click. He had the strange sensation of being suspended in time and space, watching a room filled with frozen statues, with no movement save for the falling keys. Carole staring, Garfield staring, the fat man next to him staring—everyone staring, waiting.

IGNITION
T-
T-
T-5
T-
ENGINES FIRING XXXX REPEAT
ENGINES FIRING
XXXXXXXXXXXX
FIRST MOVEMENT XXXXXXXX
LIFT OFF XXXX LIFT OFF XXXX ALL SYSTEMS GO
ALL SYSTEMS GO

"The sweet bastard's off," someone shouted. The word, relayed to the hall, brought a cheer.

"Go, baby, go," a voice prayed. The Monarch—airborne! At that instant it hung above its launching pad as if suspended in midair, its giant mainstage engines spewing vast sheets of flame, pushing it faster, faster . . .

GOING GOING GOING GOING PLUS 10 SECONDS GOING
GOING VERY NICELY XXXX GOING GOING GOING PLUS 20 SECONDS
GOING GOING VERY NICELY XXXX GOING PLUS 30 SECONDS

A strange hush gripped the room except for the clatter of the teletype keys and Elliott shifted uncomfortably, keeping his eyes pinned to the machine. Click, click, click, click. Garfield reached up and wiped his brow, his face set and intent.

PLUS 40
PLUS 50
GOING GOING XXXX PLUS 60
GOING VERY NICELY
PLUS 65
PLUS 70 AND GOING XXX

"It's doing it!" Garfield exclaimed suddenly, his voice incredulous.

"Damned tootin' it's doing it," the bald man snapped belligerently.

PLUS 75 XXX
PLUS 80
GOING GOING XXX GOING
PLUS 85
GOING GOING GOING GOING XXX
XXXXXXXXXXXXXX

PLUS 100 AND GOING GOING XXX NICE VAPOR TRAIL
GOING GOING XXX VERY NICE XXX PLUS 110 SECONDS AND GOING

"Go, baby, go . . ."

PLUS 115

"She's ready to stage . . ." The message ran through the room. Elliott clenched his hands. First stage separation—the time of trial, the instant when the big mainstage would break free, send the second stage . . .

"Go baby, go!" He broke the thought, watching the keys.

GOING GOING XXX
PLUS
HOLD XXX HOLD XXX
STANDBY XXXXXXXXXXX
XXXXXXXXXXX

"Standby!" an incredulous voice shouted.

STANDBY XXX
MONARCH EXPLODED XXXX EXPLODED AT PLUS 127
STANDBY XXX STANDBY

"Kee-rist!" the bald man swore. The word jerked Elliott back to reality. A drone of voices filled the room and suddenly exhausted, he tore his eyes from the machine and turned, seeing Carole's brave smile. Stone wore a mask of disappointment.

"The goddamn LOX tank," a voice next to Elliott exclaimed. The LOX tank. The words jolted him and momentarily he recreated the vision of the static test missile exploding in flame.

"It can't be," someone denied. "The fuel tank was damned near empty."

"The g's, the weight of the second stage . . ."

He listened to the clamor, feeling sickened as he stared at the teletype. Coldly impersonal, with no sense of drama, the keys continued to fall.

STANDBY XXX STANDBY XXX

Standby, he thought bitterly. *Standby for what? Did they think they could glue the damned bird together?*

REPEAT XXX MONARCH EXPLODED OR DESTROYED AT PLUS 127 SEC-
ONDS
XXX STANDBY FOR RANGE AND ALTITUDE XXX

"Well, that's that." Garfield blew a cloud of smoke toward the ceiling. "It's back to the old drafting board."

"Yeah." Looking morosely around, he saw the crowd had splintered into small groups, jabbering and gesticulating. Everyone had a theory. Pushing his way to Carole's side, he said brusquely: "I'd better get back. We're going to catch hell."

"I'm sorry, Jim." She touched his arm.

"It looked so good," Stone said desolately.

"Next time," he replied harshly. "There's always another missile." Turning, he elbowed his way toward the door. God, it had looked so good.

"I'm sorry, we haven't heard a thing," Elliott curtly told Jack Embry, city editor of the *Bulletin-News.* "I'll let you know the moment we hear anything definite, but in the meantime you'll have to go on the wire story."

"—— ———— ——————— —— ——— ——————— ——————————?"

"No, there's no connection." He spoke sharply, not surprised that Embry should try to couple the explosion with the earlier one involving the static test missile. They'd all get on that wagon before they were through.

"——— ——— ——————— ———————— ——————————."

"Sure, I'll do that."

"————— —— —————————."

"As early as possible, Jack."

"———— —— ——————— —— ————?"

"Okay, I'll do that." He slammed down the phone and glanced at his watch. The holds during the countdown had eaten away the hours of the day. Now it was nearly noon. Joe Stone poked in his head to say he had the *Herald-Examiner* on the phone.

"You take it," Elliott instructed. "Tell 'em we haven't heard a thing. Tell them all that."

"Roger." As Stone turned away, his secretary announced another call.

"Turn it over to Stone," he ordered. "I'm only interested in Florida."

"Yes, Mr. Elliott."

"And send in Hackleberg." Sitting back, he studied the drawing of the Monarch that hung above his desk and thought bitterly: It flew on paper, it flew in the news releases and it had flown in a thousand conferences; but that was all. Why hadn't they pulled it back, checked it from A to Z following the loss of the test missile? They were damned lucky it hadn't blown on the pad. A black eye. Not that other missiles hadn't fizzled; but they had hailed the Monarch as something special. A hundred news stories attested its reliability. Slater would slaughter them.

When Hackleberg came to the door, he instructed, "Cover the TWX room, rush over everything from Florida."

"Will do."

Elliott watched him leave, contemplating events to come. Damn, blow a bird and he had every newspaper and radio station in town on his neck, each demanding the inside scoop. But his hands were tied—would be until he heard from Florida. The hopes, the dreams. *Today a new bird cried* . . . His lead. He smiled sourly. It had cried all right—cried dying in flames, hurtling brokenly into the sea. A sparrow trying to be an eagle, and on such things the nation's power waxed and waned. Bergstrom's preparations had covered everything . . . in detail . . . except the possibility of failure. That hadn't been foreseen. What now, little man? Bail the bird out, of course. It would be the static test story all over again, except that this time they had invited the press to witness the debacle. The Nation had witnessed it. The world knew. How would Bergstrom handle that?

Carole brought in a tray, setting it on the desk.

"Coffee," she announced cheerfully.

"That I can use. Who's the good samaritan?"

"Garfield—he ordered the cafeteria to send over several pitchers. And some rolls," she added.

"Good for Harry."

"Feeling low, Jim?"

"Disappointed more than anything. I guess my expectations were too high."

"You weren't alone."

"No, I imagine Bergie's pretty sour."

"Probably too busy to feel anything," she conjectured. She looked at the coffee pitcher. "I'll be back."

"Thanks, Carole." He watched her go, then returned to his thoughts, wishing the vice-president's call would come. Still, what was there to say? The metal bird, a tin pterodactyl . . . *Today a god died under a hot Florida sun.* That's what he should write. The bird was the goddess Isis and they the clamoring temple priests. Isis, the fallen idol. To hell with it, he gritted. It's just a missile. We have a factory full. Next time . . . The phone rang and he grabbed the receiver, listening as Hackleberg reported that the explosion appeared internal.

"What does that mean?" he asked sharply, knowing the answer.

"The range safety officer didn't destroy it. The explosion resulted from a malfunction."

"Are you certain?"

"That's what they say."

"Florida?"

"Our engineers."

"To hell with our engineers. I don't want anything but Florida information," he barked.

"Okay." Hackleberg hung up.

The Florida call came through immediately afterward.

"What's happening out there?" Bergstrom sounded tired.

"We're stalling everyone . . . waiting for the official word."

"The Air Force is putting out a release, Jim."

"Can't you give us a preview?"

"Yes, you'd better cut the others in. I want to get everyone squared away."

"Hold on." Elliott cupped the phone and shouted, listening as the others came on extension lines.

"Garfield here . . ."

"Henderson . . ."

"Koepple speaking."

"Here are the facts," Bergstrom declared, as the line grew quiet. "The flight was a success. We lost the missile at plus one hundred and twenty-seven seconds but we achieved most of our major test objectives. That's the important thing."

"What percent?" Elliott asked flatly.

"Ninety percent success."

"What went wrong?" He sensed Bergstrom's hesitancy before he answered.

"We're not certain. Perhaps something quite minor."

"Any chance of structural failure . . . too much loading on the fuel tanks?" Garfield asked.

"Nonsense, Harry, we don't want anything like that getting around," the vice-president rasped. "Where'd you hear it?"

"Local chatter. Some of our engineers are saying it. I thought you ought to know."

"We're not certain of the cause," Bergstrom repeated. "We'll have to wait until we analyze the data." His voice became more brisk. "However, that's neither here nor there. The flight proved we have a good solid marketable ICBM and we have to protect it, minimize the story as much as we can." Elliott smiled bitterly at the logic.

"You can't hide it," Garfield protested. "It's not like the desert test, R. T. We had the whole press there. Everyone saw it."

"I'm not trying to hide anything," the vice-president snapped testily. "We just have to play it down."

"Every company in the business has lost missiles—lots of them." It took Elliott several seconds to place the voice as Henderson's.

"That doesn't help us," Bergstrom cut in.

"If we could show—"

"No, it's bad for the industry, Eugene." A brief silence ensued before he continued, "Let the ghosts of the missiles rest in peace."

"You're right," Henderson acknowledged abruptly.

Koepple asked hesitantly, "Any chance of human error?"

"That's a possibility, Art." Bergstrom cleared his throat. "I would venture it highly probable."

"With the bird at plus 127 seconds?" Elliott queried. He felt the stillness before Bergstrom spoke.

"You're right, Jim. It would look like a dodge. We'll play it straight, give out the affirmative aspects of the story."

"We'll have to mention the loss," Garfield counseled. "What'll we say? We'll be queried a hundred times before the day's over."

"We can't consider it as a loss, Harry." Carole came in and slipped into a chair across from Elliott. "Attaining ninety percent of our objectives is extremely successful, and that's the way we have to play it. What do you think, Jim?"

"We can state that, certainly, but we should have an answer for the missile's destruction."

"We'll have to sidestep it, Jim, say we won't know until we analyze the telemetry data. By that time the story will be forgotten."

"How about the Air Force release?"

"No conflict, Jim. They see it as we do." He spoke decisively. "Here's the way I want it handled: The flight proved a success with over ninety percent of our objectives achieved. At the end of that time the missile was destroyed through unknown causes."

"Without giving a reason?" someone asked.

"None at all. It won't be necessary. We can't afford to undersell a success."

They discussed the pros and cons for a while, and when they were through, Elliott asked, "Will you be flying in tonight?"

"Tomorrow, Jim. I want to make certain all the facts on this end come out all right."

"Check, we'll handle everything," he responded, thinking

there was nothing to handle. The vice-president had dictated the story . . . in two sentences.

"I'd appreciate that."

As the phone clicked in his ear, he swung toward Carole, saying sarcastically, "We have a good solid marketable ICBM that just scored a smashing success, or at least ninety percent of one. Wouldn't that frost you?"

"I'm sorry, Jim."

"Yeah."

"It's not a super-bird."

"No, it's not."

They stopped talking as Henderson came from the other office, followed by Koepple and Garfield. The latter smiled cynically, asking, "Where do we go from here?"

"Follow the party line, Harry." He weighed him briefly. "I'll handle it. There's nothing left but the obit."

"If I can help."

"No, we're okay."

"Well . . ."

"I'll have it out in an hour."

"Anything I can do?" Koepple offered.

"Not a thing, Art."

"Then I'll take off, leave early." He smiled apologetically. "I'm pretty tired."

"Take it easy, Art."

"I'll see you Monday." He turned wearily, pausing at the door. "I'll be home."

"Good-by, Mr. Koepple," Carole said softly.

"Good-by, Carole."

"There doesn't seem to be much reason for my staying," Henderson said.

"None at all," Elliott agreed.

As he left, Garfield said bluntly, "I don't like this."

"Neither do I," he acknowledged.

"We're trying too hard to make it sound like a roaring success. It'll work against us, Jim. We'd be better off if we acknowledged a malfunction and let it go at that."

"I agree, Harry."

"The press isn't naïve. Those boys have been watching missiles for years. They know when one flubs, and all they ask is a reason. Give 'em that and they're satisfied. After the first edition, they bury it in the second edition. If we claim a success, we'll start one hell of a controversy."

"I realize that," he replied, thinking Garfield had argued the other way on the loss of the static test missile. Still, this was different. The Nation had followed this flight.

The chief of publicity gazed at Carole, fumbling with a cigar. "If there's nothing else . . ."

"I'll handle it, and thanks, Harry." He watched him depart, listening to his footsteps recede through the outer office before turning to Carole. "This won't take long."

"I'll get more coffee," she offered.

"And a roll." As she left, he rolled a sheet of yellowcap into the typewriter and lit a cigarette, taking a few quick drags before starting.

A Monarch Intercontinental Ballistic Missile today was destroyed after 127 seconds of flight.

It was the first launching of the giant missile, sent into the sky from a launch site at Cape Canaveral, Florida. The Monarch is produced for the Air Force by Western Aerospace Division of Midwest Aeronautical Corporation.

Although the flight was of short duration, company officials reported the test highly successful, with ninety percent of the desired test data obtained.

Officials of Western Aerospace stated . . .

Finishing, he scanned the copy. Sure, the test had been a success—Bergstrom had been right on that score. They had gotten the missile off the pad, had learned a lot. *A good solid marketable ICBM* . . . The phrase ran through his mind. He had little doubt but that the vice-president was correct on that score. The Monarch would make out. They'd find the trouble, make a fix, fire another missile. There'd be successes and failures until, eventually declared fully operational, they'd begin stuffing it in caves, floating it on the seas—another deterrent. It wasn't a super-bird. He knew that now. If the Monarch grew (and it would grow), it would be at the expense of missiles just as good. Or better.

Odd, now that the bird had failed, he could view it objectively. Or had Bergstrom's glib assurance awakened him? He meditated. What did the Monarch imply? An entire new weapon system—new ground support, logistics and manning systems, new maintenance and storage facilities, so that in essence each system required hundreds of millions of dollars above the actual missile costs themselves. In that sense he could view the Monarch as a detriment, for the money spent in support systems could add that many more weapons to existing systems.

It all boils down to the question of necessity. That was Vroman's claim, and Walsh's. Was the Monarch necessary? He forced himself to examine the question. What about armies . . . navies . . . peripheral wars? What about Southeast Asia, Cuba, Berlin? Could the Monarch solve those problems? The Titan hadn't. Neither had the Minuteman. He remembered Vroman's words—*The fragmentation of nations* . . . *The slow march of inches* . . . Blow hot, blow cold, the war had many faces—propaganda, diplomacy, threat, infiltration, phony fronts, espionage, brush wars and many more—a cold-hot war that swirled unceasingly in and around the giant silver monuments that proclaimed *No War*. He'd always known that, yet had never related it to the Monarch. Or had he looked the other way?

He became aware of the stir permeating the big plant, the hum and bustle of business as usual, and thought: The firing's forgotten; they're getting ready for the next one. A forklift passed below his window and the cough of its gasoline engine made him melancholy. What was his role in all this? How true were his words, or how false? *The bird of freedom* . . . He'd proclaimed it a hundred times, but what did he actually know about it? Nothing, except what he himself said, or was told to say. He'd traveled the blind road of faith, looking neither right nor left.

What had he sacrificed in the process? His self-respect? He shifted uncomfortably, recalling how he'd tried to use Kroeber, his moves to impress Bergstrom. Had he done that for the Monarch, or for the job? Had he fought with Carole from a stance of truth, or to fool himself? The Monarch, the big metal bird.

The super-bird . . .

The ultimate bird, for who could improve on an eagle? It was there now in the factory; it must be pushed, regardless of effort or cost, or conscience. It demanded obeisance, blind faith. Nothing must stand in its way. Why? He knew the answer.

The Big Sell.

James Elliott, huckster. *I sell Birds*. He laughed bitterly. What now? Would he, like Bergstrom, go on? The question clung to his mind.

After a while he heard the click of Carole's shoes in the outer office and looked up, forcing a smile as she came through the doorway.

13

Chapter 13

BERGSTROM stared at the telegram.

Leaning back in his chair, he let it lie on the desk in front of him. That it had been sent by someone in the plant appeared obvious—someone quite close to him. So, Elissa had a play-mate. Somehow the identity of the latter didn't surprise him. He'd felt a quick stab of pain at the first instant of revelation, followed by an indignation in which he'd been the righteous husband, wrathful at discovery of his wife's infidelity; but that, too, had passed, replaced by guilt feelings tinged with remorse, in which he blamed himself for her dereliction. Brooding, he knew he had driven her to it through a constant neglect as he'd centered his drive and energies around the missile, forgetful that another world existed outside the confines of the corpora-tion. Home had been a place to hang his hat, and little more. Solely concerned with his own ambitions, or rather his ambi-tions for the company, he had forgotten that she was a woman with a woman's needs—that happiness required more than a hillside estate and a convertible. Like a fool, he'd settled for material gifts.

Not that he'd been an angel, but at least he'd had the good sense to keep his affairs away from home and work. He'd refused to mix business and pleasure, rebuffing many overtures in the process. That irritated him as much as anything—she should have been more discreet. But few people were any more. Discretion had become old-fashioned until now it seemed almost the vogue to flaunt an affair as if somehow it added extra zest. She had tried to hurt him, he reasoned, otherwise she would never have allowed such a thing with someone so close to him. He pondered the mechanisms which might underlie such an act.

He dropped his eyes to the telegram. Joan knew. He had wondered at her nervous, skittish demeanor, the way she had refused to meet his eyes when he had arrived—the way the telegram had been placed squarely on his desk instead of the usual IN basket. She knew, but how did she know? Could she have sent it? Immediately he rejected the idea. Had she read it against a strong light? He regretted that he hadn't examined the seal. No matter. What did count was that she knew, and in that respect, formed the key. He prided himself on his logical mind and liked to think of it as a precise machine, geared to reality, capable of dichotomizing between cause and effect, between black and white, an analytical probe that allowed him to reach conclusions with a facility beyond that of most men. That belief lay in the back of his mind as he studied the problem confronting him.

The telegram must have originated with one of the candidates for Vroman's job; he could see no other motive. There were cranks, people with warped senses, but that seemed farfetched in this case. The timing had been too good—too close to his moment of decision. Elliott, Garfield, Koepple . . . Mentally he ticked off the names, considering each. He could eliminate Koepple. The man might connive in the interests of his empire, but he was too forthright for that kind of thing. And too smart. But that held for Elliott as well. He would fight —had fought—but he'd made it a clean fight. *Integrity.* He let the word seep through his mind. Garfield was another matter; aggressive, enterprising, at times offensive, he'd let nothing stand in his way. Garfield very well could have sent it; but how had he gotten the information? An endless chain, he realized. An indiscretion was like a stone dropped into a still pool; the ripples inevitably followed. He weighed the assumption before moving on to the next.

Joan knew, hence she must have learned it from one of the girls, for certainly no man would tell her that kind of thing. But which girl? (And if he were right in his surmise about Garfield, how had the information reached Joan?) He perused the baffling aspects, knowing that in the end he would have to turn to Joan. Well, he seemed to have come to a dead end. *From someone to Garfield to . . . to Joan:* the chain needed filling in.

Item. Eugene Henderson was a dead duck.

He contemplated the act of dismissing him, savoring it. There'd be no preamble, no explanation; just the terse words: *We won't be requiring your services after this month, Henderson.* That, he persuaded himself, would almost make it worth while. Well, that left him at an impasse, but he needn't be for long; he leaned forward and rang for Joan. He heard her bustle around before she entered—reluctantly, he discerned— halting just inside the doorway. She avoided his eyes and nervously clasped her hands, confirming his belief that she knew. At least he'd act on that assumption. Deliberately he allowed a period of silence, keeping his eyes fixed on her before saying, "I want to ask you one question, Joan."

"Yes, Mr. Bergstrom." She spoke in a voice unnaturally high.

"You know about this?" He tapped the telegram.

"It . . . it came while you were away."

"I know," he replied dryly. "That's not what I meant." Her lips moved and she glanced away, twisting her hands together tightly. "You know what's in it," he pursued.

"Well, I . . ." He let her flounder for a few seconds.

"I know you do, Joan." Her face and actions had given her away, and he continued with more assurance: "Just tell me about it."

"Honestly . . ." She stopped, confused, and afraid she was preparing to flee, he spoke sharply:

"Joan!" As she forlornly wrung her hands, he urged gently, "Just answer the question. There's nothing to worry over." When she didn't answer, he tried again: "I'm not holding anything against you. I just want to know where the information came from. You learned this from someone," he finished more forcibly.

Her lips quivered and he caught the frantic helplessness in her eyes before she replied brokenly, "Yes, Mr. Bergstrom."

"Who told you?"

"Why . . ." She hesitated, visibly agitated.

"Go on," he prompted.

"Esther," she finally managed to gasp.

"Oh?" Again he found himself without surprise. Esther got around. He had very good reasons for knowing that. Could she have told Garfield? He found the idea intriguing. Seeing Joan's eyes fill with tears, he gently reassured her. "Please don't worry. This won't affect you in the least. We'll keep this our secret. Agreed?" He sat straighter and smiled, trying to assume a fatherly role.

"Yes, Mr. Bergstrom." She dabbed at her eyes, appearing relieved, and he wondered what she had expected of him.

"Take the rest of the day off," he encouraged. "Pull yourself together."

"Thank you, I need it." She looked at him through wet eyes and forced a smile before turning to leave. Lord, the knowledge that he had been hurt had hit her hard . . . He hadn't suspected her feelings before. Of course, plenty of secretaries grew quite close to their bosses—ten thousand stories had been written around the theme. He'd seen it in the plant, in quite high places. But she was a good girl, he thought, a thoroughbred—he'd remember her on the next wage review, show he appreciated her concern.

Inspecting the telegram again, he decided he couldn't procrastinate: he'd have to get to the bottom of it—clear the air. Nevertheless he forced himself to take the time to lock it securely in a file, light a cigarette and sort through the morning mail before going down to the director's office.

Esther glanced up, startled. "Good morning, Mr. Bergstrom," she managed to say.

"Morning, Esther." Noting her confusion, he sat alongside the desk, making himself comfortable before continuing. "Esther, we've known each other for a long time." He stopped, gauging the impact of his words. She nodded dumbly, and seeing her fright, he stated bluntly, "If you're worried over your job, you can forget it."

"I . . . I appreciate that, Mr. Bergstrom."

"You've earned it," he replied without humor.

"I . . . try," she answered lamely.

"I have no fault there." He leaned back, studying her face, the small wrinkles gathered at the corners of her eyes, the nervous twitching of her lips, before saying casually, "There's just one thing I want to ask you: Where did you get the information you gave Joan?" Her mouth worked convulsively, and the fact she didn't ask what information revealed her guilt.

He pondered the slender face, the mouth a trifle too wide, and stated curtly, "You have nothing to worry over." Still she hesitated, visibly distraught and he waited, making a steeple of his hands.

"Mr. Garfield," she uttered finally. Her eyes made little darting movements and finally settled on him. "He told me."

"That's all I want to know, Esther. Now we'll forget the whole thing, right? File it away with the rest of our secrets."

"Yes, Mr. Bergstrom." Her voice held sheer gratitude.

"We'll have you another boss before long." Smiling faintly, he rose and left, still not surprised at what he had learned. He had surmised as much. Garfield—he weighed the man, wondering where he had obtained the information. The Garfields of the world were operators, the gatherers of such things; gatherers and users, he corrected. He contemplated the knowledge as he returned to his office.

The lights were off in the front of the house when he reached home. He entered quietly, clicked on a wall lamp and went directly to the bar.

"That you, Roland?" Elissa called from the bedroom. He wanted to ask her who else it might be but instead grunted a reply and reached for the Scotch, then changed his mind and mixed a gin and tonic, sipping it as he headed toward the bedroom.

Elissa, cool and comfortable-looking against the pale blue spread, laid aside her magazine, and asked, "Hard day?" The standard question accompanied by the standard smile.

"Interesting."

"Oh?"

Instead of answering, he set down his drink, removed his coat and loosened his tie, studying himself in the mirror. His face appeared fuller, more jowly, and a small network of blue veins showed above one cheek. He rubbed the area reflectively, wondering if he looked like just another horned husband. He tilted his face—thinning hair, encroaching gray . . . Getting old, he thought, conscious of his wife's image in the mirror. Thank God he was a man of the world, or perhaps she should be thankful for that. She watched him, lips half parted, her face expectant. The image had ash-blond hair, slender, hollowed cheeks, blue eyes—blue and guileless, he perceived. Strange, she hadn't aged at the same rate as he.

She spoke again: "Had dinner?"

"Ate out."

"I waited." Her eyes became quizzical when he didn't respond, and she pursued: "Still worried over the launching?"

"No, that's history," he replied, recognizing the question as idle conversation. She really didn't give a damn. "You never expect much on the first go-round. First missile usually flubs. The Air Force expects that."

"Then it shouldn't affect the production contract?" She made it a question.

"It shouldn't, but we're not certain."

"Of the contract?"

He nodded. "Byerkoff says the winds from Washington are veering, blowing in the direction of solids . . . an expanded Polaris program . . . a larger share of the budget for conventional arms. He's quite worried. So's Cronkhill. It's going to be a fight. However, we're in a fairly strong position. We rushed Stark East. It would have been nice to have gone all the way though."

"All the way where?" she asked, puzzled.

"The Monarch," he replied, concealing his exasperation. "It would have been great to have gone the full route— smacked into the splash net. We needed that, but I guess it was too much to expect." He sat on the edge of the bed, untied his shoes and kicked them off, then reached for the glass.

"You were saying?" she encouraged.

"Saying what?"

"About the day being interesting."

"Oh, yes." Appraisingly he watched her over the rim of the glass. "I'm making some personnel changes."

"Vroman's job?" The casual way she asked caused him to wonder. She didn't sound particularly interested.

"Of course." He lowered the glass. "What else?" When her expression didn't change, he added, "I'm dumping Garfield off at Space Electronics."

"Dumping?"

"Getting the bastard out of my hair."

"I always thought him obnoxious."

Her lack of concern baffled him but, he reasoned, she didn't suspect what he knew. Still, he had expected her to display more interest in his selection of a director. He said, "He didn't stand up too well on the launching—quibbled on how it should be handled, as if there were more than one choice. I'm giving Koepple a slice of his empire."

"Koepple?"

"He's a good man. Perhaps not up to the big job, but plenty good for what he's doing."

He stopped, waiting, eying her musingly until finally she asked, "And the director's job?"

"Elliott," he announced, savoring the moment. "He's done a damn good job." A nervous twitch in her jaw betrayed her reaction, and holding her eyes, he continued, "I'm firing Henderson, of course."

If he expected shock or dismay, he was disappointed. Gazing steadily at him, she repeated, "Of course."

"You didn't expect that?"

"No, but I'm not sorry." The honesty behind the words brought a tinge of contriteness and he forced himself to be cruel.

"What's the matter—he wearing out?"

She tossed her head defiantly. "There wouldn't have been a Henderson—any others—if I'd had a husband."

"Any others?" he mocked.

"Don't act surprised. I'm a bitch, just like all the other wives in that goddamned Fourth of July factory," she rasped bitterly.

"Oh?" he murmured, surprised that he felt no shock. He surveyed her slowly: sitting with her body leaned back, supported by one arm, she looked coolly defiant. The globes of her breasts pushed against the lacy fabric of her gown, revealing the dark areolas of her nipples, and her ash-blond hair, slightly disheveled, gave a wanton appearance that touched the chord of sensuality. He briefly wondered what Henderson had felt, seeing her as he saw her now, and forcibly dismissed the thought. Strange, he felt a slow surge of desire, a pressure at the temples, a fullness, and added, "You might be right."

"We've gone our separate ways, Roland."

"So we have." He looked at the glosheen draperies and white carpeting, at the king-size bed with its pale blue spread and the woman lying on it, and added, "But that's over."

"What do you intend to do?" The undercurrent of alarm and uncertainty brought the trace of a smile to his lips, and with it an unexpected tug of gentleness.

He said calmly, "I'm going to give you a husband, Elissa. This time let's make it work."

Harry Garfield emerged from the elevator feeling old and worn, his fight gone, replaced by a sense of defeat and hopelessness. Sensing the unsteadiness of his gait, he deliberately slowed his pace, wondering at the tremble in his legs. The interview with Bergstrom—if one could call it an interview—had been short and abrupt, but in those moments he had seen a lifetime swept away, or so he felt. All the years past, wasted . . . He took a deep breath, pulling himself together. *Harry the gambler.* The phrase brought the wisp of a smile. Sometimes the cards fell wrong—the difference between a jack and an ace. The noon whistle sounded and he saw Elliott emerge from the PR offices, glancing up and down the hall. As Elliott nodded toward him, then took a closer look, Garfield glimpsed the speculation in his face.

"You look rugged," Elliott said. "Feel bad?"

"Lousy." He managed a smile.

"Need some aspirin?"

"Won't help a bit." He hesitated, trying to pull himself together before continuing, "I just came down from Bergie's."

"Oh?" This time Elliott raised his eyes, his face expectant.

"We've been suckered, Jim."

"Suckered?" The casual way he asked alerted Garfield's curiosity and he appraised the other, thinking: *He isn't alarmed. Why?* To the contrary, he appeared quite composed, more interested in looking past him down the hall than in the conversation. *He knows something,* he decided. Nevertheless he went on:

"I'm going to the bush league . . . take over Henderson's post at Space Electronics. Bergie's giving Koepple a slice of my empire, moving up Roberts." His eyes weighed the other, searching for a reaction, and seeing none, he grew puzzled. "That means you'll have a new boss—Mr. Eugene Henderson," he finished scathingly.

"Did he say that?"

"How else could it be?" He felt the rancor return and with it the slow sweep of hopelessness. The end of dreams. He continued bitterly, "He's a flak artist, Jim. There's always someone who can take someone. Look how Judas took Jesus."

"Perhaps you're better off," Elliott sympathized. The statement held no emotion, kindling Garfield's curiosity anew.

"How do you figure?"

"If you stayed, you'd be working for him. This way you'll be your own king."

"Sure, a king without a kingdom. That place is out in the weeds—no man's land," he retorted. "Twenty-two years and I'm moved to the boondocks. I have a damned good notion to quit."

"It might not be too bad."

"Not too bad? That's two steps removed from the corporation, Jim."

"I still think it's better than being stuck here. You'll be your own boss, make your own decisions, Harry. You're a chief here; you'll be a director there."

"The bush leagues—I'm going downhill." His anger stirred. "I should have sunk him while I had the chance, the cuckolding bastard." Preoccupied with wonder at Esther's evident failure to communicate the gossip to Joan, he failed to see the startled look that flashed across the other's face. He did see Elliott's lips form a question, then relax, leaving it unasked. "Anyway, that's it," he finished lamely.

"Well, hell, I hope it works out, Harry."

"How about yourself? You'll have him on your neck." Elliott started to answer when he caught sight of Carole hurrying toward him, and turned expectantly. Garfield eyed her morosely.

"Keep you waiting long?" she asked.

"Just got here." Elliott turned to Garfield. "We're going to the cafeteria. Like to join us?"

"Next time," he replied, feeling a sudden desire to be alone. "Take it easy," Elliott counseled. Carole smiled and they moved off. He stood for a moment, watching as they walked through the hall. Christ, the news hadn't shaken him one whit. Had he already known? Still, he should have reacted. He saw them move together and touch hands. Like two kids, he fancied. Two kids! An echo from years past—he and Madge, long ago. When they passed through the glass doors into the sunlight, he turned toward his office.

Roland T. Bergstrom sat in the silence of his walnut-paneled office gazing at a Janek drawing of the Monarch missile. His favorite—the one with the fire trail cleaving the sky. He sat straight, immobile, his heavy face expressionless as he contemplated his decision, and which now required but the scratch of a pen to make final.

He had never let personal considerations enter into such things before, he meditated, nor would he now. His sole criterion always had been the corporation, and that was the way it should be. Men, machines, products—even such a mighty one as the Monarch—served the same cause. For that reason he had given to the Monarch the best of him, and he would continue to. Not that the Monarch wasn't a good missile. It would require a few fixes . . . more testing . . . but in the end it would hold its own. He brought back his mind to the decision.

It hadn't been his to make after all, he reflected, but had been dictated by the corporation, or rather the corporation's needs. The confidential memo that he'd read that morning told the story: the big contract was shaky. Forces—almost too powerful to contemplate—had spoken for more diversified military forces. Southeast Asia and a renewed Berlin flare-up had shaken the nation, and the cry to do something was coming from the land. There would be more Polarises, more of the conventional weapons and ground forces, more of everything except ICBMs. And even there the solids were gaining a strategic foothold, a dangerous one. He felt a stab of trepidation at the bitter fight he faced, and all at once of loneliness.

He needed the best man he could get, the strongest—the one who could shoulder the load and push the Monarch. The missile counted, and the company counted, and that was all. Nothing else mattered, neither consideration of himself nor anyone else. He'd held off until the last, hoping for John Vroman's return. But that hope, too, was gone. Vroman wouldn't return. He weighed the memo he had prepared the night before. It lay on his desk near the pen stand, a small, blue rectangle. He knew the words by heart: *Effective immediately, Mr. James Elliott will succeed to the position of director for* . . .

A stroke of the pen, he mused, listening to the sound of Joan's typewriter as he followed the thread of his reasoning. Koepple . . . a good man . . . but he had slowed with age. Still, he'd made no mistake in giving him a slice of Garfield's empire. He'd do a good job. Garfield . . . He considered the name, picturing the man's face, and felt a slight distaste. He could overlook his personal offensiveness, but he had disqualified himself the night of the launching—his reluctance to protect the Monarch had assured that. His own judgment had been better; the story, after all, had been quite obscure, lost in the excitement of an uneasy world.

But Elliott and Henderson both were good—both had proved it. Either could handle the job and do it justice, although he considered Elliott the stronger of the two. Never mind, his personal considerations had never entered into such matters, and couldn't now. With the fight coming up, he'd need one or the other. Or rather it was a need of the corporation. The Monarch had to survive . . . be sold. His own likes and dislikes could have no part in such a critical decision. The corporation . . .

Sighing, he reached for a pen, drew the memo toward him and briefly read it. Decisively he scratched out the name James Elliott and above it wrote: Eugene Henderson. Methodically he blotted it and pushed it aside before picking up another— Elliott's resignation. Why? He'd told the man he had the job, had assured him that it was just a matter of paper work. Letting the memo flutter to his desk, he leaned back and closed his eyes. Why would a man quit at the very threshold of success?

He wished he knew.

It was over, past, almost as if it had never been. He thought it strange how quickly a few years could be erased. Not that the memory would perish, but simply that it was no longer important. Occasionally he visualized the bird—the sleek lines of her as she came down the assembly line, or how she looked, resting with her nose pointed to the sky.

From their apartment he could see the white sweep of sand leading down to the tideline, the rock ledge that split the waves. She would be there, her easel propped on the sand.

Looking back at the clutter of papers around him, he returned to his writing, occasionally stopping to edit or to read what he had written. He worked steadily until he heard her returning.

Over supper he said, "You are very lovely, Mrs. Elliott."

"Thank you, Mr. Elliott." She paused reflectively. "I heard some news today. The Monarch . . ."

"Awarded the contract?" As she nodded, he added, "I'm not surprised. I knew they'd get it."

"Jim Elliott, you knew nothing—"

"But I did," he interrupted. "Garfield explained it one night at the bar."

"Jim Elliott!"

"I love you," he said. Their eyes met across the table, then he pushed aside his plate and went around to her.

"Jim . . ." she whispered.